A COUNTRY GENTLEMAN
AND HIS FAMILY

BY

MRS. OLIPHANT

AUTHOR OF
'THE WIZARD'S SON,' 'HESTER,' ETC.

First published in 1886

British Library Cataloguing-in-Publication Data
A catalogue record for this book is available
from the British Library

CONTENTS

Margaret Oliphant

Margaret Oliphant was born in Wallyford, Scotland in 1828. When she was ten years old, her family moved to Liverpool, where she began to experiment with writing. She had her first novel, *Passages in the Life of Mrs. Margaret Maitlan* (1849), published when she was just 21. It was a moderate commercial success, and following her second novel (*Caleb Field,* published in 1851) Oliphant became a regular contributor to the famous *Blackwood's Magazine.*

By the 1860s, Oliphant was a popular and recognized author, and in order to support her family (she had become a widow in 1959) she became an incredibly prolific author. Oliphant eventually went on to write more than 120 works, including novels travelogues, histories and volumes of literary criticism. Two of her better-known fictional works are *Miss Marjoribanks* (1866) and *Phoebe Junior* (1876). Towards the end of her life, she wrote a well-received series of supernatural short stories called *Tales of the Seen and Unseen* (1885), which remains popular to this day. Oliphant died in 1897, aged 69.

CHAPTER I.

Theodore Warrender was still at Oxford when his father died. He was a youth who had come up from his school with the highest hopes of what he was to do at the university. It had indeed been laid out for him by an admiring tutor with anticipations which were almost certainties: "If you will only work as well as you have done these last two years!" These years had been spent in the dignified ranks of Sixth Form, where he had done almost everything that boy can do. It was expected that the School would have had a holiday when he and Brunson went up for the scholarships in their chosen college, and everybody calculated on the "double event." Brunson got the scholarship in question, but Warrender failed, which at first astonished everybody, but was afterwards more than accounted for by the fact that his fine and fastidious mind had been carried away by the Æschylus paper, which he made into an exhaustive analysis of the famous trilogy, to the neglect of other less inviting subjects. His tutor was thus almost more proud of him for having failed than if he had succeeded, and Sixth Form in general accepted Brunson's success apologetically as that of an "all-round" man, whose triumph did not mean so much. But if there is any place where the finer scholarship ought to tell, it should be in Oxford, and his school tutor, as has been said, laid out for him a sort of little map of what he was to do. There were the Hertford and the Ireland scholarships, almost as a matter of course; a first in moderations, but that went without saying; at least one of the Vice-Chancellor's prizes—probably the Newdigate, or some other unconsidered trifle of the kind; another first class in Greats; a fellowship. "If you don't do more than this I will be disappointed in you," the school tutor said.

The college tutors received Warrender with suppressed enthusiasm, with that excitement which the acquisition of a man who is likely to distinguish himself (and his college) naturally calls forth. It was not long before they took his measure and decided that his school tutor was right. He had it in him to bring glory and honour to their doors. They surrounded him with that genial warmth of incubation which brings a future first class tenderly to the top of the lists. Young Warrender was flattered, his heart was touched. He thought, with the credulity of youth, that the dons loved him for himself; that it was because of the attractions of his own noble nature that they vied with each other in breakfasting and dining him, in making him the companion of their refined and elevated pleasures. He thought, even, that the Rector—that name of fear—had at last found in himself the ideal which he had vainly sought in so many examples of lettered youth. He became vain, perhaps, but certainly a little self-willed, as was his nature, feeling himself to be on the top of the wave, and above those precautions for keeping himself there which had once seemed necessary. He did not, indeed, turn to any harm, for that was not in his nature; but feeling himself no longer a schoolboy, but a man, and the chosen friend of half the dons of his college, he turned aside with a fine contempt from the ordinary ways of fame-making, and betook himself to the pursuit of his own predilections in the way of learning. He had a fancy for out-of-the-way studies, for authors who don't pay, for eccentricities in literature; in short, for having his own way and reading what he chose. Signals of danger became gradually visible upon his path, and troubled consultations were held over him in the common room. "He is paying no attention to his books," remarked one; "he is reading at large whatever pleases him." Much was to be said for this principle, but still, alas, these gentlemen were all agreed that it does not pay.

"If he does not mind, he will get nothing but a pass," the Rector said, bending his brows. The learned society shrank, as if a sentence of death had been pronounced.

"Oh no, not so bad as that!" they cried, with one voice.

"What do you call so bad as that? Is not a third worse than that? Is not a second quite as bad?" said the majestic presiding voice. "In the gulf there are no names mentioned. We are not credited with a mistake. It will be better, if he does not stick to his books, that he should drop."

Young Warrender's special tutor made frantic efforts to arrest this doom. He pointed out to the young man the evil of his ways. "In one sense all my sympathies are with you," he said; "but, my dear fellow, if you don't read your books you may be as learned as ——, and as clear-sighted as ——" (the historian, being unlearned, does not know what names were here inserted), "but you will never get to the head of the lists, where we have hoped to see you."

"What does it matter?" said Warrender, in boyish splendour. "The lists are merely symbols. You know one's capabilities without that; and as for the opinion of the common mass, of what consequence is it to me?"

A cold perspiration came out on the tutor's brow. "It is of great consequence to—the college," he said. "My dear fellow, so long as we are merely mortal we can't despise symbols; and the Rector has set his heart on having so many first classes. He doesn't like to be disappointed. Come, after it's all over you will have plenty of time to read as you like."

"But why shouldn't I read as I like now?" said Warrender. He was very self-willed. He was apt to start off at a tangent if anybody interfered with him,—a youth full of fads and ways of his own, scorning the common path, caring nothing for results. And by what except by results is a college to be known and assert itself? The tutor whose hopes had been so high was in a state of depression for some time after. He even made an appeal to the school tutor, the enthusiast who had sent up this troublesome original with so many fine prognostications: who replied to the appeal, and descended one day upon the youth in his room, quite unexpectedly.

"Well, Theo, my fine fellow, how are you getting on? I hope you are keeping your eyes on the examination, and not neglecting your books."

"I am delighted to see you, sir," said the lad. "I was just thinking I should like to consult you upon"—and here he entered into a fine question of scholarship,—a most delicate question, which probably would be beyond the majority of readers, as it is of the writer. The face of the public-school man was a wonder to see. It was lighted up with pleasure, for he was an excellent scholar, yet clouded with alarm, for he knew the penalties of such behaviour in a "man" with an examination before him.

"My dear boy," he said, "in which of your books do you find any reference to that?"

"In none of them, I suppose," said the young scholar. "But, you don't think there is any sanctity in a set of prescribed books?"

"Oh no, no sanctity: but use," said the alarmed master. "Come, Theo, there's a good fellow, don't despise the tools we all must work with. It's your duty to the old place, you know, which all these newspaper fellows are throwing stones at whenever they have a chance: and it's your duty to your college. I know what you are worth, of course: but how can work be tested to the public eye except by the lists?"

"Why should I care for the public eye?" said the magnanimous young man. "*We* know that the lists don't mean everything. A headache might make the best scholar that ever was lose his place. A fellow that knows nothing might carry the day by a fluke. Don't you remember, sir, that time when Daws got the Lincoln because of that old examiner, who gave us all his own old fads in the papers? Every fellow that was any good was out of it, and Daws got the scholarship. I am sure you can't have forgotten that."

"Oh no, I have not forgotten it," said the master ruefully. "But that was only once in a way. Come, Theo, be reasonable. As long as you are in training, you know, you must keep in the beaten way. Think, my boy, of your school—and of me, if you care for my credit as a tutor."

10

"You know, sir, I care for you, and to please you," said Warrender, with feeling. "But as for your credit as a tutor, who can touch that? And even I am not unknown here," he added, with a little boyish pride. "Everybody who is of any importance knows that the Rector himself has always treated me quite as a friend. I don't think"—this with the ineffable simple self-assurance of youth, so happy in the discrimination of those who approve of it that the gratification scarcely feels like vanity—"that I shall be misunderstood here."

"Oh, the young ass!" said the master to himself, as he went away. "Oh, the young idiot! Poor dear Theo, what will be his feelings when he finds out that all they care for is the credit of the college?" But he was not so barbarous as to say this, and Warrender was left to find out by himself, by the lessening number of the breakfasts, by the absence of his name on the lists of the Rector's dinner-parties, by the gradual cooling of the incubating warmth, what had been the foundation of all the affection shown him. It was not for some time that he perceived the change which made itself slowly apparent, the gradual loss of interest in him who had been the object of so much interest. The nest was, so to speak, left cold, no father bird lending his aid to the development; his books were no longer forced on his consideration; his tutor no longer made anxious remarks. Like other silly younglings, the lad for a while rejoiced in his freedom, and believed that he had succeeded in making his pastors and teachers aware of a better way. And it was not till there flashed upon him the awful revelation that *they were taking up Brunson*, that he began to see the real state of affairs. Brunson was the all-round man whom Sixth Form despised,—a fellow who had little or no taste for the higher scholarship, but who always knew his books by heart, mastering everything that would "pay" with a determined practical faculty fertile of results. There is no one for whom the dilettante mind has a greater contempt; and when Warrender saw that Brunson figured at the Rector's dinner-parties as he himself had once done, that it was Brunson who went on the river with parties of young dons and walked out of college arm in arm with his tutor, the whole meaning of his own brief advancement burst upon him. Not for himself, as he had supposed in the youthful simplicity which he called vanity now, and characterised by strong adjectives; not in the least for him, Theo Warrender, scholar and gentleman, but for what he might bring to the college,—the honours, the scholarships, the credit to everybody concerned in producing a successful student. That he became angry, scornful, and Byronic on the spot need surprise nobody. Brunson! who never had come within a hundred miles of him or of his set at school; did not even understand the fine problems which the initiated love to discuss; was nothing but a plodding fellow, who stuck to his work, and cared no more for the real soul of Greek literature or philosophy than the scout did. Warrender laughed aloud,—that hollow laugh, which was once so grand an exponent of feeling, and which, though the Byronic mood has gone out of fashion, will never go out of fashion so long as there is youthful pride to be wounded, and patient merit has to accept the spurns of the unworthy. No, perhaps the adjective is mistaken, if Shakespeare ever was mistaken; not patient, but exasperated merit, conscious to the very finger points of its own deserts.

Warrender was well enough aware that he could, if he chose, make up the lost way and leave Brunson "nowhere" in the race for honours; but it was his first disenchantment, and he felt it deeply. Letters are dear and honours sweet, but our own beloved personality is dearer still; and there is no one who does not feel humbled and wounded when he finds out that he is esteemed, not for himself, but for what he can do,—and poor Theo was only twenty, and had been made much of all his life. He began to ask himself, too, whether his past popularity, the pleasant things that had been always said of him, the pleasant way in which his friendship had been sought, were perhaps all inspired by the same motive,—because he was likely to do credit to his belongings and friends. It is a fine thing to do credit to your belongings, to be the pride of your community, to be quoted to future generations as the hero of the past. This was what had occurred to him at school, and he had liked it immensely. Warrender had been a word to conjure withal, named by lower boys with awe, fondly cherished in the records of Sixth Form. But the glimmer in the Head Master's eye as he said good-bye, the little falter in his tutor's voice,—did these mean no more than an appreciation of his progress, and an anticipation of the honour and glory he was to bring them at the university, a name to fling in the teeth of the newspaper fellows next time they demanded what were the results of the famous public school system? This thought had a sort of maddening effect upon the fastidious, hot-headed, impatient young man. He flung his books into a corner of the room, and covered them over with a yellow cairn of railway novels. If that was all, there let them lie. He resolved that nothing would induce him to touch them more.

The result was—but why should we dwell upon the result? It sent a shiver through the college, where there were some faithful souls who still believed that Warrender could pick up even at the last moment, if he liked. It produced such a sensation in his old school as relaxed discipline entirely, and confounded masters and scholars in one dark discouragement. "Warrender has only got a —— in Mods." We decline to place any number where that blank is; it filled every division (except the lowest) with consternation and dismay. Warrender! who was as sure of a first as—why, there was nobody who was so sure as Warrender! The masters who were Cambridge men recovered their courage after a little, and said, "I told you so! That was a boy who ought to have gone to Cambridge, where individual characteristics are taken into consideration." Warrender's tutor took to his bed, and was not visible for a week, after which only the most unsympathetic, not to say brutal, of his colleagues would have mentioned before him Warrender's name. However, time reconciles all things, and after a while the catastrophe was forgotten and everything was as before.

But not to Warrender himself. He smiled, poor boy, a Byronic smile, with a curl of the upper lip such as suited the part, and saw himself abandoned by the authorities with what he felt to be a lofty disdain; and he relapsed into such studies as pleased him most, and set prescribed books and lectures at defiance. What was worst to bear was that other classes of "men" made up to him, after the men of distinction, those whom the dons considered the best men, had withdrawn and left him to pursue his own way. The men who loafed considered him their natural prey; the æsthetic men who wrote bad verses opened their arms, and were ready to welcome him as their own. And perhaps among these classes he might have found disinterested friendship, for nobody any longer sought Warrender on account of what he could do. But he did not make the trial, wrapping himself up in a Childe-Harold-like superiority to all those who would consort with him, now that he had lost his hold of those with whom only he desired to consort. His mother and sisters felt a little surprised, when they came up to Commemoration, to find that they were not overwhelmed by invitations from Theo's friends. Other ladies had not a spare moment: they were lost in a turmoil of breakfasts, luncheons, water-parties, concerts, flower-shows, and knew the interior of half the rooms in half the colleges. But with the Miss Warrenders this was not so. They were asked to luncheon by Brunson, indeed, and had tea in the rooms of a young Cavendish, who had been at school with Theo. But that was all, and it mortified the girls, who were not prepared to find themselves so much at a disadvantage. This was the only notice that was taken of his downfall at home, where there was no academical ambition, and where everybody was quite satisfied so long as he kept his health and did not get into any scrape. Perhaps this made him feel it all the more, that his disappointment and disenchantment were entirely shut up in his own bosom, and that he could not confide to any one the terrible disillusionment that had befallen him on the very threshold of his life. That the Rector should pass him with the slightest possible nod, and his tutor say "How d'ye do,

Warrender?" without even a smile when they met, was nothing to anybody except himself. Arm in arm with Brunson, the don would give him that salutation. Brunson, who had got his first in Mods, and was going on placidly, admired of all, to another first in the final schools.

But if there was any one who understood Warrender's feelings it was this same Brunson, who was in his way an honest fellow, and understood the situation. "It is all pot-hunting, you know," this youth said. "They don't care for me any more than they care for Jenkinson. It's all for what I bring to the college, just as it was for what they expected you were going to bring to the college; only I understood it, and you didn't. I don't care for them any more than they do for me. Why, they might see, if they had any sense, that to work at you, who care for that sort of thing, would be far better than to bother me, who only care for what it will bring. If they had stuck to you they might have done a deal with you, Warrender: whereas I should have done just the same whether they took any notice of me or not."

"You mean to say I'm an empty-headed fool that could be cajoled into anything!" cried the other angrily.

"I mean nothing of the sort. I mean that I'm going to be a schoolmaster, and that first classes, etc., are my stock in trade. You don't suppose I work to please the Rector? And I know, and he knows, and you know, that I don't know a tenth part so much as you do. If they had held on at you, Theo, they might have got a great scholar out of you. But that's not what they want. They want so many firsts, and the Hertford, and the Ireland, and all the rest of it. It's all pot-hunting," Mr. Brunson said. But this did not lessen the effect of the disenchantment, the first disappointment of life. Poor Theo became prone to suspect everybody after that first proof that no one was above suspicion,—not even the greatly respected head of one of the first colleges in the world.

After that dreadful fiasco in the schools, Warrender continued to keep his terms very quietly; seeing very few people, making very few friends, reading after his own fashion with an obstinate indifference to all systems of study, and shutting his eyes persistently to the near approach of the final ordeal. Things were in this condition when he received a sudden telegram calling him home. "Come at once, or you will be too late," was the message. The Rector, to whom he rushed at once, looked at it coldly. He was not fond of giving an undergraduate leave in the middle of the term. "The college could have wished for a more definite message," he said. "Too late for what, Mr. Warrender?" "Too late to see my father alive, sir!" cried the young man; and as this had all the definiteness that the college required he was allowed to go. This was how his studies were broken up just as they approached their conclusion, although, as he had been so capricious and self-willed, nobody expected that in any circumstances it could have been a very satisfactory close.

CHAPTER II.

The elder Mr. Warrender was a country gentleman of an undistinguished kind. The county gentry of England is a very comprehensive class. It includes the very best and most delightful of English men and English women, the truest nobility, the finest gentlemen; but it also includes a number of beings the most limited, dull, and commonplace that human experience knows. In some cases they are people who do well to be proud of the generation of gentlefolk through whom they trace their line, and who have transmitted to them not only the habit of command, but the habit of protection, and that easy grace of living which is not to be acquired at first hand; and there are some whose forefathers have handed down nothing but so many farms and fields, and various traditions, in which father and son follow each other, each smaller and more petty of soul than he that went before. The family at the Warren were of this class. They were acknowledged gentry, beyond all question, but their estates and means were small and their souls smaller. Their income never reached a higher level than about fifteen hundred a year. Their paternal home was a house of rather mean appearance, rebuilt on the ruins of the old one in the end of last century, and consequently as ugly as four square walls could be. The woods had grown up about it, and hid it almost entirely from sight, which was an advantage, perhaps, to the landscape, but not to those who were condemned to dwell in the house, which was without light and air and everything that was cheering. The name of the Warren was very well adapted to the place, which, except one corner of the old house which had stood fast when the rest was pulled down, might almost have been a burrow in the soft green earth, damp and warm and full of the mould of ages, though it was a mere new-comer in the world. Its furniture was almost entirely of the same date as the house, which means dingy carpets, curtains of harsh and unpliable stuff, and immense catafalques of mahogany in the shape of sideboards, arm-chairs, and beds. A four-poster of mahogany, with hangings of red moreen, as stiff as a board and much less soft,—that was the kind of furnishing; to be sure, it was full of feather-beds and pillows, warm blankets and fresh linen, which some people thought made amends.

The family consisted of Mr. and Mrs. Warrender, two daughters, and the son, with whom the reader has already made acquaintance. How he had found his way into such a nest was one of those problems which the prudent evolutionist scarcely cares to tackle. The others were in their natural place: the father a Warrender like the last dozen Warrenders who had gone before him, and the girls cast exactly in the mould of all the previous Minnies and Chattys of the family. They were all dull, blameless, and good—to a certain extent; perfectly satisfied to live in the Warren all the year long, to spend every evening of their lives round the same hearth, to do the same thing to-day as they had done yesterday and should do to-morrow. To be so easily contented, to accommodate one's self with such philosophy to one's circumstances,—what an advantage that is! But it required no philosophy on the part of the girls, who had not imagination enough to think of anything different, and who devoutly believed that nothing on earth was so virtuous, so dignified, so praiseworthy, as to keep the linen in order, and make your own underclothing, and sit round the fire at home. When any one would read aloud to them they wanted no better paradise; but they were not very exacting even in the matter of reading aloud. However exciting the book might be, they were quite willing that it should be put away at a quarter to ten, with a book-marker in it to keep the place. Once Chatty had been known to take it up clandestinely after prayers, to see whether the true murderer was found out; but Minnie waited quite decorously till eight o'clock next evening, which was the right hour for resuming the reading. Happy girls! They thus had in their limited little world quite a happy life, expecting nothing, growing no older from year to year. Minnie was twenty-five, Chatty twenty-three: they were good-looking enough in their quiet way, very neat and tidy, with brown hair so well brushed that it reflected the light. Theodore was the youngest, and he had been very welcome when he came; for otherwise the property would have gone to a distant heir of entail, which would not have been pleasant for any of the family. He had been a very quiet boy so long as he was at home, though not perhaps in the same manner of quietness as that of the girls; but since he was thirteen he had been away for the greater part of the years, appearing only in the holidays, when he was always reading for something or other,—so that nobody was aware how great was the difference between the fastidious young scholar and the rest of his belongings.

Mr. Warrender himself was not a scholar. He had got through life very well without ever being at the university. In his day it was not considered such a necessity as now. And he was not at all critical of his son. So long as the boy got into no scrapes he asked no more of him. He was quite complacent when Theo brought home his school prizes, and used to point them out to visitors. "This is for his Latin verses," he would say. "I don't know where the boy got a turn for poetry. I am sure it was not from me." The beautiful smooth binding and the school arms on the side gave him great gratification. He had a faint notion that as Theo brought home no prizes from Oxford he was not perhaps getting on so well; but naturally he knew nothing of his son's experiences with the Rector and the dons. And by that time he was ill and feverish, and far more taken up about his beef-tea than about anything else in the world. They did not make it half strong enough. If they only would make it strong he felt sure he would soon regain his strength. But how could a man pick up, who was allowed nothing but slops, when his beef-tea was like water? This was the matter that occupied him most, while his son was going through the ordeal above described,—there never was any taste in the beef-tea. Mr. Warrender thought the cook must make away with the meat; or else send the best of the infusion to some of her people in the village, and give it to him watered. When it was made over the fire in his room he said his wife had no skill; she let all the goodness evaporate. He never could be satisfied with his beef-tea; and so, grumbling and indignant, finding no savour in anything, but thoroughly convinced that this was "their" fault, and that they could make it better if they were to try, he dwindled and faded away.

It was a long illness; a family gets used to a long illness, and after a while accepts it as the natural course of events. And the doctor had assured them all that no sudden "change" was to be looked for. Nevertheless, there was a sudden change. It had become the routine of the house that each of the ladies should spend so many hours with papa. Mrs. Warrender was with him, of course, the greater part of the day, and went out and in to see if he was comfortable every hour or two during the night; but one of the girls always sat with him in the evening, bringing her needlework upstairs, and feeling that she was doing her duty in giving up the reading just when the book was at its most interesting point. It was after Chatty had fulfilled this duty, and everybody was serenely preparing to go to bed, that the change came. "How is he?" Mrs. Warrender had said, as they got out the Prayer-Book which was used at family prayers. "Just as usual, mamma: quite quiet and comfortable. I think he was asleep, for he took no notice when I bade him good-night," Chatty said; and then the servants came in, and the little rites were accomplished. Mrs. Warrender then went upstairs, and received the same report from her maid, who sat with the patient in the intervals when the ladies were at prayers. "Quite comfortable, ma'am, and I think he is asleep." Mrs. Warrender went to the bedside and drew back the curtain softly,—the red moreen curtain which was like a board suspended by the head of the bed,—and lo, while they all had been so calm, the change had come.

The girls thought their mother made a great deal more fuss than was necessary; for what could be done? It might be right to send for the doctor, who is an official whose presence is essential at the last act of life; but what was the good of sending a man on horseback into Highcombe, on the chance of the telegraph office being still open? Of course it was not open; and if it had been, Theo could not possibly leave Oxford till next morning. But then it was a well-known fact that mamma was excitable, and often did things without thought. He lingered all night, "just alive, and that is all," the doctor said. It was Chatty who sent for the rector, who came and read the prayers for the sick at the bedside, but agreed with Dr. Durant that it was of no use attempting to rouse the departing soul from the lethargy in which he lay. And before Theodore arrived all was over. He knew it before he entered the house by the sight of the drawn blinds, which received him with a blank whiteness of woe as soon as he caught sight of the windows. They had not sent to meet him at the station, thinking he would not come till the later train.

"Try and get mamma to lie down," Minnie said, as she kissed her brother. "She is going on exciting herself for nothing. I am sure everything was done that could be done, and we can do him no good by making ourselves more miserable now."

Minnie had cried in the early morning as much as was right and natural,—her eyes were still a little red; but she did not think it necessary to begin over again, as Chatty did, who had a tendency to overdo everything, like mamma. As for Theodore, he did not cry at all, but grew very pale, and did not say a word when he was taken into the chamber of death. The sight of that marble, or rather waxen, figure lying there had a greater effect upon his imagination than upon that of either of the girls, who perhaps had not got much imagination to be affected. He was overawed and silenced by that presence, which he had never met before so near. When his mother threw herself into his arms, with that excess of emotion which was peculiar to her, he held her close to him with a throb of answering feeling. The sensation of standing beside that which was not, although it was, his father, went through and through the being of the sensitive young man. Death is always most impressive in the case of a commonplace person, with whom we have no associations but the most ordinary ones of life. What had come to him?—to the mind which had been so much occupied with the quality of his beef-tea? Was it possible that he could have leaped all at once into the contemplation of the highest subjects, or must there not be something intermediate between the beef-tea and the *Gloria in Excelsis*? This was the thought, inappropriate, unnatural, as he felt it, which came into his mind as he stood by the bed upon which lay that which had been the master of the Warren yesterday, and now was "the body"; a solemn, inanimate thing arranged with dreadful neatness, presently to be taken away and hid out of sight of the living. Tears did not come even when he took his mother into his arms, but only a dumb awe not unmixed with horror, and even that sense of repulsion with which some minds regard the dead.

It was the height of summer, the time at which the Warren looked its best. The sunshine, which scarcely got near it in the darker part of the year, now penetrated the trees on every side, and rushed in as if for a wager, every ray trying how far it could reach into the depths of the shade. It poured full into the drawing-room by one window, so that Minnie was mindful at all times to draw down that blind, that the carpet might not be spoiled; and of course all the blinds were down now. It touched the front of the house in the afternoon, and blazed upon the lawn, making all the flowers wink. Inside, to people who had come out of the heat and scorching of other places more open to the influences of the skies, the coolness of the Warren in June was delightful. The windows stood open, the hum of bees came in, the birds made an unceasing chorus in the trees. Neither birds nor bees took the least notice of the fact that there was death in the house. They carried on their jubilation, their hum of business, their love-making and nursery talk, all the same, and made the house sound not like a house of mourning, but a house of rejoicing; all this harmonious noise being doubly audible in the increased stillness of the place, where Minnie thought it right to speak in a whisper, and Chatty was afraid to go beyond the example of her sister. Mrs. Warrender kept her room, except in the evening, when she would go out with Theo for a little air. Only in the grounds! no farther,—through the woods, which the moonlight pierced with arrows of silver, as far as the pond, which shone like a white mirror with all the great leaves of the water-lilies black upon its surface. But the girls thought that even this was too much. They could not think how she could feel able for it before the funeral. They sat with one shaded lamp and the shutters all closed, "reading a book," which was their severest estimate of gravity. That is to say, each had a book: one a volume of sermons, the other *Paradise Lost*, which had always been considered Sunday reading by the Warrenders, and came in very conveniently at this moment. They had been busy all day with the maid and the dressmaker from the village, getting their mourning ready. There were serious doubts in their minds how high the crape ought to come on their skirts, and whether a cuff of that material would be enough without other trimmings on the sleeves; but as it was very trying to the eyes to work at black in candlelight, they had laid it all aside out of sight, and so far as was possible out of thought, and composed themselves to read as a suitable occupation for the evening, less cheerful than either coloured or white needlework, and more appropriate. It was very difficult, especially for Minnie, upon whom the chief responsibility would rest, to put that question of the crape out of her thoughts; but she read on in a very determined manner, and it is to be hoped that she succeeded. She felt very deeply the impropriety of her mother's proceedings. She had never herself stirred out-of-doors since her father's death, and would not till after the funeral, should the interests of nations hang on it. She, at least, knew what her duty was, and would do it. Chatty was not so sure on this subject, but she had been more used to follow Minnie than to follow mamma, and she was loyal to her traditions. One window was open a little behind the half-closed shutters, and let in something of the sounds and odours of the night. Chatty was aware that the moon was at the full, and would have liked to stretch her young limbs with a run; but she dared not even think of such a thing in sight of Minnie's face.

"I wonder how long mamma means to stay. One would think she was *enjoying* it," Minnie said, with a little emphasis on the word. As she used it, it seemed the most reprehensible verb in the world.

"She likes to be with Theo," said Chatty; "and she is always such a one for the air."

"Likes!" said her sister. "Is this a time to think of what one likes, with poor dear papa in his coffin?"

"She never left him as long as he wanted her," said the apologetic sister.

"No, indeed, I should hope not; that would have been criminal. Poor dear mamma would never do anything really bad; but she does not mind if she does a thing that is unusual. It is *very* unusual to go out before the funeral; it is a thing that is never done, especially by the ladies of the house."

"Shall we be able to go out on Friday, Minnie?" Friday was the funeral day.

"It would be very bad taste, I think. Of course, if it does not prove too much for us, we ought to go to church to meet the procession. Often it is thought to be too much for the ladies of a family."

"I am sure it would not be too much for me. Oh, I shall go as far as we can go with him—to the grave, Minnie."

"You had better wait till you see whether it will not be too much for you," said the elder sister, while Chatty dried her eyes. Minnie's eyes had no need of drying. She had cried at the right time, but it was little more than levity to be always crying. It was nearly as bad as enjoying anything. She did not like extravagance of any kind.

And then they turned to their reading again, and felt that, whatever mamma might think herself at liberty to do, they, at least, were paying that respect to their father's memory which young women in a well-regulated household should always be the first to pay.

CHAPTER III.

Meanwhile the mother and son took their walk. It was a very silent walk, without much outward trace of that enjoyment which Minnie had felt so cruelly out of place: but no doubt to both there was a certain pleasure in it. Mr. Warrender had now been lying in that silent state which the most insignificant person holds immediately after death, for three days, and there was still another to come before he could be laid away in the dark and noisome bed in the family vault, where all the Warrenders made their last assertion of superiority to common clay. This long and awful pause in the affairs of life was intolerable to the two people now walking softly through the paths of the little wood, where the moonbeams shone through the trees; to the son, because he was of an impatient nature, and could not endure the artificial gloom which was thus forced upon him. He had felt keenly all those natural sensations which the loss of a father calls forth: the breaking of an old tie, the oldest in the world; the breach of all the habits of his life; the absence of the familiar greeting, which had always been kind enough, if never enthusiastic; the general overturn and loss of the usual equilibrium in his little world. It was no blame to Theo if his feelings went little further than this. His father had been no active influence in his life. His love had been passive, expressing itself in few words, without sympathy in any of the young man's pursuits, or knowledge of them, or desire to know,—a dull affection because the boy belonged to him, and satisfaction in that he had never got into any scrapes or given any trouble. And the return which the son made was in the same kind. Theo had felt the natural pang of disruption very warmly at the moment; he had felt a great awe and wonder at sight of the mystery of that pale and solemn thing which had lately been so unmysterious and unsolemn. But even these pangs of natural sensation had fallen into a little ache and weariness of custom, and his fastidious soul grew tired of the bonds that kept him, or would have kept him, precisely at the same point of feeling for so many hours and days. This is not possible for any one, above all for a being of his temper, and he was restless beyond measure, and eager to get over this enforced pause, and emerge into the common life and daylight beyond. The drawn blinds somehow created a stifling atmosphere in his very soul.

Mrs. Warrender felt it was indecorous to begin to speak of plans and what was to be done afterwards, so long as her dead husband was still master of the oppressed and melancholy house; but her mind, as may be supposed, was occupied by them in the intervals of other thoughts. She was not of the Warrender breed, but a woman of lively feelings; and as soon as the partner of her life was out of her reach she had begun to torment herself with fears that she had not been so good to him as she ought. There was no truth, at least no fact, in this, for there could have been no better wife or more careful nurse. But yet, as every individual knows more of his or her self than all the rest of the world knows, Mrs. Warrender was aware that there were many things lacking in her conjugal devotion. She had not been the wife she knew how to be; in her heart she had never given herself credit for fulfilling her duty. Oh yes, she had fulfilled all her duties. She had been everything to him that he wanted, that he expected, that he was capable of understanding. But she knew very well that when all is said, that is not everything that can be said; and now that he was dead, and could no longer look in her face with lack-lustre eyes, wondering what the deuce the woman meant, she threw herself back upon her own standard, and knew that she had not come up to it. Even now she could not come up to it. Her heart ought to be desolate; life ought to hold nothing for her but perhaps resignation, perhaps despair. She ought to be beyond all feeling for what was to come. Yet she was not so. On the contrary, new ideas, new plans, had welled up into her mind,—

how many, how few hours after she had laid down the charge, in which outwardly she had been so faithful, but inwardly so full of shortcomings? These plans filled her mind now as she went by her son's side through the mossy paths where, even in the height of summer, it was always a little cold. She could not speak of them, feeling a horror of herself, an ashamed sense that to betray the revulsion of her thoughts to her boy would be to put her down from her position in his respect for ever. Between these mutual reluctances to betray what was really in them the two went along very silently, as if they were counting their steps, their heads a little bowed down, the sound of their feet making far more commotion than was necessary in the stillness of the place. To be out-of-doors was something for both of them. They could breathe more freely, and if they could not talk could at least think, without the sense that they were impairing the natural homage of all things to the recently dead.

"Take care, Theo," she said, after a long interval of silence. "It is very damp here."

"Yes, there is a good deal of timber that ought to go." He caught his breath when he had said this, and she gave a slight shiver. They both would have spoken quite freely had the father been alive. "The house is damp, too," said he, taking courage.

"In winter, perhaps, a little, when there is much rain."

And then there was a long pause. When they came within sight of the pond, which glistened under the moonlight, reflecting all the trees in irregular masses, and showing here and there a big white water-lily bud couched upon a dark bank of leaves, he spoke again: "I don't think it can be very healthy, either, to have the pond so near the house."

"You have always had your health, all of you," she said.

"That is true; but not very much of it. We are a subdued sort of family, mother."

"That is because the Warrenders——" She stopped here, feeling the inappropriateness of what she was about to say. It very often happens that a wife has but little opinion of the race to which her husband belongs. She attributes the defects of her own children to that side instinctively. "It is character," she said, "not health."

"But all the same, if we had a little more air and a little less shade——"

He was becoming bolder as he went on.

"Theo," she said tremulously, "it is too soon to begin to talk of that."

And then there was a pause again. When they came to the edge of the pond, and stopped to look at the water-lilies, and at the white flood of the moonlight, and all the clustering masses of the trees that hung round as if to keep it hidden and sheltered, it was she who spoke: "Your father was very fond of this view. Almost the last time he was out we brought him here. He sat down for a long time, and was quite pleased. He cared for beautiful things much more than he ever said."

The thought that passed through Theo's mind was very rapid, that it might well be so, seeing nothing was ever said on the subject; but his remark was, "Very likely, mother," in a soft and soothing voice.

"I should be very sorry to see any—I mean I hope you will not make much alteration here."

"It is too soon," he said hastily, "to speak of that."

"Much too soon," she replied, with a quick sense of shame, taking her son's arm as they turned back. Even to turn back made the burden heavier, and dispelled the little advantage which they had got by the walk.

"There will be, I suppose, a great number of people—on Friday."

"Yes, I think a great number; everybody about."

"What a nuisance! People might have sense enough to know that at such a moment we don't want a lot of strange faces peering at us, finding out how we bear up."

"My dear, it would have pleased him to know everybody would be there."

"I suppose so," said Theo, in a tone which was half angry and half resigned.

"We will have to take a little thought how they are to go. Lord Markland must come first, after the relations."

"Why? They never took much notice of us, and my father never liked him. I don't see why he should come at all."

"Oh yes, he will come, and your dear father would have liked it. The Warrenders have always thought a great deal of such things."

"I am a Warrender, I hope, and I don't."

"Ah, Theo, you! But you are much more like my family," she said, with a little pressure of his arm.

This did not give him so much pleasure as it did her; for, after all, however near a man may be to his mother's family, he generally prefers his own, and the name which it is his to bear. They got back under the thick shadow of the trees when the conversation came to this point, and once more it was impressed upon both that the path was very damp, and that even in June it was difficult to get through without wet feet; but Mrs. Warrender had felt herself checked by her son's reply about the alterations, and Theo felt that to betray how much he was thinking of them would be horrifying to his mother: so they both stepped into the marshy part without a word.

"You are still decided to go on Friday,—you and the girls?"

"Surely, Theo: we are all in good health, Heaven be praised! I should not feel that I had done everything if I did not go."

"You are sure it will not be too much for you, mother?"

This question went to her heart. She knew that it ought to be too much for her. Had she been the wife she ought to have been, the widow with a broken heart, then, perhaps, there might have been a doubt. But she knew also that it would not be too much for her. Her heart ached for the ideal anguish, which nobody looked for, nor would have understood. "He would have liked it," she said, in a subdued voice. That, at least, was quite true: and to carry out all his wishes thus faithfully was something, although she could not pay him the homage which was his due,—the supreme compliment of a broken heart.

At last Friday came. It was a dull day, of the colour most congenial to such a ceremony. A gentle shower fell upon the wreaths and crosses that covered the coffin. There was a large assembly from all the country round, for Mr. Warrender had been a man who never harmed anybody, which is perhaps a greater title to respect than those possess who have taken more trouble. When you try to do good, especially in a rural place, you are sure to stir up animosities; but Mr. Warrender had never stirred up anybody. He was greatly respected. Lord Markland was what the farmers called "a wild young sprig," with little regard to the proprieties; but he was there, and half the clergymen of the diocese, and every country gentleman on the west side of the county. The girls from behind their crape veils watched the procession filing into church, and were deeply gratified; and Mrs. Warrender felt that he would have liked it, and that everything was being done according to his wishes. She said to herself that this was what he would have done for her if she had died first; and immediately there rose before her eyes (also behind her crape veil) a picture of what might have been, had the coffin in the middle of the church been hers; how he would have stepped and looked, and the way in which he would have held out his hand silently to each of the company, and the secret pleasure in the fulfilment of all that was just and right which would have been in his mind. It was instantaneous, it was involuntary, it made her smile against her will; but the smile recalled her to herself, and overwhelmed her with compunction and misery. Smile— when it was he who lay there in the coffin, under that black pall, expecting from her the last observances, and that homage which ought to come from a breaking heart!

The blinds were drawn up when they returned home, the sunshine pouring in, the table spread. Minnie, leading Chatty with her, not without a slight struggle on that young lady's part, retired to her room, and lay down a little, which was the right thing to do. She had a tray brought upstairs, and was not disinclined for her luncheon: mercifully, their presence at the funeral had not been too much for them. And all the mourning was complete and everything in order, even so far as to the jet necklaces which the girls put on when they went down to tea. Mrs. Warrender had been quite overcome on re-entering the house, feeling, though she had so suffered from the long interval before the funeral, that to come back to a place from which he had now been solemnly shut out for ever was more miserable than all that had gone before; for it will be perceived that she was not of the steady mettle of the others, but a fantastic woman, who changed her mind very often, and whose feelings were always betraying her. The funeral had been early, and the distant visitors had been able to leave in good time, so that there was no need for a large luncheon party; and the lawyer and a cousin of Mr. Warrender's were the only strangers who shared that meal with the mother and son. Then, as a proper period had now been arrived at, and as solicitors rush in where heirs fear to tread, open questions were asked about the plans of the family and what Theo meant to do. He said at once, "I see no need for plans. Why should there be any discussion of plans? So far as outward circumstances go, what change is there? My mother and the girls will just go on as usual, and I, of course, will go back to Oxford. It will be more than a year before I can take my degree."

He thought—but no doubt he must have been mistaken—that a blank look came over his mother's face; but it was so impossible that she could have thought of anything else that he dismissed the idea from his mind. She said nothing, but Mr. Longstaffe replied—

"At present that is no doubt the wisest way; but I think it is always well that people should understand each other at once and provide for all emergencies, so that there may be no wounded feeling, or that sort of thing, hereafter. You know, Mrs. Warrender, that the house in Highcombe has always been the jointure house?"

"Yes," she said, with a certain liveliness in her answer, almost eagerness. "My husband has often told me so."

"We are authorised to put it in perfect repair, and you are authorised to choose whatever you please out of the furniture at the Warren to make it according to your taste. Perhaps we had better do that at once, and put it into your hands. If you don't live there, you can let it, or lend it, or make some use of it."

"It might be convenient," Mrs. Warrender said, with a slight hesitation, "if Theodore means, as I suppose he does, to carry out improvements here."

And yet she had implored him yesterday not to make many alterations! Theo felt a touch of offence with his mother. He began to think there was something in the things the girls used to say, that you never knew when you had mamma, or whether she might not turn upon you in a moment. She grew much more energetic, all at once, and even her figure lost the slight stoop of languor that was in it. "If you are going to cut any trees, or do any drainage, Theo, we could all live there while the works went on."

He gave a slight start in person, and a much greater in spirit, and a fastidious curve came to his forehead. "I don't know that I shall cut any trees now. You know you said the other day, We can talk of that after."

"Oh yes, it is early days," said the lawyer. "Of course it is not as if there were other heirs coming in, or any compulsory division were to be made. You can take your time. But I have always observed that things went smoother when it was understood from the first, in case of a certain emergency arising, or new conditions of any kind, so and so should follow. You understand what I mean."

"It is always wisest," said the Warrender cousin, "to have it all put down hard and fast, so that nobody may be disappointed, whatever should happen. Of course Theo will marry."

"I hope so," said his mother, permitting herself to smile.

"Of course he will marry," said the lawyer.

"But he had better take his degree first," the cousin added, feeling that he had distinguished himself; "and in the meantime the girls and you will have time to look about you. Highcombe is rather a dull place. And then the house is large. You could not get on in it with less than four or five servants."

"Four would do," said Mr. Longstaffe.

"And supposing my cousin kept a pony chaise, or something? She could not get on without a pony chaise. That means another."

Theodore pushed back his chair from the table with a harsh peremptoriness, startling them all. "I am sure my mother doesn't want to go into these calculations," he said; "neither do I. Leave us alone to settle what we find to be best."

"Dear me," said cousin Warrender, "I hope you don't imagine me to have any wish to interfere." Theo did not make any reply, but gave his mother his arm, and led her upstairs.

"I did not wish you to be troubled with business at all; certainly not to-day," he said to her, half apologetically. But there was something in her face which he did not quite understand, as she thanked him and smiled, with an inclination to cry. Was it possible that she was a little disappointed to have the discussion stopped, and that she took much interest in it, and contemplated not at all with displeasure the prospect of an entire change in her life?

CHAPTER IV.

It will be divined from what has been said that there was one element in the life at the Warren which has not yet been entered into, and that was Mrs. Warrender. The family were dull, respectable, and proper to their fingers' ends. But she was not dull. She had been Mr. Warrender's wife for six-and-twenty years,— the wife of a dull, good man, who never wanted any variety in his life, who needed no change, no outbursts of laughter or tears, nothing to carry away the superabundance of the waters of life. With him there had been no superabundance, there had never been any floods; consequently there was no outlet necessary to carry them away. But she was a woman of another sort: she was born to hunger for variety, to want change, to desire everything that was sweet and pleasant. And lo! fate bound her to the dullest life,—to marry Mr. Warrender, to live in the Warren. She had not felt it so much in the earlier part of her life, for then she had to some extent what her spirit craved. She had children: and every such event in a woman's life is like what going into battle is to a man,—a thing for which all his spirits collect themselves, which she may come out of or may not, an enormous risk, a great crisis. And when the children were young, before they had as yet betrayed themselves what manner of spirits they were, she had her share of the laughter and the tears; playing with her babies, living for them, singing to them, filling her life with them, and expecting as they grew up that all would be well. Many women live upon this hope. They have not had the completion of life in marriage which some have; they have failed in the great lottery, either by their own fault or the fault of others: but the children, they say to themselves, will make all right. The *désillusionment* which takes this form is the most bitter of all. The woman who has not found in her husband that dearest friend, whose companionship can alone make life happy, when she discovers after a while that the children in whom she has placed her last hope are his children, and not hers,—what is to become of her? She is thrown back upon her own individuality with a shock which is often more than flesh and blood can bear. In Mrs. Warrender's case this was not, as in some cases, a tragical discovery, but it had an exasperating and oppressive character which was almost more terrible. She had been able to breathe while they were children; but when they grew up they stifled her, each with the same "host of petty maxims" which had darkened the still air from her husband's lips. How, in face of the fact that she had been their teacher and guide far more than their father ever was, they should have learned these, and put aside everything that was like her or expressed her sentiments, was a mystery which she never could solve; but so it was. Mr. Warrender was what is called a very good father. He did not spoil them; bonbons of any kind, physical or spiritual, never came to them from his hands. He could not be troubled with them much as babies, but when they grew old enough to walk and ride with him he liked their company; and they resembled him, which is always flattering. But he had taken very little notice of them during the first twelve years or so of their life. During that time they had been entirely in their mother's hands, hearing her opinions, regulated outwardly by her will: and yet they grew up their father's children, and not hers! How strange it was, with a touch of the comic which made her laugh!—that laugh of exasperation and impatience which marks the intolerable almost more than tears do. How was it? Can any one explain this mystery? She was of a much more vivacious, robust, and vigorous race than he was, for the level of health among the Warrenders, like the level of being generally, was low; but this lively, warm-blooded, energetic creature was swallowed up in the dull current of the family life, and did not affect it at all. She nursed them, ruled them, breathed her life into them, in vain: they were their father's children,—they were

Warrenders born.

This was not precisely the case with Theo, her only son. To him she had transmitted something; not her energy and love of life, but rather something of that exasperated impatience which was so often the temper of her mind in later years, though suppressed by all the powers of self-control she possessed, and modified, happily, by the versatility of her nature, which could not brood and mope over one subject, however deeply that might enter into her life. This impatience took in him the form of a fastidious intolerance, a disposition to start aside at a touch, to put up with nothing, to hear no reason even, when he was offended or crossed. He was like a restive horse, whom the mere movement of a shadow, much more the touch of a rein or the faintest vibration of a whip, sets off in the wildest gallop of nervous self-will or self-assertion. The horse, it is to be supposed, desires his own way as much as the man does when he bolts or starts. Theo was in this respect wonderfully unlike the strain of the Warrenders, but he was not on that account more like his mother; and he had so much of the calm of the paternal blood in his veins along with this unmanageableness that he was as contented as the rest with the quiet of the home life, and so long as he was permitted to shut himself up with his book wished for no distraction,—nay, disliked it, and thought society and amusements an intolerable bore.

Thus it was the mother alone to whom the thought of change was pleasant. A woman of forty-five in widow's weeds, who had just nursed her husband through a long illness and lost him, and whose life since she was nineteen had been spent in this quiet house among all these still surroundings, amid the unchangeable traditions of rural life,—who could have ventured to imagine the devouring impatience that was within her, the desire to flee, to shake the dust off her feet, to leave her home and all her associations, to get out into the world and breathe a larger air and be free? Sons and daughters may entertain such sentiments; even the girls, whose life, no doubt, had been a dull one, might be supposed willing enough, with a faint pretence of natural and traditionary reluctance, and those few natural tears which are wiped so soon, to leave home and see the world. But the mother! In ordinary circumstances it would have been the duty of the historian to set forth the hardness of Mrs. Warrender's case, deprived at once, by her husband's death, not only of her companion and protector, but of her home and position as head of an important house. Such a case is no doubt often a hard one. It adds a hundred little humiliations to grief, and makes bereavement downfall, the overthrow of a woman's importance in the world, and her exile from the sphere in which she has spent her life. We should be far more sure of the reader's sympathy if we pictured her visiting for the last time all the familiar haunts of past years, tearing herself away from the beloved rooms, feeling the world a blank before her as she turned away.

On the contrary, it is scarcely possible to describe the chill of disappointment in her mind when Theo put an abrupt stop to all speculations, and offered her his arm to lead her upstairs. She ought, perhaps, to have wanted his support to go upstairs, after all, as her maid said, that she had "gone through": but she did not feel the necessity. She would have preferred much to know what was going to be done, to talk over everything, to be able to express without further sense that they were premature and inappropriate, as much as it would be expedient to express of her own wishes. The absolute repression of those five dark days, during which she had said nothing, had been almost more intolerable to her than years of the repression which was past. When you know that nothing you can do or say is of any use, and that whatsoever struggle you may make will be wholly ineffectual to change your lot, it is comparatively easy, in the composure of impossibility, to keep yourself down; but when all at once you become again master of your own fate, even a temporary curb becomes intolerable. Mrs. Warrender went into her room by the compulsion of her son and conventional propriety, and was supposed to lie down on the sofa and rest for an hour or two. Her maid arranged the cushions for her, threw a shawl over her feet, and left her on tip-toe, shutting the door with elaborate precautions. Mrs. Warrender remained still for nearly half an hour. She wept, with a strange mixture of feelings; partly out of a poignant sense of the fictitiousness of all these observances by which people were supposed to show "respect" to the dead, and partly out of a real aching of the heart and miserable sense that even now, that certainly by and by, the man who had been so all-important a little while ago would be as if he had not been. She wept for him, and yet at the same time wept because she could not weep more for him, because the place which knew him had already begun to know him no more, and because of the sham affliction with which they were all supplementing the true. It was she who shed the truest tears, but it was she also who rebelled most at the make-believe which convention forced upon her; and the usual sense of hopeless exasperation was strong in her mind. After a while she threw off the shawl from her feet and the cushions that supported her shoulders, and got up and walked about the room, looking out upon the afternoon sunshine and the trees that were turning their shadows to the east. How she longed, with a fervour scarcely explainable, not at all comprehensible to most people, to leave the place, to open her wings in a large atmosphere, to get free!

At half-past four o'clock Minnie and Chatty went down to tea. They were to the minute, and their mother heard them with a half smile. It was always time enough for her to smooth her hair and her collar, and take a new handkerchief from her drawer, when she heard the sisters close their door. She went downstairs after them, in her gown covered with crape, with her snowy cap, which gave dignity to her appearance. Her widow's dress was very becoming to her, as it is to so many people. She had a pretty complexion, pure red and white, though the colour was perhaps a little broken, and not so smooth as a girl's; and her eyes were brown and bright. Notwithstanding the weeks of watching she had gone through, the strain of everything that had passed, she made little show of her trouble. Her eye was not dim, nor her natural force abated. The girls were dull in complexion and aspect, but their mother was not so. As she came into the room there came with her a brightness, a sense of living, which was inappropriate to the hour and the place.

"Where is Theo?" she asked.

"He is coming in presently; at least, I called to him as he went out, and told him tea was ready, and he said he would be in presently," Chatty replied.

"I wish he would have stayed, if it had even been in the grounds, to-day," said Minnie. "It will look so strange to see him walking about as if nothing had happened."

"He has been very good; he has conformed to all our little rules," said the mother, with a sigh.

"Little rules, mamma? Don't you think it of importance, then, that every respect——"

"My dear," said Mrs. Warrender, "I am tired of hearing of every respect. Theo was always respectful and affectionate. I would not misconstrue him even if it should prove that he has taken a walk."

"On the day of dear papa's funeral!" cried Minnie, with a voice unmoved.

Mrs. Warrender turned away without any reply; partly because the tears sprang into her eyes at the matter-of-fact statement, and partly because her patience was exhausted.

"Have you settled, mamma, what he is going to do?" said Chatty.

"It is not for me to decide. He is twenty-one; he is his own master. You have not," Mrs. Warrender said, "taken time to think yet of the change in our circumstances. Theo is now master here. Everything is his to do as he pleases."

"Everything!" said the girls in chorus, opening their eyes.

"I mean, of course, everything but what is yours and what is mine. You know your father's will. He has been very just, very kind, as he always was." She paused a little, and then went on:

"But your brother, as you know, is now the master here. We must understand what his wishes are before we can settle on anything."

"Why shouldn't we go on as we always have done?" said Minnie. "Theo is too young to marry; besides, it would not be decent for a time, even if he wanted to, which I am sure he does not. I don't see why he should make any change. There is nowhere we can be so well as at home."

"Oh, nowhere!" said Chatty.

Their mother sat and looked at them, with a dull throb in her heart. They had sentiment and right on their side, and nature too. Everybody would agree that for a bereaved family there was no place so good as home,—the house in which they were born and where they had lived all their life. She looked at them blankly, feeling how unnatural, how almost wicked, was the longing in her own mind to get away, to escape into some place where she could take large breaths and feel a wide sky over her. But how was she to say it, how even to conclude what she had been saying, feeling how inharmonious it was with everything around?

"Still," she said meekly, "I am of Mr. Longstaffe's opinion that everything should be fully understood between us from the first. If we all went on just the same, it might be very painful to Theo, when the time came for him to marry (not now; of course there is no question of that now), to feel that he could not do so without turning his mother and sisters out-of-doors."

"Why should he marry, so long as he has us? It is not as if he had nobody, and wanted some one to make him a home. What would he do with the house if we were to leave it? Would he let it? I don't believe he could let it. It would set everybody talking. Why should he turn his mother and sisters out-of-doors? Oh, I never thought of anything so dreadful!" cried Minnie and Chatty, one uttering one exclamation, and another the other. They were very literal, and in the minds of both the grievance was at once taken for granted. "Oh, I never could have thought such a thing of Theo,—our own brother, and younger than we are!"

The mother had made two or three ineffectual attempts to

stem the tide of indignation. "Theo is thinking of nothing of the kind," she said at last, when they were out of breath. "I only say that he must not feel he has but that alternative when the time comes, when he may wish—when it may be expedient——No, no, he has never thought of such a thing. I only say it for the sake of the future, to forestall after-complications."

"Oh, I wish you wouldn't frighten one, mamma! I thought you had heard about some girl he had picked up at Oxford, or something. I thought we should have to turn out, to leave the Warren—which would break my heart."

"And mine too,—and mine too!" cried Chatty.

"Where we have always been so happy, with nothing to disturb us!"

"Oh, so happy! always the same, one day after another! It will be different," said the younger sister, crying a little, "now that dear papa—— But still no place ever can be like home."

And there was the guilty woman sitting by, listening to everything they said; feeling how good, how natural, it was,—and still more natural, still more seemly, for her, at her age, than for them at theirs,—yet conscious that this house was a prison to her, and that of all things in the world that which she wanted most was to be turned out and driven away!

"My dears," she said, not daring to betray this feeling, "if I have frightened you, I did not mean to do it. The house in Highcombe, you know, is mine. It will be our home if—if anything should happen. I thought it might be wise to have that ready, to make it our headquarters, in case—in case Theo should carry out the improvements."

"Improvements!" they cried with one voice. "What improvements? How could the Warren be improved?"

"You must not speak to me in such a tone. There has always been a question of cutting down some of the trees."

"But papa would never agree to it; papa said he would never consent to it."

"I think," said Mrs. Warrender, with a guilty blush, "that he—

had begun to change his mind."

"Only when he was growing weak, then,—only when you over-persuaded him."

"Minnie! I see that your brother was right, and that this is not a time for any discussion," Mrs. Warrender said.

There was again a silence: and they all came back to the original state of mind from which they started, and remembered that quiet and subdued tones and an incapacity for the consideration of secular subjects were the proper mental attitude for all that remained of this day.

It was not, however, long that this becoming condition lasted. Sounds were heard as of voices in the distance, and then some one running at full speed across the gravel drive in front of the door, and through the hall. Minnie had risen up in horror to stop this interruption, when the door burst open, and Theo, pale and excited, rushed in. "Mother," he cried, "there has been a dreadful accident. Markland has been thrown by those wild brutes of his, and I don't know what has happened to him. It was just at the gates, and they are bringing him here. There is no help for it. Where can they take him to?"

Mrs. Warrender rose to her feet at once; her heart rising too almost with pleasure to the thrill of a new event. She hurried out to open the door of a large vacant room on the ground floor. "What was Lord Markland doing here?" she said. "He ought to have reached home long ago."

"He has been in *that* house in the village, mother. They seemed to think everybody would understand. I don't know what he has to do there."

"He has nothing to do there. Oh, Theo, that poor young wife of his! And had he the heart to go from—from—us, in our trouble—there!"

"He seems to have paid for it, whatever was wrong in it. Go back to the drawing-room, for here they are coming."

"Theo, they are carrying him as if he were——"

"Go back to the drawing-room, mother. Whatever it is, it

43

cannot be helped," Theodore said. He did not mean it, but there was something in his tone which reminded everybody—the servants, who naturally came rushing to see what was the matter, and Mrs. Warrender, who withdrew at his bidding—that he was now the master of the house.

CHAPTER V.

Markland was a much more important place than the Warren. It was one of the chief places in the county in which the family had for many generations held so great a position. It was a large building, with all that irregularity of architecture which is dear to the English mind,—a record of the generations which had passed through it and added to it, in itself a noble historical monument, full of indications of the past. But it lost much of its effect upon the mind from the fact that it was in much less good order than is usual with houses of similar pretensions; and above all because the wood around it had been wantonly and wastefully cut, and it stood almost unsheltered upon its little eminence, with only a few seedling trees, weedy and long, like boys who had outgrown their strength, straggling about the heights. The house itself was thus left bare to all the winds. An old cedar, very large but very feeble, in the tottering condition of old age to which some trees, like men, come, with two or three of its longest branches torn off by storm and decay, interposed its dark foliage over the lower roof of the west wing, and gave a little appearance of shelter, and a few Lombardy poplars and light-leaved young birches made a thin and interrupted screen to the east; but the house stood clear of these light and frivolous young attendants in a nakedness which made the spectator shiver. The wood in the long avenue had been thinned in almost the same ruthless way, but here and there were shady corners, where old trees, not worth much in the market, but very valuable to the landscape, laid their heads together like ancient retainers, and rustled and nodded their disapproval of the devastation around.

Young Lady Markland, with her boy, on the afternoon of the June day on which Mr. Warrender was buried, walked up and down for some time in front of the house, casting many anxious looks down the avenue, by which, in its present denuded state, every approaching visitor was so easily visible. She was still very young, though her child was about eight; she having been married, so to speak, out of the nursery, a young creature of sixteen, a motherless girl, with no one to investigate too closely into the character of the young lover, who was not much more than a boy himself, and between whom and his girlish bride a hot, foolish young love had sprung up like a mushroom, in a week or two of acquaintance. She was twenty-five, but did not look her age. She was small in stature,—one of those exquisitely neat little women whose perfection of costume and appearance no external accident disturbs. Her dress had the look of being moulded on her light little figure; her hair was like brown satin, smooth as a mirror and reflecting the light. She did not possess the large grace of abstract beauty. There was nothing statuesque, nothing majestic, about her, but a kind of mild perfection, a fitness and harmony which called forth the approval of the more serious-minded portion of humanity as well as the admiration of the younger and more frivolous.

It was generally known in the county that this young lady had far from a happy life. She had been married in haste and over-confidence by guardians who, if not glad to be rid of her, were at least pleased to feel that their responsibility was over, and the orphan safe in her husband's care, without taking too much pains to prove that the husband was worthy of that charge, or that there was much reasonable prospect of his devotion to it. Young Markland, it was understood, had sown his wild oats somewhat plentifully at Oxford and elsewhere; and it was therefore supposed, with very little logic, that there were no more to sow. But this had not proved to be the case, and almost before his young wife had reached the age of understanding, and was able to put two and two together, he had run through the fortune she brought him—not a very large one—and made her heart ache, which was worse, as hearts under twenty ought never to learn how to ache. She was not a happy wife. The country all about, the servants, and every villager near knew it, but not from Lady Markland. She was very loyal, which is a noble quality, and very proud, which in some cases does duty as a noble quality, and is accepted as such. What were the secrets of her married life no one ever heard from her; and fortunately those griefs which were open to all the world never reached her, at least in detail. She did not know, save vaguely, in what society her husband spent the frequent absences which separated him from her. She did not know what kind of friends he made, what houses he frequented, even in his own neighbourhood; and she was still under the impression that many of her wrongs were known by herself alone, and that his character had suffered but little in the eyes of the world.

There was one person, however, from whom she had not been able to hide these wrongs, and that was her child;—her only child. There had been two other babies, dead at their birth or immediately after, but Geoff was the only one who had lived, her constant companion, counsellor, and aid. At eight years old! Those who had never known what a child can be at that age, when thus entrusted with the perilous deposit of the family secrets, and elevated to the post which his father ought but did not care to fill, were apt to think little Geoff's development unnatural; and others thought, with reason, that it was bad for the little fellow to be so constantly with his mother, and it was said among the Markland relations that as he was now growing a great boy he ought to be sent to school Poor little Geoff! He was not a great boy, nor ever would be. He was small, *chétif*, unbeautiful; a little sandy-haired, sandy-complexioned, insignificant boy, with no features to speak of and no stamina, short for his age and of uncertain health, which had indeed been the first reason of that constant association with his mother which was supposed to be so bad for him. During the first years of his life, which had been broken by continual illness, it was only her perpetual care that kept him alive at all. She had never left him, never given up the charge of him to any one; watched him by night and lived with him by day. His careless father would sometimes say, in one of those brags which show a heart of shame even in the breast of the vicious, that if he had not left her so much to herself, if he had dragged her about into society, as so many men did their wives, she never would have kept her boy; and perhaps there was some truth in it. While he pursued his pleasures in regions where no wife could accompany him, she was free to devote all her life, and to find out every new expedient that skill or science had thought of to lengthen out the child's feeble days, and to gain time to make a cure possible. He would never be very strong was the verdict now, but with care he would live: and it was she who had over again breathed life into him. This made the tie a double one; not out of gratitude, for the child knew of no such secondary sentiment, but out of the redoubled love which their constant association called forth. They did not talk together of any family sorrows. It was never intimated between them that anything wrong happened when papa was late and mamma anxious, or when there were people at Markland who were not *nice*,—oh, not a word; but the child was anxious as well as mamma. He too got the habit of watching, listening for the hurried step, the wild rattle of the phaeton with those two wild horses, which Lord Markland insisted on driving, up the avenue. He knew everything, partly by observation, partly by instinct. He walked with his mother now, clinging with both hands to her arm, his head nearly on a level with her shoulder, and close, close to it, almost touching, his little person confused in the outline of her dress. The sunshine lay full along the line of the avenue, just broken in two or three places by the shadow of those old and useless trees, but without a speck upon it or a sound.

"I don't think papa can be coming, Geoff, and it is time you had your tea."

"Never mind me. I'll go and take it by myself, if you want me to, and you can wait here."

"Why?" she said. "It will not bring him home a moment sooner, as you and I know."

"No, but it feels as if it made him come; and you can see as far as the gate. It takes a long time to drive up the avenue. Oh yes, stop here; you will like that best."

"I am so silly," she said, which was her constant excuse. "When you are grown up, Geoff, I shall always be watching for you."

"That you shan't," said the boy. "I'll never leave you. You have had enough of that."

"Oh yes, my darling, you will leave me. I shall want you to leave me. A boy cannot be always with his mother. Come, now, I am going to be strong-minded. Let us go in. I am a little tired, I think."

"Perhaps the funeral was later than he thought," said the boy.

"Perhaps. It was very kind of papa to go. He does not like things of that kind; and he was not over-fond of Mr. Warrender, who, though he was very good, was a little dull. Papa doesn't like dull people."

"No. Do you like Theo Warrender, mamma?"

"Well enough," said Lady Markland. "I don't know him very much."

"I like him," said the child. "He knows a lot: he told me how to do that Latin. He is the sort of man I should like for my tutor."

"But he is a gentleman, Geoff. I mean, he would never be a tutor. He is as well off as we are,—perhaps better."

"Are men tutors only when they are not well off?"

"Well, dear, generally when they require the money. You could not expect young Mr. Warrender to come here and take a great deal of trouble, merely for the pleasure of teaching you."

"Why not?" said Geoff. "Isn't it a fine thing to teach children? It was you that said so, mamma."

"For me, dear, that am your mother; but not for a gentleman who is not even a relation."

"Gentlemen, to be sure, are different," said Geoff, with an air of deliberation. "There's papa, for instance——"

His mother threw up her hand suddenly. "Hark, Geoff! Do

you hear anything?"

They had come indoors while this talk was going on, and were now seated in a large but rather shabby sitting-room, which was full of Geoff's toys and books. The windows were wide open, but the sounds from without came in subdued; for this room was at the back of the house, and at some distance from the avenue. They were both silent for some moments, listening, and then Lady Markland said, with an air of relief, "Papa is coming. I hear the sound of the phaeton."

"That is not the phaeton, mamma; that is only one horse," said Geoff, whose senses were very keen. When Lady Markland had listened a little longer, she acquiesced in this opinion.

"It will be some one coming to call," she said, with an air of resignation; and then they went on with their talk.

"Gentlemen are different; they don't take the charge of the children like you. However, in books," said Geoff, "the fathers very often are a great deal of good; they tell you all sorts of things. But books are not very like real life; do you think they are? Even Frank, in Miss Edgeworth, though you say he is so good, doesn't do things like me. I mean, I should never think of doing things like him; and no little girl would ever be so silly. Now, mamma, say true, what do you think? Would any little girl ever be so silly as to want the big bottle out of a physic shop? Girls may be silly, but not so bad as that."

"Perhaps, let us hope, she didn't know so much about physic shops, as you call them, as you do, my poor boy. I wonder who can be calling to-day, Geoff! I should have thought that everybody near would be thinking of the Warrenders, and——
It is coming very fast, don't you think? But it does not sound like the phaeton."

"Oh no, it is not the phaeton. I'll go and look," said Geoff. He came back in a moment, crying, "I told you—it's a brougham! Coming at such a pace!"

"I wonder who it can be!" Lady Markland said.

And when the boy resumed his talk she listened with

inattention, trying in vain to keep her interest fixed on what he was saying, making vague replies, turning over a hundred possibilities in her mind, but by some strange dulness, such as is usual enough in similar circumstances, never thinking of the real cause. What danger could there be to Markland in a drive of half a dozen miles, in the daylight; what risk in Mr. Warrender's funeral? The sense that something which was not an ordinary visit was coming grew stronger and stronger upon her, but of the news which was about to reach her she never thought at all.

At last the door opened. She rose hastily, unable to control herself, to meet it, whatever it was. It was not a ceremonious servant announcing a visit, but Theo Warrender, pale as death itself, with a whole tragic volume in his face, but speechless, not knowing, now that he stood before her, what to say, who appeared in the doorway. He had hurried off, bringing his mother's little brougham to carry the young wife to her husband's bedside; but it was not until he looked into her face and heard the low cry that burst from her that he realised what he had to tell. He had forgotten that a man requires all his skill and no small preparation to enable him to tell a young woman that her husband, who left her in perfect health a few hours before, was now on the brink of death. He stopped short on the threshold, awed by this thought, and only stared at her, not knowing what to say.

"Mr. Warrender!" she said, with the utmost surprise; then, with growing wonder and alarm, "You have come—— Something has happened!"

"Lady Markland—yes, there has been an accident. My mother—sent me with the brougham. I came off at once. Will you go back with me? The horse is very fast, and you can be there in half an hour."

This was all he could find to say. She went up to him, holding out her hands in an almost speechless appeal. "Why for me? Why for me? What has it got to do with me?"

He did not know how to answer her question. "Lady Markland!" he cried, "your husband——" and said no more.

She was at the door of the brougham in a moment. She had not taken off her garden hat, and she wanted no preparation. The child sprang to her side, caught her arm, and went with her without a word or question, as if that were undeniably his place. Everybody knew and remarked upon the singular union between the neglected young wife and her only child, but Warrender felt, he could scarcely tell why, that it annoyed and irritated him at this moment. When he put her into the carriage, and the boy clambered after her, he was unaccountably vexed by it,—so much vexed that his profound sympathy for the poor lady seemed somehow checked. Instead of following them into the carriage, which was not a very roomy one, he shut the door upon them sharply. "I will walk," he said. "I am not needed. Right, Jarvis, as fast as you can go." He stood by to see them dash off, Lady Markland giving him a surprised yet half-relieved look, in the paleness of her anxiety and misery. Then it suddenly became apparent to him that he had done what was best and most delicate, though without meaning it, out of the sudden annoyance which had risen within him. It was the best thing he could have done: but to walk six miles at the end of a fatiguing and trying day was not agreeable, and the sense of irritation was strong in him. "If ever I have anything to do with that boy——" he said involuntarily within himself. But what could he ever have to do with the boy, who probably by this time, little puny thing that he was, was Lord Markland, and the owner of all this great, bare, unhappy-looking place, eaten up by the locusts of waste and ruin.

The butler, an old servant, had been anxiously trying all this time to catch his eye. He came up now, as Warrender turned to follow on foot the carriage, which was already almost out of sight. "I beg your pardon, sir," he said, with the servant's usual formula, "but I've sent round for the dogcart, if you'll be so kind as to wait a few minutes. None of us, sir, but feels your kindness, coming yourself for my lady, and leaving her alone in her trouble, poor dear. Mr. Warrender, sir, if I may make so bold, what is the fact about my lord? Yes, sir, I heard what you told my lady; but I thought you would nat'rally say the best, not to frighten her. Is there any hope?"

"Not much, I fear. He was thrown out violently, and struck against a tree; they are afraid that his spine is injured."

"Oh, sir, so young! and oh, so careless! God help us, Mr. Warrender, we never know a step before us, do we, sir? If it's the spine, it will be no pain; and him so joky, more than his usual, going off them very steps this morning, though he was going to a funeral. Oh, Mr. Warrender, that I should speak so light, forgetting—— God bless us, what an awful thing, sir, after what has happened already, to happen in your house!"

Warrender answered with a nod,—he had no heart to speak; and, refusing the dogcart, he set out on his walk home. An exquisite summer night: everything harsh stilled out of the atmosphere; the sounds of labour ceasing; a calm as of profoundest peace stealing over everything. The soft and subdued pain of his natural grief, hushed by that fatigue and exhaustion of both body and mind which a long strain produces, was not out of accord with the calm of nature. But very different was the harsh note of the new calamity, which had struck not the house in which the tragedy was being enacted, but this one, which lay bare and naked in the last light of the sinking sun. So young and so careless! So young, so wasteful of life and all that life had to give, and now parted from it, taken from it at a blow!

CHAPTER VI.

Lord Markland died at the Warren that night. He never recovered consciousness, nor knew that his wife was by his side through all the dreadful darkening of the summer evening, which seemed to image forth in every new tone of gathering gloom the going out of life. They told her as much as was necessary of the circumstances,—how, the distance between the Warren and the churchyard being so short, and the whole cortège on foot, Lord Markland's carriage had been left in the village; how he had stayed there to luncheon (presumably with the rector, for no particulars were given, nor did the bewildered young woman ask for any), which was the reason of his delay. The rest was very easily explained: everybody had said to him that "some accident" would happen one day or other with the horses he insisted on driving, and the prophecy had been fulfilled. Such prophecies are always fulfilled. Lady Markland was very quiet, accepting that extraordinary revolution in her life with a look of marble, and words that betrayed nothing. Was she broken-hearted? was she only stunned by the suddenness, the awe, of such a catastrophe? The boy clung to her, yet without a tear, pale and silent, but never, even when the words were said that all was over, breaking forth into any childish outburst. He sat on the floor in her shadow, even when she was watching by the deathbed, never left her, keeping always a hold upon her arm, her hand, or her dress. Mrs. Warrender would have taken him away, and put him to bed,—it was so bad for him; but the boy opposed a steady resistance, and Lady Markland put down her hand to him, not seeing how wrong it was to indulge him, all the ladies said. After this, of course nothing could be done, and he remained with her through all that followed. What followed was strange enough to have afforded a scene for a tragedy. Lady Markland asked to speak to Warrender, who had retired, leaving his mother, as was natural, to manage everything. He came to her at the door of the room which had so suddenly, with its bare, unused look, in the darkness of a few flickering candles, become a sort of presence chamber filled with the solemnity of dying. Her little figure, so neat and orderly, an embodiment of the settled peace and calm of life having nothing to do with tragedies, with the child close pressed against her side, his pale face looking as hers did, pale too and stony—never altogether passed from the memory of the man who came, reluctant, almost afraid, to hear what she had to say to him. It was like a picture against the darkness of the room,—a darkness both physical and moral, which centred in the curtained gloom behind, about which two shadowy figures were busy. Often and with very different sentiments he saw this group again, but never wholly forgot it, or had it effaced from the depths of his memory.

"Mr. Warrender," she said, in a voice which was very low, yet he thought might have been heard all over the house, "I want you to help me."

"Whatever I can do," he began, with some fervour, for he was young, and his heart was touched.

"I want," she continued, "to carry him home at once. I know it will not be easy, but it is night, and all is quiet. You are a man; you will know better how it can be done. Manage it for me."

Warrender was entirely unprepared for such a commission. "There will be great difficulties, dear Lady Markland," he said. "It is a long way. I am sure my mother would not wish you to think of her. This is a house of death. Let him stay."

She gave him a sort of smile, a softening of her stony face, and put out her hand to him. "Do it for me," she said. She was not at all moved by his objections,—perhaps she did not even hear them; but when she had thus repeated her command, as a queen might have done, she turned back into the room, and sat down, to wait, it seemed, until that command should be accomplished.

Warrender went away with a most perplexed and troubled mind. He was half pleased, underneath all, that she should have sent for him and charged him with this office, but bewildered with the extraordinary commission, and not knowing what to do.

"What is it, Theo? What did she want with you?" his sisters cried, in subdued voices, but eager to know everything about Lady Markland, who had been as the stars in the sky to them a little while before.

He told them in a few words, and they filled the air with whispered exclamations. "How odd, how strange; oh, how unusual, Theo! People will say it is our doing. They will say, How dreadful of the Warrenders! Oh, tell her you can't do it! How could you do it, in the middle of the night!"

"That is just what I don't know," Warrender rejoined.

"Mr. Theo," said the old man, who was not dignified with the name of butler, "the lady is quite right. I can't tell you how it's to be done, but gardener, he is a very handy man, and he will know. The middle of the night—that's just what makes it easy, young ladies; and instead o' watching and waiting, the 'holl of us 'ull get to bed."

"That is all you're thinking of, Joseph."

"Well, it's a deal, sir, after all that's been going on in this house," Joseph said, with an aggrieved air. He had to provide supper, which was a thing unknown at the Warren, after all the trouble that every one had been put to. He was himself of opinion that to be kept up beyond your usual hours, and subjected to unexpected fatigues, made a "bit of supper" needful even for the uncomfortable and incomprehensible people whom he called the quality. They were a poorish lot, and he had a mild contempt for them, and to get them supper was a hardship; still, it was his own suggestion, and he was bound to carry it out.

It is unnecessary to enter into all Warrender's perplexities and all the expedients that were suggested. At last the handy gardener and himself hit upon a plan by which Lady Markland's wishes could be carried out. She sat still in the gloomy room where her husband lay dead, waiting till they should be ready; doubting nothing, as little disturbed by any difficulty as if it had been the simplest commission in the world which she had given the young man. Geoff sat at her feet, leaning against her, holding her hand. It is to be supposed that he slept now and then, as the slow moments went on, but whenever any one spoke to his mother his eyes would be seen gleaming against the darkness of her dress. They sat there waiting, perfectly still, with the candles flickering faintly about the room in the night air that breathed in through the open windows. The dark curtains had been drawn round the bed. It was like a catafalque looming darkly behind. Mrs. Warrender had used every persuasion to induce her guest to come into another room, to take something, to rest, to remember all that remained for her to do, and not waste her strength,— all those formulas which come naturally to the lips at such a moment. Lady Markland only answered with that movement of her face which was intended for a smile and a shake of her head.

At last the preparations were all complete. The night was even more exquisite than the evening had been; it was more still, every sound having died out of the earth except those which make up silence,—the rustling among the branches, the whirr of unseen insects, the falling of a leaf or a twig. The moon threw an unbroken light over the broad fields; the sky spread out all its stars, in myriads and myriads, faintly radiant, softened by the larger light; the air breathed a delicate, scarcely perceptible fragrance of growing grass, moist earth, and falling dew. How sweet, how calm, how full of natural happiness! Through this soft atmosphere and ethereal radiance a carriage made its way that was improvised with all the reverence and tenderness possible, in which lay the young man, dead, cut off in the very blossom and glory of his days, followed by another in which sat the young woman who had been his wife. What she was thinking of who could tell? Of their half-childish love and wooing, of the awaking of her own young soul to trouble and disappointment, of her many dreary days and years; or of the sudden severance, without a moment's warning, without a leave-taking, a word, or a look? Perhaps all these things, now for a moment distinct, now mingling confusedly together, formed the current of her thoughts. The child, clasped in her arms, slept upon her shoulder; nature being too strong at last for that which was beyond nature, the identification of his childish soul with that of his mother. She was glad that he slept, and glad to be silent, alone, the soft air blowing in her face, the darkness encircling her like a veil.

Warrender went with this melancholy cortége, making its way slowly across the sleeping country. He saw everything done that could be done: the dead man laid on his own bed; the living woman, in whom he felt so much more interest, returned to the shelter of her home and the tendance of her own servants. His part in the whole matter was over when he stepped back into the brougham which she had left. The Warrenders had seen but little of the Marklands, though they were so near. The habits of the young lord had naturally been little approved by Theo Warrender's careful parents; and his manners, when the young intellectualist from Oxford met him, were revolting at once to his good taste and good breeding. On the other hand, the Warrenders were but small people in comparison, and any intimacy with Lord and Lady Markland was almost impossible. It was considered by all the neighbours "a great compliment" when Lord Markland came to the funeral. Ah, poor Markland, had he not come to the funeral! Yet how vain to say so, for his fate had been long prophesied, and what did it matter in what special circumstances it came to pass! But Warrender felt, as he left the house, that there could be no longer distance and partial acquaintance between the two families. Their lines of life—or was it of death?—had crossed and been woven together. He felt a faint thrill go through him,—a thrill of consciousness, of anticipation, he could not tell what Certainly it was not possible that the old blank of non-connection could ever exist again. *She*, to whom he had scarcely spoken before, who had been so entirely out of his sphere, had now come into it so strangely, so closely, that she could never be separated from his thoughts. She might break violently the visionary tie between them,—she might break it, angry to have been drawn into so close a relation to any strangers,—but it never could be shaken off.

He drove quickly down the long bare avenue, where all was so naked and clear, and put his head out of the carriage window to look back at the house, standing out bare and defenceless in the full moonlight, showing faintly, through the white glory which blazed all around, a little pitiful glimmer of human lights in the closed windows, the watch-lights of the dead. It seemed a long time to the young man since in his own house these watch-lights had been extinguished. The previous event seemed to have become dim to him, though he was so much more closely connected with it, in the presence of this, which was more awful, more terrible. He tried to return to the thoughts of the morning, when his father was naturally in all things his first occupation, but it was impossible to do it. Instead of the thoughts which became him, as being now in his father's place, with the fortunes and comfort of his family more or less depending upon him, all that his mind would follow were the events of this afternoon, so full of fate. He saw Lady Markland stand, with the child clinging to her, in the dim room, the shrouded bed and indistinct attendant figures behind, the dimly flickering lights. Why had she so claimed his aid, asked for his service, with that certainty of being obeyed? Her every word trembled in his ear still:—they were very few; but they seemed to be laid up there in some hidden repository, and came out and said themselves over again when he willed, moving him as he never had been moved before. He made many efforts to throw off this involuntary preoccupation as the carriage rolled quickly along; the tired horse quickening its pace as it felt the attraction of home, the tired coachman letting it go almost at its own pleasure, the broad moonlight fields, with their dark fringes of hedge, spinning past. Then the village went past him, with all its sleeping houses, the church standing up like a protecting shadow. He looked out again at this, straining his eyes to see the dark spot where his father was lying, the first night in the bosom of the earth: and this thought brought him back for a moment to himself. But the next, as the carriage glided on into the shadow of the trees, and the overgrown copses of the Warren received him into their shadow, this other intrusive tragedy, this story which was not his, returned and took possession of him once more. To see her standing there, speaking so calmly, with the soft tones that perhaps would have been imperious in other circumstances: "Do it for me." No question whether it could be done, or if he could do it. One thing only there was that jarred throughout all,—the child that was always there, forming part of her. "If ever I have anything to do with that boy"—Warrender said to himself; and then there was a moment of dazzle and giddiness, and the carriage stopped, and a door opened, and he found himself standing out in the fresh, soft night with his mother, on the threshold of his own home. There was a light in the hall behind her, where she stood, with the whiteness of the widow's cap, which was still a novelty and strange feature in her, waiting till he should return. It was far on in the night, and except herself the household was asleep. She came out to him, wistfully looking in his face by the light of the moon.

"You did everything for her, Theo?"

"All that I could. I saw him laid upon his bed. There was nothing more for me to do."

"Are you very tired, my boy? You have done so much."

"Not tired at all. Come out with me a little. I can't go in yet. It is a lovely night."

"Oh, Theo, lovely and full of light!—the trees, and the bushes, and every blade of grass sheltering something that is living; and yet death, death reigning in the midst."

She leaned her head upon his arm and cried a little, but he did not make any response. It was true, no doubt, but other thoughts were in his mind.

"She will have great trouble with that child, when he grows up," he said, as if he had been carrying on some previous argument.

"It is ridiculous to have him always hanging about her, as if he could understand."

Mrs. Warrender started, and the movement made his arm which she held tremble, but he did not think what this meant. He thought she was tired, and this recalled his thoughts momentarily to her. "Poor mother!" he said; "you sat up for me, not thinking of your own fatigue and trouble, and you are over-tired. Am I a trouble to you, *too*?" His mind was still occupied with the other train of thinking, even when he turned to subjects more his own.

"Do you know," she said, not caring to reply, "it is the middle of the night?"

"Yes, and you should be in bed. But I couldn't sleep. I have never had anything of the kind to do before, and it takes all desire to rest out of one. It will soon be daylight. I think I shall take my bath, and then get to work."

"Oh no, Theo. You would not work,—you would think; and there are some circumstances in which thinking is not desirable. Come out into the moonlight. We will take ten minutes, and then, my dear boy, good-night."

"Good-morning, you mean, mother, and everything new,—a new life. It has never been as it will be to-morrow. Have you thought of that?" She gave a sudden pressure to his arm, and he perceived his folly. "That I should speak so to you, to whom the greatest change of all has come!"

"Yes," she said, with a little tremor. "It is to me that it will make the most difference. And that poor young creature, so much younger than I, who might be my child!"

"Do you think, when she gets over all this, that it will be much to her? People say——"

"That is a strange question to ask," she said, with agitation,—"a very strange question to ask. When we get over all this,—that is, the shock, and the change, and the awe of the going away,—what will it be then, to all of us? We shall just settle down once more into our ordinary life, as if nothing had happened. That is what will come of it. That is what always comes of it. There is nothing but the common routine, which goes on and on for ever."

She was excited, and shed tears, at which he wondered a little, yet was compassionate of, remembering that she was a woman and worn out. He put his hand upon hers, which lay on his arm. "Poor mother!" he murmured, caressing her hand with his, and feeling all manner of tender cares for her awake in him. Then he added softly, returning in spite of himself to other thoughts, "The force of habit and of the common routine, as you say, cannot be so strong when one is young."

"No," she said; and then, after a pause, "If it is poor Lady Markland you are thinking of, she has her child."

This gave him a certain shock, in the softening of his heart. "The child is the thing I don't like!" he exclaimed, almost sharply. Then he added, "I think the dawn must be near; I feel very chilly. Mother, come in; as you say, it is the best thing not to think, but to go to bed."

CHAPTER VII

The morning rose, as they had said to each other, upon a new life.

How strange it is to realise, after the first blow has fallen, that this changed life is still the same! When it brings with it external changes, family convulsions, the alteration of external circumstances, although these secondary things increase the calamity, they give it also a certain natural atmosphere; they are in painful harmony with it. But when the shock, the dreadful business of the moment, is all over, when the funeral has gone away from the doors and the dead has been buried, and everything goes on as before, this commonplace renewal is, perhaps, the most terrible of all to the visionary soul. Minnie and Chatty got out their work,—the coloured work, which they had thought out of place during the first week. They went in the afternoon for a walk, and gathered fresh flowers, as they returned, for the vases in the drawing-room. When evening came they asked Theo if he would not read to them. It was not a novel they were reading; it was a biography, of a semi-religious character, in which there were a great many edifying letters. They would not, of course, have thought of reading a novel at such a time. Warrender had been wandering about all day, restless, not knowing what to do with himself. He was not given to games of any kind, but he thought to-day that he would have felt something of the sort a relief, though he knew it would have shocked the household. In the afternoon, on a chance suggestion of his mother's, he saw that it was a sort of duty to walk over to Markland and ask how Lady Markland was. Twelve miles—six there and six back again—is a long walk for a student. He sent up his name, and asked whether he could be of any use, but he did not receive encouragement.

Lady Markland sent her thanks, and was quite well ("she says," the old butler explained, with a shake of the head, so that no one might believe he agreed in anything so unbecoming). The Honourable John had been telegraphed for, her husband's uncle, and everything was being done; so that there was no need to trouble Mr. Warrender. He went back, scarcely solaced by his walk. He wanted to be doing something. Not Plato; in the circumstances Plato did not answer at all. When he opened his book his thoughts escaped from him, and went off with a bound to matters entirely different. How was it possible that he could give that undivided attention which divine philosophy requires, the day after his father's funeral, the first day of his independent life, the day after——! That extraordinary postscript to the agitations of yesterday told, perhaps, most of all. When the girls asked him to read to them, opening the book at the page where they had left off, and preparing to tell him all that had gone before, so that he might understand the story ("although there is very little story," Minnie said, with satisfaction; "chiefly thoughts upon serious subjects"), he jumped up from his chair in almost fierce rebellion against that sway of the ordinary of which his mother had spoken. "You were right," he said to her; "the common routine is the thing that outlasts everything. I never thought of it before, but it is true."

Mrs. Warrender, though she had herself been quivering with the long-concentrated impatience for which it seemed even now there could be no outlet, was troubled by her son's outburst, and, afraid of what it might come to, felt herself moved to take the other side. "It is very true," she said, faltering a little, "but the common routine is often best for everything, Theo. It is a kind of leading-string, which keeps us going."

The girls looked up at Theo with alarm and wonder, but still they were not shocked at what *he* said. He was a man; he had come to the Warren from those wild excitements of Oxford life, of which they had heard with awe; they gazed at him, trying to understand him.

"I have always heard," said Minnie, "that reading aloud was the most tranquillising thing people could do. If we had each a book it would be unsociable; but when a book is read aloud, then we are all thinking about the same thing, and it draws us together;" which was really the most sensible judgment that could have been delivered, had the two fantastic ones been in the mood to understand what was said.

Chatty did not say anything, but after she had threaded her needle looked up with great attention to see how the fate of the evening was to be decided. It was a great pleasure when some one would read aloud, especially Theo, who thus became one of them, in a way which was not at all usual; but perhaps she was less earnest about it this evening than on ordinary occasions, for the biographical book was a little dull, and the letters on serious subjects were dreadfully serious. No doubt, just after papa's death, this was appropriate; but still it is well known there are stories which are also serious, and could not do any one harm, even at the gravest moments.

"There are times when leading-strings are insupportable," Theo said; "at any time I don't know that I put much faith in them. We have much to arrange and settle, mother, if you feel able for it."

"Mamma can't feel able yet," returned Minnie. "Oh, why should we make any change? We are so happy as we are."

"I am quite able," said Mrs. Warrender. She had been schooling herself to the endurance which still seemed to be expected of her, but the moment an outlet seemed possible the light kindled in her eye. "I think with Theo that it is far better to decide whatever has to be done at once." Then she cried out suddenly, carried away by the unexpected unhoped-for opportunity, "O children, we must get away from here! I cannot bear it any longer. As though all our own trouble and sorrow were not enough, this other—this other tragedy!" She put up her hands to her eyes, as though to shut out the sight that pressed upon them. "I cannot get it out of my mind. I suppose my nerves and everything are wrong; all night long it seemed to be before me,—the blood on his forehead, the ghastly white face, the labouring breath. Oh, not like your father, who was good and old and peaceful, who was just taken away gently, led away,—but so young and so unprepared! Oh, so unprepared! What could God do with him, cut off in the midst of——"

Minnie got up hastily, with her smelling-salts, which always lay on the table. "Go and get her a glass of water, Theo," she said authoritatively.

Mrs. Warrender laughed. It was a little nervous, but it was a laugh. It seemed to peal through the house, which still was a house of mourning, and filled the girls with a horror beyond words. She put out her hands to put their ministrations away. "I do not want water," she said, "nor salts either. I am not going into hysterics. Sit down and listen to me. I cannot remain here. It is your birthplace, but not mine. I am dying for fresh air and the sight of the sun. If you are shocked, I cannot help it. Theo, when you go back to Oxford I will go to—I don't know where; to some place where there is more air; but here I cannot stay."

This statement was as a thunderbolt falling in the midst of them, and the poor woman perceived this instinctively. Her son's impatience had been the spark which set the smouldering fire in her alight, but even he was astounded by the quick and sudden blaze which lit up the dull wonder in his sisters' faces. And then he no longer thought of going to Oxford. He wanted to remain to see if he could do anything,—perhaps to be of use. A husband's uncle does not commend himself to one's mind as a very devoted or useful ministrant, and even he would go away, of course; and then a man who was nearer, who was a neighbour, who had already been so mixed up with the tragedy,—that was what he had been thinking of; not of Oxford, or his work.

"It is not worth while going back to Oxford," he said; "the term is nearly over. One can read anywhere, at home as well as—I shall not go back at present." He was not accustomed yet to so abrupt a declaration of his sentiments, and for the moment he avoided his mother's eye.

Minnie went back to her seat, and put down the bottle of salts on the table, with an indignant jar. "I am so glad that you feel so, Theo, *too*."

Mrs. Warrender looked round upon her children with despairing eyes. They were all *his* children,—all Warrenders born; knowing as little about her and her ways of thinking as if she had been a stranger to them. She was indeed a stranger to them in the intimate sense. The exasperation that had been in her mind for years could be repressed no longer. "If it is so," she said, "I don't wish to interfere with your plans, Theo; but I will go for—for a little change. I must have it. I am worn out."

"Oh, mamma, you will not surely go by yourself, without us! How could you get on without us!" cried Chatty. She had perhaps, being the youngest, a faint stir of a feeling in her mind that a little change might be pleasant enough. But she took her mother at her word with this mild protest, which made Mrs. Warrender's impatient cry into a statement of fixed resolution: and the others said nothing. Warrender was silent, because he was absorbed in the new thoughts that filled his mind; Minnie, because, like Chatty, she felt quite apart from any such extraordinary wishes, having nothing to do with it, and nothing to say.

"It will be very strange, certainly, for me to be alone,—very strange," Mrs. Warrender said, with a quiver in her voice. "It is so long since I have done anything by myself; not since before you were all born. But if it must be," she added, "I must just take courage as well as I can, and—go by myself, as you say."

Once more there was no response. The girls did not know what to say. Duty, they thought, meant staying at home and doing their crewel-work; they were not capable of any other identification of it all at once. It was very strange, but if mamma thought so, what could they do? She got up with nervous haste, feeling now, since she had once broken bounds, as though the flood of long-restrained feeling was beyond her control altogether. The natural thing would have been to rush upstairs and pack her things, and go off to the railway at once. That, perhaps, might not be practicable; but neither was it practicable to sit quietly amid the silence and surprise, and see her wild, sudden resolution accepted dully, as if a woman could contemplate such a severance calmly. And yet it was true that she must get fresh air or die. Life so long intolerable could be borne no longer.

"I think in the meantime," she said, with a forced smile, "I shall go upstairs."

"You were up very late last night," returned Theo, though rather by way of giving a sort of sanction to her abrupt withdrawal than for any other reason, as he rose to open the door.

"Yes, it was very late. I think I am out of sorts altogether. And if I am to make my plans without any reference to the rest of the family——"

"Oh, that is absurd," he said. "Of course the girls must go with you, if you are really going. But you must not be in a hurry, mother. There is plenty of time; there is no hurry." He was thinking of the time that must elapse before the doors of Markland would be open even to her who had received Lord Markland into her house. Till then he did not want her to go away. When she had left the room he turned upon his sisters and slew them.

"What do you mean, you two? I wonder if you have got hearts of stone, to hear the poor mother talk of going away for a little change, and to sit there like wooden images, and never open your mouths!"

The girls opened their mouths wide at this unexpected reproach. "What could we say? Mamma tells us all in a moment she wants to go away from home! We have always been taught that a girl's place is at home."

"What do you call home?" he asked.

It was a brutal speech, he was aware. Brothers and sisters are permitted to be brutal to each other without much harm done. Minnie had begun calmly, with the usual, "Oh, Theo!" before the meaning of the question struck her. She stopped suddenly, looked up at him, with eyes and lips open, with an astonished stare of inquiry. Then, dull though she was, growing red, repeated in a startled, awakened, interrogative tone, "Oh, Theo!" with a little gasp as for breath.

"I don't mean to be disagreeable," he said. "I never should have been, had not you begun. The mother has tried to make you understand half a dozen times, but I suppose you did not want to understand. Don't you know everything is changed since—since I was last at the Warren? Your home is with my mother now, wherever she chooses to settle down."

It must be said for Warrender that he meant no harm whatever by this. He meant, perhaps, to punish them a little for their heartlessness. He meant them to see that their position was changed,—that they were not as of old, in assured possession; and he reckoned upon that slowness of apprehension which probably would altogether preserve them from any painful consciousness. But it is astonishing how the mind and the senses are quickened when it is ourselves who are in question. Minnie was the leader of the two. She was the first to understand; and then it communicated itself partly by magnetism to Chatty, who woke up much more slowly, having caught as it were only an echo of what her brother said.

"You mean—that this is not our home any more," said Minnie. Her eyes filled with sudden tears, and her face was flushed with the shock. She had seldom looked so well, so thoroughly awakened and mistress of her faculties. When she was roused she had more in her than was apparent on the surface. "I did not think you would be the one to tell us that. Of course we know that it is quite true. Chatty and I are older than you are, but we are only daughters, and you are the boy. You have the power to turn us out,—we all know that."

"Minnie!" cried Chatty, struck with terror, putting out a hand to stop these terrible words,—words such as had never been said in her hearing before.

"But we did not think you would have used it," the elder sister said simply, and then was silent. He expected that she would end the scene by rushing from the room in tears and wrath. But what she did was much more embarrassing. She dried her tears hastily, took up her crewel-work, sat still, and said no more. Chatty threw an indignant but yet at the same time an inquiring glance at him. She had not heard or observed the beginning of the fray, and did not feel quite sure what it was all about.

"I am sure Theo would never do anything that was unkind," she remarked mildly; then after a little pause, "Wouldn't it have been much better to have had the reading? I have noticed that before: when one reads and the others work, there is, as the rector says, a common interest, and we have a nice evening; but when we begin talking instead—well, we think differently, and we disagree, and one says more than one means to say, and then—one is sorry afterwards," Chatty said, after another pause.

On the whole, it was the girls who had the best of it in this encounter. It is impossible to say how much Theo was ashamed of himself when, after Chatty's quite unaccustomed address, which surprised herself as much as her brother and sister, and after an hour of silence, broken by an occasional observation, the girls put aside their crewels again, and remarked that it was time to go to bed. A sense of opposition and that pride which prevents a man from being the first to retire from a battle-field, even when the battle is a failure and the main armies have never engaged, had kept him there during the evening, in spite of himself. But when they left him master of the ground, there can be no doubt that he felt much more like a defeated than a triumphant general. This first consequence of the new *régime* was not a beautiful or desirable one. There were thus three parties in the house on the evening of the first day of their changed existence: the mother, who was so anxious to leave the scene of her past existence behind her; the girls, who clung to their home; the brother, the master, who, half to show that he took his mother's side, half out of instinctive assertion of himself, had let them know roundly that their home was theirs no longer. He was not proud of himself at all as he thought of what he had said; but yet when he recalled it he was not perhaps so sorry for having said it as he had been the minute after the words left his lips. It was better, possibly, as the lawyer, as the mother, as everybody, had said, that the true state of affairs should be fully understood from the first. The house was theirs no longer. The old reign and all its traditions had passed away; a new reign had begun. What that new reign might turn to, who might share it, what wonderful developments it might take, who could tell?

His imagination here went away with a leap into realms of sheer romance. He seemed to see the old house transformed, the free air, the sweet sunshine pouring in, the homely rooms made beautiful, the inhabitants—— What was he thinking of? Did ever imagination go so fast or so far? He stopped himself, with vague smiles stealing to his lips. All that enchanted ground was so new to him that he had no control over his fancy, but went to the utmost length with a leap of bewildering pleasure and daring almost like a child. Yet mingled with this were various elements which were not lovely. He was not, so far as had been previously apparent, selfish beyond the natural liking for his own comfort and his own way, which is almost universal. He had never wished to cut himself off from his family, or to please himself at their expense. But something had come into his mind which is nearer than the nearest,—something which, with a new and uncomprehended fire, hardens the heart on one side while melting it on the other, and brings tenderness undreamed of and cruelty impossible to be believed, from the same source. He felt the conflict of these powers within him when he was left alone in the badly furnished, badly lighted drawing-room, which seemed to reproach him for the retirement of those well-known figures which had filled it with tranquil dulness for so many years, and never wished it different. With something of the same feeling towards the inanimate things about him which he had expressed to his sisters, he walked up and down the room. It too would have to change, like them, to acknowledge that he was master, to be moulded to new requirements. He felt as if the poor old ugly furniture, the hard curtains that hung like pieces of painted wood, the dingy pictures on the walls, contemplated him with pain and disapproval. They were easier to deal with than the human furniture; but he had been accustomed to them all his life, and it was not without a sense of impiety that the young iconoclast contemplated these grim household gods, harmless victims of that future which as yet was but an audacious dream. He was standing in front of the great chiffonnier, with its marble top and plate-glass back, looking with daring derision at its ugliness, when old Joseph came in at his usual hour—the hour at which he had fulfilled the same duty for the last twenty years—to put out the lamps. Warrender could horrify the girls and insult the poor old familiar furniture, but he was not yet sufficiently advanced to defy Joseph. He turned round, with a blush and quick movement of shame, as if he had been found out, at the appearance of the old man with his candle in his hand, and murmuring something about work, hurried off to the library, with a fear that even that refuge might perhaps be closed upon him. Joseph remained master of the situation. He followed Warrender to the door with his eyes, with a slight contemptuous shrug of his shoulders, as at an unaccountable being whose "ways" were scarcely important enough to be taken into account, and trotted about, putting out one lamp after another, and the twinkling candles on the mantelpiece, and the little lights in the hall and corridor. It was an office Joseph liked. He stood for a moment at the foot of the back stairs looking with complacency upon the darkness, his candle lighting up his little old wry face. But when his eye caught the line of light under the library door, Joseph shook his head. He had put the house to bed without disturbance for so long: he could not abide, he said to himself, this introduction of new ways.

CHAPTER VIII.

It was a violent beginning; but perhaps it was as well, on the whole, that the idea of Theo's future supremacy should have been got into the heads of the duller portion of the family. Warrender was so anxious that there should be no unnecessary haste in his mother's departure, and so ready to find out a pleasant place where they could all go, that everything that had been harsh was forgotten. Indeed, it is very possible in a family that a great many harsh things may be said and forgotten, with little harm done— boys and girls who have been brought up in the same nursery having generally insulted as well as caressed each other with impunity from their earliest years. This happy effect of the bonds of nature was no doubt made easier by the placid characters of the girls, who had no inclination to brood over an unkindness, nor any habit of thinking what was meant by a hasty word. On the contrary, when they remembered it in the morning, after their sound night's sleep, they said to each other that Theo could not possibly have meant it; that he must have been out of temper, poor fellow. They even consented to listen and to look when, with unusual amiability, he called them out to see what trees he intended to cut down, and what he meant to do. Minnie and Chatty indeed bewailed every individual tree, and kissed the big, tottering old elm, which had menaced the nursery window since ever they could remember, and shut out the light. "Dear old thing!" they said, shedding a tear or two upon its rough bark. "It would be dear indeed if it brought down the wall and smashed the old play-room," their brother said,—an argument which even to these natural conservatives bore, now that the first step had been taken, a certain value. Sometimes it is not amiss to go too far when the persons you mean to convince are a little obtuse.

73

They entered into the question almost with warmth at last. The flower garden would be so much improved, for one thing; there never had been sun enough for the flowers, and the big trees had taken, the gardener said, all the goodness out of the soil. Perhaps after all Theo might be right. Of course he knew so much more of the world!

"And, mother, before you go, you should see—Lady Markland," Theo said.

There was a little hesitation in his voice before he pronounced the name, but of this no one took any notice, at the time.

"I have been wondering what I should do. There has been no intimacy, not more than acquaintanceship."

"After what has happened you surely cannot call yourselves mere acquaintances, you and she."

"Perhaps not that: but it is not as if she had thrown herself upon my sympathy, Theo. She was very self-contained. Nobody could doubt that she felt it dreadfully; but she did not fling herself upon me, as many other women would have done."

"I should not think that was at all her character," said Warrender.

"No, I don't suppose it is her character; and then there were already two of her, so to speak,—that child——"

"The only thing I dislike in her," he said hastily, "is that child. What good can a creature of that age do her? And it must be so bad for the boy."

"I don't know about the good it can do her. You don't any of you understand," Mrs. Warrender said, with a moistening of her eyes, "the good there is in a child. As young people grow up they become more important, no doubt,—oh yes, far more important,—and take their own place. But a little thing that belongs to you, that has no thoughts but what are your thoughts, that never wants to be away from you——"

"Very unnatural," said the young man severely, "or else fictitious. The little thing, you may be sure, would much rather be playing with its own companions; or else it must be an unhealthy little sentimental——"

Mrs. Warrender shook her head, but said no more. She gave him a look half remonstrating, half smiling. I had a little boy once, it was on her lips to say: but she forbore. How was the young man, beginning his own individual career, thinking of everything in the world rather than of such innocent consolation as can be given to a woman by a child, to understand that mystery? She whose daughters, everybody said, must be "such companions," and her son "such a support," looked back wistfully upon the days when they were little children; but then she was an unreasonable woman. She was roused from a little visionary journey back into her own experiences by the sound of Theo's voice going on:—

"——should call and ask," he was saying. "She might want you. She must want some one, and they say she has no relations. I think certainly you should call and ask. Shall I order the brougham for you this afternoon? I would drive you over myself, but perhaps, in the circumstances, it would be more decorous——"

"It must be the brougham; if you think I ought to go so soon——"

"Well, mother, you are the best judge; but I suppose that if women can be of any use to each other it must be at such a—at a time when other people are shut out."

Mrs. Warrender was much surprised by his fervour: but she remembered that her husband had been very punctilious about visiting, as men in the country often are, the duty of keeping up all social connections falling upon their wives, and not on themselves. The brougham was ordered, accordingly, and she set out alone, though Minnie would willingly have strained a point to accompany her. "Don't you think, mamma, that as I am much nearer her own age she might like me to go?" that young lady said. But here Theo came in again with his newly acquired authority. "Mother is the right person," he said.

She did not feel much like the right person as she drove along. Lady Markland had not wanted consolation; the shock had turned her to stone. And then she had her child, and seemed to need no other minister. But if it pleased Theo, that was motive enough. Mrs. Warrender reflected, as she pursued her way, upon the kind of squire he would make, different from his father,—oh, very different; not the ordinary type of the English country gentleman. He would not hunt, he would shoot very little; but her husband had not been enthusiastic in either of these pursuits. He would not care, perhaps, for county business or for the quarter sessions; he would have too much contempt for the country bumpkins to be popular with the farmers or wield political influence. Very likely (she thought), he would not live much at the Warren, but keep rooms at Oxford, or perhaps go to London. She had no fear that he would ever "go wrong." That was as great an impossibility as that he should be prime minister or Archbishop of Canterbury. But yet it was a little odd that he should be so particular about keeping up the accidental connection with Lady Markland. This showed that he was not so indifferent to retaining his place in the county and keeping up all local ties as she thought. As for any other ideas that Theo might associate with the young widow,—the widow whose husband lay still unburied,—nothing of the kind entered Mrs. Warrender's head.

The nakedness of the house seemed to be made more conspicuous by the blank of all the closed windows, the white blinds down, the white walls shining like a sort of colourless monument in the blaze of the westering sun. The sound of the wheels going up the open road which was called an avenue seemed a kind of insult to the stillness which brooded over the house of death. When the old butler came solemnly down the great steps, the small country lady, who was not on Lady Markland's level, felt her little pretence at intimacy quite unjustifiable. The butler came down the steps with a solemn air to receive a card and inquiries, and to give the stereotyped reply that her ladyship was as well as could be looked for: but lifted astonished eyes, not without a gleam of insolence in them, when Mrs. Warrender made the unexpected demand if Lady Markland would see her. See *you*! If it had been the duchess, perhaps! was the commentary legible in his face. He went in, however, with the card in his hand, while she waited, half indignant, half amused, with little doubt what the reply would be. But the reply was not at all what she expected. After a minute or two of delay, another figure, quite different from that of the butler, appeared on the steps: a tall man, with very thin, unsteady legs, a face on which the ravages of age were visibly repaired by many devices unknown to its simpler victims, with an eye-glass in his eye and a hesitation in his speech. He was not unknown to the society about, though he showed himself but rarely in it, and was not beloved when he appeared. He was Lord Markland's uncle, the late lord's only brother,—he who was supposed to have led the foolish young man astray. Mrs. Warrender looked at him with a certain horror, as he came walking gingerly down the steps. He made a very elaborate bow at the carriage door,—if he were really Satan in person, as many people thought, he was a weak-kneed Satan,—and gulped and stammered a good deal (in which imperfections we need not follow him) as he made his compliments. His niece, he said, had charged him with the kindest messages, but she was ill and lying down. Would Mrs. Warrender excuse her for to-day?

"She is most grateful for so much kindness; and there is a favour—ah, a favour which I have to ask. It is, if you would add to your many kind services——"

"I have rendered no kind services, Mr. Markland. The accident happened at our doors."

"Ah, no less kind for that. My niece is very grateful, and I—and I, too,—that goes without saying. If we might ask you to come to-morrow, to remain with her while the last rites——"

"To remain with her! Are you sure that is Lady Markland's wish?"

"My dear lady, it is mine, and hers,—hers, too; again, that goes without saying. She has no relations. She wants countenance,—countenance and support; and who could give them so fitly as yourself? In the same circumstances: accept my sincerest regrets. Mr. Warrender was, I have alway heard, an excellent person, and must be a great loss. But you have a son, I think."

"Yes, I have a son."

"Who has been here twice to inquire? Most friendly, most friendly, I am sure. I see, therefore, that you take an interest— Then may we calculate upon you, Wednesday, as early as will suit you?"

"I will come," said Mrs. Warrender, still hesitating, "if you are quite sure it is Lady Markland's wish."

While he repeated his assurances, another member of the family appeared at the door, little Geoff, in a little black dress, which showed his paleness, his meagre, small person, insignificance, and sickliness more than ever. He had been there, it would seem, looking on while his uncle spoke. At this moment he came down deliberately, one step at a time, till his head was on a level with the carriage window. "It is quite true," he said. "Mother's in her own room. She's tired, but she wants you, if you'll come; anyhow, *I* want you, please, if you'll come. They say I'm to go, but not mamma: and you know she couldn't be left by herself; uncle thinks so, and so do I."

The little thing stood shuffling from one foot to another, his hands in his pockets, his little gray eyes looking everywhere but at the compassionate face turned to him from the carriage window. There was a curious ridiculous repetition in the child's attitude of Theo's assertion of his rights. But Mrs. Warrender's heart was soft to the child. "I don't think she wants me," she said. "I will do anything at such a time, but——"

"I want you," said Geoff. He gave her a momentary glance, and she could see that the little colourless eyes had tears in them. "I shall have to go and leave her, and who will take care of her? She is to have a thing like yours upon her head." He was ready to sob, but kept himself in with a great effort, swallowing the little convulsion of nature. His mother's widow's cap was more to Geoff than his father's death; at least it was a visible sign of something tremendous which had happened, more telling than the mere absence of one who had been so often absent. "Come, Mrs. Warrender," he said, with a hoarseness of passion in his little voice. "I can leave her if you are there."

"I will come for your sake, Geoff," she said, holding out her hand, and with tears in her eyes. He was not big enough to reach it from where he stood, and the tears in her voice affected the little hero. He dug his own hands deeper into his pockets, and shuffled off without any reply. It was the uncle, whose touch she instinctively shrank from, who took and bowed over Mrs. Warrender's hand. The Honourable John bowed over it as if he were about to kiss it, and might have actually touched the black glove with his carmine lips (would they have left a mark?) had not she drawn it away.

What a curious office to be thus imposed upon her! To give countenance and support, or to take care of, as little Geoff said, this young woman whom she scarcely knew, who had not in the depth of trouble made any claim upon her sympathy. Mrs. Warrender looked forward with anything but satisfaction to the task. But when she told her tale it was received with a sort of enthusiasm. "Oh, how nice of her!" cried Minnie and Chatty; and their mother saw, with half amusement, that they thought all the more of her because her companionship had been sought for by Lady Markland. And in Warrender's eyes a fire lighted up. He turned away his head, and after a moment said, "You will be very tender to her, mother." Mrs. Warrender was too much confused and bewildered to make any reply.

When the next day came she went, with reluctance and a sense of self-abnegation, which was not gratifying, but painful, to fulfil this office. "She does not want me, I know," Mrs. Warrender said to her son, who accompanied her, to form part of the cortége, in the little brougham which had been to Markland but once or twice in so many years, and this last week had traversed the road from one house to another almost every day. "I think you are mistaken, mother; but even so, if you can do her any good," said Theo, with unusual enthusiasm. His mother thought it strange that he should show so much feeling on the subject; and she went through the great hall and up the stairs, through the depths of the vast silent house, to Lady Markland's room, with anticipations as little agreeable as any with which woman ever went to an office of kindness. Lady Markland's room was on the other side of the house, looking upon a landscape totally different from that through which her visitor had come. The window was open, the light unshaded, and Lady Markland sat at a writing-table covered with papers, as little like a broken-hearted widow as could be supposed. She was dressed, indeed, in the official dress of heavy crape, and wore (for once) the cap which to Geoff had been so overpowering a symbol of sorrow; but, save for these signs, and perhaps a little additional paleness in her never high complexion, was precisely as Mrs. Warrender had seen her since she had risen from her girlish bloom into the self-possession of a wife, matured and stilled by premature experience. She came forward, holding out her hand, when her visitor, with a reluctance and diffidence quite unsuitable to her superior age, slowly advanced.

"Thank you," she said at once, "for coming. I know without a word how disagreeable it is to you, how little you wished it. You have come against your will, and you think against my will, Mrs. Warrender; but indeed it is not so. It is a comfort and help to me to have you."

"If that is so, Lady Markland——"

"That is why you have come," she said. "It is so. I know you have come unwillingly. You heard—they have taken the boy from me."

"But only for this day."

"Only for the hour, I hope. It is supposed to be too much for me to go." Here she smiled, with a nervous movement of her face. "Nothing is too much for me. You know a little about it, but not all. Do you remember him when we were married, Mrs. Warrender? I recollect you were one of the first people I saw."

This sudden plunge into the subject for which she was least prepared—for all her ideas of condolence had been driven out of her mind by the young woman's demeanour, the open window, the cheerful and commonplace air of the room—confused Mrs. Warrender greatly. "I remember Lord Markland almost all his life," she said.

"Here is the miniature of him that was done for me before we were married," said Lady Markland, rising hurriedly, and bringing it from the table. "Look at it; did you ever see a more hopeful face? He was so fresh; he was so full of spirits. Who could have thought there was any canker in that face?"

"There was not then," said the elder woman, looking through a mist of natural tears—the tears of that profound regret for a life lost which are more bitter, almost, than personal sorrow—at the miniature. She remembered him so well, and how everybody thought all would come right with the poor young fellow when he was so happily married and had a home.

"Ah, but there was!—nobody told me; though if all the world had told me it would not have made any difference. Mrs. Warrender, he is like that now. Everything else is gone. He looks as he did at twenty, as good and as pure. What do you think it means? Does it mean anything? Or is there only some physical interpretation of it, as these horrible men say?"

"My dear," said Mrs. Warrender, quite subdued, "they say it means that all is pardoned, and that they have entered into peace."

"Peace," she said. "I was afraid you were going to say rest; and he who had never laboured wanted no rest. Peace,—where the wicked cease from troubling, is that what you mean? He had no time to repent."

"My dear—oh, I am not clear, I can't tell you; but who can tell what was in his mind between the time he saw his danger and the blow that stunned him? If my boy had done everything against me, and all in a moment turned and called to me, would I refuse him? And is not God," cried one mother to the other, taking her hands, "better than we?"

It was she who had come to be the comforter who wept, tears streaming down her cheeks. The other held her hands, and looked in her face with dry feverish eyes. "Your boy," she said slowly, "he is good and kind,—he is good and kind. Will my boy be like him? Or do you think there is an inheritance in that as in other things?"

CHAPTER IX.

The post town for the Warren was Highcombe, which was about four miles off. To drive there had always been considered a dissipation, not to say a temptation, for the Warrenders; at least for the feminine portion of the family. There were at Highcombe what the ladies called "quite good shops,"—shops where you could get everything, really as good as town, and if not cheaper, yet still quite as cheap, if you added on the railway fare and all the necessary expenses you were inevitably put to, if you went to town on purpose to shop. Accordingly, it was considered prudent to go to Highcombe as seldom as possible; only when there was actually something wanted, or important letters to post, or such a necessity as balanced the probable inducement to buy things that were not needed, or spend money that might have been spared. The natural consequence of this prudential regulation was that the little shop in the village which lay close to their gates had been encouraged to keep sundry kinds of goods not usually found in a little village shop, and that Minnie and Chatty very often passed that way in their daily walks. Old Mrs. Bagley had a good selection of shaded Berlin wools and a few silks, and even, when the fashion came in for that, crewels. She had a few Berlin patterns, and pieces of muslin stamped for that other curious kind of ornamentation which consisted in cutting holes and sewing them round. And she had beads of different sizes and colours, and in short quite a little case of things intended for the occupation of that super-abundant leisure which ladies often have in the country. In the days with which we are concerned there were not so many activities possible as now. The village and parish were not so well looked after. There was no hospital nearer than the county hospital at Highcombe, and the "Union" was in the parish of Standingby, six miles off, too far to be visited; neither had it become the fashion then to visit hospitals and workhouses. The poor of the village were poor neighbours. The sick were nursed, with more or less advantage, at home. Beef-tea and chicken broth flowed from the Warren, whenever it was necessary, into whatsoever cottage stood in need, and very good, wholesome calf's-foot jelly, though perhaps not quite so clear as that which came from the Highcombe confectioners. Everything was done in a neighbourly way, without organisation. Perhaps it was better, perhaps worse. In human affairs it is always so difficult to make certain. But at all events the young ladies had not so much to do. And lawn tennis had not been yet invented, croquet even was but in the mild fervour of its first existence. Schools of cookery and ambulances were unknown. And needle-work, bead-work, muslin-work, flourished. Crochet, even, was still pursued as a fine-art occupation. That period is as far back as the Crusades to the sympathetic reader, but to the Miss Warrenders it was the natural state of affairs. They went to Mrs. Bagley's very often, in the dulness of the afternoon, to turn over the Berlin wools and the crochet cottons, to match a shade, or to find a size they wanted. The expenditure was not great, and it gave an object to their walk. "I must go out," they would say to each other, "for there is that pink to match;" or "I shall be at a stand-still with my antimacassar; my cotton is almost done." It was not the fault of Minnie and Chatty that they had nothing better to do.

Mrs. Bagley was old, but very lively, and capable, even while selling soap, or sugar, or a piece of bacon, or a tin tea-kettle, of seeing through her old spectacles whether the tint selected was one that matched. She was a woman who had "come through" much in her life. Her children were all grown up, and most of them dead. Those who remained were married, with children of their own, making a great struggle to bring them up, as she herself had done in her day. She had two daughters, widows,—one in the village, one at some distance off; and living with herself, dependent on her, yet not dependent altogether, was all that remained of another daughter, the one supposed to have been her favourite. It seemed to the others rather hard that granny should lavish all her benefits upon Eliza, while their own families got only little presents and helps now and then. But Lizzie was always the one with mother, they said, though goodness knows she had cost enough in her lifetime without leaving such a charge on granny's hands. Lizzie Bagley, who in her day had been the prettiest of the daughters, had married out of her own sphere, though it could not be said to be a very grand marriage. She had married a clerk, a sort of gentleman,—not like the ploughman and country tradesman who had fallen to the lot of her sisters. But he had never done well, had lost one situation after another, and had gone out finally to Canada, where he died,—he and his wife both; leaving their girl with foreign ways and a will of her own, such as the aunts thought (or at least said) does not develop on the home soil. As poor little Lizzie, however, had been but two years away, perhaps the blame did not entirely lie with Canada. Her mother's beauty and her father's gentility had given to Lizzie many advantages over her cousins. She was prettier and far more "like a lady" than the best of them; she had a slim, straight little person, without the big joints and muscles of the race, and with blue eyes which were really blue, and not whitey-gray. And instead of going out to service, as would have been natural, she had learned dressmaking, which was a fine lady sort of a trade, and put nonsense into her head, and led her into vanity. To see her in the sitting-room behind the shop, with her hair so smooth and her waist so small and collars and cuffs as nice as any young lady's, was as gall and wormwood to the mothers of girls quite as good (they said) as Lizzie, and just as near to granny, but never cosseted and petted in that way. And what did granny expect was to become of her at the end? So long as she was sure of her 'ome, and so long as the young ladies at the Warren gave her a bit of work now and again, and Mrs. Wilberforce at the Rectory had her in to make the children's things, all might be well enough. But the young ladies would marry, and the little Wilberforces would grow up, and granny—well, granny could not expect to live for ever. And what would Miss Lizzie do then? This was what the aunts would say, shaking their heads. Mrs. Bagley, when she said anything at all in her own defence, declared that poor little Lizzie had no one to look to her, neither father nor mother, and that if her own granny didn't take her up and do for her, who should? And that, besides, she did very well with her dressmaking. But nevertheless, by time, Mrs. Bagley had her own apprehensions too.

Minnie and Chatty were fond of making expeditions into the shop, as has been said. They liked to have a talk with Lizzie, and to turn over her fashion-books, old and new, and perhaps to plan, next time they had new frocks, how the sleeves should be made. It was a pleasant "object" for their walk, a break in the monotony, and gave them something to talk about. They went in one afternoon, shortly after the events which have been described. Chatty had occasion for a strip of muslin stamped for working, to complete some of her new underclothing which she had been making. The shop had one large square window, in which a great many different kinds of wares were exhibited, from bottles full of barley sugar and acid drops to bales of striped stuff for petticoats. Bunches of candles dangled from the roof, and nets of onions, and the old lady herself was weighing an ounce of tea for one of her poor customers when the young ladies came in. "Is Lizzie at home, Mrs. Bagley?" said Minnie. "Don't mind us,— we can look for what we want; and you mustn't let your other customers wait."

"You're always that good, miss," said the old woman. Her dialect could only be expressed by much multiplication of vowels, and would not be a satisfactory representation even then, so that it is not necessary to trouble the eye of the reader with its peculiarities. A certain amount of this pronunciation may be taken for granted. "If all the quality would be as considerate, it would be a fine thing for poor folks."

"Oh, but people with any sense would always be considerate!

How is your mother, Sally? Is it for her you are buying the tea? Cocoa is very nourishing; it is an excellent thing for her."

"If you please, miss," said Sally, who was the purchaser, "mother do dearly love a cup of tea."

"You ought to tell her that the cocoa is far more nourishing," said Minnie. "It would do her a great deal more good."

"Ah, miss, but there isn't the heart in it that there is in a cup o' tea," said Mrs. Bagley. "It do set a body up when so be as you're low. Coffee and cocoa and that's fine and warming of a morning; but when the afternoon do come, and you feels low——"

"Why should you feel low more in the afternoon than in the morning, Mrs. Bagley? There's no reason in that."

"Ain't there, miss? There's a deal of 'uman nature, though. Not young ladies like you, that have everything as you want; but even my Lizzie, I find as she wants her tea badly afternoons."

"And so do we," said Chatty, "especially when we don't go out. Look here, this is just the same as the last we had. Mrs. Wilberforce had such a pretty pattern yesterday,—a pattern that made a great deal of appearance, and yet went so quick in working. She had done a quarter of a yard in a day."

"You'll find it there, miss," said the old woman. "Mrs. Wilberforce don't get her patterns nowhere but from me. Lizzie chose it herself, last time she went to Highcombe. And they all do say as the child has real good taste, better nor many a lady. Lizzie! Why, here's the young ladies, and you never showing. Lizzie, child! She's terribly taken up with a—with a—no, I can't call it a job,—with an offer she's had."

"An offer! Do you mean a real *offer*?" cried the girls together, with excitement, both in a breath.

"Oh, not a hoffer of marriage, miss, if that's what you're thinking of, though she's had them too. This is just as hard to make up her mind about. Not to me," said the old woman. "But perhaps I've give her too much of her own way, and now when I says, Don't, she up and says, Why, granny? It ain't always so easy to say why; but when your judgment's agin it, without no reason, I'm always for following the judgment. Lizzie! Perhaps, miss, you'd give her your advice."

Lizzie came out, as this was said, through the little glass door, with a little muslin curtain veiling the lower panes, which opened into the room beyond. She made a curtsey, as in duty bound, to the young ladies, but she said with some petulance, "I ain't deaf, granny," as she did so.

"She has always got her little word to say for herself," the old woman replied, with a smile. She had opened the glass case which held the muslin patterns, and was turning them over with the tips of her fingers,—those fingers which had so many different kinds of goods to touch, and were not, perhaps, adapted for white muslin. "Look at this one, miss; it's bluebells that is, just for all the world like the bluebells in the woods in the month o' May."

"I've got the new Moniture, Miss Warrender, and there are some sweet things in it,—some sweetly pretty things," said Lizzie, holding up her paper. Minnie and Chatty, though they were such steady girls, were not above being fluttered by the Moniteur de la Mode. They both abandoned the muslin-work, and passed through the little door of the counter which Mrs. Bagley held open for them. The room behind, though perhaps not free from a little perfume of the cheese and bacon which occupied the back part of the shop, was pleasant enough; it had a broad lattice window, looking over the pleasant fields, under which stood Lizzie's work-table, a large white wooden one, very clean and old, with signs of long scrubbing and the progress of time, scattered over with the little litter of dressmaking. The floor was white deal, very clean also, with a bit of bright-coloured carpet under Lizzie's chair. As it was the sitting-room and kitchen and all, there was a little fire in the grate.

"Now," said Mrs. Bagley, coming in after them and shutting the door, for there was no very lively traffic in the shop, "the young ladies is young like yourself, not to take too great a liberty, and you think as I'm old and old-fashioned. Just you tell the young ladies straight off, and see what they'll say."

"It ain't of such dreadful consequence, granny. A person would think my life depended on it to hear you speak. Sleeves are quite small this summer, as I said they would be; and if you'll look at this trimming, Miss Chatty, it is just the right thing for crape."

"People don't wear crape, Miss Muffler tells us, nearly so much as they used to do," said Miss Warrender, "or at least not nearly so long as they used to do. Six months, she says, for a parent."

"Your common dresses will be worn out by then, miss," said Lizzie. "I wouldn't put any on your winter frocks, if I was you, for black materials are always heavy, and crape don't show on those thick stuffs. I'd just have a piping for the best, and——"

"What's that," said Chatty, who was the most curious, "that has such a strong scent—and gilt-edged paper? You must have got some very grand correspondent, Lizzie."

Lizzie made a hasty movement to secure a letter which lay on the table, and looked as if about to thrust it into her pocket. She changed her mind, however, with a slight scowl on her innocent-seeming countenance, and, reluctantly unfolding it, showed the date in large gilt letters: "The Elms, Underwood, Highcombe." Underwood was the name of the village. Minnie and Chatty repeated it aloud; and one recoiled a few steps, while the other turned upon Lizzie with wide-open, horrified eyes. "The Elms! Lizzie, you are not going there!"

"That's what I say, miss," cried Mrs. Bagley with delight; "that's what I tells her. Out o' respect to her other customers she couldn't go there!"

"To the Elms!" repeated Minnie. She became pale with the horror of the idea. "I can only say, Lizzie, in that case, that mamma would certainly never employ you again. Charlotte and I might be sorry as having known you all our lives, but we could do nothing against mamma. And Mrs. Wilberforce too," she added. "You may be sure she would do the same. The Elms—why, no respectable person—I should think not even the Vidlers and the Drivers——"

"That is what I tells her, miss,—that's exactly what I tells her—nobody—much less madam at the Warren, or the young ladies as you're so fond of: that's what I tells her every day."

Lizzie, whose forehead had been puckered up all this time into a frown, which entirely changed the character of her soft face, here declared with some vehemence that she had never said she was going to the Elms,—never! Though when folks asked her civilly, and keeping a lady's-maid and all, and dressing beautiful, and nothing proved against them, who was she that she should say she wouldn't go? "And I thought it might be such a good thing for granny, who is always complaining of bad times, if she could get their custom. It's a house where nothing isn't spared," said Lizzie; "even in the servants' hall the best tea and everything." She was fond of the young ladies, but at such an opportunity not to give them a gentle blow in passing was beyond the power of woman; for not even in the drawing-room did the gentlefolks at the Warren drink the best tea.

"I wouldn't have their custom, not if it was offered to me," said Mrs. Bagley with vehemence. "And everybody knows as every single thing they have comes from Highcombe, if not London. I hope as they mayn't find an empty nest some fine morning, and all the birds away. It would serve that nasty Molasis right, as is always taking the bread out of country folk's mouth."

"That's just what I was thinking, granny," said the girl. "If I'd gone it would have been chiefly for your sake. But since the young ladies and you are both so set against it, I can't, and there's an end."

"I am sure she never meant it," said the younger sister. "She was only just flattered for a moment, weren't you, Lizzie? and pleased to think of some one new."

"That's about the fact, that is," said the old woman. "Something new; them lasses would just give their souls for something new."

"But Lizzie must know," said Miss Warrender, "that her old customers would never stand it. I was going to talk about some work, and of coming up two days next week to the Warren. But if there is any idea of the—other place——"

"For goodness' sake speak up and say, No, miss, there ain't no thought of it, Lizzie!"

"Now I know you're so strong against it, of course I can't, and there's an end," said Lizzie; but she looked more angry than convinced.

CHAPTER X.

The girls went round by the rectory on their way home. It was a large red brick house, taller almost than the church, which was a very old church, credibly dating from the thirteenth century, with a Norman arch to the chancel, which tourists came to see. The rectory was of the days of Anne, three stories high, with many twinkling windows in framework of white, and a great deal of ivy and some livelier climbing plants covering the walls, with the old mellow red bricks looking through the interstices of all this greenery. The two Miss Warrenders did not stop to knock or ring, but opened the door from the outside, and went straight through the house, across the hall and a passage at the other end, to the garden beyond, where Mrs. Wilberforce sat under some great limes, with her little tea-table beside her. She was alone; that is, as near alone as she ever was, with only two of the little ones playing at her feet, and the little Skye comfortably disposed on the cushions of a low wicker-work chair. The two sisters kissed her, and disturbed the children's game to kiss them, and displaced the little Skye, who did not like it at all. Mrs. Wilberforce was a little roundabout woman, with fair hair and a permanent pucker in her forehead. She was very well off,—she and all her belongings; the living was good, the parish small, the work not overpowering: but she never was able to shake off a visionary anxiety, the burden of some ancestral trouble, or the premonition of something to come. She was always afraid that something was going to happen: her husband to break down from overwork (which for clergymen, as for most other people in this generation, is the fashionable complaint), the parish to be invaded with dissent and socialism, the country to go to destruction. This latter, as being the greatest, and at the same time the most distant, a thing even which might happen without disturbing one's individual comfort, was most certain; and she waited till it should happen, with always an anxious outlook for the first symptoms. She received Minnie and Chatty, who were her nearest neighbours, and whom she saw almost daily, with a tone of interest and attachment beyond the ordinary, as she had done ever since their father's death. Indeed, they had found this everywhere, a sort of natural compensation for their "great loss." They were surrounded by the respect and reawakened interest of all the people who were so familiar with them. A bereaved family have always this little advantage after a death.

"How are you, dears," Mrs. Wilberforce said, "and how is your dear mother?" Ordinarily Mrs. Warrender was spoken of as their mother, *tout court*, without any endearing adjective.

"Mamma is quite wonderful," said Minnie. "She thinks of everything and looks after everything almost as if—nothing had ever happened."

"She keeps up on our account," said Chatty, "and for Theo's sake. It is so important, you know, to keep home a little bright—oh, I mean as little miserable as possible for him."

"Bright, poor child!" said Mrs. Wilberforce pathetically. "You have not realised as yet what it is. When the excitement is all over, and you have settled down in your mourning, then is the time when you will feel it. I always tell people the first six weeks is nothing; you are so supported by the excitement. But afterwards, when everything falls into the old routine. I suppose, however, you are going away."

"Mamma said something about it: but we all preferred, you know——"

"You had much better go away. I told you so the moment I heard it. And as Theo has all the summer to himself before he requires to go back to Oxford, what is there to stop you?" Mrs. Wilberforce took great pleasure in settling other people's plans for them, and deciding what they were to do.

"That wasn't what we came to talk about," said the elder

Miss Warrender, who was quite able to hold her own. "Mrs. Wilberforce, we have just come from old Mrs. Bagley's at the shop, and there we made quite a painful discovery. We said what we could, but perhaps it would be well if you would interfere. I think, indeed, you ought to interfere with authority, or even, perhaps, the rector."

"What is it? I always thought that old body had a turn for Dissent. She will have got one of those people from Highcombe to come out and hold a meeting: that is how they always begin."

"Oh no,—a great deal worse than that."

"Minnie means worse in our way of thinking," the younger sister explained.

"I don't know anything worse," said the clergyman's wife, "than the bringing in of Dissent to a united parish such as ours has been. But I know it will come. I am always expecting to hear of it every day; things go so fast nowadays. What with radicalism, and the poor people all having votes, and what you call progress, one never knows what to expect, except the worst. I always look for the worst. Well, what is it then, if it isn't Dissent?"

Then Miss Warrender gave an account of the real state of affairs. "The letter was there on the table, dated the Elms, Underwood, Highcombe, as if—as if it was a county family; just as we put it ourselves on our paper."

"But far finer than ours,—gilt, and paper so polished and shining, and a quarter of an inch thick. Oh, much finer than ours!"

"Ours, of course, will be black-edged for a long, long time to come; there could not be any comparison," said Minnie, with a sigh. "But think of the assurance of such people! I am so glad to have found you alone, for we couldn't have talked about it before the rector. And I believe if we hadn't gone there just at the right moment she would have accepted. I told her mamma would never employ her again."

"I never had very much opinion of that little thing," said Mrs. Wilberforce. "She is a great deal too fine. If her grandmother was a sensible person, she would have put a stop to all those feathers and flowers and things."

"Still," said Minnie, with some severity, "a young woman who is a dressmaker and gets the fashion-books, and is perhaps in the way of temptation, may wear a feather in her hat; but that is not to say that she should encourage immorality, and make for anybody who asks her: especially considering the way we have all taken her up."

"Who is it that encourages immorality?" said a different voice, over Mrs. Wilberforce's head,—quite a different voice; a man's voice, for one thing, which always changes the atmosphere a little. It was the rector himself, who came across the lawn in the ease of a shooting-coat, with his hands in his pockets. He wore a long coat when he went out in the parish, but at home there can be no doubt that he liked to be at his ease. He was a man who was too easy in general, and might, perhaps, if his wife had not scented harm from the beginning, have compromised himself by calling at the Elms.

"Oh, please!" cried Minnie, with a blush. "Mrs. Wilberforce will tell you. We really have not time to stay any longer. Not any tea, thank you. We must be running away."

"There is nothing to be so sensitive about," said the clergyman's wife. "Of course Herbert knows that you must know: you are not babies. It is Lizzie Hampson, the dressmaker, who has been asked to go and work at the Elms."

"Oh!" said the rector. He showed himself wonderfully reasonable,—more reasonable than any one could have expected. "I wouldn't let her go there if I was you. It's not a fit place for a girl."

"We are perfectly well aware of that," said Mrs. Wilberforce. "I warned you from the beginning. But the thing is, who is to prevent her from going? Minnie has told her plainly, it appears, and I will speak to her, and as her clergyman I should say it was your duty to say a word; but whether we shall succeed, that is a different matter. These creatures seem to have a sort of real attraction for everything that is wrong."

"We all have that, I'm afraid, my dear."

"But not all in that way. There may be a bias, but it doesn't take the same form. Do sit down, girls, and take your tea, like reasonable creatures. She shall never enter the rectory, of course, if—and if you are sure Mrs. Warrender will do the same. But you know she is very indulgent,—more indulgent than I should be in her place. There was that story, you know, about Fanny, the laundry-maid. I don't think we shall do much if your dear mother relents, and says the girl is penitent as soon as she cries. She ought to know girls better than that. A little thing makes them cry: but penitence,—that is getting rarer and rarer every day."

"There would be no need for penitence in this case. The girl is a very respectable girl. Don't let her go there, that's all: and give me a cup of tea."

"Isn't that like a man!" said Mrs. Wilberforce. "Don't let her go there, and give him a cup of tea!—the one just as easy as the other. I am sure I tell you often enough, Herbert, what with all that is done for them and said about them, the poor people are getting more and more unmanageable every day."

"Our family has always been Liberal," said Minnie. "I think the poor people have their rights just as we have. They ought to be educated, and all that."

"Very well," said the other lady; "when you have educated them up to thinking themselves as good—oh, what am I saying? far better—than their betters, you'll see what will come of it. I for one am quite prepared. I pity the people who deceive themselves. Herbert chooses to laugh, but I can't laugh; it is much too serious for that."

"There will be peace in our days," said the rector, "and after all, Fanny, we can't have a revolution coming because Lizzie Hampson——"

"Lizzie Hampson," said his wife solemnly, "is a sign of the times. She may be nothing in herself,—none of them are anything in themselves,—but I call her a sign of the times."

"What a grand name for a little girl!" he said, with a laugh. But he added seriously, "I wish that house belonged to Theo, or some one we could bring influence to bear upon; but what does a city man care? I wish we could do as the Americans do, and put rollers under it, and cart it away out of the parish."

"Can the Americans do that?"

"They say so. They can do every sort of wonderful thing, I believe."

"And that is what we are coming to!" said Mrs. Wilberforce, with an air of indignant severity, as if this had been the most dreadful accusation in the world.

"I suppose," said the rector, strolling with the young ladies to the gate, "that Theo holds by the family politics? I wonder whether he has given any attention to public questions. At his age a young fellow either does—or he does not," he added, with a laugh. "Oxford often makes a change."

"We don't approve of ladies taking any part in politics," said Minnie, "and I am sure I have never mentioned the subject to Theo."

"But you know, Minnie, mamma said that Theo was—well, I don't remember what she said he was, but certainly not the same as he was brought up."

"Then let us hope he has become a Conservative. Landholders should be and clergy must," said the rector, with a sigh. Then he remembered that this was not a style of conversation likely to commend itself to the two girls. "I hope we shall see you back next Sunday at the Sunday school," he said. "Of course I would not hurry you, if you found it too much; but a little work in moderation I have always thought was the very best thing for a grief like yours. Dear Mrs. Warrender, too," he added softly. He had not been in the habit of calling her dear Mrs. Warrender; but it seemed a term that was appropriate where there had been a death. "I hope she does not quite shut herself up."

"Mamma has been with Lady Markland several times,"

said Minnie, with a mixture of disapproval and satisfaction. "Naturally, we have been so much thrown together since——"

"To be sure. What a sad thing!—twice in one house, within a week, was it not, the two deaths?"

"Just a week," said Chatty, who loved to be exact.

"But you know Lord Markland was no relation," added Minnie, too conscientious to take to herself the credit of a grief which was not hers. "It was not as if we felt it in that way."

"It was a dreadful thing to happen in one's house, all the same. And Theo, I hear, goes a great deal to Markland. Oh, it is quite natural. He had so much to do for her from the first. And I hear she is a very attractive sort of woman, though I don't know much of her, for my own part."

"Attractive? Well, perhaps she may be attractive, to some people," said Minnie; "but when a woman has been married so long as she has, one never thinks—and her attractiveness has nothing to do with Theo," she added, with some severity.

"Oh no, I suppose not," said the rector. "Tell him I hope we shall soon see him here, for I expect his friend Dick Cavendish in the end of the week. You remember Cavendish? He told me he had met you at Oxford."

"Oh yes," said Chatty quickly. Minnie, who was not accustomed to be forestalled in speech, trod upon this little exclamation, as it were, and spoilt its effect. "Cavendish! I am not sure. I think I do recollect the name," she said.

And then they shook hands with the rector across the gate, and went upon their way. But it was not for the first moment quite a peaceful way. "You were dreadfully ready to say you remembered Mr. Cavendish," said the elder sister. "What do you know of Mr. Cavendish? If I were you, I would not speak so fast, as if Mr. Cavendish were of such importance."

"Oh no, he is of no importance; only I do recollect him quite well. He gave us tea. He was very——"

"He was exactly like other young men," said Miss Warrender. And then they proceeded in silence, Chatty having no desire to contest the statement. She did not know very much about young men. Their way lay across the end of the village street, beyond which the trees of the Warren overshadowed everything. There was only a fence on that side of the grounds, and to look through it was like looking into the outskirts of a forest. The rabbits ran about by hundreds among the roots of the trees. The birds sang as if in their own kingdom and secure possessions. To this gentle savagery and dominion of nature the Miss Warrenders were accustomed; and in the freshness of the early summer it was sweet. They went on without speaking, for some time, and then it seemed wise to the younger sister to forestall further remark by the introduction of a new subject, which, however, was not a usual proceeding on Chatty's part.

"Minnie," she said, "do you know what the rector meant when he spoke of Lady Markland, that she was an attractive woman? You took him up rather sharply."

"No, I didn't," said Minnie, with that ease which is noticed among near relations. "I said she was rather old for that."

"She is scarcely any older than you. I know that from the Peerage. I looked her up."

"So did I," said Miss Warrender. "That does not make her a day younger or more attractive. She is four years older than Theo: therefore she is as if she were not to him. Four years is a dreadful difference when it is on the wrong side."

Chatty was ridiculously simple for a person of three-and-twenty. She said, "I cannot think what that has to do with it. The rector is really very silly at times in what he says."

"I don't see that he is silly. What he means is that Lady Markland will take advantage of Theo, and he will fall in love with her. I should say, for my part, that it is very likely. I have seen a great many things of the kind, though you never open your eyes. He is always going to Markland to see what he can do, if there is anything she wants. He is almost sure to fall in love with her."

"Minnie, a married woman!"

"Oh, you little simpleton! She is not a married woman, she is a widow; and she is left extremely well off and with everything in her hands,—that is to say, she would be very well off if there was any money. A widow is in the best position of any woman. She can do what she likes, and nobody has any right to object."

"Oh, Minnie!" protested the younger sister again.

"You can ask mamma, if you don't believe me. But of course she would not have anything to say to Theo," Miss Warrender said.

CHAPTER XI.

"When is Dick Cavendish coming?" said Mrs. Wilberforce to her husband. "I wish he hadn't chosen to come now, of all times in the world, just when we can do nothing to amuse him; for with the Warrenders in such deep mourning, and those other horrible people on the other side, and things in general getting worse and worse every day——"

"He is not acquainted with the parish, and he does not know that things are getting worse and worse every day. It is a pity about the mourning; but do you think it is so deep that a game of croquet would be impossible? Croquet is not a riotous game."

"Herbert!" cried Mrs. Wilberforce. She added in a tone of indignant disapproval, "If you feel equal to suggesting such a thing to girls whose father has not yet been six weeks in his grave, I don't."

The rector was reduced to silence. He was aware that the laws of decorum are in most cases better understood by ladies than by men, and also that the girls at the Warren would sooner die than do anything that was not according to the proper rule that regulated the conduct of persons in their present circumstances. He withdrew, accordingly, to his study, with rather an uneasy feeling about the visit of Dick Cavendish. The rector's study was on the opposite side of the hall, at the end of a short passage, which was a special providence; for nothing that Mrs. Wilberforce could do would prevent him from smoking, and by this means the hall, at least, and the chief sitting-room were kept free of any suggestions of smoke. He said of himself that he was not such a great smoker, but there was no doubt that it was one of the crosses which his wife said everybody had to bear. That was her cross, her husband's pipe, and she tried to put up with it like a Christian. This is one of the cases in which there is very often a conflict of evidence without anything that could be called perjury on either side: for Mrs. Wilberforce declared to her confidants (she would not have acknowledged it to the public for worlds) that her husband smoked morning, noon, and night; whereas he, when the question was put to him casually, asserted that he was not at all a great smoker, though he liked a pipe when he was working, and a cigar after dinner. "When you are working! Then what a diligent life you must lead, for I think you are always working," the wife would remark. "Most of my time, certainly, dear," said the triumphant husband. There are never very serious jars in a family where smoke takes so important a place. Mr. Wilberforce retired now, and took a pipe to help him to consider. The study was a commodious room, with a line of chairs against the further wall, which the parish mostly took when the bumpkins had anything to say to the parson. A large writing-table, fitted with capacious drawers, stood in the middle of the room, of which one side was for parish business, the other magisterial: for the rector of Underwood was also a justice of the peace, and very active in that respect. He was a man who did not fail in his duty in any way. His sermons he kept in a handsome old carved-oak bureau against the wall, where—for he had been a dozen years in Underwood, and had worked through all the fasts and feasts a great many times—he had executed a classification, and knew where to put his hand on the Christmas sermons, and those for the saints' days, and even for exceptional occasions, such as funerals, almost in the dark. Two large windows, one of which opened upon the lawn, and the other, round the corner, in the other wall of the house, commanded a pretty view of the village, lying with its red roofs in the midst of a luxuriant greenness. Saint Mary-under-wood was the true name of the parish, for it lay in a part of the country which was very rich in trees.

Here he sat down with his friend's letter, and thought. The Cavendishes had once held an important position in the county, and lived in one of the greatest "places" in the neighbourhood. But they had met with a fate not unknown to the greatest favourites, and had descended from their greatness to mediocrity, without, however, sacrificing everything, and indeed with so good a margin that, though they were no longer included among the most eminent gentry of England, they still held the place of a county family. They had shifted their headquarters to a much smaller house, but it was one which had already been possessed by them before they became great. The younger sons, however, had very little to look to, and Dick, who was considered clever, was going to the bar. He was a friend, more or less, of young Warrender's, and had been at Oxford with him, where he was junior to Theo in the university, though his senior in years. For Dick had been a little erratic in his ways. He had not been so orderly and law-abiding as a young English gentleman generally is. He had gone away from home very young, and spent several years in wandering before he would address himself to serious life. He had been in Canada and in the backwoods, and though California was not known then as now, had spent a few months at the gold diggings, in the rude life and strife which English families, not yet acquainted with farming in Manitoba and ranches in the far West, heard of with horror, and where only those sons who were "wild," or otherwise unmanageable, had as yet begun to go. When he returned, and announced that he was going to Oxford, and after that to the bar, it was like the vision of the madman clothed and in his right mind to his parents. This their son who had been lost was found. He came into a little fortune, left him by his godfather, when he returned; and, contrary to the general habit of families in respect to younger sons, his parents were of opinion that if some "nice girl" could be found for Dick it would be the best thing that could happen,—a thing which would lighten their own responsibilities, and probably confirm him in well-doing.

But with all the new-fashioned talk about education and work for women, which then had just begun, nice girls were not quite so sure as they used to be that to reclaim a prodigal, or consolidate a penitence, was their mission in life. Perhaps they were right; but the old idea was good for the race, if not for the individual woman, human sacrifices being a fundamental principle of natural religion, if not of the established creed. And it cannot be said that it was altogether without a thought of finding the appropriate victim that the prodigal had been invited to Underwood. He was not altogether a prodigal, nor would she be altogether a victim. People do not use such hard words. He was a young fellow who wanted steadying, for whom married life (when he had taken his degree), or even an engagement, might be expected to do much. And the Miss Warrenders were "nice girls," whose influence might be of the greatest advantage to him. What need to say any more?

But it was tiresome that, after having made up this innocent little scheme for throwing them together, Dick should choose, of all times in the world, to arrive at the rectory just after Mr. Warrender's death, when the family were in mourning, and not "equal to" playing croquet, or any other reasonable amusement. It was hard, the rector thought. It was he, and not his wife, strangely enough, who had thrown himself into this project of match-making. The Warrender girls were the most well-regulated girls in the world, and the most likely to keep their respective husbands straight; and Mr. Wilberforce also thought it would be a very good thing for the girls themselves, who were so much out of the way of seeing eligible persons, or being sought. The rector felt that if Minnie Warrender once took the young man in hand he was safe. And they had already met at Oxford during Commemoration, and young Cavendish had remembered with pleasure their fresh faces and slightly, pleasantly rustic and old-fashioned ways. He was very willing to come when he was told that the Wilberforces saw a great deal of Warrender's nice sisters. "Why, I am in love with them both! Of course I shall come," he had said, with his boyish levity. But with equal levity had put it off from time to time, and at last had chosen the moment which was least convenient, the most uncomfortable for all parties,—a moment when there was nothing but croquet, or picnics, or other gentle pleasures which require feminine co-operation, to amuse the stranger, and when the feminine co-operation which had been hoped for was for the time altogether laid on the shelf and out of the question. Few things could be more trying than this state of affairs.

Notwithstanding which Dick Cavendish arrived, as had been arranged. There was nothing remarkable about his appearance. He was an ordinary brown-haired, blue-eyed young man,— not, perhaps, ordinary, for that combination is rather rare,— and there were some people who said that something in his eye betrayed what they called insincerity; indeed there was generally about him an agreeableness, a ready self-adaptation to everybody's way of thinking, a desire to recommend himself, which is always open to censure. Mrs. Wilberforce was one of the people who shook her head and declared him to be insincere. And as he went so far as to agree that the empire very possibly was dropping to pieces, and the education of the poor tending to their and our destruction, in order to please her, it is possible that she was not far wrong. As a matter of fact, however, his tactics were successful even with her; and though she did not relinquish her deep-seated conviction, yet the young man succeeded in flattering and pleasing her, which was all that he wanted, and not that she should vouch for his sincerity. He was very sorry to hear that the Warrenders were in mourning. "I saw the death in the papers," he said, "and thought for a moment that I had perhaps better write and put off; for some people look their worst in mourning. But then I reflected that some others look their best; and their hearts are soft, and a little judicious consolation nicely administered——"

Though it was not perhaps of a very high quality, the rector was delighted with his young friend's wit.

"It must be nicely administered," he said, "and you will not find them inaccessible. They are the best girls in the world, but too natural to make a fuss, as some girls do. He was a very insignificant, neutral-tinted kind of man. I cannot think why they should be supposed to be so inconsolable."

"Oh, Herbert!" said his wife.

"Yes, I know, my dear; but Oh, Herbert, is no argument. Nobody is missed so much as we expect, not the very best. Life may have to make itself a new channel, but it flows always on. And when the man is quite insignificant, like poor Mr. Warrender——"

"Don't blaspheme the dead, Herbert. It is dreadful to hear you, you are so cynical; and when even a clergyman takes up such opinions, what can we expect of other people?" Mrs. Wilberforce said, with marked disapproval, as she left the gentlemen after dinner. She left them in a novel sort of way, going out of the window of the dining-room to the lawn, which ran along all that side of the house. The drawing-room, too, opened upon it, and one window of the rector's study; and the line of limes, very fine trees, which stood at a little distance, throwing a delightful shadow with their great silken mass of foliage over the velvety grass, made the lawn into a kind of great withdrawing-room, spacious and sweet. Mrs. Wilberforce had a little settlement at one end of this, with wicker-work chairs and a table for her work and one for tea, while her husband, at the other end, clinging to his own window, which provided a mode of escape in case any one should appear to whom his cigar might be offensive, smoked at the other, throwing now and then a few words at her between the puffs. While thus indulging himself he was never allowed to approach more near.

"I am afraid we have not very much amusement for you," the rector said. "There is nothing going on at this season, and the Warren, as my wife says, is shut up."

"Not so much shut up but that one may go to see Warrender?"

"Oh no."

"And in that case the ladies must be visible, too: for I entertained them, you know, in my rooms at Commem. They must at least ask me to tea. They owe me tea."

"Well, if you are content with that. My wife is dreadfully particular, you know. I daresay we may be able to manage a game, for all Mrs. Wilberforce says; and if the worst comes to the worst, Dick, I suppose you can exist without the society of ladies for a few days."

"So long as I have Mrs. Wilberforce to fall back upon, and Flo. Flo is growing very pretty, perhaps you don't know? Parents are so dull to that sort of thing. But there is somebody else in the parish I have got to look after. What is their name? I can't recollect, but I know the name of the house. It is the Elms."

"The Elms, my dear fellow!" cried the rector, with consternation. He turned pale with fright and horror, and, rising, went softly and closed the window, which his wife had left open. "For Heaven's sake," he said, "don't speak so loud; my wife might hear."

"Why shouldn't she hear?" said Dick undaunted. "There's nothing wrong, is there? I don't remember the people's name——"

"No, most likely not; one name will do as well as another," said the rector solemnly. "Dick, I know that a young fellow like you looks at things in another light from a man of my cloth; but there are things that can be done, and things that can't, and it is simply impossible, you know, that you should visit at a place like that from my house."

"What do you mean by a place like that? I know nothing about the place. It belongs to my uncle Cornwall, and there is something to be done to it, or they won't stay."

The rector drew a long breath. "You relieve me very much," he said. "Is the Mr. Cornwall that bought the Elms your uncle Cornwall—without a joke? Then you must tell him, Dick, there's a good fellow, to do nothing to it, but for the love of Heaven help us to get those people away."

"Who are the people?" said the astonished Dick. It is uncertain whether Mr. Wilberforce managed to make any articulate reply, but he sputtered forth some broken words, which, with the look that accompanied them, gave to his visitor an idea of the fact which had been for a month or two whispered, with bated breath, by the villagers and people about. Dick, who was still nominally of the faction of the reprobates, fell a-laughing when the news penetrated his mind. It was not that his sympathies were with vice as against virtue, as the rector was disposed to believe; but the thought of the righteous and strait-laced uncle, who had sent him into what would have been to Mr. Cornwall the very jaws of hell, and of all that might have happened had he himself, Dick, announced in Mrs. Wilberforce's presence his commission to the Elms, was too comical to be resisted, and the peals of his laughter reached the lady on the lawn, and brought the children pressing to the dining-room window to see what had happened. Flo, of whom Dick had said that she was getting pretty, but who certainly was not shy, and had no fear of finding herself out of place, came pertly and tapped at the window, and, looking in with her little sunny face, demanded to know what was the fun, so that Dick burst forth again and again. The rector did not see the fun, for his part; he saw no fun at all. Even when Dick, almost weeping with the goodness of the joke, endeavoured to explain how droll it was to think of his old uncle sending him there, Mr. Wilberforce did not see it. "My wife will ask me what you were laughing about, and how am I to tell her? She will see no joke in it, and she will not believe that I was not laughing with you—at all that is most sacred, Emily will say." No one who had seen the excellent rector at that moment would have accused him of sharing in the laughter, for his face was as blankly serious as if he had been at a funeral: but he knew the view which Mrs. Wilberforce was apt to take.

And his fears came so far true that he did undergo a rigid cross-questioning as soon as the guest was out of the way. And though the rector was as discreet as possible, it yet became deeply impressed upon the mind of his wife that the fun had something to do with the Elms. That gentlemen did joke on such subjects, which were not fit to be talked about, she was fully aware; but that her own husband, a man privileged beyond most men, a clergyman of the Church of England, should do it, was bitter indeed to her. "I know what young men are," she said; "they are all the same. I know there is nothing that amuses and attracts them so much as improper people. But, Herbert, you! and when vice is at our very doors, to laugh! Oh, don't say another word to me on the subject!" Mrs. Wilberforce cried.

CHAPTER XII.

The recollection of that unexplained and ill-timed merriment clouded over the household horizon even next morning; but Dick was so cheerful and so much at his ease that things ameliorated imperceptibly. The heart of a woman, even when most disapproving, is softened by the man who takes the trouble to make himself agreeable to her children. She thought that there could not be so very much harm in him, after all, when she saw the little ones clustering about him, one on his knees and one on his shoulders. "There is a sort of instinct in children," she said afterwards: and most people would be in this respect of Mrs. Wilberforce's opinion. And about noon the rector took his guest to call at the Warren. Though this was not what an ordinary stranger would have been justified in doing, yet when you consider that he had known Theo at Oxford and entertained the ladies at Commem., you will understand why the rector took this liberty. "I suppose I may ask the girls and Theo to come over in the afternoon," said Mr. Wilberforce.

"Oh, certainly, Herbert, you may *ask* them," she replied, but with a feeling that if Minnie accepted it would be as if the pillars of the earth were shaken; though indeed in the circumstances with a young man on her hands to be amused for all the lingering afternoon, Mrs. Wilberforce herself would have been very willing that they should come. Dick Cavendish was a pleasant companion for a morning walk. He admired the country in its fresh greenness, as they went along, though its beauty was not striking. He admired the red village, clustering under the warmth and fulness of the foliage, and pleased the rector, who naturally felt his own *amour propre* concerned in the impression made by his parish upon a new spectator. "We must come to old England for this sort of thing," said Dick, looking back upon the soft rural scene with the half-patronising experience of a man *qui en a vu bien d'autres*. And the rector was pleased, especially as it was not all undiscriminating praise. When they got within the grounds of the Warren criticism came in. "What does Warrender mean," Dick said, "by letting everything run up in this wild way? the trees have no room to breathe."

"You must recollect that Theo has just come into it And the old gentleman was long feeble, and very conservative,—though not in politics, as I could have wished."

"Ah, I thought Warrender was a bit of a radical: but they say a man always becomes more or less a Tory when he comes into his property. I have no experience," said Dick, with his light-hearted laugh. Had Mrs. Wilberforce heard him, she would have found in it that absence of respect for circumstances which she considered to be one of the signs of the times; and it had a startling and jarring effect upon the individual who did hear it, who was disturbed by it in the stillness of his morning walk and thoughts. It broke the silence of the brooding air, and awakened impertinent echoes everywhere, Nature being always glad of the opportunity. The young owner of the place was himself absorbed in a warm haze of visions, like his own trees in the hush of the noon. Any intrusion was disagreeable to him. Nevertheless, when he saw the rector he came forward with that consciousness of the necessity of looking pleased which is one of the vexations of a recluse. What did he mean by bringing men here, where nobody wanted either them or him? But when he saw who it was who accompanied the rector, Warrender's face and the line of annoyance in his forehead softened a little; for Dick was one of the men who are everywhere welcome. Warrender even smiled as he held out his hand.

"You, Cavendish! Who could have thought of seeing you here?"

"I am afraid I am rather presuming: but I could not be so near without coming to see you." Dick grew grave, as was incumbent in the circumstances, and though he had no doubt whatever of seeing the ladies added a sort of humble suggestion: "I am afraid I can scarcely hope to pay my respects?"

"You must come in and see my mother," Warrender said.

The house, as has been said, looked its best when shade and coolness were a necessity of the season; but the visitor who came with keen eyes, observing everything, not because he had any special object, but because he could not help it, took in in a moment the faded air of solid respectability, the shabbiness which does not mean poverty, the decent neglect, as of a place whose inhabitants took no thought of such small matters, which showed everywhere. It was not neglect, in the ordinary sense of the word, for all was carefully and nicely arranged, fresh flowers on the tables, and signs of living—but rather a composed and decorous content. The girls, as they were always called, were found, Chatty with her hands full of flowers and a number of china vases before her, standing at an old buffet in the hall, and Minnie just coming out of the dining-room, where she had been doing her morning needle-work, which was of a plain and homely description, not calculated to be seen by visitors. The old buffet in the hall was not like the mahogany catafalque in the other rooms, and the flowers were very fresh and the china of unappreciated antiquity. Perhaps these accessories helped to make the modest little picture of Charlotte arranging the flowers a pretty one; and she was young and fresh and modest and unconscious; her figure was pretty and light; her look, as she raised her head and blushed to see the little party of men, so guileless, frank, and good that, though the others, who were used to her, thought nothing of her, to Dick it appeared that Chatty was a very pleasant thing to see against the dim background of the old respectable house.

"It is Mr. Cavendish," said Minnie. "How curious! It is true sometimes, no doubt, as everybody says, that talk of an angel and you see its wings; but generally it is just the person whom one least thinks of who appears."

"That is very hard upon me," said Dick. "My mind has been so full of you for twenty-four hours that you ought to have thought a little upon me, if only on the theory of brain waves."

"I hope you don't believe in anything of that sort. How should you think of people when there is nothing to put you in mind of them? If we had been in Oxford, indeed—Come into the drawing-room; we shall find mamma there. And how is dear Mrs. Wilberforce?"

"She wants you all," said the rector, in a low voice aside, "to come over this afternoon to tea."

"To tea, when you have company! Oh, she could not—she never could expect such a thing!"

"Do you call one of your brother's friends company,—one? I should say it took three at least to constitute company. And I want Theo to come. Mind what I say. If you don't amuse him, Theo will think of nothing but going to Markland. He goes to Markland more than I like already."

"Mr. Wilberforce, I am not one that believes in love being blind, and I know all Theo's faults; but to think that he is courting amusement,—amusement, and papa only dead six weeks!"

"I did not say amusement," said the rector crossly. "I said to be amused, which is quite different; not to be left for ever in the same state of mind, not to lie vacant."

"You must have a very poor opinion of him and of all of us," said Miss Warrender, leading the way into the drawing-room, where the others had gone before them. Chatty remained behind, being still busy with her flowers. The rector and Minnie were supposed to be talking parish talk, and to have lingered with that purpose. Chatty thought it sounded too animated to be all about the clothing club and the mothers' meetings, but she supposed that some one must have gone wrong, which was generally the exciting element in parish talk. She was not herself excited by it, being greatly occupied how to make the big white Canterbury bells stand up as they ought in the midst of a large bouquet, in a noble white and blue Nankin vase, which was meant for the table in the hall.

Mrs. Warrender was very glad to see young Cavendish. She asked at once if they were going to take him to Hurst Hill and the old castle at Pierrepoint, and entered almost eagerly into a description of what could be done for a stranger. "For we have scarcely anything, except the country itself, to show a stranger," she said. "There is nothing that is exciting, not much society, and unfortunately, at this moment, the little that there was——"

"I know," said Dick, "it is my misfortune. I was deeply sorry to hear——" He had never seen Mr. Warrender, and naturally could have no profound regret on the subject, but his eyes expressed so much tender sympathy that her heart was touched, and tears came to her own.

"You are very kind to take a part in our sorrows," she said. "If all had been well with us, there would have been no one more pleased than he to make our country pleasant to you. He was always so much interested in Theo's friends. But even as things are, if you do not find it too sad, we shall always be glad to see you. Not that we have anything to tempt you," she added, with a smile.

"Then, Mrs. Warrender," said the rector, "may I tell my wife that you are not going away?"

Mrs. Warrender cast a wistful look round her,—at her son, at the remorseless inclosure of those dull walls, which were like those of a prison. "It appears not, for the present," she said.

"No," said Minnie; "for where can we be so well as at home? For my part, I don't believe in change. What do you change? Only the things about you. You can't change yourself nor your circumstances."

"The skies, but not the soul," said Dick.

"That is just what I mean, Mr. Cavendish. I see you understand. Mamma thinks it would be more cheerful to go away. But we don't really want to be cheerful. Why should we be cheerful?—at least for six months, or I should say a year. We can't be supposed to be equal to anything, after our great loss, in less than a year."

At this they were all silent, a little overawed; and then Mrs.

Warrender returned to her original discourse upon Pierrepoint Castle and the Hurst at Cleveland: "They are both excellent places for picnics. You should take Mr. Cavendish there."

"That was all very well," said the rector, "when there was all of you to fall back upon; but he must be content with the domestic croquet and the mild gratification of walks, in present circumstances. Has Theo come to any decision about the improvements? I suppose you will not begin to cut down till the autumn?"

"Everything is at a standstill, Mr. Wilberforce."

"Well," said Theo, almost angrily, turning to the rector, "there is no hurry, I hope. One need not start, axe in hand, as if one had been waiting for that. There is time enough, in autumn or in spring, or when it happens to be convenient. I am in no haste, for my part."

There was again a little pause, for there had been temper in Theo's tones. And then it was that the rector distinguished himself by the most ill-timed question,—a question which startled even Chatty, who was coming in at the moment with a bowl full of roses, carried in both hands. Yet it was a very innocent-seeming question, and Cavendish was not aware of any significance in it till he saw the effect it produced. "How," said Mr. Wilberforce very distinctly, "is Lady Markland?" He was looking straight at Theo, but as the words came out of his mouth, struck too late by their inappropriateness, turned and looked Mrs. Warrender somewhat severely in the face.

"Oh!" she said, as if some one had struck her; and as for Warrender, he sprang to his feet, and walked across the room to one of the windows, where he stood pulling to pieces one of Chatty's bouquets. She put down her roses, and stood with her hands dropped and her mouth a little open, a picture of innocent consternation, which, however, was caused more by the effect upon the others than by any clear perception in herself. All this took place in a moment, and then Mrs. Warrender replied sedately, "The last time I saw her she was well enough in health.

Sor—trouble," she added, changing the word, "does not always affect the health."

"And does she mean to stay *there*?" the rector said, feeling it necessary to follow up his first question. Mrs. Warrender hesitated, and began to reply that she did not know, that she believed nothing was settled, that—when Theodore suddenly turned and replied:—

"Why shouldn't she stay? The reason is just the same for her as for us. Death changes little except to the person immediately concerned. It is her home: why shouldn't she stay?"

"Really," said the rector, "you take it so seriously I—when you put the question to me, I—— As a matter of fact," he added, "I did not mean anything, if I must tell the truth. I just said the first thing that occurred. And a change is always the thing that is first thought of after such a—after such a——" The rector sought about for a word. He could not say calamity, or affliction, or any of the words that are usually employed. He said at last, with a sense of having got triumphantly over the difficulty—"such a shock."

"I agree with the rector," said Minnie. "It would be far better that she should go away, for a change. The circumstances are quite different. For a lady to go and look after everything herself, when it ought not to be supposed possible that she could do anything: seeing the lawyers, and giving the orders, and acting exactly as if nothing had happened,—oh, it is too dreadful! It is quite different from us. And she does not even wear a widow's cap! That would be reason enough for going away, if there was nothing else. She ought to go away for the first year, not to let anybody know that she has never worn a widow's cap."

"Now that is a very clever reason," said Dick Cavendish, who felt it was time for him to interfere, and lessen the serious character of the discussion. "Unaided, I should never have thought of that. Do at Rome as Rome does; or if you don't, go out of Rome, and don't expose yourself. There is a whole system of social philosophy in it."

"Oh, I am not a philosopher," cried Minnie, "but I know what I think. I know what my opinion is."

"We are not here to criticise Lady Markland," said her mother; and then she burst into an unpremeditated invitation, to break the spell. "You will bring Mr. Cavendish to dine with us one evening?" she said. "He and you will excuse the dulness of a sad house."

The rector felt his breath taken from him, and thought of what his wife would say. "If you are sure it will not be too much for you," he replied.

Dick's eyes and attention were fixed upon the girls. Minnie's face expressed the utmost horror. She opened her mouth to speak; her sharp eyes darted dagger thrusts at her mother; it was evident that she was bursting with remonstrance and denunciation. Chatty, on the contrary, looked at her mother, and then at the stranger, with a soft look of pleasure stealing over her face. It softened still more the rounded outline, the rose tints, which were those of a girl of seventeen rather than twenty-three, and which her black dress brought out with double force. Dick thought her quite pretty,—nay, very pretty,—as she stood there, her sleeves thrust a little back on her arms,—her hands a little wet with the flowers, her face owning a half guilty pleasure of which she was half ashamed. The others were involved in thoughts quite different: but innocent Chatty, relieved by the slightest lifting of the cloud, and glad that somebody should be coming to dinner, was to him the central interest of the group.

"You put your foot in it, I think," he said to the rector, as they walked back, "but I could not quite make out how. Who is the unhappy woman, lost to all sense of shame, who wears no widow's cap?"

"I meant no harm," said the rector. "It was quite natural that I should ask for Lady Markland. Of course it stands to reason that as he died there, and they were mixed up with the whole business, and she is not in my parish, they should know more of her than I."

"And so old Warrender is mixed up with a beautiful widow," said Dick. "He doesn't seem the sort of fellow: but I suppose something of that sort comes to most men, one time or another," he added, with a half laugh.

"What, a widow?" said the rector, with a smile. "Eh? What are you saying? What is that? Well, as you ask, that is the Elms, Cavendish, where I suppose you no longer have any desire to go."

"Oh, that is the Elms, is it?" said Cavendish. His voice had not its usual cheerful sound. He stood quite still, with an interest which the rector thought quite uncalled for. The Elms was a red brick house, tall like the rectory, and of a similar date, the upper stories of which appeared over a high wall. The quick shutting of a door in this wall was the thing which had awakened the interest of Cavendish. A girl had come hurriedly, furtively, out, and with the apparent intention of closing it noiselessly had let the door escape from her hand, and marked her departure by a clang which for a moment filled the air. She glanced round her hastily, and with a face in which a very singular succession of emotions were painted looked in the faces of the gentlemen. The first whom she noticed was evidently the rector, to whom she gave a glance of terror: but then turned to Dick, with a look of amazement which seemed to take every other feeling away,— amazement and recognition. She stared at him for a moment as if paralysed, and then, fluttering like a bird in her light dress, under the high, dark line of the wall, hurried away.

"Bless me," said the rector troubled, "Lizzie Hampson! Now I recollect that was what the ladies were saying. Silly girl, she has gone, after all; but I must put a stop to that. How she stared at you, Dick, to be sure!"

"Yes, she has got a sharp pair of eyes. I think she will know me again," said Dick, with what seemed to the rector rather forced gaiety. "Rather a pretty little girl, all the same. What did you call her? Is she one of your parishioners? She looked mighty frightened of you."

"Lizzie Hampson," said the rector. "She is the granddaughter

118

of the old woman at the shop. She is half a foreigner I believe: but I always thought—Bless me! Emily will be very sorry, but very angry too, I am afraid. I wish I had not seen it. I wish we had not come this way."

"Do you think you are obliged to tell? It was only by accident that we saw her," said Cavendish. "It would hurt nobody if you kept it to yourself."

"I daresay the poor little thing meant no harm," said the rector to himself; "it is natural to want to make a little more money. I am entering into temptation, but I cannot help it. Do you think, after all, I might say nothing about seeing her? We should not have seen her, you know, if we had come home the other way."

"Give her the benefit of the possibility," said Dick, with a short laugh. But he seemed to be affected too, which was wonderfully sympathetic and nice of him, with what troubled the rector so much. He scarcely talked at all for the rest of the way. And though he was perhaps as gay as ever at lunch, there came over him from time to time a curious abstraction, quite out of character with Dick Cavendish. In the afternoon, Warrender and Chatty came in, as they had been invited to tea (not Minnie, which satisfied Mrs. Wilberforce's sense of right), and a very quiet game of croquet, a sort of whisper of a game, under their breath, as it were, was played. And in this way the day passed. The visitor declared in the evening that he had enjoyed himself immensely. But he had a headache, and instead of coming in to prayers went out in the dark for a walk; which was not at all the sort of thing which Mrs. Wilberforce liked her visitors to do.

CHAPTER XIII.

Dick Cavendish went out for a walk. It was a little chilly after the beautiful day; there was rain in the air, and neither moon nor stars, which in the country, where there are no means of artificial lighting, makes it unpleasant for walking. He went right into the big clump of laurels, and speared himself on the prickles of the old hawthorn before he emerged from the Rectory gates. After that it was easier. Many of the cottage people were indeed going to bed, but by the light which remained in a window here and there he was able to preserve himself from accident as he strolled along. Two or three dogs, sworn enemies to innovation, scented him, and protested at their loudest against the novelty, not to say wickedness, of a passenger at that hour of the night. It was, perhaps, to them what Lizzie Hampson's independence was to Mrs. Wilberforce,—a sign of the times. He made his way along, stumbling here and there, sending into the still air the odour of his cigar, towards the spot where the window of the little shop shone in the distance like a low, dim, somewhat smoky star, the rays of which shaped themselves slightly iridescent against the thick damp atmosphere of the night. Cavendish went up to this dull shining, and stared through the window for a moment through the sticks of barley sugar and boxes of mustard and biscuits. He did not know there was any special significance in the sight of Lizzie Hampson seated there within the counter, demurely sewing, and apparently unconscious of any spectators, but it was enough to have startled any of the neighbours who were aware of Lizzie's ways. The old grandmother had gone to see her daughter in the village, who was ill; but in such cases it was Lizzie's way to leave the door of the room in which she sat open, and to give a very contemptuous attention to the tinkle of the little bell attached to the door which announced a customer. Now, however, she sat in the shop, ready to supply anything that might be wanted. Dick strolled past quietly, and went a little way on beyond, but then he came back. He did not linger at the window, as one of Lizzie's admirers might have done. He passed it twice; then, with a somewhat anxious gaze round him, went in. He asked for matches, with a glance at the open door of the room behind. Lizzie said nothing, but something in her look gave him as well as words could have done an assurance of safety. He had closed the door of the shop behind him. He now said quickly, "Then I was not mistaken, and it is you, Lizzie."

There was not the slightest appearance in her of the air of a rustic flirt waiting for a lover, still less of anything more objectionable. Her look was serious, full of resistance and even of defiance, as if the encounter was against her will, though it was necessary that it should be. "Yes, sir," she said shortly, "you were not mistaken, and it is me."

"And what are you doing here?"

"Nothing that isn't right," said Lizzie. "I'm living with my grandmother, as any one will tell you, and working at my trade."

"Well—that is all right," he said, after a moment's hesitation.

"I don't suppose that you sought me out just for that, sir—to give me your approbation," the girl said quickly.

"For which you don't care at all," he said, with a half laugh.

"No more than you care for what I'm doing, whether it's good or bad."

"Well," he said, "I suppose so far as that goes we are about even, Lizzie: though I, for one, should be sorry to hear any harm of you. Do you ever hear anything—of your mistress—that was?"

She gave him a keen look. All the time her hands were busy with a little pile of match-boxes, the pretence which was to explain his presence had any one appeared. "She is—living, if that is what you mean," Lizzie said.

"Living! Oh yes, I suppose so—at her age. Is she—where she was?"

Lizzie looked at him, again investigating his face keenly, and he at her. They were like two antagonists in a duel, each on his guard, each eagerly observant of every point at which he could have an advantage. At last, "Where was that, sir?" she said. "I don't know where you heard of her last."

Dick made no answer. It was some moments before he spoke at all. Then, "Is she in England?" he said.

"I'm not at liberty, sir, to say where she is."

"You know, of course. I can see that in your face. Is she——But perhaps you don't intend to answer any question I put to you."

"I think not, sir," said Lizzie firmly. "What would be the good? She don't want you, nor you——"

"Nor I her: it is true," he said. His face became very grave, almost stern. "I have little reason to wish to know. Still you must be aware that misery is the end of such a way of life."

"Oh, you need give yourself no trouble about that," cried Lizzie, with something like scorn; "she is a deal better off and more thought upon than ever she would have been if——"

"Poor girl!" he said. These words and the tone in which they were spoken stopped the quick little angry speech that was on Lizzie's lips. She wavered for a moment, then recovered herself.

"If you please," she said, "to take your matches, sir. It ain't general for gentlemen like you to come into granny's shop: and we think a deal of little things here. It is not as if we were—on the other side."

He laughed with a sort of fierce ridicule that offended the girl. "So—I might be supposed to be coming after you," he said.

She flung the matches to him across the counter. "There may be more difference here than there was *there*; but a gentleman, if he is a gentleman; will be civil wherever he is."

"You are quite right," said Dick, recovering himself, "and I spoke like a fool. For all that you say, misery is the end of such a life; and if I could help it I should not like her to come to want."

"Oh!" said Lizzie, with exasperation, stamping her foot. "Want yourself! You are more like to come to it than she is. I could show you in a moment—I could just let you see——" Here she paused, and faltered, and grew red, meeting his eyes. He did not ask any further questions. He had grown pale as she grew red. Their looks exchanged a rapid communication, in which neither Lizzie's reluctance to speak nor his hesitation in asking was of any avail. He put down the sixpence which he had in his hand upon the counter, and went out into the night in a dumb confusion of mind, as if he had received a blow.

Here, breathing the same air, seeing the same sights, within reach! He went a little further on in the darkness, not knowing where, nor caring, in the bewilderment of the shock which had come to him unawares, and suddenly in the dark was aware of a range of lighted windows which seemed to hang high in the air—the windows of the Elms appearing over the high garden wall. He went along towards the house mechanically, and only stopped when his shoulder rubbed against the bricks, near the spot where he had seen Lizzie come out, as he walked past. The lights moved about from window to window; the house seemed full of movement and life; and within the wall there was a sound of conversation and laughter. Did he recognise the voices, or any one among them? He did not say so even to himself, but turned round and hurried back, stumbling through the darkness which hid and blinded him. In the village he met a woman with a lantern, who he did not doubt was Lizzie's grandmother, the village authority; no doubt a gossip, quite disposed to search into other people's mysteries, quite unaware of the secret story which had connected itself with his own. She passed him in a little mist of light in the midst of the dark, raising her head instinctively as he passed with a sense of something unfamiliar, but of course not seeing who he was. Presently he found his way again into the Rectory garden, avoiding the prickles of the tree against which he had spiked himself on his way out. Mrs. Wilberforce was on her way upstairs with her candle as he came in. She looked at him disapprovingly, and hoped, with something like irony, that he had enjoyed his walk. "Though you must have had to grope along in the dark, which does not seem much of a pleasure."

"The air is delightful," said Dick, with unnecessary fervour. "I like a stroll in the dark, and the lights in the cottages are pretty to see."

"Dear me, I should have thought everybody was in bed; but late hours are creeping in with other things," said the rector's wife as she went upstairs. The rector himself was standing at the door of his study, with an unlighted pipe in his hand. "Come and have a smoke," he said. For a moment it occurred to Cavendish, though rather as a temptation than as a relief, to tell the story which seemed to fill his mind like something palpable, leaving room for nothing else, to his simple-minded rural friend, an older man than himself and a clergyman, and therefore likely to have received other confidences before now. But something sealed his lips; the very atmosphere of the house, the narrow life with its thousand little occupations, in which there was an ideal yet prosaic innocence, an incapacity even to understand those elements of which tragedy is made. How could he say it—how reveal anything so alien to every possibility! He might have told the good Wilberforce had he been in debt or in love, or any light difficulty in which the parson might have played the part of mediator, whether with an angry father or an irritated creditor. He would have made an excellent confidant in such cases, but not in this.

In debt or in love—in love! Dick Cavendish's character was well known; or so, at least, everybody thought. He was always in love, just as he was always in good spirits,—a fellow full of frolic and fun, only too light-hearted to take life with sufficient seriousness; and life must be taken seriously if you are going to make anything of it. This had been said to him a great many times since he came home. There was no harm known of him, as there generally is of a young man who lets a few years drop in the heyday of life. He liked his fun, the servants said, which was their way of putting it: and his parents considered that he did not take life with sufficient seriousness; the two verdicts were the same. But the people most interested in him had almost unanimously agreed in that theory, of which mention has been already made, about the "nice girl." He was himself aware of the plan and had got a great deal of amusement out of it. Whether it came to anything else or not, it at least promised him a great deal of pleasure. Scores of nice girls had been invited to meet him, and all his relatives and friends had laid themselves out thus to make a reformed character of Dick. He liked them all, he declared; they were delightful company, and he did not mind how many he was presented to; for what can be nicer than a nice girl? and to see how many of them there were in the world was exhilarating to a man fresh out of the backwoods. As he had never once approached the limits of the serious, or had occasion to ask himself what might be the end of any of these pleasant triflings into which his own temperament, seconding the plots of his friends, carried him lightly, all had gone quite well and easily, as Dick loved the things about him to go. But suddenly, on this occasion, when there was an unexpected break in the pleasant surface of affairs, and dark remembrances, never forgotten, had got uppermost in his mind; in this night of all others, when those two words, "in love," floated through his mind, there rose up with them a sudden apparition,—the figure, light, yet not shadowy, of Chatty Warrender holding the bowl of roses with both hands, and with that look of innocent surprise and pleasure in her face. Who can account for such appearances? She walked into his imagination at the mere passage of these words through his head, stepping across the threshold of his fancy with almost as strong a sensation of reality as if she had pushed open his door and come into the room in which he was to all appearance quite tranquilly taking off his boots and changing his coat to join the rector in the study below. He had seen a great many girls more beautiful, more clever, more striking in every way, than Chatty. He had not been aware, even, that he had himself distinguished her; yet there she was, with her look, which was not addressed to him, yet perhaps was more or less on account of him,—that look of unexpected pleasure. Was it on his account? No; only because in the midst of the dulness some one was asked to dinner. Bah! he said to himself, and tossed the boot he had taken off upon the floor—in the noisy way that young men do before they learn in marriage how to behave themselves, was the silent comment of Mrs. Wilberforce, who heard him, as she made her preparations for bed, next door.

Dick was not so jolly as usual, in the hour of smoke and converse which ensued. It was usually the rector's favourite hour, the moment for expansion, for confidences, for assurances on his part, to his young friends, that life in the company of a nice woman, and with your children growing up round you, was in reality a far better thing than your clubs and theatres—although a momentary regret might occasionally cross the mind, and a strong desire for just so many reasonable neighbours as might form a whist-party. Dick was in the habit of making fun of the rector's self-congratulations and regrets, but on this evening he scarcely made a single joke. Three or four times he relapsed into that silence, meditative or otherwise, which is permitted and even enjoyable in the midst of smoke, when two men are confidential without saying anything, and are the best of company without exchanging one idea. But in the midst of one of those pauses, which was more remarkable, he suddenly sat bolt upright in his chair, and said, "I am afraid I must leave you to-morrow," taking away the rector's breath.

"Leave us to-morrow! Why in the name of wonder should you leave us to-morrow?" Mr. Wilberforce cried.

"Well, the truth is," said Dick, "you see I have been away from home a considerable time: and my people are going abroad very soon; and then I've been remiss, you know, in my home duties."

"But you knew all that, my dear fellow, yesterday as well as to-day."

"That's true," said Dick, with a laugh. "The fact is that's not all, Wilberforce. I have had letters."

"Letters! Has there been a delivery? Bless my soul!" said the rector, "this is something quite new."

"Look here," said Dick. "I have been out, and I passed by the—the post-office, and there I got news—Come, don't look at me in that violent way. I have got news, and there is an end of it, which makes me think I had better clear out of this."

"If you want to make a mystery, Cavendish," said the rector, slowly knocking out the ashes of his pipe.

"I don't want to make any mystery," said Dick; then he added, "If I did, it would be, of course, because I could not help it. Sometimes a man is mixed up in a mystery which he can't throw any light upon, for—for other people's sake."

"Ah!" said Mr. Wilberforce. He refilled the pipe very deliberately, and with a very grave face. Then, with a sudden flash of illumination, "I make no doubt," he cried, "it's something about those tenants of your uncle's. He is urging you to go to the Elms."

"Well, since you have guessed, that is about it," said Cavendish. "I can't carry out my commission, and as I'd rather not explain to him——"

"Why shouldn't you explain to him? I have quite been calculating that you would explain to him, and get him to take action, and free us of a set of people so much—so entirely," cried the indignant rector, "out of our way!"

"Well, you see," said Dick, "it's not such an easy thing to get people out of a house. I know enough about law to know that; and the old fellow would be in a terrible way if he knew. I don't want to worry him, don't you see? so the best thing I can do is to say I left very soon, and had not the time to call."

"Well, for one thing, I am rather glad to hear you say so," said the rector; "for I thought at first, by the way you introduced the subject, that your uncle himself, who has always borne such an excellent character, was somehow mixed up——"

Cavendish replied by a peal of laughter so violent as almost to look hysterical. He laughed till the tears ran down his cheeks. "Poor old uncle," he said,—"poor old fellow! After a long and blameless life to be suspected, and that by a clergyman!"

"Cavendish," said the rector severely, "you are too bad; you make fun of things the most sacred. It is entirely your fault if I ever associated in my mind for a moment—— However," he added, "there is one thing certain: you can't go away till you have dined at the Warren, according to Mrs. Warrender's invitation. In her circumstances one must be doubly particular, and as she made an effort for Theo's sake, and yours as his friend——"

"Oh, she made an effort! I did not think of that."

"If you are in such a hurry, Emily can find out in the morning whether to-morrow will suit them, and one day longer will not matter, surely. I can't conceive why you should feel such an extreme delicacy about it."

"Oh, that's my way," said Dick lightly. "I am extremely delicate about everything, though you don't seem to find it out."

"I wish you could be a little serious about something," said the rector, with a sigh. "Things are not all made to get a laugh out, though you seem to think so, Dick."

"It is as good a use as another," said Dick. But as he went upstairs shortly after, the candle which he carried in his hand lighted up, in the midst of the darkness of the peaceful, sleeping house, a face which revealed anything rather than an inclination to get laughter out of everything. Nevertheless, he had pledged himself to stay for the dinner at the Warren which was to cost Mrs. Warrender an effort. It might cost him more than an effort, he said to himself.

CHAPTER XIV.

"One day is the same to us as another. We see nobody."

"Oh, of course!" said Mrs. Wilberforce. "Dear Mrs. Warrender, it is so noble of you to make such an effort. I hope Theo will appreciate it as it deserves."

Mrs. Warrender coloured a little, as one is apt to do when condemned by too much praise. It is difficult sometimes to tell which is worse, the too little or the too much: but she did not make any reply.

"But I am glad it does not make any difference to have us to-night; that is, if you meant me to come?—or perhaps it was only the two gentlemen? I see now: to be sure, two gentlemen is no party; they need not even come back to the drawing-room at all. I am so glad I came to inquire, for now I understand perfectly. And you are sure it will quite suit you to have them to-night?"

"Of course," said Minnie, "Mamma does not look upon you as company, dear Mrs. Wilberforce; it will be only a relief if you come, for gentlemen, and especially new people, who don't know what we have lost nor anything about us, are trying. Mr. Cavendish, I remember, was quite nice when we had tea in his rooms at Commemoration, and if all had been well—— But I am sure mamma forms too high an estimate of her own powers. What I am afraid of is that she will break down."

"To be sure, dear Minnie, if you are afraid of that——" said the rector's wife, and so it was settled. Chatty took no part at all in the arrangements. She had not joined in her sister's severe animadversions as to the dinner-party. For herself, she was glad of the change; it might be wrong, but she could not help being glad. It was, she acknowledged to herself, rather dull never to see any but the same faces day after day. And Mr. Cavendish was very nice; he had a cheerful face, and such a merry laugh. To be sure, it would not be right for Chatty herself to laugh, in the circumstances, in her deep mourning, but it was a mild and surely innocent gratification to listen to the laugh of another. The Wilberforces were very great friends and very nice, but they always remembered what had happened, and toned themselves—these were the words Mrs. Wilberforce used—toned themselves to the subdued condition of the family. Chatty thought that, however nice (and most thoughtful) that might be, it was pleasant now and then to be in company with somebody who did not tone himself, but laughed freely when he had a mind to do so. And accordingly she kept very quiet, and took no part, but inclined silently to her mother's side.

This day was to Dick Cavendish like a bad dream. He could not move outside the inclosure of the rectory grounds without seeing before him in the distance the high garden wall, the higher range of windows, the big trees which gave its name to the Elms. Going through the village street, he saw twice—which seemed a superfluity of ill-fortune—Lizzie Hampson, with her demure air, passing without lifting her eyes, as if she had never seen him before. Had any one else known what he alone knew, how extraordinary would his position have appeared! But he had no leisure to think of the strangeness of his position, all his faculties being required to keep himself going, to look as if everything was as usual. The terror which was in his mind of perhaps, for anything he could tell, meeting some one in these country roads, without warning, to meet whom would be very different from meeting Lizzie Hampson, by times got the better of his composure altogether. He did not know what he would do or say in such an emergency. But he could do nothing to avoid it. The Wilberforces, anxious to amuse him, drove him over in the waggonette, in the morning, to Pierrepoint, making a little impromptu picnic among the ruins. Under no circumstances could the party have been very exciting, except to the children, who enjoyed it hugely, with the simple appetite for anything that is supposed to be pleasure which belongs to their age. They passed the Elms both coming and going. Mrs. Wilberforce put her parasol between her and that objectionable house, but all the same made a rapid inspection of it through the fringes. Dick turned his head away; but he, too, saw more than any one could be supposed to see who was looking in the other direction, and at the same time, with an almost convulsion of laughter, which to himself was horrible, perceived the double play of curiosity and repugnance in his hostess with a fierce amusement. He had to make some sort of poor jest, he did not know what, to account for the laugh which tore him asunder, which he could not keep in. What the joke was he did not know, but it had an unmerited success, and the carriage rattled along past the garden wall in a perfect riot of laughter from the fine lungs of the rector and Flo and Georgie and all the little ones. If any one had but known! The tragedy was horrible, but the laughter was fresh and innocent on all lips but his own. Coming back he laughed no more. The gates were being opened; a sound of horses' hoofs and the jingle of their furniture was audible. The inhabitants were about to drive out. "If you look back you may catch a glimpse of—those people," the rector whispered. But Dick did not look back. The danger made him pale. Had they met face to face, what would have happened? Could he have sat there safe among the innocent children, and made no sign? But when the evening came, and it was time for the dinner at the Warren, he had regained his composure, which, so far as his companions were aware, had never been lost.

In the Warren there were strong emotions, perhaps passions, which he did not understand, but which gave him a sort of fellow-feeling more sympathetic than the well-being of the rector and his wife. Nothing is more pleasant to see than the calm happiness of a wedded pair, who suit each other, who have passed the youthful period of commotion, and have not reached that which so often comes when the children in their turn tempt the angry billows. But there is something in that self-satisfied and self-concentrated happiness which jars upon those who in the turmoil of existence have not much prospect of anything so peaceful. And then domestic comfort is often so sure that nothing but its own virtue could have purchased such an exemption from the ills of life. The Warren had been a few months ago a pattern of humdrum peacefulness. The impatience that sometimes lit up a little fire in Mrs. Warrender's eyes was so out of character, so improbable, that any one who suspected it believed himself to have been deceived; for who could suppose the mother to be tired of her quiet existence? And the girls were not impatient; they lived their half-vegetable life with the serenest and most complacent calm. Now, however, new emotions were at work. The young master of the house was full of abstraction and dreams, wrapped in some pursuit, some hope, some absorbing preoccupation of his own. His mother was straining at her bonds like a greyhound in a leash. Minnie, who had been the chief example of absolute self-satisfaction and certainty that everything was right, had developed a keenness of curiosity and censure which betrayed her conviction that something had gone wrong. These three were all, as it were, on tiptoe, on the boundary line, the thinnest edge which divided the known from the unknown; conscious that at any moment something might happen which would disperse them and shatter all the remains of the old life.

Chatty alone, amid these smouldering elements of change, sat calm in her accustomed place as yet unawakened except to the mild pleasure of a new face among those to which she was accustomed, and of a cheerful voice and laugh which broke the monotony. She had not even gone so far as to say to herself that such a cheerful presence coming and going might make life more interesting. The new-comer, she was quite well aware, was going away to-morrow, nor was there any reason within her power of divination why he should not go; but he was a pleasant break. Chatty reasoned with herself that though a love of novelty is a bad thing and quite unjustifiable in a woman, still that when something new comes of itself across one's point of vision, there is no harm in taking the good of it. And accordingly she looked up with her face of pleasure, and smiled at the very sound of Dick's cheerful voice, thinking how delightful it must be to be so cheerful as that. What a happy temperament! If Theo had been as cheerful! But then to think of Theo as cheerful was beyond the power of mortal imagination. Thus they sat round the table, lighted by a large lamp standing up tall in the midst, according to the fashion of the time. In those days the light was small, not because of æsthetic principles, but because people had not as yet learned how to make more light, and the moderator lamp was the latest invention.

"We took Mr. Cavendish to Pierrepoint, as you suggested," said Mrs. Wilberforce. "We had a very nice drive, but the place is really infested by persons from Highcombe; the woman at the gate told us there had been a party of thirty people from the works the day before yesterday. Sir Edward will soon find the consequences if he goes on in that way. If everybody is allowed to go, not only will they ruin the place, but other people, people like ourselves, will give up going. He might as well make it a penny show."

"It is a show without the penny," said the rector.

"If the poor people did any harm, he would, no doubt, stop their coming," said Mrs. Warrender mildly.

"Harm! but of course they do harm. The very idea of thirty working-people, with their heavy boots, and their dinner in a basket, and smoking, no doubt!"

"That is bad," said Dick. "Wilberforce and I did nothing of that kind. We only made explorations in the ruins, and used a little tobacco to keep off the bad air. The air in the guard-room was close, and Georgie had a puff at a cigarette, but only with a sanitary view. And our dinner was in a hamper; there are distinctions. By the way, it was not dinner at all; it was only lunch."

"And we, I hope, Mr. Cavendish, are very different from——"

"Oh, very different. We have most things we wish to have, and live in nice houses, and have gardens of our own, and woods to walk in."

"That is quite true," said Minnie; "and we have always been Liberal,—not against the people, as the Conservatives are; but still it cannot be good to teach them to be discontented with what they have. We should all be contented with what we've got. If it had not been the best for us, it would not have been chosen for us."

"Perhaps we had better not go into the abstract question, Minnie. I suppose, Mr. Cavendish, you go back to Oxford after the vacation?"

"For hard work," he said, with a laugh. "I am such an old fellow I have no time to lose. I am not an honour man, like Warrender."

"And you, Theo,—you are going too?" said the rector.

Warrender woke up as out of a dream. "I have not made up my mind. Perhaps I shall, perhaps not; it is not of much importance."

"Not of much importance! Your first class——"

"I should not take a first class," he said coldly.

"But, my dear fellow!——" The rector's air of puzzled consternation, and the look he cast round him, as if to ask the world in general for the reason of this extraordinary self-sacrifice, was so seriously comic that Dick's gravity was in danger, especially as all the other members of the party replied to the look with a seriousness, in some cases disapproval, in some astonishment, which heightened the effect.

"Where does he expect to go to?" he said solemnly.

"Theo thinks," said his mother, "that a first class is not everything in the world as it is in the University."

"But my dear Mrs. Warrender! that is precisely one of the things that ladies never understand."

"I have no chance of one, so I agree with Warrender," said Dick. "The Dons will bother, but what does that matter? They have no souls beyond the class lists."

"This is all extremely unnecessary," said Warrender, with an air of suppressed irritation. "Perhaps you will allow me to know best. I have no more chance of a first class than you have,

Cavendish. I have not worked for it, and I have no expectation of it. All that was over long ago. I thought every one knew."

"Every one knew that you could have whatever you chose to have, Warrender. Some thought it foolish, and some fine; but every one knew exactly the cause."

"Fine!" said the young master of the house, growing red. "But it is of no consequence to me what they say. I may go back, or I may not; it is not of the slightest importance to any one but myself." He added in a tone which he tried to make lighter, "What use is a class of any kind to a small country gentleman? To know the cost of cultivation and what pays best is better than a dozen firsts. I want to find out how to cut my trees, and how to manage my farmers, and how not to make a fool of myself at petty sessions. Neither Plato nor Aristotle could throw any light on these subjects."

"For the last you must come to me," said Dick; "on that point you'll find me superior to all the sages put together. And as for drawing leases—but I suppose you have some beggar of a man of business who will take the bread out of a poor beginner's mouth."

"Though Mr. Cavendish talks in that way," said Mrs. Wilberforce aside to Minnie, "as though he wanted employment so much, he has a very nice little fortune of his own. It is just his way of talking. And as for connection, there is no one better. His father is a cousin—it may be a good many times removed, but still it is quite traceable—of the Duke. I am not sure, even, that they are not in the peerage as collaterals; indeed, I am almost sure they are, and that we should find him and everything about him, if we looked."

"Of course everybody knows he is very well connected," said Minnie, "but young men all talk nonsense. Listen to Theo! Why shouldn't he go back to Oxford and take his degree, like other people? I don't care about the class. A gentleman need not be particularly clever; but if he has been at the University and does not take his degree, it is always supposed that there is some reason. I don't think it is respectable, for my part."

"Ah, my dear, the young men of the present day, they are a law to themselves," said her friend. "They don't care for what is respectable. Indeed, so far as I can see, they make it a sort of reproach; they let nobodies pick up the prizes. And what do they expect it is all to end in? I could tell them very well, if they would listen to me. The French Revolution is what it will end in; but of course they will not listen to anything one can say."

"Oh, you know we are Liberals," cried Minnie; "we don't go in with that."

"If you are going to town to-morrow, Cavendish, I don't mind if I go with you," said Warrender. "I have some business to look after. At least, it is not exactly business," for he saw his mother's eyes turned on him inquiringly; "it is a commission from a friend. I shall only stay a night, mother; you need not look so surprised."

"It will do you good," she said quietly. "And why should you hurry back? You will be the better for the change."

He gave her a suspicious, half-angry look, as if he saw more in her words than met the eye. "I shall only be gone a single night," he said.

"I will do all I can to upset his good resolutions, Mrs. Warrender. He shall go to all sorts of notorious places, to keep me in countenance. If he can be beguiled into any little improprieties, I am your man."

"Don't be afraid," said the rector. "Dick's wickednesses are all theoretical. I'd trust Georgie in the worst haunt he knows."

Dick looked up with a laugh, with some light word of contradiction, and in a moment there gleamed before him, as by the touching of a spring, as by the opening of a door, the real state of the case so far as he was himself concerned. The present scene melted away to give place to another,—to others which were burnt upon his memory in lines of fire; to one which he could see in his imagination, with which he had a horrible connection, which he could not dismiss out of his thoughts, though he was in reality a fugitive from it, flying the vicinity, the possible sight, the spectre of a ruin which was beyond description. Merely to think of this amid an innocent company, around this decorous table, brought a sickening sensation, a giddiness both mental and physical. He turned his head away from the eyes of the mother, who, he felt, must, in her experience, divine something from the expression in his, to meet the pleased and guileless look with which Chatty was listening to that laughing disclaimer which he had just made. She was sitting by his side, saying nothing herself, listening to the talk, amused and almost excited by the new voice, the little play of light intercourse; even the charm of a new voice was something to Chatty. And she was so certain that what the rector said was true, that Georgie, or even she herself, more delicate still, a simple-hearted young woman, might have been trusted in his worst haunt. He read her look with a keen pang of feelings contradictory, of sharp anguish and a kind of pleasure. For indeed it was true; and yet—and yet—— Did they but know!

Warrender walked back with the party as far as the Rectory gate. Indeed, so simple was the place, the entire family came out with them, straying along under the thick shade of the trees to the little gate which was nearest the Rectory. It was a lovely summer night, as different as possible from the haze and chill of the preceding one, with a little new moon just disappearing, and everything softened and whitened by her soft presence in the sky. Mrs. Wilberforce and Minnie went first, invisible in the dimness of the evening, then the two solid darknesses of the rector and Warrender. Dick came behind with Mrs. Warrender, and Chatty followed a step in the rear of all. The mother talked softly, more than she had done as yet. She told him that their home henceforward would probably be in Highcombe, not here,—"That is, not yet, perhaps, but soon," she said, with a little eagerness not like the melancholy tone with which a new-made widow talks of leaving her home,—and that it would please her to see him there, if, according to the common formula, "he ever came that way." And Dick declared with a little fervour which was unnecessary that he would surely go, that it would be always a pleasure. Why should he have said it? He had no right to say it;

for he knew, though he could not see, with once more that pang of mingled pleasure and misery, that there was a look of pleased satisfaction on Chatty's face as she came softly in the darkness behind.

CHAPTER XV.

Dick was astir very early next morning. He did his packing hurriedly, and strolled out in the freshness of the early day. But not to enjoy the morning sunshine. He walked along resolutely towards the house which had suddenly acquired for him so painful an interest. For why? With no intention of visiting it; with a certainty that he would see no one there; perhaps with an idea of justifying himself to himself for flying from its neighbourhood, for putting distance, at least the breadth of the island, between him and that place, which he could not henceforward get out of his mind. To think that he had come here so lightly two days ago with his old uncle's commission, and that now no inducement in the world, except death or hopeless necessity, could induce him to cross that threshold. If the woman were on her death-bed, yes; if she was abandoned by all and without other help, as well might be, as would be, without doubt, one time or another. But for nothing else, nothing less. He walked along under the wall, and round the dark shrubberies behind which enveloped the house. All was quiet and peace, for the moment at least; the curtains drawn over the windows; the household late of stirring; no lively housewife there to rouse maids and men, and stir up a wholesome stir of living. The young man's cheerful face was stern as he made this round, like a sentinel, thinking of many things that were deep in the gulf of the past. Two years of his life which looked like a lifetime, and which were over, with all the horrors that were in them, and done with, and never to be recalled again. He was still young, and yet how much older than any one was aware! Twenty-seven, yet with two lives behind him: one that of youth, to which he had endeavoured to piece his renewed existence; and the other all complete and ended, a tragedy, yet like many tragedies in life, cut off not by death. Not by death, for here were both the actors again within reach of each other,—one within the sleeping house, one outside in the fresh air of the morning,—with a gulf like that between Dives and Lazarus, a gulf which no man might cross, of disgust and loathing, of pain and hatred, between.

The door in the wall opened stealthily, softly, and some one came out. It was so early that such precautions seemed scarcely necessary. Perhaps it was in fear of seeing him, though that was so unlikely, that Lizzie looked round so jealously. If so, her precautions were useless, as she stepped out immediately in front of the passenger whom she most desired to avoid. He did not speak to her for a moment, but walked on, quickening his pace as hers fluttered into a run, as if to escape him. "Stop," he said at length. "You need not take the trouble to conceal yourself from me."

"I'm not concealing—anything," said Lizzie, half angry, half sullen, with a flush on her face. "I've done nothing wrong," she added quickly.

"I don't say you've done anything wrong; for what I can tell you may be doing the work of an angel."

She looked up at him eagerly, and the tears sprang to her eyes. "I don't know for that. I—I don't ask nothing but not to be blamed."

"Lizzie," he said, "you were always a good girl—and to be faithful as you seem, may, for anything I know, be angels' work. I could not do it, for my part."

"Oh no," she said, hurriedly. "It could not be looked for from you,—oh no, no!"

"But think if you were to ruin yourself," he said. "The rector saw you the other day, but he will say nothing. Yet think if others saw you."

"Sir," cried Lizzie, drawing back, "it will do me more harm and vex granny more to see a gentleman walking by my side and talking like that, as if he took an interest in me,—which you don't, all the same," she added, with a little bitterness, "only for—others."

"I do," he cried, "if I could help you without harming you. But it is chiefly for the other. I want you to act for me, Lizzie. If trouble should come, as come, of course, it will——"

"I am none so sure. You never saw her half so pretty—and he——"

"Silence!" cried Dick, with a voice that was like the report of deep guns. "If trouble comes, let me know. She must not want or be miserable. There is my address. Do not apply to me unless there is absolute need; but if that comes, write, telegraph,—no matter which; help shall come."

"And what am I to do with a gentleman's card?" said Lizzie. "Granny or some one will be sure to see it. It will drop out of my pocket, or it will be seen in my drawers, or something. And if I were to die it would be found, and folks would think badly of me. I will not take your card."

"This is folly, Lizzie."

"If it is, folly's natural. I don't believe there will be any need; if there is, I'll find you out, if you're wanted, but I won't take the card. Will you please, sir, to walk on? I've got my character to think of."

The girl stopped short, leaning against the corner of the wall, defying him, though she was not hostile to him. He put back his card in his pocket, and took off his hat, which was a recognition which brought the colour to Lizzie's cheek.

"Go away, sir; I've got my character to think of," she said. Then she curtsied deeply, with a certain dignity in her rustic manners. "Thank you," she said, "all the same."

Dick walked into the rector's dining-room with little Georgie seated on his shoulder. "Fancy where we found him, mamma," said Flo. "Buying barley sugar from old Mrs. Bagley at the shop. What does a gentleman want with barley sugar? He is too old. You never eat it, nor papa."

"He give it all to me," said Georgie, "and Fluffy had some.

141

Fluffy and me, we are very fond of Mr. Cavendish. Don't go away, Mr. Cavendish, or come back to-morrow."

"Yes, tum back to-morrow," cried the other little ones. Flo was old enough to know that the future had vistas deeper than to-morrow. She said, "Don't be so silly, all you little things. If he was coming back to-morrow, why should he go to-day? He will come back another time."

"When dere's need ob him," said his little godson gravely, at which there was much laughing. But for his part Dick did not laugh. He hid his serious countenance behind little Dick's curly head, and thus nobody knew that there was not upon it even a smile.

At Underwood, which is a very small village, there is no station; so that Dick had to be driven to the railway in the waggonette, the rector making this an occasion to give the children and the governess a drive, so that the two gentlemen could not say much to each other. They had a moment for a last word solely at the door of the railway carriage, in which Warrender had already taken his place. The rector, indeed, had to speak through the carriage window at the last moment. He said, hesitating, "And you won't forget? Tell Mr. Cornwall if he refuses to do anything, so as to drive these people away, it will be the kindest thing he can do for the parish. Tell him——" But here the guard interposed to examine the tickets, and there was a slamming of doors and a shriek of whistles, and the train glided away.

"I think I understand what the rector means," said Warrender. "He is speaking of *that* house. Oh, you need not smile; nothing could be more entirely out of my way."

"I did not smile," said Dick, who was as grave as all the judges in a row.

"Perhaps you have not heard about it. It was there Markland spent the last afternoon before his accident, almost the last day of his life. It gives her a bitter sort of association with the place."

"Markland?" said Dick. "Oh yes, I remember. Lord Markland, who—— He died, didn't he? It may not be a satisfactory household, but still he might have gone there without any harm."

"Oh, I don't suppose there was any harm, except the love of bad company; that seems a fascination which some men cannot resist. I don't care two straws myself whether there was harm or not; but it is a bitter sort of recollection for *her*."

"They were both quite young, were they not?"

"Markland was over thirty," said the young man, who was but twenty-two; "and she is—oh, she is, I suppose, about my age."

He knew, indeed, exactly what was her age; but what did that matter to a stranger? She was superior to him, it was true, in that as in all other things.

"I have heard they were not very happy," Dick said. He cared no more for the Marklands than he did for the domestic concerns of the guard who had looked at his ticket two minutes ago; but anything answered for conversation, which in the present state of his mind he could not exert himself to make brilliant.

"Oh, happy!" cried Warrender. "How could they be happy? She a woman with the finest perceptions, and a mind—such as you seldom find in a woman; and he the sort of person who could find pleasure in the conversation that goes on in a house like that."

Dick did not say anything for some time; he felt as though all the people he met in these parts must go on like this, in absolute unconsciousness, giving him blow after blow. "I don't mean to take up the cudgels for that sort of people," he said at last; "but they are—not always stupid, you know." But to this semi-defence his companion gave no heed.

"She was no more than a child when she was married," said Warrender, with excitement, "a little girl out of the nursery. How was she to know? She had never seen anybody, and to expect her to be able to judge at sixteen——"

"That is always bad," said Dick, musing. He was like the other, full of his own thoughts. "Yet some girls are very much developed at sixteen. I knew a fellow once who—— And she went entirely to the bad."

"What are you talking of?" cried Warrender, almost roughly. "She was like a little angel herself, and knew nothing different— and when that fellow—who had been a handsome fellow they say—fell in love with her, and would not leave her alone for a moment, I, for one, forgive her for being deceived. I admire her for it," he went on. "She was as innocent as a flower. Was it possible she could suspect what sort of a man he was? It has given her such a blow in her ideal that I doubt if she will ever recover. It seems as if she could not believe again in genuine, unselfish love."

"Perhaps it is too early to talk to her about such subjects."

"Too early! Do you think I talk to her about such subjects? But one cannot talk of the greatest subjects as we do without touching on them. Lady Markland is very fond of conversation. She lets me talk to her, which is great condescension, for she is—much more thoughtful, and has far more insight and mental power, than I."

"And more experience," said Dick.

"What do you mean? Well, yes; no doubt her marriage has given her a sort of dolorous experience. She is acquainted with actual life. When it so happens that in the course of conversation we touch on such subjects I find she always leans to the darker side." He paused for a moment, adding abruptly, "And then there is her boy."

"Oh," said Dick, "has she a boy?"

"That's what I'm going to town about. She is very anxious for a tutor for this boy. My opinion is that he is a great deal too much for her. And who can tell what he may turn out? I have brought her to see that he wants a man to look after him."

"She should send him to school. With a child who has been a pet at home that is the best way."

"Did I say he had been a pet at home? She is a great deal too wise for that. Still, the boy is too much for her, and if I could hear of a tutor—— Cavendish, you are just the sort of fellow to know. I have not told her what I am going to do, but I think if I could find some one who would answer I have influence enough——"

Warrender said this with a sudden glow of colour to his face, and a conscious glance; a glance which dared the other to form any conclusions from what he said, yet in a moment avowed and justified them. Dick was very full of his own thoughts, and yet at sight of this he could not help but smile. His heart was touched by the sight of the young passion, which had no intention of disclosing itself, yet could think of nothing and talk of nothing but the person beloved.

"I don't know how you feel about it, Warrender," he said, "but if I had a—friend whom I prized so much, I should not introduce another fellow to be near her constantly, and probably to—win her confidence, you know; for a lady in these circumstances must stand greatly in need of some one to—to consult with, and to take little things off her hands, and save her trouble, and—and all that."

"That is just what I am trying to do," said Warrender. "As for her grief, you know—which isn't so much grief as a dreadful shock to her nerves, and the constitution of her mind, and many things we needn't mention—as for that, no one can meddle. But just to make her feel that there is some one to whom nothing is a trouble, who will go anywhere, or do anything——"

"Well: that's what the tutor will get into doing, if you don't mind. I'll tell you, Warrender, what I would do if I were you. I'd be the tutor myself."

"I am glad I spoke to you," said the young man. "It is very pleasant to meet with a mind that is sympathetic. You perceive what I mean. I must think it all over. I do not know if I can do what you say, but if it could be managed, certainly—— Anyhow, I am very much obliged to you for the advice."

"Oh, that is nothing," said Dick; "but I think I can enter into your feelings."

"And so few do," said Warrender; "either it is made the subject of injurious remarks—remarks which, if they came to her ears, would—or a succession of feeble jokes more odious still, or suggestions that it would be better for me to look after my own business. I am not neglecting my own business that I am aware of; a few trees to cut down, a few farms to look after, are not so important. I hope now," he added, "you are no longer astonished that the small interests of the University don't tell for very much in comparison."

"I beg you a thousand pardons, Warrender. I had forgotten all about the University."

"It does not matter," he said, waving his hand; "it does not make the least difference to me. It would not change my determination in any way, whatever might depend upon it; and nothing really depends upon it. I can't tell you how much obliged I am to you for your sympathy, Cavendish." He added, after a moment, "It is doubly good of you to enter into my difficulties, everything being so easy-going in your own life."

Cavendish looked at his companion with eyes that twinkled with a sort of tragic laughter. It was natural for the young one to feel himself in a grand and unique position, as a very young man seized by a *grande passion* is so apt to do; but the fine superiority and conviction that he was not as other men gave a grim amusement to the man who was so easy-going, whose life was all plain sailing in the other's sight. "All the more reason," he said, with a laugh, "being safe myself, that I should take an interest in you." He laughed again, so that for the moment Warrender, with momentary rage, believed himself the object of his friend's derision. But a glance at Cavendish dispelled this fear, and presently each retired into his corner, and they sat opposite to each other saying nothing, while the long levels of the green country flew past them, and the clang of the going swept every other sound away. They were alone in their compartment, each buried in his thoughts: the one in all the absorption of a sudden and overwhelming passion, not without a certain pride in it and in himself, although consciously thinking of nothing but of *her*, going over and over their last interviews, and forming visions to himself of the future; while the other, he who was so easy-going, the cheerful companion, unexpectedly found to be so sympathetic, but otherwise somewhat compassionately regarded as superficial and commonplace by the youth newly plunged into life,—the other went back into those recollections which were his, which had been confided to none, which he had thought laid to rest and half forgotten, but which had suddenly surged up again with so extraordinary a revival of pain. The presence of Warrender opposite to him, and the unconscious revelation he had made of the condition of his own mind and thoughts, had transported Dick back again for a moment into what seemed an age, a century past, the time when he had been as his friend was, in the ecstasy of a youthful passion. He remembered that; then with quick scorn and disdain turned from the thought, and plunged into the deep abysses of possibility which he now saw opening at his feet. He had said to himself that the past was altogether past, and that he could begin in his own country, far from the associations of his brief and unhappy meddling with fate, a new existence, one natural to him, among his own people, in the occupations he understood. He had not understood either himself or life in that strange, extravagant essay at living which he had made and ended, as he had thought, and of which nobody knew anything. How could he tell, he asked himself now, how much or how little was known? Was anything ever ended until death had put the finis to mortal history?

These young men sat opposite to each other, two excellent examples of the well-born, well-bred young Englishman, admirably dressed, with that indifference to and ease in their well-fitting garments, that easy and careful simplicity, which only the Anglo-Saxon seems able to attain to in such apparel; Warrender, indeed, with something of that dreamy look about the eyes which betrays the abstraction of the mind in a realm of imagination, but nothing besides which could have suggested to any spectator the presence of either mystery in the past or danger in the future, beyond the dangers of flood or field. They were both above the reach of need, but both with that wholesome necessity for doing which is in English blood, and all the world before them—public duty and private happiness, the inheritance of the class to which they belonged. Yet to one care had come in the guise of passion; and the other was setting out upon a second beginning, no one knew how heavily laden and handicapped in the struggle of life.

CHAPTER XVI.

By this time London was on the eve of its periodical moment of desertion; the fashionable people all gone or going; legislators weary and worn, blaspheming the hot late July days, and everything grown shabby with dust and sunshine; the trees and the grass no longer green, but brown in the parks; the flowers in the balconies overgrown; the atmosphere all used up and exhausted; and the great town, on the eve of holiday, grown impatient of itself. Although fashion is but so small a part of the myriads of London, it is astonishing how its habits affect the general living, and how many, diversely and afar off, form a certain law to themselves of its dictates, though untouched by its tide.

Warrender had never known anything about London. His habits were entirely distinct from those of the young men, both high and low, who find their paradise in its haunts and crowds. When he left Cavendish on their arrival, not without a suggestion on Dick's part of an after meeting which the other did not accept, for no reason but because in his present condition it was more pleasant to him to be alone, Warrender, who did not know where to go or what to do in order to carry out the commission which he had so vaguely taken upon him, walked vaguely along, carrying about him the same mist of dreams which made other scenes dim. Where was he to find a tutor in the streets of London? He turned to the Park by habit, as that was the direction in which, half mechanically, he was in the habit of finding himself when he went to town. But he was still less likely to find a tutor for Lady Markland's boy in the lessened ranks of the loungers in Rotten Row than he was in the streets. He walked among them with his head in the clouds, thinking of what she had said when last he saw her; inquiring into every word she had uttered; finding, with a sudden flash of delight, a new meaning which might perchance lurk in a phrase of hers, and which could be construed into the intoxicating belief that she had thought of him in his absence. This was far more interesting than any of the vague processional effects that glided half seen before his eyes, the streams of people with no apparent meaning in them, who were going and coming, flowing this way and the other, on their commonplace business. The phantasmagoria of moving forms and faces went past and past, as he thought, altogether insignificant, meaning nothing. She had said, "I wondered if you remarked"—something that had happened when they were apart from each other; a sunset it was, now he remembered, of remarkable splendour, which she had spoken of next day. "I wondered if you remarked," not I wonder, which would have meant that at that moment she was in the act of wondering, but I wonder*ed*, in the past, as if, when the glorious crimsons and purples struck her imagination, and gave her that high delight which nature can give to the lofty mind (the adjectives too were his, poor boy), she had thought of him, perhaps, as the one of all her friends who was most likely to feel as she was feeling. Poor Warrender was conscious, with bitter shame and indignation against himself, that at that moment he was buried in his father's gloomy library, deep in the shadow of those trees which he had no longer leisure to think of cutting, and was not so much as aware that there was a sunset at all; and this he had been obliged to confess, with passionate regret (since she had seen it, and given it thus an interest beyond sunsettings): but afterwards recalled, with the tempestuous sudden joy and misery that seized upon him all at once now.

In the middle of Rotten Row! with still so many pretty creatures on so many fine horses cantering past, and even what was more wonderful, Brunson, that inevitable competitor, the substance of solid success to Warrender's romance of shadowy glory, walking along with his arm in that of another scholar, and pointing to the man of dreams who saw them not. "He is working out that passage in the Politics that your tutor makes such a pother about," said the other. "Not a bit of it," cried Brunson, "for that would pay." But they gave him credit, at all events, for some classic theme, and not for the discoveries he was making in that other subject which is not classic, though universal; whereas the only text that entered into his dreams was that past tense, opening up so many vistas of thought which he had not realised before. Was there ever a broken sentence of Aristotle that moved so much the scholar to whom a new reading has suddenly appeared? There is no limiting the power of human emotion which can flow in almost any channel, but enthusiastic indeed must be the son of learning in whose bosom the difference of the past and the present tense would raise so great a ferment. "I wondered if you remarked." It lit up heaven and earth with new lights to Warrender. He wanted no more to raise his musings into ecstasy. He pictured her standing looking out upon the changing sky, feeling perhaps a loneliness about her, wanting to say her word, but with no one near whose ear was fit to receive it. "I wondered"—and he all the while unconscious, like a dolt, like a clod, with his dim windows already full of twilight, his mossy old trees hanging over him, his back turned, even, could it have penetrated through dead walls and heavy shade, to the glow in the west! While he thought of it his countenance too glowed with shame. He said to himself that never, should he live a hundred years, would he again be thus insensible to that great and splendid ceremonial which ends the day. For that moment she had wanted him, she had need of him: and not even in spirit had he been at hand, as her knight and servant ought to be.

And all this, as we have said, in the middle of Rotten Row! He remembered the spot afterwards, the very place where that revelation had been made to him: but never was aware that he had met Brunson, who was passing through London on his way to join a reading party, and was in the meantime, in passing, making use of all the diversions that came in his way, in the end of the season, as so reasonable and practical a person naturally would do.

Warrender went long and far in the strength of this marvellous supply of spiritual food, and wanted no other; but at last, a long time after, when it was nearly time to go back to his train, bethought himself that it would be better to lunch somewhere, for the sake of the questions which would be certainly put to him when he got home on this point. In the meantime he had occupied himself by looking out and buying certain new books, which he had either heard her inquire about or thought she would like to see—and remembered one or two trifles she had mentioned which she wanted from town, and even laid in a stock of amusements for little Geoff,—boys' books, suited rather to his years than to his precocity. About the other and more serious part of his self-constituted mission Warrender, however, had done nothing. He had passed one of those "Scholastic Agencies," which it had been his (vague) intention to inquire at, had paused and passed it by. There was truth, he reflected, in what Cavendish said. How could he tell who might be recommended to him as tutor for Geoff? Perhaps some man who would be his own superior, to whom she might talk of the sunset or even of other matters, who might worm his way into the place which had already begun to become Warrender's place,—that of referee and executor of troublesome trifles, adviser at least in small affairs.

He then began to reflect that in all probability a tutor in the house would be a trouble and embarrassment to Lady Markland: one who could come for a few hours every day (and was there not one who would be too happy of the excuse to wait upon his mistress daily?) one who could engage Geoff with work to be done, so that the mother might be free; one, indeed, who would thus supplement the offices already held, and become indispensable where now he was only precariously necessary, capable of being superseded. It is very possible that in any case, even had he not asked the valuable advice of Dick Cavendish, his journey to London would have come to nothing; for he was in the condition to which a practical proceeding of such a kind is inharmonious, and in which all action is somewhat against the grain. But with the support of Dick's advice his reluctance was justified to himself, and he returned to Underwood with a consciousness of having given up his first plan for a better one, and of having found by much thought an expedient better calculated to answer all needs. Meanwhile he carried with him everywhere the delight of that discovery which he had made. To say over the words was enough,—I wondered if you remarked. Had Cavendish been with him on the return journey, or had any stranger addressed him on the way, this was the phrase which he would have used in reply. He watched the sunset eagerly as he walked home from the station, laden with his parcel of books. It was not this time a remarkable sunset. It was even a little pale, as if it might possibly rain to-morrow, but still he watched, with an eye to all the changes of colour. Perhaps nature had not hitherto called him with a very strong voice; but there came a great many scraps of poetry floating in his head which might have given an interest to sunsets even before Lady Markland. There was something about that very golden greenness which was before his eyes, "beginning to fade in the light he loves on a bed of daffodil sky." He identified that and all the rims of colours that marked the shining horizon. Perhaps she would ask him if he had remarked; and he would be able to reply.

"Books?" cried Minnie—"are all those books? Don't you know we have a great many books already, more than we have shelves for? The library is quite full, and even the little bookcase in the drawing-room. You should get rid of some of the old ones if you bring in so many new."

"And who did you see in town, Theo?" said his mother. He had no club, being so young and so little accustomed to London; but yet a young man brought up as he had been can scarcely fail to have many friends.

"Most people seem to have gone away," he said. "I saw nobody. Yes, there were people riding in the Row, and people walking too, I suppose, but nobody I knew."

"And did you go up all that way only to buy books? You might have written to the bookseller for them, and saved your fare."

Theo made his sister no reply, but when Chatty asked, rather shyly, if he had seen much of Mr. Cavendish, answered warmly that Cavendish was a very good fellow; that he took the greatest interest in his friends' concerns, and was always ready to do anything he could for you. "I had no idea what a man he was," he said, with fervour. Mrs. Warrender looked up at this with a little anxiety, for according to the ordinary rules which govern the reasoning of women she was led from it to the deduction, not immediately visible to the unconcerned spectator, that her son had got into some scrape, and had found it necessary to have recourse to his friend's advice. Theo in a scrape! It seemed impossible: but yet there are few women who are not prepared for something happening of this character even to the best of men.

"I hope," she said, "that he is a prudent adviser, Theo; but he is still quite a young man."

"Not so young; he must be six or seven and twenty," said the young man; and then he paused, remembering that this was the perfect age,—the age which she had attained, which he had described to Cavendish as "about my own,"—and he blushed a little and contradicted himself. "Yes, to be sure, he is young: but that makes him only the more sympathetic; and it was not his advice I was thinking of so much as his sympathy. He is full of sympathy."

"You have us to sympathise with you," said Minnie. "I don't know what you want from strangers. We ought to stand by each other, and not care what outsiders say."

"I hope Theo will never despise the sympathy of his own people, but—a friend of your own choosing is a great help," said Mrs. Warrender. Yet she was uneasy. She did not think young Cavendish's sympathy could be on account of Theo's late bereavement, and what trouble could the boy have that he confided to Cavendish, and did not mention to his mother?

She became more and more convinced that there must be some scrape, or at least that something had gone wrong. But save in these speeches about Cavendish there was no proof of anything of the kind. He gave no further explanation, however, of the business which had taken him to town, unless the fact that he drove over to Markland next morning with the half of the pile of books which he had brought from town, in his dog-cart, should afford an explanation; and that was so vague that it was hard to say what it did or did not prove.

He went over to Markland with his books, but left them in the dog-cart, shy, when he was actually in her presence, of carrying her that bribe. Books were a bribe to her; she had been out of the way of gratifications of this kind, and too solitary and forsaken during the latter part of her married life to know what was going on and to supply herself. She was sitting with Geoff upon the terrace, which ran along one side of the house, when Warrender appeared, and both teacher and pupil received him with something that looked very like relief; for the day was warm, and the terrace was but ill chosen as a schoolroom. The infinite charm of a summer day, the thousand invitations to idleness with which the air is full, the waving trees (though there were not many of them), the scent of the flowers, the singing of the birds, all distracted Geoff's attention, and sooth to say his mother's too. She would have been glad to sit quiet, to escape the boy's questioning, to put away the irksome lessons which she herself did not much more than understand, and to which she brought a mind unaccustomed and full of other thoughts. Of these other thoughts there were so many, both of the future and the past: it was very hard to keep her attention to the little boy's Latin grammar. And Geoff on his side was weary too; he should have been in a schoolroom, shut out from temptation, with maps hung along the walls, instead of waving trees, and where he could not have stopped to cry out, "I say, mamma, there's a squirrel. I am certain it is a squirrel," in the midst of his exercises. That, of course, was very bad. And then up to a recent period he had shared all, or almost all, his mother's thoughts; but since his father's death these had become so full of complications that a child could no longer share them, though neither quite understood the partial severance which had ensued. Both were relieved, however, when the old butler appeared at the end of the terrace, pointing out to Warrender where the little group was. The man did not think it necessary to expose himself to the full blaze of the sunshine in order to lead "a great friend" like Mr. Warrender close up to my lady's chair.

"We are very glad to see you; in fact, we are much too glad to see you," said Lady Markland, with a smile. "We are ashamed to say that we were not entering into our work as we ought. Nature is always so busy doing a hundred things, and calling us to come and look what she is about. We take more interest in her occupations than in our own."

"Mamma makes a story of everything," said Geoff, half aggrieved; "but I'm in earnest. Grammar is dreadful stuff; there are no reflections in it. Why can't one begin to read books straight off, without nasty, stupid rules?"

Warrender took little note of what the boy said. Meanwhile he had shaken hands and made his salutations, and his sovereign lady, with a smile, had given him a chair. He felt himself entering, out of the blank world outside, into the sphere of her existence, which was his Vita Nuova, and was capable for the moment of no other thought.

"I think," said Lady Markland,—"for we have really been at it conscientiously for a long time and doing our best,—I think, Geoff, we may shut up our books for to-day. You know there will be your lessons to prepare to-night."

"I'll go and look at Theo's horse. Have you got that big black one? I shall be back in a moment, mamma."

"If you look behind you will find some books, Geoff; some that perhaps you will like."

"Oh, good!" said the boy, with his elfish little countenance lighting up. He was very slight and small for his age, a little shadow darting across the sunshine. The half of the terrace lay in a blaze of light, but all was cool and fresh in the corner where Lady Markland's light chairs and table were placed in the angle of the balustrade, there half hidden by a luxuriant climbing rose. Above Lady Markland's head was a cluster of delicate golden roses, tinged in their hearts with faint red, in all the wealth of their second bloom. Her black dress, profound black, without any relief, was the only dark point in the scene. A little faint colour of recovering health, and perhaps of brightening life, had come to her face. She was very tranquil, resting as people rest after a long illness, in a sort of convalescence of the heart.

"You must forgive his familiarity, Mr. Warrender; you are so good to him, and at his age one is so apt to presume on that."

Warrender had no inclination to waste the few minutes in which he had her all to himself in any discussion of Geoff. He said hastily, "I have brought some other books to be looked at,— things which people are talking of. I don't know if you will care for them, but there is a little novelty in them, at least. I was in town yesterday——"

"You are very good to me too," she said. "A new book is a wonderful treat. I thought you must be occupied or absent that we did not see you here."

Again that past tense, that indication that in his absence—— Warrender felt his head grow giddy with too much delight. "I was afraid to come too often, lest you should think me—importunate."

"How so?" she said simply. "You have been like a young brother ever since—— How could I think you other than kind? The only thing is that you do too much for me. I ought to be trying to walk alone."

"Why, while I am here?" cried the young man; "asking nothing better, nothing half so good as to be allowed to do what I can,— which, after all, is nothing."

She gave a slight glance at him under her eyelids, with a faint dawning of surprise at the fervour of his tone. "The world which people say is so hard is really very kind," she said. "I never knew till now how kind—at least when one has a great evident claim upon its sympathy,—or pity, should I say? Those who find it otherwise are perhaps those whose troubles cannot be made public, and yet who expect their fellow-creatures to divine."

Warrender was sadly cast down to be considered only as the world, a type, so to speak, of mankind in general, kind to those whose claims were undeniable. He replied with a swelling heart, "There must always be individuals who divine, though perhaps they may not dare to show their sympathy,—ah, don't say pity, Lady Markland!"

"You humour me," she said, "because you know I love to talk. But pity is very sweet; there is a balm in it to those who are wounded."

"Sympathy is better.
"'Mighty love would cleave in twain
    The lading of a single pain,
    And part it, giving half to him.'"

"Ah," she cried, with a glimmer in her eyes, "if you go to the poets, Mr. Warrender! And that is more than sympathy. What did he call it himself? 'Such a friendship as had mastered time.'"

"Mamma, mamma, look here!" came in advance of his appearance the voice of Geoff. He came panting, flying round the other angle of the terrace, with his arms full of books. And here, as if it were a type of all that was coming, the higher intercourse, the exchange of thought, the promotion of the man over the child, came suddenly to an end.

CHAPTER XVII.

Lady Markland had recovered in a great degree from the shock of her husband's death. It had been, as Mrs. Warrender said, a shock rather than a sorrow. There is no such reconciler of those who have been severed, no such softener of the wounds which people closely connected in life so often give to each other, as death. A long illness ending so has often the effect of blotting out altogether the wrongs and bitternesses of many troubled years. The unkind husband becomes once more a hero, the child who has stung its parents to the quick a young and tender saint, by that blessed process. Nor when death comes in a moment is it of less avail. The horror, the pity, the intolerable pang of sympathy, with which we realise what the sudden end must have been to him who met it, without time to think, without time to repent, without a moment to prepare himself for that incalculable change, affects every mind, even that of the merest spectator; how much more that of one whom the victim had left a few hours before with a careless word, perhaps an insult, perhaps a jest! What changes of mood, what revelations, what sudden adaptation to the supreme necessity, may come with the blow, the spectator, even if he be nearest and dearest to the sufferer, cannot know. He knows only what was and is, and his soul is overwhelmed with pity. In that moment those who are most deeply injured forgive and forget. They remember the time when all was well,—the sweet childhood, the blooming youth, the first love, the halcyon days before trouble came.

Lady Markland had felt this universal influence. But when she showed her husband's portrait to Mrs. Warrender, it was not so much with a renewal of love as with a great anguish of pity that her mind was filled. This for a time veiled even in her mind the relief, which was not altogether to be ignored even then, but which gradually gained upon her, yet still with great gravity and pain. She was free from a bondage which had become intolerable to her, which day by day she had felt herself less able to bear; but this gain was at his cost. To gain anything at the cost of another is painful to a generous mind; but to gain at such a price,—the price as seemed not only of another's life, but of a life to which it had seemed almost impossible that there could be any harmonious completion or extension! For what could he do in another world, in a world of spirits? He had been all fleshly; nothing in him that was not of the earth. In the majority of cases it is a hard thing to understand how a spirit, formed apparently for nothing but the uses of earth, should be able to adapt itself in a moment to those occupations and interests which are congenial to another state of existence; and with young Lord Markland this was peculiarly the case. He had seemed to care for nothing except things which he could not carry with him into the unseen. Had other capacities, other desires, developed in a moment into the new life? This is a question which no one could answer, and his wife could only think of him as he had been. There seemed nothing but suffering, deprivation, for him, in such a change. The wind, when it blew wildly of nights, seemed to her like the moan of a wandering spirit trying vainly to get back to the world which it understood, to the pleasures of which it was capable. And had she bought relief and freedom by such a sacrifice exacted from another? When comforters bid her believe that he had gone to a better place, that it was her loss but his gain,—which in all probability is true in all cases, not only in those of the saints whose natural home is heaven,—her heart rose against them, and contradicted them, though she said nothing. It was—alas that it should be so!—her gain. She dared not, even to herself, deny that; but how could it be his—a man who had no thought but of the beggarly elements of life, no aspiration beyond its present enjoyments? and it was by this dreadful overturn in his existence, this taking from him of everything he cared for, that she had been made free. Such a thought as this is more terrible than sorrow, it is sadder than death. It left her for a long time very grave, full of something which was almost remorse, as if she had done it; wondering whether God himself could make up to poor Geoffrey, who had never thought of Him, for the loss of everything which he had ever thought of or cared for. She could not confide this thought to any spiritual guide,—and indeed she was not a woman to whom a spiritual guide was possible. Her problems, her difficulties, remained in her own breast, where she worked them out as she could, or, perhaps, in process of time, forgot them, which, in the darkness of human understanding, was probably the better way.

But in one respect he had been just, nay, generous, to his wife. He had left the burdened estates, the no-money, the guardianship of her child, entirely to her. His old uncle, indeed, was associated with her in that guardianship; but this was merely nominal, for old John Markland was very indifferent, more interested in his own comforts than in all the children in the world, and had no mind to interfere. She found herself thus not only a free woman, but with what was equal to a new profession upon her shoulders,—the care of her boy's fortune and of considerable estates, though at the moment in as low a condition and as badly managed as it was possible for estates to be. It was not the fault of Mr. Longstaffe, who had all the business of the county in his hands, and who had tried in vain to save from incumbrance the property which Lord Markland had weighed down almost beyond redemption. Mr. Longstaffe, indeed, when he heard of the fatal accident to his client, had been unable to refrain from a quick burst of self-congratulation over a long minority, before he composed his countenance to the distress and pity which were becoming such an occasion. When the funeral was over, indeed, he permitted himself to say piously that, though such an end was very shocking, it was an intervention of Providence for the property, which could not have stood another year of Lord Markland's going-on. He was a little dubious of Lady Markland's wisdom in taking the burden of the business upon her own shoulders; but on the whole he respected her and her motives, and gave her all the help in his power. And Lady Markland let no grass grow under her feet. She began proceedings at once with an energy which nobody had expected from her. The horses were sold, and the establishment reduced without any delay. The two other houses, both expensive,—the villa in the Isle of Wight, the shooting-box in the Highlands,—both of which had been necessary to Lord Markland's pursuits, were let as soon as it was possible to secure tenants. And Geoff and his mother began, in one wing of the big barracks at Markland, a life not much different from their past life, except in so far that it was free from interruption and anxiety. The pang of loss in such a case does not last; and Lady Markland entered with all the zest of an active-minded and intelligent woman into the work from which she had been debarred all her previous life. No man, perhaps,— seeing that men can always find serious occupation when they choose to do so,—can throw himself with the same delight into unexpected work as such a woman can do, a woman to whom it is salvation from many lesser miseries, as well as an advantage in itself. She had known nothing hitherto, except that everything was going badly, and that she was helpless to interfere, to arrest the ruin which stared them in the face. And now to feel that she might stop that ruin, might even make up for all the losses of the past, and place her son in the position his father had lost, was a happiness beyond description, and gave new life and exhilaration to all her thoughts.

This change, however, occasioned other changes, which marked the alteration from the old life to the new with difficulties and embarrassments which were inevitable. One of those, and the most important, has been already indicated. It concerned Geoff. The change in Geoff's existence was great. Into the morning-room, where his mother and he had constantly sat together, where he had his lessons, where all the corners were full of his toys, where his little life had been spent from morning till night in such a close and absorbing companionship as can only exist between a parent and an only child, there suddenly intruded things and thoughts with which Geoff had little to do. First came a large writing table, occupying the centre of the room, with all sorts of drawers full of papers, and so many letters and notes and account-books that Geoff looked with astonishment, mingled with awe and admiration, at the work which went on upon it. "Did you write all these?" he said to his mother, touching with a finger a pile of letters. He was proud of the achievement, without remembering that he had himself sat very forlorn all the morning, in the light of the great bow windows, with his lesson books, and had asked a great many questions, without more response than a smile and a "Presently, dear," from the mother who was generally so ready to meet and reply to every word he said. Geoff kept his place in the window, as he had always done, and after Lady Markland had got through her morning's work there would be an attempt at the lessons, which heretofore had been the pleasant occupation of the whole morning,—a delightful dialogue, in which the mind of the teacher was as much stimulated as that of the pupil, since Geoff conducted his own education by means of a multitude of questions, to which it was not always very easy to reply. Under the new *regime*, however, this long process was not possible, and the lessons had to be said in a summary manner which did not at all suit Geoff's way of thinking. He did not complain, but he was puzzled, turning it over in his mind with slow but progressive understanding. The big writing-table seemed typical to Geoff. It threw a deep shadow behind it, making the thick, light-coloured, much-worn carpet, on which he had trotted all his life, dark and gloomy, like the robbers' cave he had often found so much difficulty in inventing in the lightness of the room. He had a robbers' cave to his desire now in the dark, dark hole between the two lines of drawers; but it was dearly bought.

Geoff, however, without being as yet quite clear in his mind as to his grievance, had instinctively taken what means were in

163

his power to make up for it. There was that robbers' cave, for one thing, which had many dramatic possibilities. And he was a boy who took a great interest in his fellow-creatures, and liked to listen to talk, especially when it was of a personal character. He was delighted to be there, notwithstanding the strange silence to which he was condemned, when Dickinson, the bailiff, came in to make his report and to receive his orders. Geoff took the greatest interest in Dickinson's long-winded stories about what was wanted in the village, the cottages that were tumbling to pieces, the things that must be done for the farmers. Lady Markland was at first greatly amused and delighted to see how her boy entered into everything, and even made a gentle boast that Geoff understood better than she did. It was only when Mr. Longstaffe and her clergyman simultaneously snubbed her that this foolish woman came to herself. Mr. Longstaffe said, in his brusque way, that he thought Master Geoff—he begged his pardon, little Lord Markland—would be better at his lessons; while Mr. Scarsdale put on a very grave air, and remarked that he feared Dickinson might have things to tell his mistress which were not fit for a little boy's ears. This last address had disconcerted the young mother sadly, and cost her some tears; for she was as innocent as Geoff, and the idea that there were in the village things to tell her that were unfit for the child's ears threw her into daily terror, not only for him, but for herself. This was one of the things that made it apparent that a new rule was necessary. Her business grew day by day, as she began to understand it better, and the lessons fell more and more into the background. Geoff was the soul of loyalty, and did not complain. He developed a quite new faculty of silence, as he sat at his table in the window, now and then stealing a glance at her to see if she were free. That little figure, seated against the light, was all that Lady Markland had to cheer her, as she set out upon this new and stony path of life. He represented everything that made her task possible and her burden grateful to her. Without him always there in the background, what, she asked herself, would existence be to her? She asked herself this question when it first began to be suggested by her friends that Geoff should be sent to school. It is one special feature in the change and downfall that happens to a woman when she becomes a widow that all her friends find themselves at liberty to advise her. However bad or useless her husband may be, so long as he lives she is safe from this exercise of friendship; but when he is dead all mouths are opened. Mr. Scarsdale paid her a visit solemnly, in order to deliver his soul in this respect. "I came on purpose," he said, as if that was an additional virtue, "to speak to you, dear Lady Markland, very seriously about Geoff." And whether it was by his own impulse, or because he was written to on the subject, and inspired by zealous friends nearer home, old Mr. Markland wrote to his dear niece in the same strain, assuring her that it would be far the best thing to send him to school. To school! Her little delicate boy, not nine till April, who had never been out of his mother's care! Lady Markland suffered a great deal from these attacks, and she tried hard, by getting up early, by sitting up late, to find time for Geoff, as of old; but Geoff himself had fallen into the new ways, and the lessons languished. What was she to do?

And then it was that the alternative of a tutor was suggested to her. A tutor! That did not seem so terrible. She confided her troubles to Warrender, who had fallen into the way of riding over to Markland two or three times a week, of checking Dickinson's accounts for her, and looking up little bits of law as between landlord and tenant, and doing his best to make himself necessary; not with any deep-laid plan, but only because to be near her, and serve her, was becoming more and more the desire of his life. Warrender was not fond of Geoff. It is possible, indeed, that his spirits rose with a sense of relief at the suggestion of sending that inevitable third in all their interviews away; but he was at that stage when the wish of a person beloved is strong enough in a young mind to make all endurance possible, and to justify the turning upside down of heaven and earth. He had replied boldly that there would be nothing more easy than to find a tutor; that he himself would go to town, and make inquiries; and that she need contemplate the other dreadful alternative no more. Lady Markland was more grateful to Theo than words could say, and she told all her friends, with a serene countenance, that she had made up her mind to the tutor. It is a great thing to have made up one's mind. It gave a satisfaction and calm to her spirits that nothing else could have done. Indeed, she was so satisfied that she avoided the subject thereafter, and said nothing more to Warrender, who had constituted himself her agent, and took great care not to question him about what he had been doing in London, when she heard that he had been there. For after all, to come to a determination is the great thing. The practical part may be put in operation at any moment. What is really necessary is to make up one's mind.

Something of the same feeling moved Warrender when he returned from that expedition to London, which has been already recorded. Dick Cavendish's suggestion had been to him a suggestion from heaven. But when he returned home, and as he began to think, there were a great many secondary matters to be taken into account. He began to realise the interest that would be taken by the entire county in a matter which did not concern them in the very least. He realised the astonished look of his mother, and felt already his ear transfixed by Minnie's persistent "Why?" Theo saw all these hindrances by degrees. He said to himself, indignantly, that it was nobody's business but his own, and that he hoped he was able to judge for himself. But these reflections do not make an end of a difficulty; they only show more distinctly a consciousness of it. And thus it was that he put off making to Lady Markland the proposal he intended to make, just as she, on her side, put off asking him whether he had done anything in the matter. In the meantime, while the summer lasted, there were many reasons and excuses for putting off from day to day.

CHAPTER XVIII.

The moment, however, was approaching when Warrender had to declare for himself what he intended to do. It is true that he had given indications of previous intention which had put his family on their guard. He had said to Cavendish and to others that it was doubtful whether he would return to Oxford,—words which had made the ladies look at each other, which had drawn a sharp exclamation from Minnie, but which even she had consented to say nothing of until his resolution was more evident. It might be but a caprice of the moment, one of the hasty expressions which Theo was not unaccustomed to launch at his little audience, making them stare and exclaim, but which were never meant to come to anything. Most likely this was the case now. And the preparations went on as usual without anything further said. Mrs. Warrender had curbed her own impatience; she had yielded to his wishes and remained at the Warren, with a sympathy for his sudden fascination and for the object of it which no one else shared; but she looked not without longing for the time when he should return to his studies,—when there should no longer be any duty to keep her to the Warren, nothing to make self-denial necessary. The thought of the free air outside this little green island of retreat almost intoxicated her by times, as the autumn days stole on, and October came red and glowing, with sharp winds but golden sunsets which tinged the woods. By this time, Chatty, too, began to have sensations unusual to her,—such as must thrill through the boat upon the shore, when the little waves run up and kiss its sides, wooing it to the water, for which it was made. Chatty had been almost as much a piece of still life as the boat: but the baptism of the spray had been flung in her face, and dreams of triumphant winds and dazzling waves outside had crept into her cave. Minnie was conscious of no longings, but she knew that it was time to prepare Theo's linen, to see that everything was marked, so that he might have a chance at least of getting his things back from the wash. And Chatty had knitted him half a dozen pairs of silk socks,—some in stripes of black and white, some violet, like a cardinal's,—suitable for his mourning. No one, however, mentioned the subject until the beginning of October, when, as they sat at luncheon one day, it was suddenly introduced by Miss Warrender without timidity, or recollection that there was any doubt about it. "When does term begin, Theo?" his sister asked, in the midst of the usual conversation. The other ladies, who were more quick to sympathise with his feelings, held their breath; but Minnie put her question quite simply, as if she expected him (as she did) to say "the 15th" or "the 17th," as the case might be.

Theo paused a moment, and cast a glance round them all. Then he answered in a voice which seemed louder than usual because it was somewhat defiant. "I don't know," he said slowly; "and if you want the truth, I don't care."

"Theo!" cried Minnie, with a little scream. Chatty, who had been contemplating at her ease, when this conversation began, the bubbles rising in a glass of aerated water which she was holding up to the light, set it down very quickly, and gave him an appealing look across the table. Mrs. Warrender looked at him too, pretending, poor lady, not to understand. "But, my dear," she said, "we must get everything ready; so it is very necessary to know."

"There is nothing to be got ready, so far as I am aware," he replied, with a flush on his face, and the look of a man who is making a stand against his opponents. "I am not going up this term, if that is what you mean."

Then all three looked at him with different degrees of remonstrance, protest, or appeal. Mrs. Warrender was much too sensible of her incapacity to prevail against him to risk any controversy. And even Minnie was so confounded by the certainty of his tone that, except another resounding "Theo!" the tone of which was enough to have made any man pause in an evil career, she too, for the moment, found nothing to say.

"My dear, don't you think that's a great pity?" his mother remarked very mildly, but with a countenance which said much more.

"I don't wish to discuss the question," he said. "I thought I had told you before. I don't mean to be disagreeable, mother; but don't you think that in my own case I should know best?"

"Theo!" cried Minnie for the third time, "you are more than disagreeable; you are ridiculous. How should you know best,—a boy like you? You think you can do what you like because poor papa is dead, and we are nothing but women. Oh, it is very ungenerous and undutiful to my mother, but it is ridiculous too."

"My mother can speak for herself," said the young man. "I don't owe any explanations to you."

"You will have to give explanations to every one, whether you owe them or not!" cried Minnie. "I know what people think and what they say. There is always supposed to be some reason for it when a young man doesn't go back to his college. They think he has got into disgrace; they think it is some bad scrape. We shall have to make up excuses and explanations."

"They may think what they please, so far as I am concerned," he replied.

"But, my dear, she is right, though that does not matter very much," said Mrs. Warrender. "There will be a great many inquiries; and explanations will have to be given. That is not the most important, Theo. Didn't you tell me that if you lost this term you could not go in, as you call it, for honours? I thought you had told me so."

"Honours!" he said contemptuously. "What do honours mean? I found out the folly of that years ago. They are a sort of trade-mark, very good for business purposes. Brunson has sense on his side when he goes in for honours. They are good for the college to keep up its reputation as a teaching machine; and they are good for a schoolmaster in the same way. But what advantage would all the honours of the University be to me?" he added, with a laugh of scorn. "There's an agricultural college somewhere. There would be some meaning in it if I took honours there."

"You have a strange idea of your own position, Theo," said Mrs. Warrender, roused to indignation. "You are not a farmer, but a country gentleman."

"Of the very smallest," he said,—"a little squire. If I were a good farmer and knew my trade, I should be more good."

"A country gentleman," cried Minnie, who had kept silence with difficulty, and seized the first opportunity to break in, "is just the very finest thing a man can be. Why, what are half the nobility compared to us? There are all sorts of people in the nobility,—people who have been in trade, brewers and bankers and all sorts; even authors and those kind of people. But I have always heard that an English country gentleman who has been in the same position for hundreds of years—Why, Theo, there is not such a position in the world! We are the bulwark of the country. We are the support of the constitution. Where would the Queen be, or the church, or anything, without the gentry? Why, Theo, an English country gentleman——"

She paused from mere want of breath. On such a subject Miss Warrender felt that words could never have failed; and she devoutly believed everything she said.

"If he's so grand as that," said Theo, with a laugh, "what do you suppose is the consequence of a little more Latin and Greek?"

Minnie would have said with all sincerity, Nothing at all; but she paused, remembering that there were prejudices on this subject. "You might as well say, What's the use of shoes and stockings," she said, "or of nice, well-made clothes, such as a gentleman ought to wear? By the bye, Mr. Cavendish, though I did not care so much for him this time as the last, had his clothes very well made. Education is just like well-made things," she added, with a sense that she had made, if not an epigram, something very like it,—a phrase to be remembered and quoted as summing up the discussion.

"If that's all," said Warrender, "I've got enough for that." The reference to Cavendish and the epigram had cleared the atmosphere and given a lighter tone to the family controversy, and the young man felt that he had got over the crisis better than he hoped. He waved his hand to Minnie amicably as he rose from the table. "I thank thee, Jew," he said with a lighter tone and laugh than were at all usual with him, as he went away. The ladies sat silent, listening to his steps as he went through the hall, pausing to get his hat; and no one spoke till he suddenly appeared again, crossing the lawn towards the gate that led into the village. Then there was a simultaneous long breath of fulfilled expectation, not to be called a sigh.

"Ah!" said Minnie, "I thought so. He always goes that way."

"It is the way that leads to all the places Theo would be likely to go to."

"You mean it leads to Markland, mamma. Oh, I know very well what Theo means. He thinks he is very deep, but I see through him; and so would you, if you chose. I never thought him so clever as you all did—but that he should let that woman twist him round her little finger, and give up everything for her!—I could not have supposed he would have been so silly as that."

Mrs. Warrender made no reply except a brief reproof to her daughter for speaking of Lady Markland as that woman. Perhaps she was herself a little vexed with Lady Markland, though she was aware it was unjust. But she was not vexed with Theo. She followed his foolishness (for to be sure it was foolishness, poor boy!) with a warmth of sympathy such as very rarely animates a mother in such circumstances. In her growing anxiety about him, in the commotion of mind with which she had watched the rising passion in his, there had been something which seemed to Mrs. Warrender like a new vicarious life. She had been, as it were, the spectator of this drama from the day when, to her great surprise, Theo had urged, almost compelled her to offer her services and society to the young widow. His vehemence then and a look in his eyes with which she was noways acquainted, but of which, as a woman capable of similar emotion, she divined the meaning, had awakened her, with a curious upspringing of her whole being, to the study of this new thing, to see what was going to come of it, and how it would develop. She had never known in her own person what passion was; she had never been the object of it, nor had she felt that wild and all-absorbing influence; but she recognised it when she saw it in her son, with the keenest thrill of sympathetic feeling. She watched him with a kind of envy, a kind of admiration, a wondering enthusiasm, which absorbed her almost as much as his love absorbed him. She who had been surrounded by dulness all her life, mild affections, stagnant minds, an easy, humdrum attachment which had all the external features of indifference,—it brought a curious elation to her mind to see that her boy was capable of this flaming and glowing passion. It had curbed her impatience as nothing else could have done, and made her willing to wait and watch, to withstand the pressure of the long monotonous days, and content herself with the dead quiet of her life. She had not known even anxiety in the past. That of itself was a vivifying influence now.

A little later Mrs. Warrender drove into Highcombe with Chatty, an expedition which she had made several times of late, as often as the horses could be spared. The house in Highcombe, which was her own, which she was to live in with the girls if Theo married or anything happened, was being put in order, and that too was a gentle interest. Fortunately, upon this afternoon Minnie was occupied in the parish. It was her "day," and nothing in heaven or earth was ever permitted to interfere with Minnie's "day." The other two were pleased to be alone together, though they never said so, but kept up even between themselves the little fiction of saying, What a pity Minnie could not come! Chatty sympathised with her mother more than Minnie had ever done, and was very glad in her heart to ask a question or two about what was happening and what Theo could mean, to which Mrs. Warrender answered with much greater ease and fulness than if her elder daughter had been present to give her opinion. Chatty asked with bated breath whether there was not something wicked and terrible in the thought that Lady Markland, a woman who was married, and who had been consoled in her affliction by the clergyman and all her friends reminding her that her husband was not lost but gone before, and that she would meet him again,—that she should be loved and wooed by another man. Chatty grew red with shame as she asked the question. It seemed to her an insult to any woman. "As if our ties were for this world only!" she said. Mrs. Warrender in her reply waived the theological question altogether, and shook her head, and declared that it was not the thought that Lady Markland was a widow or that she was Theo's senior which troubled her. "But she will never think of him," said the mother. "Oh, Chatty, my heart is sore for my poor boy. He is throwing away his love and the best of his life. She will never think of him. She is full of her own affairs and of her child. She will take all that Theo gives her, and never make him any return."

"Then, mamma, would you wish——" cried Chatty, astonished.

"I wish anything that would make him happy," her mother said. "It is a great thing to be happy." She said this more to herself than to her daughter; and to be sure, to a young person, it was a most unguarded admission for a woman to make.

"Does being happy always mean——?" Here Chatty paused, with the sudden flame of a blush almost scorching her cheeks. She had turned her head in the opposite direction, as if looking at something among the trees; and this was perhaps why Mrs. Warrender did not hear what she said. Always mean love— Chatty did not say. Various events had suggested this question, but on the whole she was very glad her mother did not hear.

CHAPTER XIX.

Warrender went off very quickly upon his long walk. He could not but feel, notwithstanding his little bravado of indifference, that it was a very important decision, which he had made irrevocable by thus publishing it. For some time it had been a certainty in his mind; but nothing seems a certainty until it has been said, and now that it had been said, the thought that he had absolutely delivered himself over into the nameless crowd, that he had renounced all further thought of distinction in the only way he knew of for acquiring it, was somewhat awful to him. The unimaginable difference which exists between a man within whose reach a first class is still dangling and him who has no hope but to be "gulfed," is little comprehensible by the unacademical mind; but it is one not to be contemplated without a shudder. When he thought of what he was resigning, when he thought of what he must drop into, the blood seemed to boil in Theo's veins and to ring in his ears. To be a passman; to descend among the crowd; to consort with those who had "pulled through," perhaps with difficulty, who had gone through all sorts of dull workings and struggles, and to whom their books were mere necessary instruments of torture, to be got done with as soon as possible,—these were things terrible to contemplate. And in the silence of his own soul, it was difficult to console himself with those theories about the trade-mark, and the merely professional use of academic distinction. It was all true enough, and yet it was not true. Even now he thought of his tutor with a pang; not the tutor at college, who had dropped him for Brunson, but the genial old tutor at school, who had hoped such great things for him. He said, "Poor old Boreas!" to himself, sympathising in the disappointment with which the news would be received. Warrender a passman! Warrender "gulfed"! Nobody would believe it. This gave him many pangs as he set out upon his walk. He had sacrificed his early glories to the fastidious fancy of youth; but he had never really intended to be distanced by Brunson, to fall out of the ranks at the end.

Softer thoughts began to steal over him as he pursued his way, as he began to draw near the other country in which she abode. Half-way between the houses was a little wood, through which the road passed, and which was like a vestibule to the smiling place where her throne and empire was. To other eyes it was no more smiling than the other side, but as soon as Theo became conscious, in the distance, of the bare height, all denuded of trees, on which Markland stood, the landscape seemed to change for him. There was sunshine in it which was nowhere else, more quiet skies and warmer light. He threw down the burden of his thoughts among the autumn leaves that strewed the brook in that bit of woodland, and, on the other side, remembered with an elation that went to his head, that he had this sacrifice, though she might never know it, to lay at her feet; the flower of his life, the garland of honour, the violet crown, all to scatter on her path. He would rather she should put her foot on them than that they should decorate his brow,—even if she never knew.

With these thoughts, he sped along the country road, which no longer was so green, so warm with sunshine, as before. Markland looked already cold in its bareness against the distant sky, all flushed with flying clouds, the young saplings about, bending before the wind, as if they supplicated for shelter and a little warmth, and the old tottering cedar behind the house, looking as if the next blast would bring it down with a crash. There had been a great deal of planting going on, but this only added to the straggling lines of weak-kneed, uncomfortable younglings, who fluttered their handful of leaves, and shivered in every wind that blew. Lady Markland no longer sat on the terrace. She received her familiar visitor where only intimate friends were allowed to come, in the morning-room, to which its new distinction gave something of the barrenness and rigidity of a room of business. The big writing-table filled up the centre, and nothing remained of its old aspect except Geoff's little settlement within the round of the window; a low table for his few lesson books, where less lawful publications, in the shape of stories, were but too apt to appear, and a low, but virtuously hard chair, on which he was supposed to sit, and—work; but there was not much work done, as everybody knew.

Lady Markland did not rise to receive her visitor. She had a book in her right hand, which she did not even disturb herself to put down. It was her left hand which she held out to Warrender, with a smile: and this mark of a friendship which had gone beyond all ceremony made his heart overflow. By an unusual chance, Geoff was not there, staring with his little sharp eyes, and this made everything sweeter. He had her to himself at last.

"Do I disturb you? Are you busy?" he said.

"Not at all. At least, if I am busy, it is nothing that requires immediate attention. I am a little stupid about those drainages, and what is the landlord's part. I wonder if you know any better? You must have the same sort of things to do?"

"I am ashamed to say I don't, now; but I'll get it all up," he said eagerly,—"that must be perfectly easy,—and give you the result."

"You will cram me, in short," said Lady Markland, with a smile. "You ought to be somebody's private secretary. How well you would do it! That was all right about the lease. Mr. Longstaffe was very much astonished that I should know so much. I did not tell him it was you."

"It was not me!" cried Warrender. "I had only the facts, and you supplied the understanding. I suppose that is to be my trade too; it will be something to think that you have trained me for it."

"That we have studied together," she said, "with most of the ignorance on my side, and most of the knowledge on yours. Oh, I am not too humble. I allow that I sometimes see my way out of a difficulty, with a jump, before you have reasoned it out. That sort of thing is conceded to a woman. I am 'not without intelligence,'

Mr. Longstaffe himself says. But what do you mean to imply by that tone of regret—you suppose it is to be your trade?"

"I don't mean anything,—to make you ask, perhaps. I have no doubt I mean that finding out what was the exact pound of flesh the farmers could demand, and how much on our side we could exact, did not seem very lofty work: until I remembered that you were doing it too."

"My doing it makes no difference," said Lady Markland. "You ought to know better than to make me those little compliments. But for all that, it is a fine trade. Looking after the land is the best of trades. Everything must have begun with it, and it will go on for ever. And the pleasure of thinking one can improve, and hand it over richer and better for the expenditure of a little brains upon it, as well as other condiments—" she said, with a laugh. "Guano, you will say, is of more use perhaps than the brains."

She carried off a little enthusiasm, which had lit up her eyes, with this laugh at the end.

"I don't think so," said Warrender. "Do you think I meant any compliment? but to see you giving yourself up to this, you, who— and to remember that I had been perhaps grumbling, thinking of the schools, and other such paltry honours."

"Oh, not paltry,—not paltry at all; very, very much the reverse. I am sure no one interested in you can think so."

"I think so myself," he said. "I must tell you my little experiences on that subject." And with this he told her all his little story about the devotion of the Dons; about their discovery of his pursuits, and the slackening of their approbation; and about how Brunson (a very good fellow, and quite aware of their real meaning) had taken his place. Lady Markland was duly interested, amused, and indignant; interested enough to be quite sincere in her expressions, and yet independent enough to smile a little at the conflict between wounded feeling and philosophy on Warrender's part.

"But," she added, with a woman's liking for a practicable medium, "you might have postponed your deeper reading till you had done what was necessary, and so pleased both them and yourself."

"I thought one could not serve two masters," said Theo; "and that is why I encourage myself, by your example, to take to the land and its duties, and give up the other poor little bubble of reputation."

"Don't talk of my example," she said. "I am not disinterested. I am making no choice. What I am doing is for the only object I have in life, the only thing I have in the world."

He did not ask any question, but he fixed her with intent, inquiring eyes.

"You need not look as if you had any doubt what it was. It is Geoff, of course. I don't care very much for anything else. But to hand back his inheritance unburdened, to make a man of my poor little Geoff——" Her bright eyes moistened with quick-springing tears. She smiled, and her face looked to Theo like the face of an angel; though he was impatient of the motive, he adored her for it. And she gave her head a little toss, as if to shake off this undue emotion. "I need not talk any high-flown nonsense about such a simple duty, need I?" she said, once more with a soft laugh. Instead of making the most of her pathetic position, she would always ignore the claims she had upon sympathy. Her simple duty,—that was all.

"We must not discuss that question," he said; "for if I were to say what I thought—— And this brings me to what I wanted to talk to you about, Lady Markland. Geoff——"

She looked at him, with a sudden catching of her breath. She had no expectation of a sudden invasion of the practical into the vague satisfaction of the pause, which kept Geoff still by his mother's side. And yet she knew that it was her duty to listen, to accept any reasonable suggestion that might be made.

"There was that question,—between a school and a tutor," he said. "I have been thinking a great deal about it. We settled, you remember, that to send him away to school would be too much; not good for himself, as he is delicate: and for you it would be hard. You would miss him dreadfully."

"Miss him!" she said. As if these common words could express the vacancy, the blank solitude, into which her life without Geoff would settle down!

"But it seems to me now that there is another side to the question," he continued, with what seemed to Lady Markland a pitiless persistency. "A tutor here would be too much in your way. You would not like to let him live by himself altogether. His presence would be a constant embarrassment. You could not have him with you, nor could you, for Geoff's sake, keep him quite at a distance."

She held out her hands to stop this too clear exposition. "Don't!" she cried. "Do you think I have not considered all that? You only make me see the difficulties more and more clearly, and I see them so clearly already. But what am I to do?"

"Dear Lady Markland," he said, rising from his chair, "I want to propose something to you." The young man had grown so pale, yet by moments flushed so suddenly, and had altogether such an air of agitation and passionate earnestness, that a certain alarm flashed into her mind. The word had an ominous sound. Could he be thinking—was it possible—— She felt a hot flush of shame and a cold shiver of horror and fear at the thought, which after all was not a thought, but only a sharp pang of fright, which went through her like an arrow. He saw that she looked nervously at him, but that was easily explained by what had gone before.

"It is this," he said. "It is quite simple; it will cost nobody anything, and give a great deal of pleasure to me. I want you to let *me* be Geoff's tutor. Wait a moment before you answer. It will be no trouble. I have absolutely nothing to do. My father left all his affairs in complete order; all my farms are let, everything going on quite smoothly. And you must remember our little bit of a place is very different from all you have to think of. No, I don't want to thrust myself upon you. I will ride over, or drive over, or walk over, every day. The distance is nothing; it will do me all the good in the world. And, honours or no honours, I have plenty of scholarship for Geoff. Ah, don't refuse me; it will be such a pleasure. I have set my heart on being tutor to Geoff."

She had listened to him with a great many endeavours to break in. She stopped him at last almost by force, putting out her hand and taking his when he came to a little pause for breath. "Mr. Warrender," she said, almost as breathless as he, tears in her eyes, her voice almost choked, "how can I thank you for the thought! God bless you for the thought. Oh, how good, how kind, how full of feeling! I hope if you are ever in trouble you will have as good a friend as you have been to me."

"If you will be my friend, Lady Markland—"

"That I will," she cried, "all my life; but never be able to make up to you for this." She had put out both her hands, which he held trembling, but dared not stoop to kiss lest he should betray himself. After a moment, half laughing, half sobbing, she bade him sit down again beside her. "You are very, very good," she said; "but there are a few things to be talked over. First, you are going back to Oxford in a week or two."

"I am not going up this term; that is settled already."

"Not going up! But I thought you must go up. You have not taken your degree."

"Oh, that is not till next year," he said lightly, confident in her ignorance of details. "There is no reason why I should hurry; and, in fact, I had made up my mind some time since, so there is no difficulty so far as that goes."

She looked at him with keen scrutiny; her mind in a moment flashing over the whole course of their conversation like a light over a landscape, yet seeing it imperfectly, as a landscape under a sudden flash can only be seen with a perception of its chief features, but nothing more. The young man had been tenderly kind to her all through. Since the moment when he came into this very room to tell her of her husband's accident he had never forsaken her. She had not thought that such chivalrous kindness existed in the world, but she was yet young enough and inexperienced enough to believe in it and in its complete disinterestedness; for what return could she ever make for all he had done? And now, was this a crowning service, an offer of brotherly kindness which was almost sublime, or—what was it? She looked at him as if she could see into his soul. "Oh," she said, "I know your generosity. I feel as if I could not trust you when you say it doesn't matter. How could I ever forgive myself if you were injuring your own prospects for Geoff!—if it was for Geoff."

For Geoff! Warrender laughed aloud, almost roughly, in a way which half offended her. Could anybody suppose for a moment that for that ugly, precocious little boy—? "You need not distress yourself on that account, Lady Markland," he said. "It is not for Geoff,—I had made up my mind on that question long ago,—but by way of occupying my idle time—And if you think me good enough——"

"Oh, good enough!" she said. But she was too much alarmed and startled to make any definite reply. Almost for the first time she became conscious that Theo was neither a boy nor a visionary young hero of the Sir Galahad kind, but a man like other men. The further discovery which awaited her, that she herself was not a dignified recluse from life, a queen mother ruling the affairs of her son's kingdom for him and not for herself: but in other people's eyes, at least, a young woman, still open to other thoughts, was still far from Lady Markland's mind.

CHAPTER XX.

"You will give me my answer after you have thought it all over."

"Certainly you shall have an answer: and in the meantime my thanks; or if there is any word more grateful than thanks,—more than words can say——"

He turned to look back as he closed the little gate for foot passengers at the end of the bare road which was called the avenue, and took off his hat as she waved her hand to him. Then she turned back again towards the house. It was a ruddy October afternoon, the sun going down in gold and crimson, with already the deeper, more gorgeous colours of winter in the sky. Geoff was hanging upon her arm, clinging to it with both of his, walking in her very shadow, as was his wont.

"Why do you thank Theo Warrender like that? What has he done for us?" asked Geoff.

"I don't think, dear, that you should talk of him in that familiar way. Theo! He is old enough to be"—here she paused for a moment, not pleased with the suggestion, and then added—"he might be your elder brother, at least."

"Not unless I had another mamma," said Geoff. "Theo is about as old as you."

"Oh no; much younger than I am. Do you remember you once said you would like him for your tutor, Geoff?"

"I don't think I should now," said the little boy. "That was because he was so clever. I begin to think now, perhaps it would be better not to have such a clever one. When you are very small you don't understand."

"You are not very big still, my dear boy."

"No, but things come different." Geoff had a way of twisting his little face, as he made an observation wiser than usual, which amused the world in general, but not his mother. He was not a pretty boy; there was nothing in his appearance to satisfy a pretty young woman in her ambition and vanity for her child; but his little face was turned into a grotesque by those queer contortions. She put her hand upon his arm hastily.

"Don't make such faces, Geoff. Why should you twist your features out of all shape, with every word you say?"

This was perhaps too strong, and Geoff felt it so. "I don't want to make faces," he said, "but what else have you got to do it with when you are thinking? I'll tell you how I have found out that Theo Warrender would be too clever. That day when he showed me how to do my Latin"—The boy here paused, with a curious elfish gravity. "It was a long time ago."

"I remember, dear."

"Well, you were all talking, saying little speeches, as people do, you know, that come to pay visits; and he was out of it, so he talked to me. But now, when he comes, he makes the speeches, and you answer him, and you two run on till I think you never will be done; and it is I who am out of it," said Geoff, with great gravity, though without offence. His mother pressed his clinging arms to her side, with a sudden exclamation.

"My own boy, *you* feel out of it when I am talking!—you, my only child, my only comfort!" Lady Markland held him close to her, and quick tears sprang to her eyes.

"It is nothing to make any fuss about, mamma. Sometimes I like it. I listen, and you are very funny when you talk. That is, not you, but Theo Warrender. He talks as if nothing was right but only as you thought. I suppose he thinks you are very clever." Geoff paused for a moment, and gave her an investigating look; and then added in a less assured tone, "And I suppose you are clever, ain't you, mamma?"

She was moved to a laugh, in the midst of other feelings. "Not that I know of, Geoff. I was never thought to be clever, so far as I am aware."

"You are, though," he said, "when you don't make speeches as all the people do. I think you are cleverer with Theo than with anybody. What was he talking of to-day, for instance, when I was away?"

The question was put so suddenly that she was almost embarrassed by it. "He was saying that he wished to be your tutor, Geoff. It was very kind. To save me from parting with you,—which I think would be more than I could bear,—and to save me the trouble of having a—strange gentleman in the house."

"But he would be a strange gentleman, just the same."

"He is a friend, the kindest friend; and then he would not be in the house. He wants to come over every day, just for your lessons. But it is too much,—it is too much to accept from any one," she said suddenly, struck for the first time with this view.

"That would be very jolly!" cried Geoff. "I should like that: if he came only for my lessons, and then went away: and afterwards there would be only you and me,—nobody but you and me, just as we used to be all the time, before——"

"Oh, don't say that! We were not always alone—before; there was——"

"I know," said the little boy; but after a moment's pause he resumed: "You know that generally we were alone, mamma. I like that,—you and me, and no one else. Yes, let Theo come and teach me; and then when lessons are over go away."

Lady Markland laughed. "You must think it a great privilege to teach you, Geoff. He is to be allowed that favour,—to do all he can for us,—and as soon as he has done it to be turned from the door. That would be kind on his part, but rather churlish on ours, don't you think?"

"Oh," said the boy, "then he does it for something? You said tutors worked for money, and that Theo was well off, and did not want money. I see; then he wants something else. Is no one kind just for kindness? Must everybody be paid?"

"In kindness, surely, Geoff."

The boy looked at her with his little twinkling eyes and a twist in the corner of his mouth. Perhaps he did not understand the instinctive suspicion in his mind,—indeed, there is no possibility that he could understand it; but it moved him with a keen premonition of danger. "I should think it was easiest to pay in money," he said, with precocious wisdom. "How could you and me be kind?"

They strolled homeward during this conversation along the bare avenue, through the lines of faint, weak-kneed young trees which had been planted with a far-off hope of some time, twenty years hence, filling up the gaps. Little Geoff, with all the chaos of ideas in his mind, a child unlike other children, just saved from the grave of his race, the last little feeble representative of a house which had been strong and famous in its day, was not unlike one of the feeble saplings which rustled and swayed in the wailing autumn wind. The sunshine slanted upon the two figures, throwing long shadows across the wet grass and copse, which only differed from the long slim shadows of the young trees in their steadiness as they moved along by their own impulse, instead of blowing about at the mercy of the breeze, like the heirs of the old oaks and beeches. The scene had a mixture of desolation and hopefulness which was very characteristic: everything young and new, where all should have been mature and well established, if not old—yet in the mere fact of youth conveying a promise of victory against the winds and chills of winter, against the storms and tribulations of life. If they survived, the old avenue would rustle again with verdant wealth, the old house would raise up its head; but for the present, what was wanted was warmth and shelter and protection, tempered winds and sunshine and friends, protection from the cold north and blighting east. The little human sapling was the one most difficult to guard: and who can tell before the event which alternative is best? Happily no serious question keeps possession long of a child's brain, and the evening passed as all their quiet evenings passed, without any further discussion. But Geoff's question echoed in Lady Markland's mind after the child had forgotten it and was fast asleep; "How could you and me be kind?" How was she to repay Theo for a devotion so great? It was like the devotion of a knight in the times of chivalry. She had said both to herself and others, many times, how kind he was, how could she ever repay him?—like a brother. But it was true, after all, that everybody had to be paid. How could she reward Theo for his devotion? What could she do for him? There was nothing within her power; she had no influence to help him on, no social advantage, no responsive favour of any kind. He was better off, better educated, more befriended, more surrounded, than she was. He wanted nothing from her. How could she show her gratitude, even? "How can you and me be kind?" she said to herself, with a forlorn pride that Geoff always saw the heart of the difficulty. But this did not help her to any reply.

Next morning Mr. Longstaffe, the "man of business" who had the affairs of half the county in his hands, came to Markland to see her, and any idea there might have been of attending to Geoff's lessons had to be laid aside. He had to be dismissed even from his seat in the window, where he superintended, on ordinary occasions, everything that went on. With an internal reflection how it would have been had Theo begun his labours, Lady Markland sent the boy away. "Take care of yourself, Geoff. If you go out, take Bowen with you, or old Black." Bowen was the nurse, whom Geoff felt himself to have long outgrown, and Black was an old groom, whose company was dear to Geoff on ordinary occasions, but for whom he felt no particular inclination to-day. The little boy went out and took a meditative walk, his thoughts returning to the question which had been put before them last night: Theo Warrender for his tutor, to come daily for his lessons, and then to go away. With the unconscious egotism of a child, Geoff would have received this as perfectly reasonable, a most satisfactory arrangement; and indeed it appeared to him, on thinking it over, that his mother's suggestion of a payment in kindness was on the whole somewhat absurd. "Kindness!" Geoff said to himself, "who's going to be unkind?" He proceeded to consider the subject at large. After a time he slapped his little thigh, as Black did when he was excited. "I'll tell you!" he cried to himself. "I'll offer to go over *there* half the time." He paused at this, for, besides the practical proof of kindness to Theo which he felt would thus be given, a sudden pleasure seized upon and expanded his little soul. To go over *there*: to save Theo the trouble, and for himself to burst forth into a new world, a universe of sensations unknown,—into freedom, independence, self-guidance! An exhilaration and sentiment hitherto unexperienced went up in fumes to Geoff's brain. It was scarcely noon, a still and beautiful October day; the sky as blue as summer, the trees all russet and gold, the air with just enough chill in it to make breathing a keen delight. Why not now? These words, Geoff said afterwards, came into his mind as if somebody had said them: and the boldness and wildness of daring suggested ran through his little veins like wine. He rather flew than ran to the stables, which were sadly shorn of their ancient splendour, two horses and Geoff's pony being all that remained. "Saddle me my pony, Black!" the boy cried. "Yes, Master Geoff" (the old man would not say my lord); "but the cob's lame, and I can't take Mirah without my lady's leave." "Never mind. I'm going such a little way. Mamma never says anything when I go a little way." Was it a lie, or only a fib? This question of casuistry gave Geoff great trouble afterwards; for (he said to himself) it *was* only a little way, nothing at all, though mamma of course thought otherwise, and was deceived. "You'll be very careful, Master Geoff," said the old man. Black had his own reasons for not desiring to go out that day, which made him all the more willing to give credence to Geoff's promise; and the boy had never shown any signs of foolhardiness to make his attendants nervous. With an exultation which he could scarcely restrain, Geoff found himself on his pony, unrestrained and alone. When he got beyond the park, from which he made his exit by a gate which the servants used, and which generally stood open in the morning, a sort of awful delight was in his little soul. He was on the threshold of the world. The green lane before him led into the unknown. He paused a moment, rising in his stirrups, and looked back at the house standing bare upon the ridge, with all its windows twinkling in the sun. His little heart beat, as the heart beats when we leave all we love behind us, yet rose with a thrill and throb of anticipation as he faced again towards the outer universe. Not nine till Christmas, and yet already daring adventure and fortune! This was the consciousness that rose in the little fellow's breast, and made his small gray eyes dance with light, as he turned his pony's head towards the Warren, which meant into the world.

Geoff was very confident that he knew the road. He had gone several times with his mother in the carriage direct to the Warren; one time in particular, when the route was new to him,—when he went clinging to her, as he always did, but she, frozen into silence, making no reply to him, leant back in Mrs. Warrender's little brougham, like a mother made of marble. Very clearly the child remembered that dreadful drive. But others more cheerful had occurred since. He had got to know the Warren, which was so different from Markland, with those deep old shadowing trees, and everything so small and well filled. And they had all been kind to Geoff. He liked the ladies more than he liked Theo. On the whole, Geoff found ladies more agreeable than men. His father had not left a very tender image in his mind, whereas his mother was all the world to the invalid boy. It occurred to him that he would get a very warm reception at the Warren, whither he meant to go to convey to Theo his gracious acceptance of the offered lessons; and this gave brightness and pleasure to the expedition. But the real object of it was to show kindness which his mother had suggested as the only payment Theo would accept. Geoff in his generosity was going to give the price beforehand, to intimate his intention of saving Theo trouble by coming to the Warren every second day, and generally to propitiate and please his new tutor. It was a very important expedition, and nobody after this could say that Theo's kindness was not repaid.

The pony trotted along very steadily so long as Geoff remembered to keep his attention to it; and it cantered a little, surprising Geoff, when it found the turf under its hoofs, along another stretch of sunny road which Geoff turned into without remembering it, with a thrill of fresh delight in its novelty and in the long vista under its over-arching boughs. Then he went through the little wood, making the pony walk, his little heart all melting with the sweetness and shade as he picked his way across the brook, in which the leaves lay as in Valombrosa. The pony liked that gentle pace; perhaps he had thoughts of his own which were as urgent, yet as idle, as Geoff's, and like the boy felt the delight of the unknown. Anyhow, he continued to walk along the level stretch of road beyond the wood; and Geoff, upon his back, made no remonstrance. The boy began to get a little confused by the turnings, by the landscape, by the effect of the wide atmosphere and the wind blowing in his face. He forgot almost that he was Geoff. He was a little boy on his way to fairyland, riding on and on in a dream.

CHAPTER XXI.

The pony walked on, sometimes a little quicker, sometimes a little slower, while Geoff dreamed. No doubt the pony too had his own thoughts. His opinion was that summer had come again. He was rather a pampered little pony, who had never been put to any common use, who had never felt harness on his back, or a weight behind him, or even the touch of a whip beyond that of Geoff's little switch; and he had come so far and had trotted so long that he was hot, and did not like it. He had come so far that he no longer knew which was the direction of home and the comfortable cool stable, for which he began to puff and sigh. When they came to a cross-road he sniffed at it, but never could be sure. The scent seemed to lie one time in one way, another time in another. Not being able to make sure of the way home, the pony made it up to himself in a different direction. He sauntered along, and cooled down. He took a pull at the grass, nearly snatching the loose reins out of Geoff's small hands. Then, after having thus secured the proper length, he had a tolerable meal, a sort of picnic refreshment, not unpleasant; and the grass was very crisp and fresh. He began to think that it was for this purpose, to give him a little beneficial change of diet, that he had been brought out. It was very considerate. Corn is good, and so even is nice dry, sweet-smelling hay. But of all things in the world, there is nothing so delightful as the fresh salad with all its juices, the nice sweet grass with the dew upon it, especially when it is past the season for grass, and you have been ridden in the sun.

Geoff's mind was pleasurably moved in a different way. The freedom, the silence, the fresh air, entered into his little being like wine. He had not much experienced the delights of solitude.

A sickly child, who has to be watched continually, and who is alone in the sense of having no playmates, no one of his own age near him, has less experience than the robust of true aloneness. He had been always with his mother, always, in his mother's brief absences,—so brief that they scarcely told in the little story of his life,—under the charge of the nurse, who was entirely devoted to him. He knew all the stories she had to tell by heart, and yet would have them repeated, with a certain pleasure in the sound of the words. But his mother,—he never could be sure what she was going to say. To question her was the chief occupation of his life, and she never was weary of replying. His days were full of this perpetual intercourse. So it happened that to get out alone into the absolute stillness, broken only by the rustle of the leaves, the sound of the wind as it brought them down, the twitter of the birds, the tinkle of the little stream, was a new delight to Geoff, unlike anything that had gone before. And to see miles and miles before him, to see all round, roads stretching into the unknown, houses and churches and woods, all nameless and new; was he riding out to seek his fortune, was he going to conquer the world, was he the prince riding to the castle where the Sleeping Beauty lay? Or was he going on unawares to the ogre's castle, where he was to kill the giant and deliver the prisoners?

The little boy did not, perhaps, put these questions into form, but they were all in his mind, filling him with a vague, delicious exhilaration. He was all of them put together, and little Geoff Markland beside. He was afraid of nothing: partly, perhaps, because of his breeding, which had made it apparent to him that the world chiefly existed for the purpose of taking care of Geoff; and partly from an innate confidence and friendliness with all the world. He had no serious doubt that ogres, giants, and other unpleasant people did exist to be overcome; but so far as men and women were considered, Geoff had no fear of them, and he was aware that even in the castle of the ogre these natural aids and auxiliaries were to be found. He wandered on, accordingly, quite satisfied with his fancies, until the pony gave that first jerk to the reins and began his meal. Geoff pulled him up at first, but then began to reflect that ponies have their breakfast earlier than boys, and that even he himself was beginning to feel that the time for eating had come. "We can't both have luncheon," said the little man, "and I think you might wait, pony;" but he reflected again that, if he could put out his hand and reach some bread and butter, he would not himself, at that moment, be restrained by the thought that pony's hunger was unsatisfied. This thought induced him to drop his wrists and leave pony free. They formed an odd little vignette on the side of the road: the pony, with his head down, selecting the juicy spots; the little boy amicably consenting, with his hands upon its neck. Geoff, however, to those who did not know that he was consenting, and had philosophically made up his mind to sanction, in default of luncheon for himself, his pony's meal, looked a somewhat helpless little figure, swayed about by the movements of his little steed. And this was how he appeared to the occupants of a phaeton which swept past, with two fine bay horses, and all their harness glittering and jingling in the sun. There was a lady in it, by the driver's side, and both greeted the little boy with a burst of laughter. "Shall I touch him up for you?" the gentleman cried, brandishing his whip over the pony's head. This insult went to Geoff's soul. He drew himself up out of his dreaming, and darted such a glance at the passers-by as produced another loud laugh, as they swept past. And he plucked the pony's head from the turf with the same startled movement, and surprised the little animal into a canter of a dozen paces or so, enough, at least, he hoped, to show those insolent people that he could go, when he liked. But after that the pony took matters into his own hand.

It was beginning to be afternoon, which to Geoff meant the decline of the day, after his two o'clock dinner. He had no dinner, poor child, and that afternoon languor which the strongest feel, the sense of falling off and running low, was deepened in him by unusual emptiness, and that consciousness of wrong which a child has who has missed a meal. Pony, after *his* dinner, had a more lively feeling than ever that the stable at home would be cool and comfortable, and, emboldened by so much salad, wanted to turn back and risk finding the way. He bolted twice, so that all Geoff's horsemanship and all his strength were necessary to bring the little beast round. The little man did it, setting his teeth with childish rage and determination, digging his heels into the fat refractory sides, and holding his reins twisted in his little fists with savage tenacity. But a conflict of this sort is very exhausting, and to force an unreasonable four-footed creature in the way it does not want to go requires a strain of all the faculties which it is not easy to keep up, especially at the age (not all told) of nine. Geoff felt the tears coming to his eyes; he felt that he would die of shame if any one saw him thus almost mastered by a pony, yet that he would give anything in the world to see a known face, some one who would help him home. Not the phaeton, though, or that man who had offered to "touch him up." When he heard the wheels again behind him Geoff grew frantic. He laid his whip about the pony's sides, with a maddening determination not to be laughed at again. But circumstances were too strong for Geoff. The pony made a spring forward, stopped suddenly: and Geoff, with a giddy sense of flying through the air, a horrible consciousness of great hoofs coming down, lost all knowledge of what was going to happen to him, and ended in insensibility this wild little flight into the unknown.

It was well for Geoff that some one who had been crossing a field close by, at this climax of his little history, saw the impending accident, and sprang over the stile into the road at the decisive moment; for the driver of the phaeton could scarcely, with the best will in the world, have otherwise avoided mischief, though he pulled his horses back on their hindquarters in the sudden alarm. Theo Warrender flung himself under the very hoofs of the dashing bays. He seized the child and flung him out on the edge of the road, but was himself knocked down, and lay for a moment not knowing how much he was himself hurt, and paralysed by terror for the child, whom he had recognised in the flash of the catastrophe. There was a whirl of noise for a moment, loud shrieks from the lady, the grinding of the suddenly stopped wheels, the prancing and champing of the horses, the loud exclamations of the man who was driving, to the groom who sprang out from behind, and to his shrieking companion. The groom raised Geoff's head, and propped him on the grass at the roadside, while Warrender crept out from the dangerous position he occupied, his heart sick with alarm. "He's coming to," said the groom. "There is no harm done. The gentleman's more hurt than the boy." "There is nothing the matter with me," cried Warrender, though the blood was pouring from his forehead, making bubbles in the dust. When Geoff opened his eyes he had a vision first of that anxious, blood-stained countenance; then of a bearded face in an atmosphere of cigar smoke, which reminded him strangely, in the dizziness of returning consciousness, of his father, while the carriage, the impatient bays, the lady looking down from her high seat, were like a picture behind. He could not remember at first what it was all about. The bearded man knelt beside him, feeling him all over. "Does anything hurt you, little chap? Come, that's brave. I think there's nothing wrong."

"But look at Theo! Theo's all bleeding," said Geoff, trying to raise himself up.

"It's nothing,—a trifle," said Warrender, feeling, though faint, angry that the attention of the stranger should be directed to his ghastly countenance. He added, "Don't wait on account of him. If you will let your man catch the pony, I'll take him home."

Then the lady screamed from the phaeton that the little darling must be given to her, that he was not fit to get on that pony again, that he must be driven to Underwood. She called her companion to her, who swore by Jove, and plucked at his moustache, and consulted with the groom, who by some chance knew who the child was. The end of the discussion was that Geoff, to his own great surprise, and not without a struggle, was lifted to the phaeton and placed close to the lady, who drew him to her, and kept him safe within her arm. Geoff looked up at the face that bent so closely over him with a great deal of curiosity and a mingled attraction and repulsion. In his giddy state, it seemed to him another phase of the dream. The sudden elevation, the rush of rapid motion, so different from his slow and easy progress, the two bays dashing through the air, the lady's perfumery and her caresses, all bewildered the boy. Where were they taking him? After all, was there really some ogre's castle, some enchanted palace, to which he was being swept along without any will of his? The little boy was disturbed by the kisses and caresses of his new friend. He was neither shy nor forward; but he felt himself too old to be kissed, and a little indignant, and slightly alarmed, in the confusion of his shaken frame, as to where he was being taken and what was going to happen to him. The bays were grand and the lady was beautiful; but as Geoff looked at her, holding himself as far away as was possible within the tight reach of her arm holding him, he thought her more like the enchantress than the good, lovely fairy queen, which had been his first idea. She was not like the ogre's wife he knew so well,—that pathetic, human little person, who did what she could to save the poor strayed boys; but rather of ogre kind herself, kissing him as if she would like to put a tooth in him, with loud laughter at his shrinking and indisposition to be caressed. Geoff also felt keenly the meanness of forsaking Theo, and even the pony, who by this time, no doubt, must be very sorry for having thrown him, and very much puzzled how to get home. Would the groom (left behind for the purpose) be able to catch him? All these things much disturbed Geoff's thoughts. He paid little attention to the promises that were made to him of tea and nice things to eat, although he was faint and hungry; feeling not altogether certain, in his little confused brain, that he might not, instead of eating, be eaten, although he was quite aware at the same time that this was nonsense, and could not be.

But when the phaeton turned in at the gate of the Elms, and Geoff saw the high red brick house, surrounded with its walls, like a prison, or like the ogre's castle itself, his perturbation grew to a climax. The vague alarm which takes complete possession of a child when once aroused in him rose higher and higher in his mind. When the lady sprang lightly down, and held out her arms to receive him as he alighted, the little fellow made a nervous leap clear of her, and stood shaking and quivering with the effort, on his guard, and distrustful of any advance. "Nobody is going to harm you, my little fellow," said the man, kindly enough: while the lady asked why he was frightened, with laughter, which confused and alarmed him more and more; for Geoff was accustomed to be taken seriously, and did not understand being laughed at. He wanted to be civil, notwithstanding, and was about to follow in-doors, plucking up his courage, when a glance round, which showed him how high the walls were, and that the gates had been closed, and that in the somewhat strait inclosure inside there was no apparent outlet by which he could communicate with the world in which his mother and Theo and everybody he knew were left behind, brought a thrill of panic, which he could not overcome, through him. As he paused, scared and frightened, on the threshold, he saw at the farther end of the inclosure a door standing a little ajar, at which some one had entered on foot. Geoff did not pause to think again, but made for the opening with a sudden start, and, when outside, ran like a hunted hare. He ran straight on seeing houses before him where he knew there must be safety,—houses with no high walls, cottages such as a small heart trusts in, be it beggar or prince. He ran, winged with fear, till he got as far as Mrs. Bagley's shop. It was not far, but he was unused to violent exertion, and his little body and brain were both quivering with excitement and with the shock of his fall. The dread of some one coming after him, of the house that looked like a prison, of the strangeness of the circumstances altogether, subsided at the sight of the village street, the church in the distance, the open door of the little shop. All these things were utterly antagonistic to ogres, incompatible with enchantresses. Geoff became lively again when he reached the familiar and recognisable; and when he saw the cakes in Mrs.

Bagley's window, his want of a dinner became an overpowering consciousness. He stopped himself, took breath, wiped his little hot forehead, and went in in a very gentlemanly way, taking off his hat, which was dusty and crushed with his fall, to the astonished old lady behind the counter. "Would you mind giving me a cake or a biscuit?" he said. "I don't think I have any money, but I am going to Mrs. Warrender's, if you will show me where that is, and she will pay for me. But don't do it," said Geoff, suddenly perceiving that he might be taken for an impostor, "if you have any doubt that you will be paid."

"Oh, my little gentleman," cried Mrs. Bagley, "take whatever you please, sir! I'm not a bit afraid; and if you was never to pay me, you're but a child, if I may make bold to say so; and as for a cake or a—— But if you'll take my advice, sir, a good bit of bread and butter would be far more wholesome, and you shall have that in a moment."

"Thank you very much," said Geoff, though he cast longing eyes at the cakes, which had the advantage of being ready; "and please might I have a chair or a stool to sit down upon, for I am very tired? May I go into that nice room there, while you cut the bread and butter? My mother," said the boy, with a sigh of pleasure, throwing himself down in Mrs. Bagley's big chair, which she dragged out of its corner for him, "will be very much obliged to you when she knows. Yes, I am only a child," he continued, after a moment; "but I never thought I was so little till I got far away from home. Will you tell me, please, where I am now?"

Mrs. Bagley was greatly impressed by this little personage, who looked so small and talked with such imposing self-possession. She set down before him a glass of milk with the cream on it, which she had intended for her own tea, and a great slice of bread and butter, which Geoff entered upon without further compliment. "This is Underwood," she said, "and Mrs. Warrender's is close by, and there's nobody but will be ready to show you the way; but I do hope, sir, as you haven't run away from home."

"Oh no," said Geoff, with his mouth full of bread and butter, "not at all. I only came to see Theo,—that is Mr. Warrender's name, you know. To be sure," he added, "mamma will not know where I am, and probably she is very frightened; that is something like running away, isn't it? I hope they have caught my pony, and then when I have rested a little I can ride home. Is that a nice house, that tall red house with the wall round it, or do they shut up people there?"

"Ah, that's the Elms," said the old lady, and she gave a glance which Geoff did not understand to the young woman who was sitting at work behind. "I don't know as folks is ever shut up in it," she said, significantly; "but don't you never go there, my little gentleman, for it ain't a nice house."

"The like of him couldn't get no harm—if even, Granny, it was as bad as you think."

"There is nobody as wouldn't get harm, man or woman, or even children," cried Granny dogmatically. "It was the last place as poor Lord Markland was ever in afore his accident, and who knows——"

Geoff put down his bread and butter. "That's my father," he said. He did not use the more familiar title when talking to strangers. "Did he know those people? Perhaps his horses got wild escaping from them."

Mrs. Bagley lifted up her hands in awe and wonder. "My stars!" she said, "I thought I had seen him before. Lizzie, it's the little lord."

"That is what the lady called me," said Geoff, "as if it was my fault. Do they set traps there for people who are lords?"

CHAPTER XXII.

It may be supposed what the sight of Theo all bound up and bleeding was to the family in the Warren. He had not at all the look of a benevolent deliverer, suffering sweetly from a wound received in the service of mankind. He had a very pale and angry countenance, and snorted indignant breath from his dilated nostrils. "It's nothing; a little water will make it all right," he answered to the eager questions of his mother and sisters. "Has the brat got here?"

"The brat? What brat? Oh, Theo! You've been knocked down; your coat is covered with dust. Run for a basin, Chatty, and some lint. You've been fighting, or something." These cries rose from the different voices round him, while old Joseph, who had seen from a window the plight in which his master was, stood gazing, somewhat cynical and very curious, in the background. The scene was the hall, which has been already described, and into which all the rooms opened.

"Well," said Theo angrily, "I never said I hadn't. Where's the boy? Little fool! and his mother will be distracted. Oh, don't bother me with your bathing. I must go and see after the boy."

"Let me see what is wrong," pleaded Mrs. Warrender. "The boy? Who is it? Little Markland? Has he run away? Oh, Theo, have patience a moment. Joseph will run and see. Minnie will put on her hat."

"Running don't suit these legs o' mine," grumbled Joseph, looking at his thin shanks.

"And what am I to put on my hat for?" cried Minnie. "Let Theo explain. How can we tell what he wants, if he won't explain?"

"I'll run," said Chatty, who had already brought her basin, and who flew forth in most illogical readiness, eager to satisfy her brother, though she did not know what he wanted. Good-will, however, is often its own reward, and in this instance it was emphatically so, for Chatty almost ran into a little group advancing through the shrubbery,—Mrs. Bagley, with her best bonnet hastily put on, and holding little Geoff Markland by the hand. The little boy was in advance, dragging his guardian forward, and Mrs. Bagley panted with the effort. "Oh, Miss Chatty," she cried, "I'm so thankful to see you! The little gentleman, he's in such a hurry. The little gentleman——"

Geoff left go in a moment of the old lady's hand, nearly throwing her off her balance; but he was full of his own affairs, as was natural. "It is me," he said to Chatty. "I came to see Theo; but I had an accident and he had an accident. And they wanted to take me to that tall house, but I wouldn't. Has Theo come back? and where is pony? This old lady has to be paid for the bread and butter. She was very kind, and took care of me when I ran away."

"Oh," cried Chatty, "did you run away? And Lady Markland will be so unhappy."

No one paid attention to Mrs. Bagley declaring that she wanted no payment for her bread and butter; and Geoff, very full of the importance of the position, hurried Chatty back to the house. "Can I go in?" he said, breathless; "and will you send me home, and find pony for me? Oh, here is Theo. Was it the horse that tipped you on the head?" He came forward with great gravity, and watched the bathing of Warrender's head, which was going on partly against his will. Geoff approached without further ceremony, and stood by the side of the table, and looked on. "Did he catch you with his forefoot?" said the boy. "I thought it was only the back feet that were dangerous. What a lot of blood! and oh, are they going to cut off your hair? When I got a knock on the head, mamma sent for the doctor for me."

"Dear Theo, be still, and let me do it. How could you get such a blow?"

"I will tell you, Mrs. Warrender," said the little boy, drawing closer and closer, and watching everything with his little grave face. "Pony threw me, and the big bays were coming down to crush my head. I saw them waving in the air, like that, over me! and Theo laid hold of me *here* and tore me, and they crushed him instead."

"What is all this about a pony and the bays? Theo, tell me."

"He tore me all here, look, in the back of my knickerbockers," said Geoff, putting his hand to the place; "but I'd rather have that than a knock on my head. Theo, does it hurt? Theo, what a lot you have bled! Were you obliged to tear my knickerbockers? I say, Theo, the lady was pretty, but I didn't much like her, after all."

Theo, though his head was over the basin, put out his hand and seized the child by the shoulders. "What did you run away for, you little——? Do you know your mother will be wretched about you?—your mother, who is worth a hundred of you." This was said through his teeth, with a twist of Geoff's shoulder which was almost savage.

"I say!" cried the child; then he added indignantly, "I never ran away, I came to see you, because you are going to be my tutor. I didn't think it was such a long way. And pony got hungry. And so was I."

"Going to be his tutor!" It was Minnie's voice that said this so sharply that the air tingled with the words: and even Mrs. Warrender started a little; but it was not a moment at which any more could be said. The bathing was done, and Theo's wound had now to be brought together by plaster and bound up. It was not very serious. A hoof had touched him, but that was all, and fortunately not on a dangerous place.

"Take him away and give him something to eat," said the patient, but not in a hospitable voice.

"I want to see it all done," said Geoff, pressing closer. "Is that how you do it? Don't you want another piece of plaster? Will you have to take it off again, or will it stay till it is all well? Oh, look, that corner isn't fast. Press it there, a little farther. Oh, Theo, she has done it so nicely. You can't see a bit of the bad place. It is all covered with plaster, like that, and then like this. I wish now it had been me, just to know how it feels."

"Take him away, mother, for Heaven's sake!" cried Warrender under his breath.

"My dear, you must not worry Theo. He is going to lie down now, and be quiet for a little. Go with Minnie, and have something to eat."

"I am not so hungry now," said the boy, "but very much interested. When you are interested you don't feel hungry: and the old woman gave me something to eat. Would you pay her, please? Won't you tie something on, Mrs. Warrender, to hide the plaster? It doesn't look very nice like that."

"Come," said Chatty, taking him by the hand. The elder sister had thrown herself into a chair at the mention of the tutorship, and seemed unable for further exertion.

"Oh yes, I am coming; but I am most interested about Theo. Theo, you have got a stain upon your cheek; and your coat is torn, too, as bad as my—— Well, but he did tear my knickerbockers. Look! I felt the cold wind, though I did not say anything; not upon the open road, but when we got among your trees. It is so dark among your trees. Theo!"

"Come, come; I want you to come with me," Chatty said, hurrying Geoff away; and perhaps the sight of the table in the dining-room, and the tray which Joseph, not without a grumble, was placing upon it, became about this time as interesting as Theo's wound.

"We ought to send and tell his mother that the child is here."

"Or send him back," said Minnie sharply, "and get rid of him. A little story-teller! Theo his tutor! If I were his mother, I should whip him, till he learned what lies mean!"

Mrs. Warrender looked with some anxiety at her son. "Children," she said, "make such strange misrepresentations of what they hear. But we should send——"

"I have sent already," said Theo. "She will probably come and fetch him: and, mother——"

"My dear, keep still, and don't disturb yourself. There might be a little fever."

"Oh, rubbish, fever! I shall not disturb myself, if you don't disturb me. Look here. It is quite true; I've offered myself to be his tutor."

"His tutor!" cried Minnie once more, in a voice which was like the report of a pistol. Mrs. Warrender said nothing, but looked at him with a boundless pity in her eyes, slightly shaking her head.

"Well! and what have you to say against it?" cried Theo, facing his sister, with a glow of anger mounting to the face which had been almost ghastly with loss of blood.

"This is not a moment for discussion. Go and see to the child, Minnie. Theo, my dear boy, if you care so much for Geoff as that—; at another time you must tell us all about it."

"There is nothing to tell you, save that I have made up my mind to it," he said, looking at her with that prompt defiance which forestalls remark. "Geoff! Do you think it is for Geoff? But neither at this time nor at any other time is there more to say."

He looked at her so severely that Mrs. Warrender's eyes fell. He felt no shame, but pride, in his self-sacrifice, and determination to stand by it and uphold his right to do it in the face of all the world. But this very determination, and a consciousness of all that would be said on the subject, gave Warrender a double intolerance in respect to Geoff himself. To imagine that it was for the boy's sake was, he already felt, the most unbearable offence. For the boy's sake! The boy would have been swept away before now if thought could have done it. From the first hour he had been impatient of the boy. The way in which he clung to his mother had been a personal offence. And his mother!—ah no, she could do no wrong. Not even in this matter, which sometimes tortured him, could he blame Lady Markland. But that she or any one should imagine for a moment that he was ready to sacrifice his time, his independence, so much of his life, for the sake of Geoff! That was a misconception which Warrender could not bear. "Don't let that little—— come near me," he said to his mother, as he finally went off, somewhat feebly, to the old library, where he could be sure of quiet. "Make the girls take care of him and amuse him. She will probably come and fetch him, and I will rest—till then."—That little—— Warrender did not add any epithet; the adjective was enough.

"Till then,—till she comes! Is that all your thought?" said his mother. "Oh, my poor boy!"

He met her eyes with a pride which scorned concealment. Yes, he would own it here, where it would be in vain to deny it. He would not disavow the secret of his heart. Mothers have keen eyes, but hers were not keen, they were pitying,—more sad than tears. She looked at him, and once more softly shook her head. The blood had rushed again to his face, dyeing it crimson for a moment, and he held his head high as he made his confession. "Yes, mother, that is all my thought." And then he walked away, tingling with the first avowal he had ever made to mortal ears. As for Mrs. Warrender, she stood looking after him with so mingled an expression that scarcely the most delicate of casuists could have divined the meaning in her. She was so sorry for him, so proud of him. He was so young, not more than a boy, yet man enough to give all his heart and his life—to sacrifice everything, even his pride—for the sake of the woman he loved. His mother, who had never before come within speaking distance of a passion like this, felt her heart glow and swell with pride in him, with tender admiration beyond words. She had neither loved nor been loved after this sort; and yet it was no romance of the poets, but had a real existence, and was here, here by her side, in the monotonous little world which had never been touched by such a presence before. She said to herself that it would never come to anything but misery and pain; yet even misery was better than nothingness, and he who had loved had lived. To think that a quiet, middle-aged Englishwoman, a pattern of domestic duty, should think thus, and exult in her son's inconceivable and, as she believed, unhappy passion, is almost too much to be credible. Yet so it was.

Geoff's absence was not discovered until two o'clock, when

Lady Markland, at the end of a long and troublesome consultation over matters only partially understood, suggested luncheon to her man of business. "Geoff will be waiting and very impatient," she said, with a smile. Mr. Longstaffe was not anxious to see Geoff, nor disturbed that the little boy's midday meal should have been postponed to business, though this disturbed Geoff's mother, who had been in the habit of thinking his comfort the rule of her life. She was much startled not to find him in the dining-room, and to hear that he had not come back. "Not come back! and it is two o'clock! But Black will take good care of him," she said, with a forced smile, to Mr. Longstaffe, "and I must not keep you waiting." "If you please, my lady," said the butler, "Black's not gone with him." At this Lady Markland stared at the man, the colour dying out of her face. "You have let him go out alone!" "I had nothing to do with it, my lady. The colt's lame, and Black——" "Oh," she cried, stamping her foot, "don't talk to me of excuses, but go, go, and look for my child!" Then she was told that Black had gone some time since, and was scouring all the roads about; that he had come back once, having seen nothing; and that now the coachman and gardener were gone too. From this time until the hasty messenger arrived with Theo's hurried note, Lady Markland spent the time in such distraction as only mothers know, representing to herself a hundred dangers, which reason told her were unlikely, but which imagination, more strong than reason, placed again and again before her eyes, till she felt a certainty that they were true. All those stories of kidnapping, which people in their senses laugh at, Lady Markland as much as any, being when in her right mind a very sensible woman—came before her now as possible, likely, almost certain. And she saw Geoff, with his little foot caught in the stirrup, dragged at the pony's frightened heels, the stones on the road tearing him, his head knocking against every obstacle; and she saw him lying by the roadside, white and lifeless. She saw everything that could and could not happen, and accused herself for not having sent him to school, out of danger,—for not having kept him by her side night and day.

Mr. Longstaffe naturally looked on at all this anguish with a mixture of contempt and pity. He was not at all alarmed for Geoff. "The young gentleman will have gone to visit one of his friends; he will have gone farther than he intended. He may, if he doesn't know the country very well, have missed his way: but we don't live in a country of brigands and bandits, my dear lady; somebody will be sure to direct him safely back." He managed to eat his luncheon by himself, after she had begged him not to mind her absence, and had left him undisturbed to confide to the butler his regret that Lady Markland should be so much upset, and his conviction that the little boy was quite safe. "He'll be all right, sir," the butler said. "He is as sharp as a needle, is Mr. Geoff. I did ought to say his little lordship, but it's hard to get into new ways." They said this, each with an indulgent smile at her weakness, in Lady Markland's absence. The lawyer had a great respect for her, and the butler venerated his mistress who was very capable in her own house, but they smiled at her womanish exaggeration, all the same.

Warrender had been quite right in thinking she would come at once for Geoff. She had almost harnessed the horses herself, so eager was she, and they flew along the country roads at a pace very unlike their ordinary calm. Evening had fallen when she rushed into the hall at the Warren, in her garden hat, with a shawl wrapped about her shoulders, the first she had found. Terrible recollections of the former occasion when she had been summoned to this house were in her mind, and it was with a fantastic terror which she could scarcely overcome that she found herself once more, by the same waning light, in the place where she had been sent for to see her husband die. If she had been deceived. If the child should be gone, like his father! She had not, however, a second moment in which to indulge this panic, for Geoff's voice, somewhat raised, met her ears at once. Geoff was in very great feather, seated among the ladies, expounding to them his views on things in general. "Our trees at Markland are not like your trees," he was saying. "They are just as young as me, mamma says. When I am as old as you are, or as Theo, perhaps they will be grown. But I should not like them so big as yours. When Theo is my tutor I shall tell him what I think; it will be a fine opportunity. Why, mamma!"

She had him in her arms, kissing and sobbing over him for a moment, till she could overcome that hysterical impulse. Theo had come from his room at the sound of the wheels, and the party was all collected in the drawing-room, the door of which stood open. There was little light, so that they could scarcely see each other, but Minnie had full time to remark with horror that Lady Markland did not even wear a widow's bonnet, or a crape veil, for decency, but had on a mere *hat*,—a straw hat, with a black ribbon. She put her hand on her heart in the pang of this discovery, but nobody else took any notice. And, indeed, in the outburst of the poor lady's thanks and questions, there was no room for any one else to speak.

"Oh, it was all right," said Geoff, who was in high excitement, the chief spokesman, and extremely eager to tell his own story before any one could interfere. "I knew the way quite well. I wanted to see Theo, you know, to ask him if he really meant it. I wanted to speak to him all by himself; for Theo is never the same, mamma, when you are there. I knew which turn to take as well as any one. I wasn't in a hurry; it was such a nice day. But pony was not interested about Theo, like me, and he remembered that it was dinner-time. That was all about it. And then those people in the phaeton gave him a start. It was nothing. I just popped over his head. There was no danger except that the bays might have given me a kick; but horses never kick with their forefeet."

Here Lady Markland gave a shriek, and clutched her boy again. "You fell off, Geoff, among the horses' feet!"

"Oh, it didn't matter, mamma; it didn't matter a bit, Theo caught me, and tore my knickerbockers (but they're mended now). He bled a great deal, and I helped Mrs. Warrender to plaster up the cut; but I wasn't hurt,—not a bit; and my knickerbockers——"

It was Geoff's turn now to pause in surprise, for his mother left him, and flew to Theo, and, taking his hands, tried to kiss them, and, between laughing and crying, said, "God bless you! God bless you! You have saved my boy's life!"

Geoff was confounded by this desertion, by the interruption, by the sudden cry. He put his hand up to the place where Warrender's cut was, dimly realising that it might have been in his own head but for Theo. "Was that what it was?" he said, wondering and unobserved in the midst of the new commotion, which for the moment left Geoff altogether, and rose around Warrender, as if he had been the hero of the day.

CHAPTER XXIII.

They all sat round the table and took their evening meal together before Lady Markland went back. It was not a ceremonious, grand dinner, as if there had been a party. Old Joseph pottered about, and put the dishes on the table, and handed the potatoes now and then when they were not wanted, and sometimes leaned across between the young ladies to regulate the lamp, explaining why as he did so. "Excuse me, Miss Chatty, but it's a-going to smoke," he said; and in the meantime the family helped each other. But Lady Markland was not conscious of the defects in the service. She sat by Theo's side, talking to him, looking at him in a kind of soft ecstasy. They had been friends before, but it seemed that she had now for the first time discovered what he was, and could not conceal her pleasure, her gratitude, her admiration. She made him tell her how it all happened, a dozen times over, while the others talked of other things, and poured out her thanks, her happiness, her ascriptions of praise, as if he had been more than mortal, devoting herself to him alone. Lady Markland had never been the kind of woman who allows herself in society to be engrossed by a man. It was entirely unlike her, unlike her character, a new thing. She was quite unconscious of Minnie's sharp eyes upon her, of the remarks which were being made. All she was aware of, in that rapture of safety after danger and relief from pain, was Geoff, blinking with eyes half sleepy, half excited, by the side of Mrs. Warrender, nothing hurt in him but his knickerbockers; and the young man by her side, with the wound upon his head, who had saved her child's life. Theo, for his part, was wrapped in a mist of delight for which there was no name. He saw only her, thought only of her; and for the first time began to imagine what life might be if it should ever come to mean a state in which this rapture should be permanent,—when she would always look at him so, always devote herself, eyes and lips and all her being, to make him happy.

The room lay in darkness beyond the steady light of the white lamp, shining on the circle of faces. There was not much conversation. Minnie was sternly silent, on the watch; Chatty sympathetically on the alert, too, though she scarcely knew why, because her sister was; Mrs. Warrender listening with a faint smile to Geoff's little chatter, occasionally casting a glance at the other end of the table, which she could see but imperfectly. Lady Markland spoke low, addressing Theo only, so that Geoff, as before, held the chief place. He was never weary of going over the adventures of the day.

"It is that tall house before you come to the village,—a tall, tall house, with a wall all round, as if to keep prisoners in. I know there are no prisoners now. Of course not! There are people all about in the fields and everywhere, who would soon tell the policeman and set you free. I was not afraid. Still, if the gates had been shut, and they refused to open, I don't know what one would do. The lady was like a picture in the Pilgrim's Progress,— that one, you know—I thought her pretty at first. But then she held me in her arm as if I had been a baby."

"Oh, it would be Those People!" said Minnie, moved to a passing exclamation of horror.

"Never mind that now. You must not venture out again without the groom, for it makes your mother unhappy—Theo," said Mrs. Warrender, with a smile and a sigh, "when he was a little fellow like you, never did anything to make me unhappy."

"Didn't he?" said Geoff seriously. "But I didn't know. How could I tell pony would so soon get hungry? He hasn't a regular dinner-time, as we have; only munches and munches all day. But I was telling you about the tall house."

"You must tell me another time, Geoff. Theo must bring you back with him sometimes for a holiday."

"Yes," said Geoff, "that would do better. Pony would go splendid by the side of Theo's big black. I shall come often—when I do my lessons well. I have never done any lessons except with mamma. Does Theo like teaching boys?"

"I don't know, my dear. I don't think he has ever tried."

"Then why is he coming to teach me? That, at the very bottom of it, you know, is what I wanted him to tell me; for he would not tell straight out, the real truth, before mamma."

"I hope he always tells the real truth," said Mrs. Warrender gently. "I suppose, my little Geoff, it is because he is fond of you."

Upon this Geoff shook his little head for a long time, twisting his face and blinking his keen little eyes. "He is not fond of me— oh no, it is not that. I can do with Theo very well,—as well as with any one; but he is not fond of me."

"I am glad to hear that you can do with Theo," said the mother, much amused.

"Yes. I don't mind him at all: but he is not fond of me; and he is sure not to teach mamma's way, and that is the only way I know. If he were to want to punish me, Mrs. Warrender——"

"I hope, my dear, there will be no question of that."

"I shouldn't mind," said the boy, "but mamma wouldn't like it. It might be very awkward for Theo. You are flogged when you go to school, aren't you? At least, all the books say so. Mamma," he went on, raising his voice, "here is a difficulty,—a great difficulty. If Theo should want to flog me, what should you do?"

Lady Markland did not hear him for the moment. She was absorbed!—this was the remark made by Minnie, who watched with the intensest observation. Then Geoff, in defiance of good manners, drummed on the table to attract his mother's attention, and elevated his voice: "Can't you hear what I am saying, mamma? If I were to be stupid with my lessons, and Theo were to flog me——" ("It is only putting a case, for I am not stupid," he added, for Mrs. Warrender's instruction, in an undertone.)

"You must not suggest anything so dreadful," said Lady Markland from the other end of the table. "But now you must thank Mrs. Warrender, Geoff, and Mr. Theo, and every one; for the carriage has come round, and it is growing late, and we must go away."

Then Mrs. Warrender rose, as in duty bound, and the whole party with her. "I will not ask you to stay; it is late for him, and he has had too much excitement," said the mistress of the house.

"And to think I might never have brought him home at all, never heard his voice again, but for your dear son, your good son!" cried Lady Markland, taking both her hands, putting forward her head, with its smooth silken locks in which the light shone, and the soft round of her uplifted face, to the elder woman, with an emotion and tenderness which went to Mrs. Warrender's heart. She gave the necessary kiss, but though she was touched there was no enthusiasm in her reply.

"You must not think too much of that, Lady Markland. I hope he would have done it for any child in danger."

This, of course, is always perfectly true; but it chills the effusion of individual gratitude. Lady Markland raised her head, but she still held Mrs. Warrender's hands. "I wish," she said, "oh, I wish you would tell me frankly! Does it vex you that he should be so good to me? This kind, kind offer about Geoff,—is it too much? Yes, yes, I know it is too much; but how can I refuse what he is so good, so charitable, as to offer, when it is such a boon to us? Oh, if you would tell me! Is it displeasing, is it distasteful to you?"

"I don't know how to answer you," Mrs. Warrender said.

"Ah! but that is an answer. Dear Mrs. Warrender, help me to refuse it without wounding his feelings. I have always felt it was too much."

"Lady Markland, I cannot interfere. He is old enough to judge for himself. He will not accept guidance from me,—ah, nor from you either, except in the one way." She returned the pressure of her visitor's hand, which had relaxed, with one that was as significant. "It is not so easy to lay spirits when they are once raised," she said.

Lady Markland gave her a sudden, alarmed, inquiring look; but Theo came forward at that moment with her cloak, and nothing could be said more.

He came back into the dining-room, expectant, defiant, fire in all his veins, and in his heart a sea of agitated bliss that had to get an outlet somewhere; not in a litany to her, for which there was no place, but at least in defence of her and of himself. It was Minnie, as usual, who stood ready to throw down the glove; Chatty being no more than a deeply interested spectator, and the mother drawing aside with that sense of impossibility which balks remonstrance, from the fray. Besides, Mrs. Warrender did not know, in the responsive excitement in herself which Theo's passion called forth, whether she wished to remonstrate or to put any hindrance in his way.

"Well, upon my word!" said Minnie, "Mrs. Wilberforce may well say the world is coming to a pretty pass. Only six months a widow, and not a bit of crape upon her! I knew she wore no cap. Cap! why, she hasn't even a bonnet, nor a veil, nor *anything!* A little bit of a hat, with a black ribbon,—too light for *me* to wear; even Chatty would be ashamed to be seen——"

"Oh no, Minnie; in the garden, you know, we have never worn anything deeper."

"Do you call this the garden?" cried Minnie, her voice so deep with alarm and presentiment that it sounded bass, in the silence of the night. "Six miles off, and an open carriage, and coming among people who are themselves in mourning! It ought to have given her a lesson to see my mother in her cap."

"If you have nothing better to do than to find fault with Lady Markland——" said Theo, pale with passion.

"Oh," cried Minnie, "don't suppose I am going to speak about Lady Markland to you. How can you be so infatuated, Theo? You a tutor,—you, that have always been made such a fuss with, as if there was not such another in the world! What was it all he was to be? A first class, and a Fellow, and I don't know what. But tutor to a small boy, tutor to a little lord,—a sort of a valet, or a sort of a nurse—"

"Minnie! your brother is at an age when he must choose for

himself."

"How much are you to have for it?" she cried,—"how much a year? Or are you to be paid with presents, or only with the credit of the connection? Oh, I am glad poor papa is dead, not to hear of it. He would have known what to think of it all. He would have given you his opinion of a woman—of a woman——"

"Lady Markland is a very nice woman," said Chatty. "Oh, Theo, don't look as if you were going to strike her! She doesn't know what she is saying. She has lost her temper. It is just Minnie's way."

"Of a woman who wears no crape for her husband," cried Minnie, with an effort, in her bass voice.

Theo, who had looked, indeed, as if he might have knocked his sister down, here burst into an angry peal of laughter, which rang through the house; and his mother, seizing the opportunity, took him by the arm and drew him away. "Don't take any notice," she said. "You must not forget she is your sister, whatever she says. And, my dear boy, though Minnie exaggerates, she has reason on her side, from her point of view. No, I don't think as she does, altogether; but, Theo, can't you understand that it is a disappointment to us? We always made so sure you were going to do some great thing."

"And to be of a little real use once in a way, is such a small thing!"

"Oh, Theo, you must be reasonable, and think a little. It does not want a scholar like you to teach little Geoff."

"A scholar—like me. How do you know I am a scholar at all?"

Mrs. Warrender knew that no answer to this was necessary, and did not attempt it. She went on: "And you are not in a position to want such employment. Don't you see that everybody will begin to inquire what your inducement was? A young man who has nothing, it is all quite natural; but you—Theo, have you ever asked yourself how you are to be repaid?"

"You are as bad as Minnie, mother," he said, with scorn; "you think I want to be repaid."

She clasped her hands upon his arm, looking up at him with a sort of pitying pride. "*She* must think of it, Theo—everybody must think of it; ah yes, and even yourself, at the last. Every mortal, everybody that is human,—oh, Theo, the most generous!—looks for something, something in return."

The young man tried to speak, but his voice died away after he had said "Mother!" To this he had no reply.

But though he could not answer the objection, he could put it aside; and as a matter of course he had his way. At the beginning of a thing, however clearly it may be apparent that embarrassment is involved, few people are clear-sighted enough to perceive how great the embarrassment may come to be. Lady Markland was not wiser than her kind. She spoke of Theo's kindness in a rapture of gratitude, and ended always by saying that, after all, that was nothing in comparison with the fact that he had begun by saving the boy's life. "I owe my child to him," she said,—"I owe him Geoff's life; and now it almost seems natural, when he has done so much, that he should do anything that his kind heart prompts." She would say this with tears in her eyes, with such an enthusiasm of gratitude that everybody was touched who heard her. But then, everybody did not hear Lady Markland's account of the matter; and the common mass, the spectators who observe such domestic dramas with always a lively desire to get as much amusement as possible out of them, made remarks of a very different kind. The men thought that Warrender was a fool, but that the widow was consoling herself; the ladies said that it was sad to see a young man so infatuated, but that Lady Markland could not live without an adviser; and there were some, even, who began to lament "poor dear young Markland," as if he had been an injured saint. The people who heard least of these universal comments were, however, the persons most concerned: Lady Markland, because she saw few people, and disarmed, as has been said, those whom she did see; and Warrender, because he was not the sort of man, young though he was, whom other men cared to approach with uncalled-for advice. There was but one person, indeed, after his sister, who lifted up a faithful testimony to Theo. Mrs. Wilberforce, as his parish clergyman's wife, felt that, if the rector would not do it, it was her duty to speak. She took advantage of the opportunity one evening after Christmas, when Warrender was dining at the Rectory. "Are you *still* going to Markland every day?" she said. "Isn't it a great tie? I should think by the time you have ridden there and back you can't have much time for any business of your own."

"It is a good thing, then," said Theo, "that I have so little business of my own."

"You say so," said the rector's wife, "but most gentlemen make fuss enough about it, I am sure. There seems always something to be doing when you have an estate in your hands. And now that you are a magistrate—though I know you did *not* go to Quarter Sessions," she said severely.

"There are always enough of men who like to play at law, without me."

"Oh, Theo, how can you speak so? when it is one of a gentleman's highest functions, as everybody knows! And then there are the improvements. So much was to be done. The girls could talk of nothing else. They were in a panic about their trees. There is no stauncher Conservative than I am," said Mrs. Wilberforce, "but I do think Minnie went too far. She would have everything remain exactly as it is. Now I can't help seeing that those trees—— But you have no time to think of trees or anything else," she added briskly, fixing upon him her keen eyes.

"I confess," said Theo, "I never thought of the trees from a political point of view."

"There, that is just like a man!" cried Mrs. Wilberforce. "You seize upon something one says that can be turned into ridicule; but you never will meet the real question. Oh, is that you, Herbert? Have you got rid of your churchwarden so soon?"—for this was the pretext upon which the rector had been got out of the way.

"He did not want much,—a mere question. Indeed," said the

rector, remembering that fibs are not permitted to the clergy any more than to the mere laic, and perceiving that he must expect his punishment all the same—with that courage which springs from the conviction that it is as well to be hanged for a sheep as for a lamb, "it was not the churchwarden at all; it was only a mistake of John."

"Well," said his wife significantly, "it was a mistake that was quickly rectified, one can see, as you have come back so soon. And here is Theo talking already of going home. Of course he has his lessons to prepare for to-morrow; he is not a mere idle gentleman now."

Little gibes and allusions like these rained upon the young man from all quarters during the first six months, but no one ventured to speak to him with the faithfulness used by Mrs. Wilberforce; and after a time even these irritating if not very harmful weapons dropped, and the whole matter sank into the region of the ordinary. He rode, or, if the weather was bad, drove, five days in the week to his little pupil, who in himself was not to Theo's mind an attractive pupil, and who kept the temper of the tutor on a constant strain. It ought, according to all moral rules, to have been very good for Warrender to be thus forced to self-control, and to exercise a continual restraint over his extremely impatient temper and fastidious, almost capricious temperament. But there are circumstances in which such self-restraint is rather an aggravating than a softening process. During this period, however, Theo was scarcely to be accounted for by the ordinary rules of human nature. His mind was altogether absorbed by one of, if not by the most powerful influence of human life. He was carried away by a tide of passion which was stronger than life itself.

CHAPTER XXIV

It may now be necessary to indicate the outline, at least, of an incident which was the reason why, at the most critical period of the affairs both of her brother and sister, Minnie's supervising and controlling care was neutralised. Whether it is the case that nothing that did happen would have happened, as is her sincere conviction, had she been free to observe and guide the course of events, is what neither the writer of this history nor any other human looker-on can say. We are all disposed to believe that certain possibilities would have changed the entire face of history had they ever developed, and that life would have been a different thing altogether had not So-and-So got ill, or gone on a journey, or even been so ill-advised as to die at a particular juncture. Miss Warrender was of this opinion strongly, but it is possible the reader may think that everything would have gone on very much as it did, in spite of all that she could have said or done. It is a problem which never can be settled, should we go on discussing it for evermore.

The thing which deprived the family of Minnie's care at the approaching crisis was what cannot be otherwise described than as a happy event. In the early summer, before Mr. Warrender died, a new curate had come to Underwood. This, however, is not an entirely just way of stating the case. A curate, in the ordinary sense of the word, was not wanted at Underwood. The parish was small. Such a thing as a daily service had not begun to be thought of, and the rector, who was full of energy, would have thought it wasteful extravagance to give a hundred pounds a year to another clergyman, in order that he might have the lessons read for him and the responses led by an educated voice. Ideas about educated voices, as well as about vestments and lights on the altar, have all developed since that time. People in general were quite satisfied with the clerk in those days, or, if they were not satisfied, at least accepted him as a necessary evil, at which one was free to laugh, but against which there was nothing to be said. The morning service on Sunday was the only one that was of much importance, to which the whole parish came. That in the afternoon was attended only by the village people, and did not count for much. The rector would not have said in so many words, like a French curé, that vespers was *pas obligatoire*, but he had the same feeling. Both he and his wife felt kindly to the people who came, as if it were a personal compliment. It is needless to say that things ecclesiastical have very, very much changed since, and that this easy indulgence exists no longer.

Thus there was evidently no need of a curate at Underwood proper. But the parish was now a double one. Once "St Mary's Underwood," it was now "Underwood-cum-Pierrepoint;" and the condition of drawing the revenues of the latter district was, that the rector should always provide for the duty in the little church at Pierrepoint, which was considered a fine specimen of early architecture, though not much adapted to modern needs. It had been usually some shabby old parson, some poor gentleman who had been a failure in life, one of those wonderful curates who are rich in nothing but children, and to whom the old, rambling, out-at-elbows parsonage house at Pierrepoint was of itself an attraction, who had taken this appointment. And it had been a great surprise to the neighbourhood when it was known that the Honourable and Reverend Eustace Thynne (to say the Reverend the Honourable, which is now the highest fashion in such matters, postponing, as is meet, secular rank to that of the Church, was unknown in those pre-Ritualistic days), a young man, an earl's son, an entirely unexceptionable and indeed every way laudable individual, had accepted this post. A greater surprise it would be impossible to imagine. The Warrenders had been as much interested as anybody before the death in the family had made such sentiments for a time inappropriate.

But Mr. Thynne had turned out a very sympathetic young clergyman. He had left his card and kind inquiries at once. He had helped to officiate at the funeral, and afterwards Minnie had been heard to say that no one had given her so true an idea of how grief ought to be borne. He had been a frequent visitor through the summer. If Theo saw little of him, that was entirely Theo's fault. It was Mr. Thynne who persuaded the girls that to resume their duties in the Sunday school was not only right, but the best thing for them,—so soothing and comforting; and he had come a great deal to the Warren while Theo was so much away, and in many things had made himself useful to the girls, as Theo had been doing to Lady Markland. He did not, indeed, devote himself to them with the same indiscriminate devotion. There was no occasion for anything of the kind. Mrs. Warrender was quite capable of looking after things herself, and Minnie's energy was almost greater than was necessary for the needs of their position; so that it was not at all needful or desirable that he should put himself at their disposal in any exaggerated way. But all that a man and a clergyman could do to make himself useful and agreeable Eustace Thynne did. They got to call him Eustace Thynne quite naturally, when they were talking of him, though they still called him Mr. Thynne when conversing with him. They saw a great deal of him. There was very little to do at Pierrepoint, and he was a great walker, and constantly met them when they were out. And he was very sound in his views, not extreme in anything; not an evangelical, much less inclining towards the section of the Church which began to be known in the world under the name of Puseyists. Eustace Thynne had no exaggerated ideas; he was not eccentric in anything. The Thirty-Nine Articles sat as easily upon him as his very well made coat; he never forgot that he was a clergyman, or wore even a gray checked necktie, which the rector sometimes did, but always had a white tie, very neatly tied, and a tall hat, which was considered in those days the proper dress for a clergyman, even in the country. His political ideas inclined to Conservatism, whereas, as Minnie always said, the Warrenders were Liberal; but it was a very moderate Conservatism, and the difference was scarcely appreciable.

From all this it may be divined that Minnie was in the way of following the example set her by her mother and grandmother, and the majority of women generally. She had not thought herself very likely to marry for some time back; for the county had wonderfully few young men in it, and she had no desire ever to leave home. But when Providence sent Eustace Thynne in her way, there was no reason why she should shut her eyes to that divine and benevolent intention. She softened in some ways, but hardened in others, during the course of the year. In matters upon which Eustace Thynne agreed with her,—and these were the principal features of her social creed,—she was more determined than ever, having his moral support to fall back upon: and would not allow the possibility of a doubt. And this made her the more severe upon Theo, for in all questions of propriety Mr. Thynne was with her, heart and soul.

As usually happens in the forming of new bonds, the old ones were a little strained while the process was going on. Chatty, who had been very deeply interested at first, when she saw in her elder sister symptoms of a state about which she herself had entertained only the vaguest dreams, became sometimes a little tired of it, when she found one of the results to be a growing inclination to get rid of herself. When they went out together to visit a pensioner, if they met Mr. Thynne (as they often did) on the road, Minnie would stop at the end of the lane. "Will you just run in and see how old Sarah is?" she would say to Chatty. "Two of us in such a little place is too much for the poor old dear;" and Mr. Thynne would remark, in a low voice, that Miss Warrender was so considerate (if everybody would be as considerate!), and linger and talk, while Chatty went and informed herself about all old Sarah's ills. This, however, the younger sister could have borne; but when she found, on rejoining the pair, that they had been discussing Theo, and that Minnie had been asking Mr. Thynne's advice, and that he entirely agreed with her, and thought she was quite right about Lady Markland, Chatty's spirit rose. "I would not talk about Theo to any one," she said, indignantly. "Who do you call any one? Mr. Thynne takes a great interest in all of us, and he is a clergyman, and of whom should one ask advice if not of a clergyman?" Minnie replied, with triumphant logic. "If he was a bishop, I would not talk over Theo; not with him, nor any one," Chatty replied. She had always been inclined to take Theo's part, and she became his partisan in these new circumstances, standing up for him through thick and thin. And in her little expeditions up and down the lane to ask after old Sarah, while Minnie strolled slowly along with her clerical lover, Chatty began to form little opinions of her own, and to free herself more or less from that preponderating influence of the elder sister which had shaped all her previous life. And a little wistfulness began to float across Chatty's gentle mind, and little thrills of curiosity to go through it. Her surroundings at this moment gave much room for thought. Minnie, who had never shown any patience in respect to such vanity, and was always severe with the maids and their young men, wandering on ahead with Mr. Thynne; and Theo, who had always been so imperious, given up in every thought to Lady Markland, and not to be spoken to on ordinary subjects during the short time he spent at home! With these two before her eyes, it can scarcely be supposed that Chatty did not ask herself, now and then, whether for her also there was not somebody whose appearance would change everything? And for the first time she began to get impatient of the Warren, in the gloom of the winter, and to wish, like her mother, for a change.

Mr. Thynne was not ineligible, like most curates. It was not for poverty, or because he had no other place to turn to, that he had taken the curacy at Pierrepoint. There was a family living awaiting him, a very good living; and he had some money, which an uncle had left him; and he was the honourable as well as the reverend. Minnie had her own opinion, as has been seen, on matters of rank. She did not think overmuch of the nobility. She was of opinion that the country gentry were the support and salvation of England. Still, while a plain Mrs. or Miss may be anybody to those who don't know her, a dairyman's daughter or a scion of the oldest of families—an honourable to your name does at once identify you as occupying a certain position. "It is a very good thing," she said, "in that way; it is a sort of hall-mark, you know."

"It is sometimes put on very false metal, Minnie."

"Oh, I don't know," said Minnie, with an indignant flush; "no more than any other kind of distinction. The peerage does not go wrong oftener, perhaps not so often, as other people: but it does give a *cachet*. It is known then who you belong to, and that you must be more or less nice people. I like it for that."

"There could be no doubt about Mr. Thynne, any way, my dear."

"I never said I was thinking of Mr. Thynne," said Minnie, with a violent flush, as she broke off the conversation and hurried away. And, indeed, it was not at all of Mr. Thynne that she was thinking, but rather of a possible Mrs. Thynne, and what her advantages might be over other ladies who did not possess that pretty and harmless affix. She decided that, unquestionably, it was an advantage. Out of your own county it might very well happen that nobody might know who you were: but an honourable never could be mistaken. She came gradually to change her views about the peerage in general, after that discovery, and made up her mind that a title in the family was good in every way. There could never be any doubt about that. There it was in Debrett, and everybody could satisfy themselves about its genuineness and antiquity, and lay their finger upon the descendants and relatives of the house. There were inconveniences in that, especially in respect to age, but still it was an advantage; and to be sure, for those who were added to a noble family by marriage even that inconvenience did not exist.

Mr. Thynne declared himself in summer, after the year of mourning was over, and when even Miss Warrender felt that it was permitted to be lively, and wear white dresses, though with black ribbons, of course; and as the family living fell vacant immediately, the wedding took place almost at once. It made a great sensation in the parish, it need not be said; and while the few people in Pierrepoint gave the curate a teapot, in Underwood there was a great agitation in the Sunday school and much collecting to buy a fine big Bible, with a great deal of gilding outside, for Miss Warrender, which was given to her at a tea in the schoolroom, with a speech from the rector, who was chary of public speaking, and had to be egged up to it by many little moral pricks from his wife. It was considered a very suitable present for a young lady who was going to marry a clergyman, just as the teapot was most suitable for a young clergyman about to be married. In those days there was not the rain of marriage presents from everybody within reach which are the painful fashion now. But Minnie had a very excellent, solid trousseau, as might be expected, full of useful clothes; the silks very handsome, and the dinner dresses, though serious, which she thought suitable to a clergyman's wife, quite good enough to go *anywhere in*. If she had been yielded to in that respect, her going-away dress would have been lavender with black lace, quite second mourning. But not only her mother and sister, but Mrs. Wilberforce and even Mr. Thynne himself, who did not fancy a bride in mourning, remonstrated so strongly that she was obliged to yield. "I am in favour of showing every respect to our dear ones who are gone; but there are limits," the bridegroom said, and Mrs. Wilberforce declared that, though herself a Conservative and staunch upholder of the past she did think dear Minnie sometimes went a little too far, notwithstanding that the Warrenders were Liberals. This determined stand on the part of all belonging to her resulted in Minnie's departure from the Warren clothed in a suit of russet brown, which was very becoming to her,—much more so than the whiteness of her bridal dress and veil.

This withdrew Minnie's thoughts in great measure from the other events which were preparing, and finally carried her off altogether on the eve of many and great changes, such as turned topsy-turvy the life of the Warrenders. She was naturally very much taken up by her husband and her new surroundings, and the delightful trouble of settling down in her new parish and home. And she was at a considerable distance from them, half a day's journey, which made very frequent visits impossible. It has been already said that we do not pretend to give our opinion as to whether, if Minnie had not married, things might not have gone very differently in the Warrender family life.

After the wedding guests had departed Warrender ordered his horse to be brought round, as usual. He had, of course, been occupied all the morning with his own family, and with the marriage and the entertainment afterwards. Geoff had got a holiday, which he prized very much. (Lady Markland and the boy had been asked, of course, to the wedding, but it was perhaps a relief to all that they declined to come.) And if there ever was a moment in which Mrs. Warrender wanted her son it was that day. She was tired out, and in the nervous state to which the best of us are liable at agitating moments. Minnie was not, perhaps, in absolute sympathy with her mother, but Mrs. Warrender had a great deal of imagination, and partly by those recollections of the past that are called up by every great family event, and partly by inevitable anticipations of the future, she was in special need of kindness and filial care. Her heart swelled within her when she saw the black horse brought round. She went to the door in the gray gown which she had got for Minnie's marriage, and met her son as he came into the hall. "Oh, Theo, are you going to leave us to-day? I thought you would have stayed with us to-day," she said, with what an unfavourable judge would have called a querulous tone in her voice. It was in reality fatigue and weariness, and a great desire for her boy's affection and comforting care; but the other explanation was not without reason.

"Why should I stay to-day, more than any other day?" he said.

"You don't require me to tell you, Theo. It is getting late; you can't be wanted *there*, surely, to-day."

Now this was injudicious on Mrs. Warrender's part: but a woman cannot always be judicious, however it may hurt her. He looked at her with quick offence.

"Suppose I think differently?" he said; "or suppose that it is for my own pleasure I am going, as you say, *there*?"

"I meant no harm," said Mrs. Warrender. "I have not opposed you. Often I have longed to have you a little more at home: but I never said anything, Theo,—you know I have never said anything."

"I can't imagine, mother, what there was to say."

She checked herself with difficulty, but still she did check herself. "There are some things," she said, "that I wish you would attend to,—I cannot help feeling that there are several things; but to-day, dear Theo, both Chatty and I are feeling low. Stay with us this afternoon. It will do us so much good."

She thought that he wavered for an instant, but if so it was only for an instant. "I don't believe that," he said. "We should only quarrel; and what is the use of a thing that is forced? And besides, of all days, this is the one above all others that I want to go. It is my best chance"—and then he stopped and looked at her, the colour rising to his face.

"I thought Geoff was to go somewhere, for a holiday."

He gave her another look, and the red became crimson. "That is just the reason," he said enigmatically, and with a slight wave of his hand passed her, and went out to the door.

"You will be back to dinner, Theo?"

He turned round his head as he was about to ride away, looking down upon her. "Perhaps I may be back immediately," he said,—"most likely; but never mind me, one way or another. I want nothing but to be let alone, please."

Chatty had come out to the door, and they both stood and watched him as he rode along, disappearing among the trees. "I think he must be going to—seek his fortune," his mother said, restraining a sob.

"Oh, mamma!" said simple Chatty, "I would go and pray for

him, but I don't know what to ask."

"Nor I," said Mrs. Warrender. "God bless him,—that is all that one can say."

But the house looked very dreary as they went back to it, with all the confusion of the wedding feast and the signs of a great company departed. They scarcely knew where to sit down, in the confusion that had been so gay a few hours ago, and looked so miserable now.

But Theo! What was he doing? Where was he carrying the heart that beat so high, that would be silent no longer? Was he going to lay it at the feet of a woman who would spurn it? When would he come back, and how? Already they began to listen, though he had scarcely set out, for the sound of his return,—in joy or in despair, who could say?

CHAPTER XXV.

Theo came home neither late nor early; neither in joy nor in despair. He came back harassed and impatient, eaten up with disquietude and suspense. He was pale and red in succession ten times in a moment. He was so much absorbed in his own thoughts that he hardly heard what was said to him as the three sat down, a little forlorn, as the late summer twilight began to close over all the brightness of that long fatiguing day. The evening of the wedding, with its sense already of remoteness to the great event of the morning so much prepared for and looked forward to— with the atmosphere so dead and preternaturally silent which has tingled with so much emotion, with the inevitable reaction after the excitement—nothing could ever make this moment a cheerful one. It is something more than the disappearance of a member of the family, it is the end of anticipation, of excitement, of all that has been forming and accelerating the domestic life for weeks or months, perhaps. Even if there should happen to be an unexpressed and inexpressible relief in having permanently escaped a rule of sharp criticism, a keen inspecting eye which missed nothing, even that consciousness helps to take the edge off life and make it altogether blurred and brief for the moment. The very meal was suggestive: cold chickens, cold lamb, ham on the sideboard with ornamentations upon it, remains of jellies, and preparations of cream,—an altogether chilly dinner, implying in every dish a banquet past.

And there was not very much said. Joseph, who was rather more tired than everybody else, made no attempt to bring the lamp, and no one asked for it. They sat in the waning light, which had less of day and more of night in it in that room than anywhere else, and made a very slight repast in a much subdued way, very tired, and with little interest in the cold chicken. Once Mrs. Warrender made a remark about the evening. "How dark it is! I think, Theo, if you don't do something soon the trees will crush the house." "I don't see what the trees have to do with it," he answered with irritation; "I have always begged you not to wait for me when I was late." "But you were not late, dear Theo," said Chatty, with a certain timidity. "I suppose I ought to know whether I was late or not," he replied. And the ladies were silent, and the salad was handed round. Very suitable for a summer evening, but yet on the whole a depressing meal.

When they rose from the table Mrs. Warrender asked Theo to take a turn with her, which he did with great reluctance, fearing to be questioned. But she had more discretion than to begin, at least on that subject. She told him that if he did not particularly want her, she had made up her mind to go away. "Chatty will be dull without her sister. I think she wants a little change, and for that matter, so do I. And you don't want us, Theo."

"That is a hard thing to say, mother."

"I do not mean any blame. I know that the time is critical for you too, my dear boy. That is why I ask, do you wish me to remain? but I don't think you do."

He did not answer for a full minute. Then, "No," he said, "I don't think I do." They were walking slowly round the house, by the same path which they had taken together when the father was lying dead, and before there had been question of Lady Markland in the young man's life. "Mother," he said after another interval, "I ought to tell you, perhaps. I know nothing about myself or what I am going to do; it all depends on some one else. Minnie would moralise finely on that, if she were to hear it. Things have come to this, that I know nothing about what may happen to-morrow. I may start off for the end of the world,—that is the most likely, I think. I can't go on living as I am doing now. I may go to—where? I don't know and I don't care much. If I were a Nimrod, as I ought to have been, I should have gone to Africa for big game. But it will probably be Greece or something conventional of that kind."

"Don't speak so wildly, dear. Perhaps you will not go away at all. You have not made up your mind."

"When I tell you I know nothing, not even about to-morrow! But I don't entertain much hope. That is how it will end, in all probability. And of course I don't want you to stay like rooks among the trees here. Poor old house! it will soon have no daylight at all, as you say."

"Theo, I hope you will do something before it is too late. It is not a beautiful house, but you were born in it, and so was your father."

He pressed her arm almost violently within his. "Who knows, mother? great days may be coming for the old place: or if not, let it drop to pieces, what does it matter? I shall be the last of the Warrenders."

"Theo," she said with agitation, returning the pressure of his arm, "have you said anything to-night?"

Her question was vague enough, but he had no difficulty in understanding. He said, after a moment, "I had no opportunity, there were people there; but to-morrow, to-morrow——"

They came out together as these words were said upon the edge of the pond. In the depth of that dark mirror, broken by water-lilies and floating growth of all kinds, there was a pale reflected sky, very colourless and clear, the very soul and centre of the brooding evening. Everything was dark around, the heavy summer foliage black in the absence of light, the heart of June as gloomy as if the trees had been funeral plumes. The two figures, dark like all the rest, stood for a moment on the edge of the water, looking down upon that one pale, dispassionate, reflected light. There was no cheer in it, nor anything of the movement and pulsation of human existence. The whiteness of the reflection chilled Mrs. Warrender, and made her shiver. "I suppose," she said, "I am fanciful to-night; it looks to me like an unkindly spectator, who does not care what becomes of us." She added, with a little nervous laugh, "Perhaps it is not very probable that our little affairs should interest the universe, after all."

Warrender did not make any reply. He heard what was said to him and saw what was round him in a dim sort of confused way, as if every object and every voice was at a distance; and with an impatience, too, which it was painful to him to keep down. He went back with her to the house saying little; but could not rest there, and came out again, groping his way through the surrounding trees, and returned after a while to the pond, where there was that light to think by, more congenial even in its chill clearness than the oppressive dark. It changed beneath his eyes, but he took no notice; a star came into it and looked him in the face from under the shadow of the great floating shelf of the water-lily leaves; and then came the blue of the dawn, the widening round him of the growing light, the shimmer of the early midsummer morning, long, long before those hours which men claim as the working day. That sudden bursting forth of life and colour startled him in the midst of his dreams, and he went home and stole into the sleeping, darkened house, where by dint of curtains and shutters the twilight still reigned, with something of the exhaustion and neglect of the morning after the feast. It was the morning of the day which was to decide for him whether life should be miserable or divine.

These were the words which the young man used in his infatuation. He knew no others—miserable, so that he should no longer care what happened to him, or believe in any good, which was the most probable state of affairs; or divine, a life celestial, inconceivable, which was indeed not to be dwelt upon for a moment as if under any suggestion of possibility it could be.

Next day, Mrs. Warrender began at once her preparations for that removal which she had so long contemplated, which had been so often postponed, throwing Chatty into an excitement so full of conflicting elements, that it was for some time difficult for the girl to know what her own real sentiments were. She had been figuring to herself with a little wistfulness, and an occasional escapade into dreams, the part which it was now her duty to take up, that of her mother's chief companion, the daughter of the house, the dutiful dweller at home, who should have no heart and no thought beyond the Warren and its affairs. Chatty was pleased enough with the former rôle. It had been delightful both to her mother and herself to feel how much they had in common, when the great authority on all family matters, the regulator of proprieties, the mistress of the ceremonies, so to speak, was out of the way, and they were left unmolested to follow their natural bent; but Chatty felt a little sinking of the heart when she thought of being bound to the Warren for ever; of the necessity there would be for her constant services, and the unlikelihood of any further opening of life. While there had been two, there was always a possibility of an invitation, of a visit and little break of novelty: but it was one of Minnie's most cherished maxims that a young lady in the house was indispensable, and Chatty in the recollection of this felt a certain cheerful despair, if the expression is permissible, seize her. She would be cheerful, she said to herself, whatever happened. It was her duty: she loved her home, and wanted nothing else, oh, nothing else! Home and one's mother, what could one want more?

But when Chatty heard all in a moment those plans which promised, instead of the monotonous life to which she was accustomed, a new world of novelty, of undiscovered distance, of gaieties and pleasure unknown, her despair changed into alarm. Was it right, however pleasant it might be, to go away; to abandon the Warren; to be no longer the young lady of the house, doing everything for those about her, but a young woman at large, so to speak, upon the world, getting amusements in her own person, having nothing to do for anybody? Chatty did not know what to think, what to reply to her mother. She cried, "O mamma!" with a gleam of delight; and then her countenance fell, and she asked, "What will Theo do alone?" with all the conscious responsibility of a sister, the only unmarried sister left. But the question that was uppermost in her mind did not really concern Theo. It was "What will Minnie say?" She turned this over in her mind all day with a breathless sense that among so many new things Minnie's opinion was a sort of support to her in the whirlwind of change. Minnie had often said that nothing short of necessity would make her leave the Warren. But then the firmness of that assertion was somewhat diminished by the fact that Minnie had not hesitated to leave the Warren when Mr. Thynne asked her to do so. Was necessity another name for a husband? Chatty blushed at this thought, though it seemed very improbable that any husband would ever appear to suggest such a step to herself. Would Minnie still think that the only motive; would she disapprove? Chatty went out by herself to take the usual afternoon walk which her sister had always insisted upon. The day was dull and gray for midsummer, and Chatty had not yet recovered from the fatigue of yesterday. She allowed to herself that the trees were sadly overgrown, and that it was quite dark within the grounds of the Warren when it was still light beyond; and she permitted herself to think that it was a little dull having nowhere to walk to but Mrs. Bagley's shop. To be sure there was the Rectory: but Mrs. Wilberforce would be sure to question her so closely about all that had happened and was going to happen that Chatty preferred not to risk that ordeal. There was not a soul about the village on this particular afternoon. Chatty thought she had never seen it so deserted. To make her walk a little longer, she had come out by the farther gate of the Warren,—the one that Theo always used; that which was nearest Markland. The only figures she saw in all her line of vision, as she came out, making a little sound with the gate, which in the silence sounded like a noise and startled them, were two women, just parting as it seemed. One of them Chatty saw at a glance was Lizzie Hampson. The other—she came hurrying along towards Chatty, having parted, it seemed, with a kiss from her companion. They met full without any possibility of avoiding each other, and Chatty, in spite of herself, gave a long look at this woman whom she had seen before in the high phaeton, and sometimes at the gate of the Elms. She was as young, or it might be younger than Chatty, with a lovely complexion, perhaps slightly aided by art, and quantities of curled and wavy hair. But the chief feature in her was her eyes—of infantine blue, surrounded with curves of distress like a child's who has been crying its very heart out. It was evident that she had been crying, her eyelashes were wet, her mouth quivering. Altogether, it seemed to Chatty the face of a child that had been naughty and was being punished. Poor thing! she said in her soft heart, looking at the other girl with infinite pity. Oh, how miserable it must be to go wrong! Chatty felt as if she could have found in her heart to stop this poor young creature, and entreat her, like a child, not to be naughty any more. The other looked at her with those puckered and humid eyes, with a stare into which there came a little defiance, almost an intention of affronting and insulting the young lady; but in a moment had hurried past and Chatty saw her no more. Chatty, too, quickened her steps, feeling, she could not tell why, a little afraid. Why should she be afraid? She did not like to look back, but felt as if the woman she had just passed must be mocking her behind her back, or perhaps threatening her, ready to do her a mischief. And certainly it was Lizzie Hampson who was running on in front. Chatty called to her in the sudden fright that had come over her, and was glad when the girl stopped and turned round reluctantly, though Lizzie's face was also stained with crying and wore a mutinous and sullen look.

"Did you call me, Miss Warrender? I am going home, Granny is waiting."

"Wait for me a moment, Lizzie. Oh, you have been crying too. What is the matter? And that—that lady——"

"I won't tell you a lie, Miss Chatty, when you've just found me out. But—if you're going to tell upon me, this is the truth. I have been saying good-bye to her; and no one in Underwood will ever see her more." Then Lizzie began to cry again, melting Chatty's soft heart.

"Why should I tell upon you? I have nothing to say. It appears that it is some one you know; but I—don't know who it is."

"Oh, Miss Chatty, you are the real good one," said Lizzie, "you don't think everybody's wicked. I don't love her ways, but I love her, that poor, poor thing. Don't tell Granny I was with her; but it is only to say good-bye;—that was all, for the last time, just to say good-bye."

"Is she—going away?" Chatty spoke in a low and troubled voice, knowing that she ought not to show any interest, but with a pity and almost awe of the sinner which was beyond all rule.

"Oh yes, Miss Warrender, she is going away; the gentleman spoke the truth when he said it always comes to misery. There may be a fine appearance for a time, and everything seem grand and gay; but it always comes to misery in the end."

To this Chatty made no reply. It was not a lesson that she required in her innocence and absence from all temptation, to learn; but she had an awe of it as if a gulf had opened at her feet and she had seen the blackness of darkness within.

"And if you'll believe me, she once was just as good and as innocent—! Well, and she's a kind of innocent now for that matter. Oh, poor thing! Oh, Miss Warrender, don't you be angry if I'm choking and crying, I can't help it! She don't know what she's doing. She don't know bad from good, or right from wrong. There's some like that. Just what pleases them at the moment, that's all they think of. She once had as happy a life before her! and a good husband, and served hand and foot."

"Lizzie," said Chatty, with a shudder, "don't please tell me any more. If anything can be done——"

"Nothing," said the girl, shaking her head. "What could be done? If the good ladies were to get her into their hands, they would put her in a penitentiary or something. A penitentiary for her! Oh, Miss Chatty, it's little they know. If they could put her in a palace, and give her horses and carriages and plenty to amuse her, that might do. But she doesn't want to repent; she doesn't know what it means. She wants to be well off and happy. And she's so young. Oh, don't think I would be like that for the world, not for the world, don't think it! But I can't help knowing how she feels. Oh, my poor dear, my poor dear!"

The wonder with which Chatty heard this strange plea was beyond description; but she would ask no more questions, and hear no more, though Lizzie seemed ready enough to furnish her with all details. She went back with the girl to the shop, thus disarming Mrs. Bagley, who was always full of suspicions and alarm when Lizzie was out of the way, and stood talking to the old woman while Lizzie stole into the parlour behind and got rid of the traces of her tears. Chatty felt very solemn as she stood and talked about her patterns, feeling as if she had come from a death-bed or a funeral It was something still more terrible and solemnising; it was her first glimpse into a darkness of which she knew nothing, and her voice sounded in her own ears like a mockery as she asked about the bundle of new things that had come from Highcombe. "There's one as is called the honeysuckle," said Mrs. Bagley: "it will just please you, Miss Chatty, as likes nice delicate little things." The old woman thought she must be feeling her sister's loss dreadful, looking as melancholy as if it was her coffin she was buying. And Chatty accepted the honeysuckle pattern and looked out the materials for working it, without relaxing from that seriousness which was so little habitual to her. She even forgot all about her own problems, as she went home, seeing constantly before her the pretty childlike face all blurred with tears. Was it true, as Lizzie said, that there was no way to help or deliver? If she had stopped, perhaps, as she had almost been impelled to do, and said, as it was on her lips to say, "Oh, I am so sorry for you; oh, don't do wrong any more," would the unhappy creature perhaps have listened to her, and repented, though Lizzie said she did not want to repent? Chatty could not forget that pitiful face. Would she ever, she wondered, meet it again?

CHAPTER XXVI.

Markland lay as usual, bare and white against the sun, upon that day of fate. The young trees had grown a little and stood basking, scarcely shivering, leaning their feeble young heads together in the sun, but making little show as yet; all was wrapped in the warmth and stillness of the summer morning. The old butler stood upon the steps of the great door, his white head and black figure making a point in the bright, unbroken, still life about. Within, Lady Markland was in the morning-room with her business books and papers, but not doing much; and Geoff in another, alone with *his* books, not doing much; thinking, both of them, of the expected visitor now riding up in a breathless white heat of excitement to the hall door.

The entire house knew what was coming. Two or three maids were peeping at the windows above, saying, "There he is," with flutters of sympathetic emotion. That was why the butler himself stood on the steps waiting. All these spectators in the background had watched for a long time past; and a simultaneous thrill had run through the household, which no one was conscious of being the cause of, which was instinctive and incontrovertible. If not yesterday, then to-day; or to-morrow, if anything should come in the way to-day. Things had come to such a pitch that they could go no farther. Of this every one in Markland was sure. There is something that gets into the air when excitement and self-repression run high, and warns the whole world about of the approach of an event. "A bird of the air hath carried the matter." So it is said in all languages. But it is more than a bird in the air, swifter, flying, entering into the very scent of the flowers. The last thing that Warrender thought of was that the fire and passion in his own breast had been thus publicly revealed. He wondered night and day whether *she* knew, whether she had any suspicion, if it had ever occurred to her to think; but that the maids should be peeping from the windows, and the old butler watching at the door to receive the lover, was beyond his farthest conception of possibility, fortunately—since such a thought would have overwhelmed him with fury and shame.

Lady Markland sat at her table, pondering a letter from Mr. Longstaffe. She had it spread out before her, but she could only half see the words, and only half understand what they meant. She had read in Theo's eyes upon the previous day—all. Had he but known he had nothing to reveal to her, nothing that she could not have told him beforehand! She had felt that the tempest of his young passion had been about to burst, and she had been extravagantly glad of the sudden appearance of the visitors who made it impossible. She had been glad, but perhaps a little disappointed too; her expectation and certainty of what was coming having risen also to a white heat of excitement, which fell into stillness and relief at the sight of the strangers, yet retained a certain tantalised impatience as of one from whose lips a cup has been taken, which will certainly have to be emptied another day. This was what she said to herself, with a trembling and agitation which was fully justified by the scene she anticipated. She said to herself that it must be got over, that she would not try to balk him, but rather give him the opportunity, poor boy! Yes! it was only just that he should have his opportunity, and that this great crisis should be got over as best it might. Her hands trembled as she folded Mr. Longstaffe's letter and put it away; her mind, she allowed to herself, was not capable of business. Poor boy, poor foolish boy! was not he a boy in comparison with herself, a woman not only older in years, but so much older in life; a woman who had been a wife, who was a mother; a woman whose first thoughts were already pledged to other interests, and for whom love in his interpretation of the word existed no more? She would look down upon him, she thought, as from the mountain height of the calm and distant past. The very atmosphere in which such ideas had been possible was wanting. She would still him by a word; she would be very kind, very gentle with him, poor boy! She would blame herself for having unintentionally, unconsciously, put him in the way of this great misfortune. She would say to him, "How could I have ever thought that I, a woman so much older, past anything of the kind—that *I* could harm you? But it is not love, it is pity, it is because you are sorry for me! And it will pass, and you will learn to think of me as your friend." Oh, such a friend as she would be to him! and when some one younger, prettier, happier than she came in his way, as would certainly happen! Lady Markland could not help feeling a little chill at that prospect. The warmth of a young man's devotion has a great effect upon a woman. It makes many women do foolish things, out of the gratitude, the exhilaration of finding themselves lovable and beloved, especially those who are past the age and the possibility of being loved, as Lady Markland, now seven-and-twenty, had concluded herself to be.

Seven-and-twenty! ah, but that was not all! a wife already, to whom it was shame so much as to think of any other man. A second marriage appeared to her, as to many women, a sort of atheism; a giving up of the religion of the immortal. If marriage is a tie that endures for ever, as it is every happy woman's creed it is, how could she die, how dare ever to look in the face a man whom because he was dead,—no, more than that, because a change had happened to him which was no doing of his—she had abandoned for another man? This argument made it once and for ever impossible to contemplate such an act. Therefore it was to another man's wife that this poor boy, this generous enthusiast, was giving his all. But a woman cannot have such a gift laid down at her feet without a sensation of gratitude, without a certain pleasure even amid the pain in that vindication of herself and her womanhood which he makes to her, raising her in her own esteem. Therefore she could not be hard, could not be angry. Poor boy! to think of what it was he was throwing away; and of the beating heart full of foolish passion with which he was coming to say words which her imagination snatched at, then retired from, trying not to anticipate them, not to be curious, not to be moved in advance by what he must say. But then she paused to ask herself whether she could not prevent him, whether she could not spare him these fruitless words. Would not it be wrong to let him say them when it was so certain what her response must be? She might stop him, perhaps, in the utterance; tell him—with what sympathy, with what tenderness! that it must not be; that not for her were such expressions possible; that he was mistaking himself, and his own heart, in which pity was moving, not love. Could she do this? She felt a quick pang of disappointment in the thought of thus not hearing what he had to say: but it would be kinder to him—perhaps: would it be kinder?—to stop those words on his lips, words that should only be said to the woman who could listen to them; to the happy young creature whom some time or other he might still love. This was the confusion of thought in Lady Markland's mind while she sat by her writing-table among her papers, turning them over with nervous hands, now opening, now closing again the letters to which she could give no attention; letters, a cool observer might have said, much more important than a question of a foolish young fellow's love. Meanwhile the maids peeped, and the old butler looked down the avenue where Warrender's black horse was visible, marked with foam as if he had been pushed on at a great pace, and yet, now that the house was in sight, coming slowly enough. The servants had no doubt about what was going to happen so far as Warrender was concerned—but it was all the more like an exciting story to them that they had no certainty at all how it was to end. Opinions were divided as to Lady Markland; indeed so wrapped was the whole matter in mystery that those who ought to know the best, old Soames for one, and her own maid for another, could give no opinion at all.

Geoff was all this time in the room where he had his lessons, waiting for his tutor. He was biting his nails to the quick, and twisting his little face into every kind of contortion. Geoff was now ten, and he had grown a great deal during the year,—if not so very much in stature, yet a great deal in experience. A little, a very little, and yet enough to swear by, of the wholesome discipline of neglect had fallen to Geoff's share. Business and lessons had parted his day from his mother's in a way which was very surprising when it was realised; and Geoff realised it, perhaps, better than Lady Markland did. In the evenings she was, as before, his alone; though sometimes even then a little preoccupied and with other things in her mind, as she allowed, which she could scarcely speak to him about. But in the long day these two saw comparatively little of each other. At luncheon, Warrender was always there talking to Lady Markland of subjects which Geoff was not familiar with. The boy thought, sometimes, that Theo chose them on purpose to keep him "out of it." Certainly he was very often out of it, and had to sit and stare and listen, which was very good for him but did not make him more affectionate towards Theo. To feel "out of it" is not a comfortable, but it is a very maturing experience. Geoff sat by and thought what a lot Theo knew; what a lot mamma knew; what an advantage grown-up people had; and how inattentive to other people's feelings they were in using it. After luncheon, Theo frequently stayed to talk something over with Lady Markland; to show her something; now and then to help her with something which she did not feel equal to, and during these moments Geoff was supposed to "play." What he did, generally, was to resort to the stables and talk with the coachman and Black, whose conversation was perhaps not the best possible for the little lad, and who instructed him in horse-racing and other subjects of the kind. When Theo went away, Lady Markland would call for Geoff to walk down the avenue with her, accompanying the tutor to the gate. And when he had been shaken hands with and had taken his departure, then was to Geoff the best of the day. His mother and he, when it was fine, strolled about the park together for an hour, in something like the old confiding and equal friendship; a pair of friends, though they were mother and son, and though

Geoff was but ten and she twenty-seven. That moment was old times come back, and recalled what was already the golden age to Geoff, the time before anything had happened. He did not say before his father died, for his childish memory was acute enough to recollect that things had often been far from happy then. But he remembered the halcyon days of the first mourning; the complete peace; the gradual relaxation of his mother's face; the return of her dimples, and of her laughter. It had only been then, he remembered, that he had called her "pretty mamma!" her face had become so fresh, and so soft and round. But lately it had lengthened a little again; and the eyes sometimes went miles off, which made him uneasy. "Why do your eyes go so far away? do you see anything?" he asked, sometimes; and then she would come back to him with a start, perhaps with a flush of sudden colour, sometimes with a laugh, making fun of it. But Geoff did not feel disposed to make fun of it. It gave him a pang of anger to see her so; and unconsciously, without knowing why, he was more indignant with Theo at these moments, than he was when Theo sat at table and talked about matters beyond Geoff's ken. What had Theo to do with that far-away look? What could he have to do with it? Geoff could not tell; he was aware there was no sense in his anger, but yet he was angry all the same.

And now, he sat waiting for Theo to come: waiting, but not wishing for him. Geoff was not so clever as the maids and old Soames; he did not know what he was afraid of. He had never formulated to himself any exact danger; and naturally he knew nothing of the seductions of that way upon which Warrender had been drawn without intending it; without meaning any breach of Geoff's peace or of his own. Geoff did not know at all what he feared. He felt that there was something going on which was against him; and he had a kind of consciousness, like all the rest, that it was coming to a climax to-day. But he did not know what it was, nor what danger was impending over him. Perhaps Theo intended to stay longer; to come to Markland altogether; to interfere with the boy's evenings as he had done with his mornings. Or perhaps—but when he for a moment asked himself what he feared, his thoughts all fled away into vague alarms, infinitesimal in comparison with the reality, which was far too big, too terrible, for his mind to grasp. Mamma was afraid of it too, he had thought, this morning. She had looked, as the sky looks sometimes when the clouds are flying over it, and the wind is high and a storm is getting up: sometimes her face would be all overcast, and then her eyes had the look of a shower falling (though she did not shed any tears), and then there would be a clearing. She was afraid too. It was something that Theo was going to propose: some change that he wanted to carry out: and mamma was afraid of it too. This was in one way comforting, but in another more alarming: for it must be very serious indeed, if she, too, was afraid.

He roused himself from these uncomfortable thoughts, and began to pull his books about, and put his exercise upon the desk which Theo used, when he heard the sound of Theo's arrival; the heavy hoofs of the big black horse; the voice of Soames in the hall; the quick steady step coming in. The time had been when Geoff had thrown all his books on the table, and rushed out to witness the arrival, with an eager "Oh, Theo, you're five minutes late!" or "Oh, Theo, I haven't done yet!" For some time, however, he had left off doing this. Things were too serious for such vanities; he lifted his head and held his breath, listening to the approaching footstep. A kind of alarm lest it should not be coming here at all, but straight to Lady Markland's room, made him pale for the moment. That would be too bad, to come here professedly for Geoff and to go instead to mamma! it would be just like Theo; but fortunately things were not quite so bad as that. The steps came straight to Geoff's door. Warrender entered looking—the boy could not tell how—flushed, weary-eyed: something as he had seen his father look in the morning after a late night. Excitement simulates many recollections, and this was the first thought that leaped to Geoff's little mind, with its little bit of painful experience. "I say, Theo!" the boy cried; and then stared and said no more.

"Well! what is it you say? I hope you are prepared to-day, not like last time."

"Last time! but I was very well prepared! It is you who forget. I knew all my lessons."

"You had better teach me, then, Geoff, for I don't know all: no, nor half what I want to know. Oh, is this your exercise?" Warrender said, sitting down. He looked it over and corrected it with his pencil, hanging over it, seeming to forget the boy's presence. When that was done he opened the book carelessly, anywhere, not at the place, as Geoff, who watched with keen eyes everything the young man was doing, perceived instantly. "Where did you leave off last time? Go on," he said. Geoff began; but he was far too intent on watching Theo to know what he was doing; and as he construed with his eyes only, and not all of them, for he had to keep his companion's movements in sight all the time, it is needless to say that Geoff made sad work of his Cæsar. And his little faculties were more and more sharpened with alarm, and more and more blunted in Latin, when he found that, stumble as he liked, Theo did not correct him nor say a word. He sat with his head propped on his hands, and when Geoff paused said, "Go on." Either this meant something very awful in the shape of fault-finding when the culprit had come to the end of the lesson, the exemption now meaning dire retribution then, or else—there was something very wrong with Theo. Geoff's little sharp eyes seemed to leap out of their sockets with excitement and suspense.

At last Warrender suddenly, in the midst of a dreadfully boggled sentence, after Geoff had beaten himself on every side of these walls of words in bewildering endeavours to find a nominative, suddenly sprang up to his feet. "Look here," he said, "I think I'll give you a holiday to-day."

Geoff, much startled, closed his book upon his hand. "I had a holiday yesterday."

"Oh yes, to be sure! what has that to do with it? You can put away your books for to-day. As for being prepared, my boy, if my head had not been so bad——"

"Is your head bad, Theo?" Geoff put on a hypo-critical look of solicitude to divert attention from his own delinquencies.

"I think it will split in two," said Warrender, pressing his hands upon his temples, in which indeed the blood was so swelling in every vein that they seemed ready to burst. He added a minute after, "You can run out and get a little air; and——" here he paused, and the boy stopped and looked up, knowing and fearing what was coming. "And," repeated Warrender, a crimson flush coming to his face which had been so pale, "I'll—go and explain to Lady Markland."

"Oh, if you're in a hurry to go, never mind, Theo! I'll tell mamma."

Warrender looked at Geoff with a blank but angry gaze. "I told you to run out and play," he said, his voice sounding harsh and strange. "It's very bright out of doors. It will be better for you."

"And, Theo! what shall I learn for to-morrow?"

"To-morrow!" The child was really frightened by the look Theo gave him: the sudden fading out of the flush, the hollow look in his eyes. Then he flung down the book which all the time he had been holding mechanically in his hand. "Damn to-morrow!" he said.

Geoff's eyes opened wide with amazement and horror. Was Theo going mad? was that what it meant after all?

CHAPTER XXVII.

A minute after he was in the room where Lady Markland sat with her great writing table against the light. He did not know how he got there. It seemed impossible that it could have been by mere walking out of one room into another in the ordinary mechanical way. She rose up, dark against the light, when he went in, which was not at all her habit, but he was not sufficiently self-possessed to be aware of that. She turned towards him, which perhaps was an involuntary, instinctive precaution, for against the full daylight in the great window he could but imperfectly see her features. The precaution was unnecessary. His eyes were not clear enough to perceive what was before him. He saw his conception of her, serene in a womanly majesty far above his troubled state of passion, and was quite incapable of perceiving the sympathetic trouble in her face. She held out her hand to him before he could say anything, and said, with a little catch in her breath, "Oh, Mr. Warrender! I—Geoff—we were not sure whether we should see you to-day."

This was a perfectly unintentional speech and quite uncalled for; for nobody could be more regular, more punctual, than Warrender. It was the first thing she could find to say.

"Did you think I could stay away?" he asked, in a low and hurried tone, which was not at all the beginning he had intended. Then he added, "But I have given Geoff a holiday, if you can accord me a little time,—if I may speak to you."

"Geoff is not like other boys," she said, with a nervous laugh, still standing with her back to the light. "He does not rejoice in a holiday like most children; you have made him love his work."

"It is not about Geoff," he said. "I have—something to say to you, if you will hear me. I—cannot be silent any longer."

"Oh," she said, "you are going to tell me—I know what it is you are going to say—that this cannot continue. I knew that must come sooner or later. Mr. Warrender, you don't need to be told how grateful I am; I thank you, from the bottom of my heart. You have done so much for us. It was clear that it could not—go on for ever." She put out her hand for her chair, and drew it closer, and sat down, still with her back to the window; and now even in his preoccupation with his own overwhelming excitement he saw that she trembled a little, and that there was agitation in her tone.

"Lady Markland, it is not that. It is more than that. The moment has come when I must—when I cannot keep it up any longer. Ah!" for she made a little movement with her hand as if to impose silence. "Must it be so? must I go unheard?" He came closer to her, holding out his hands in the eloquence of nature, exposing his agitated countenance to the full revelation of the light. "It is not much, is it, in return for a life—only to be allowed to speak, once: for half an hour, for five minutes—once—and then to be silent." Here he paused for breath—still holding out his hands in a silent appeal. "But if that is my sentence I will accept it," he said.

"Oh, Mr. Warrender, do not speak so. Your sentence! from me, that am so deeply in your debt, that never can repay—but I know you never thought of being repaid."

"You will repay me now, tenfold, if you will let me speak."

She put out her hand towards a chair, pointing him to it, and gave him an agitated smile. "Of course you shall speak, whatever you wish or please—as if to your mother, or your elder sister, or an old, old friend."

She put up this little barrier of age instinctively, hastily snatching at the first defensive object she could find. And he sat down as she bade him, but now that he had her permission said nothing,—nothing with his tongue, but with his clasped hands and with his eyes so much, that she covered hers with an involuntary movement, and uttered a little agitated cry. For the moment he was incapable of anything more.

"Mr. Warrender," she said tremulously, "don't, oh, don't say what will make us both unhappy. You know that I am your— friend; you know that I am a great deal older than you are; Geoff's mother, not a woman to whom—not a woman open to— not a——"

"I will tell you," he said, "I know better; this one thing I know better. A woman as far above me as heaven is above earth, whom I am not worth a look or a word from. Do you think I don't know that? You will say I ought not to have come, knowing what I did, that there was no woman but you in the world for me, and that you were not for me, nor ever would have any thought of me. I should have taken care of myself, don't you think? But I don't think so," he added, almost with violence. "I have had a year of paradise. I have seen you every day, and heard you speak, and touched your hand. To-morrow, I will curse my folly that could not be content with that. But to-day, I am mad and I cannot help myself. I can't be silent, though it is my only policy. Morning and night I think of nothing but you. When I go to sleep, and when I wake, and even when I dream, I can't think of anything but only of what you say. That is what I am going over and over all day long,—every little word that you say."

He poured this forth with a haste and fluency utterly unlike his usual mode of speech, never taking breath, never taking his eyes from her, a man possessed; while she, shrinking back in her chair, her eyes cast down, her hands nervously clasping and unclasping each other, listened, beaten down by the tempest of an emotion such as she had never seen before, such as she could scarcely understand. She had been wooed long ago, lightly wooed, herself almost a child; the whole matter little more than a frolic, though it turned into a tragedy; but she did not know and had never met with anything like this. He paused a little to recover his breath, to moisten his parched lips, which were dry and hot with excitement, and then he resumed.

"You talk of a mother, a sister, a friend. I think you want to mock me, Lady Markland. If you were to say a woman I ought to be content to worship, then I could understand you. I know I ought to have been content. Except that I have gone distracted and can't be silent, can't keep quiet. Oh, forgive me for it. Here is my life which is all yours, and my heart to put your foot on if you please; all of me belongs to you; I wish no better, only forgive me for saying it—just once, once!" In his vehemence he got down on his knees—not by way of kneeling to her, only to get nearer, to come within reach. He touched her hand as if it had been the sceptre of mercy. "Speak to me," he said, "speak to me! even if to tell me that I am a castaway!"

Lady Markland got up quickly, with a look of pain at him, as if she would have fled. "How could you be a castaway?" she cried. "Oh, Mr. Warrender, have pity on me! What can I say? Why should not we live, as we have been doing, in peace and quiet? Why should these dreadful questions be raised? Listen to me a little. Can friends not be friends without this? I am old, I am married! There never could be any question of—— Oh, listen to me! All this that you have been telling me is pity: yes, it is pity. You are so sorry for me. You think I am helpless and want—some one to take care of me, like other women. Stop, stop! it is not so! You must hear me out. I am not so helpless; and you are young: and some one better than me, some fresh girl, some one like yourself—— Theo!" This name came from her lips like a cry, because he had drawn nearer as she drew away from him, and had got her hand in both his and was kissing it desperately, as if he never would let it go. She never had called him by this name, and yet it was so usual in the house that it did not sound as does a man's Christian name suddenly pronounced by the woman he loves, like a surrender and end of all contention. But she did not, even when she made that cry, withdraw her hand from him. She covered her face with the other, and stood swaying slightly backward away from him, a figure full of reluctance, pain, almost terror; yet without either word or gesture that should send him away.

"Some one," he cried, "like myself! I want no one, nothing in the world, but you! It is not I that have raised the question, it is something stronger than I. Pity! Oh, how dare you! how dare you!" He kissed her hand with a kind of fury between every word. "I sorry for the woman whom I worship—thinking she needs me! Good heavens! are you such a woman as you are and know so little? Or is it true about women that they don't know love, or want love, but only something tame, something quiet, what you call affection?" He stopped with his voice full of scorn, notwithstanding the paroxysm of passion, and looked up at her, though on his knees, in the superiority which he felt. "You want a friend that will be tame and live in peace and quiet; and I, you think, want a fresh girl, like myself. Do you mean to insult us both, Lady Markland? Yes, strike! Order me away from you; but don't mock me! don't mock me!" Then out of scorn and superiority he sank again into the suppliant. "I will be tame, if you like; anything that you like. Only don't send me away!"

She drew her hand away from him, at last, and sank into her chair, with her heart in such a commotion, that she scarcely heard what he was saying for the loud beating in her ears. Then she made a stand again, having been, as it were, beaten from the first parallels; carried away by that fiery charge. She recovered herself a little; controlled the hurrying pulses; called back her strength. She said with a trembling voice, "Oh, let us be calm, if we can! Think a little of my position, and yours. Oh, Theo! think, besides, what I have said, that I am old. How can I bid you go, I who owe to you—you will not let me say it, but I feel it in my heart—so much, so much, of the comfort of my life! I tell you again, you should have said what you have been saying to a girl who would have put her hand in yours and that would have been all——" He put out his hand to take hers once more, but this time she refused him.

"Sit there and let us talk. If I had been that girl!—but I am not, I never can be. I am a woman who have had to act for myself. I am Geoff's mother. I must think of him and what has to be done for him. How can you say I mock you? We are two reasonable beings. We must think; we cannot be carried away by—by—by fancy, by what you call——"

Her voice broke, she could not go on, with the hurrying of her blood, the scrutiny of his looks, the passion in him which infected her. She waved her hand to him to sit down, to be calm, to listen, but she had no voice to speak.

"I am not reasonable," he replied, "no, don't think it; there is no reason in me. Afterwards, I will hear all there is to say. You shall make conditions, explanations, anything you please. Now is not the time for it. Tell me, am I to go or stay?" He was hoarse, while she was dumb. With both the question had gone far beyond the bounds of that reason to which she had appealed. "That is the only thing," he repeated. "Tell me: am I to go or stay?"

Looking forward to this, it had seemed that there was so much to be said: on his side all the eloquence of passion; on hers the specious arguments of a woman who thinks she may still be able to withhold and restrain. All these possibilities had fled. They looked at each other, almost antagonists, because of being so much the reverse. She drew back, holding herself apart, unwilling to accept that necessity of decision; not knowing how to escape from it; holding her hands clasped together that he might not secure them; her heart fluttering in her throat; her head throbbing with pain and excitement. Ah, if she had been that girl! If he had sought one like himself! He felt it too, even in the scorn with which he repulsed the suggestion; and for a moment it hung on the balance of a thought, on the turn of a look, whether his patience might not give way; whether his fastidious temper might not take fire at the aspect of that reluctance with which she held away from him, kept back, would not yield. But, on the other hand, that very reluctance, was it not a subtle attraction, a charm the more; giving a sweetness beyond all speaking to the certainty that, underneath all that resistance, the real citadel was won? After this momentary armistice and pause, in which they both seemed to regain their hurried breath, and the mist of the combat dispelled a little, he threw himself down by her again, and got both the clasped hands into his own, saying with something between supplication and authority, "I am to stay?"

"I cannot bid you go," she said, trembling, almost inaudible; and in this way the long battle came to an end in a moment. They looked at each other, scarcely believing it; asking each other, could it be so? Even he scarcely ventured to presume that it was so, though he had forced it and taken the decision into his own hands.

There ensued a half hour or so of bewildered happiness, in which it seemed, to him at least, that the world had turned into a different sphere, and to her that there was in life a sweetness which had come to her too late, of which she could never taste the true flavour, nor forget the bitterness behind; yet which was sweet and wonderful; too wonderful, almost, to believe. She delivered herself over to listen, to behold the flood of the young man's rapture. It filled her with a kind of admiration and almost terror. She was like his mother, though with a difference. She had not known what love was. It was wonderful to her to see it, to know that she was the object of it; but as the warm tide touched her, invaded her being, carrying her away, there was something of fear mingled with her yielding to that delight. She had been so certain that she would not yield; and yet had made so poor a resistance! It was fortunate that he was so lost, on his side, in the wonder of the new bliss, and had so much to pour forth of triumph and ecstasy, that he accepted the silence on her part without comment even in his own mind. It was too completely unhoped for, too extraordinary, what had already happened, that he should ask for more. Her passive position, her reticence, but added to the rapture. She was his almost against her will, constrained by the torrent of love which was irresistible, which had carried all her defences away. This gave her a sort of majesty in the young man's dazzled eyes. He was giddy with joy and pride. It had seemed to him impossible that he could ever win this queen of his every thought; and it became her, as a queen still, to stand almost aloof, reluctant, although in all the sweetness of consent she had been made to yield. It was her part, too, in nature and according to all that was most seemly, to bring him back to the consideration of that invading sea of common life which surrounded his golden isle of happiness. She put up her hand as if to stop his mouth. "Oh, Theo, there are so many things which we must think of. It cannot be all happiness as you suppose. You are not thinking how many troublesome things I bring with me."

"Let trouble be for to-morrow," he cried; "nothing but joy on this white day."

She looked at him with a shiver, yet a smile. "Ah, you are so young! your heart has no ghosts like mine."

"Speak respectfully of my heart, for it is yours. The ghosts shall be laid and the troubles will fly away. What are ghosts to you and me? One may be subject to them, but two can face the world."

"O dreamer," she cried, but the reflection of the light in his face came into hers, almost against her will.

"Not dreamer: lover, a better word. Don't spend your strength for nothing, my lady and mistress. Do you really believe that you can make me afraid, to-day?"

She shook her head, not answering, which indeed he scarcely left her time to do, he had so much to say. His very nature seemed changed, the proud, fastidious, taciturn Warrender babbling like a happy boy, in the sudden overflow of a bliss which was too much for him. But while he ran on, a louder voice than hers interrupted him,—the bell that meant the commonest of all events, the bell for luncheon. It fell into the soft retirement of that paradise, which was something of a fool's paradise to Theo, scaring and startling the pair. She made a start from his side with a guilty blush, and even he for a moment paused with something like a sense of alarm. They looked at each other as if they had been suddenly cited to appear before a tribunal and answer for what they had done. Then he broke into a breathless laugh. "I shall have to leave you. I can't face that ordeal. Oh, what a falling off is here—luncheon! must I leave everything for that?"

"Yes, go, go—it is too much," she murmured, like a culprit whose accomplice may be saved, but who herself must face the judge. "I could not bear it; I could not hold up my head, if you were there."

"One moment!" She was leaning towards him, when Geoff's hasty steps were heard in the hall and his voice that seemed to sound sharp in her very ears, "Where's mamma?" Lady Markland fell back with a face like a ghost, covering it with her hands. Warrender felt as if a sudden flame was lit in his heart. He seized her almost with violence. "I will come back to-night, when he is in bed. Be in the avenue. I must see you again to-day."

"I will, Theo."

"At nine o'clock." He pulled away the hand which still was over her eyes. "You are mine, remember, mine first. I shall count the minutes till I come back. Mine first, mine always."

"Oh, Theo, yes! for the love of heaven go!"

Was that how to conclude the first meeting of happy lovers? Warrender rushed through the hall, with his blood on fire, almost knocking over Geoff, who presented himself, very curious and sharp-eyed, directly in the way.

"Oh, I say, Theo!" cried Geoff. "Where are you going, Theo? that's lunch! lunch is on the table. Don't you hear the bell? Can't you stay?"

Warrender waved his hand, he could make no reply. He could have taken the child by the collar and flung him far away into the unknown, if that had been practicable. Ghosts, she had said: Geoff was no ghost, but he was insupportable; not to be seen with composure at that tremendous moment. The young man rushed down the steps and struck across the drive at a pace like a race-horse, though he was only walking. He forgot even the big black, munching his hay tranquilly in the stable and thinking no harm.

CHAPTER XXVIII.

Lady Markland came out of her room a little after, paler than usual, with a great air of stateliness and gravity, conscious to her finger points of the looks that met her, and putting on an aspect of severity which was very unusual to her. Geoff seized and clung to her arm as he was wont, and found it trembling. He had begun to pour forth his wonder about Theo even before he made this discovery.

"Why, Theo has gone away! He wouldn't stop for lunch. I shouted to him, but he never paid any attention. Is he ill, or is he in trouble, or what's the—— Why, mamma! you are all trembling!"

"Nonsense, Geoff, I have been—sitting with the window open: and it is a little cold to-day."

"Cold!" Geoff was so struck by the absurdity of the statement that he stopped to look at her. "Ah," he said, "you have not been running up and down to the stables or you never would think that."

"No, I have been sitting—writing."

"Oh!" said the child again, "were you writing all the time Theo was there? I thought you were talking to Theo. He gave me a holiday because he had something he wanted to say to you."

"I have told you a great many times, Geoff, that you should not call Mr. Warrender Theo. It is much too familiar. You must not presume because he is so very kind to you——"

"Oh, he doesn't mind," said Geoff lightly. "What was he saying to you, mamma?"

By this time they were at table, that is, she was at the bar, seated indeed as a concession to her weakness, about to be tried for her life before those august judges, Geoff and old Soames,

255

both of whom had their attention fixed on her with an intentness which the whole bench could scarcely equal. She held her head very high, but she did not dare to lift up her eyes.

"Will you have this, or some of the chicken?" she asked, with a voice of solemnity not quite adapted to the question.

"I say, mamma, was it about me? or was it some trouble he was in?"

"My dear Geoff, let us attend to our own business. The chicken is better for you. And why have you been running up and down to the stables? I thought I had said that I objected to the stables."

By dint of thus carrying the war into the enemy's country, she was able to meet her boy's keen eyes, which were sharp with curiosity, "like needles," as old Soames said. Soames, the other of her judges, gave his verdict without hesitation. "She have given him the sack," he said confidentially to the housekeeper, as soon as he could spare a moment. "And a very good thing too." The housemaids had come to the same conclusion, seeing Theo's hurried exit, and the rate at which he walked down the avenue. The news ran through the house in a moment. "My lady has given him the sack." The old servants were glad, because there would thus be no change; and the young ones were sorry for the same reason, and partly, too, because of their sympathy for the young lover dismissed, whose distracted departure without his horse went to their tender hearts.

Geoff had to enter into an explanation as to why he had sought the stables as soon as he was dismissed from his books,—an explanation which involved much; for it had already been pointed out to him on various occasions that the coachman and Black were not improving society. Geoff had to confess that it was dull when he had a holiday, that he didn't know where to go, that Black and the coachman were more fun than—any one else—with an expressive glance over his shoulder at old Soames, all which pleas went like so many arrows to Lady Markland's heart. Had she been so neglecting her boy that Black and the coachman had become his valued allies? She who believed in her heart that up to this moment her life had been devoted to Geoff.

The day passed to her like a day in a fever. Geoff liked it, on the whole. There was no Theo to linger after lunch and interfere with his possession of his mother. The long afternoon was all his, and Lady Markland, though she was, he thought, dull, and sometimes did not hear what he said, letting her attention stray, and her eyes go far away, over his head, was yet very tender, more affectionate than ever, anxious to inquire into all his wishes and to find out everything he wanted. He talked to her more than he had done at a stretch for a long time, and made it so apparent how completely he calculated upon her as always his companion that Lady Markland's guilty soul was troubled within her. She faltered once, "But, Geoff, you know you will have to go to school, they all say, and then to Oxford, when you are a man." "Yes, and you can come and live close by college," the boy said. "Many boys' mothers do, Mr. Sargent told me." Her heart sank more and more as he opened up his plans before her. It was all quite simple to Geoff. He did not dream of any change in himself, and what change could ever come to her? Presently the manner in which the child calculated upon her, ignoring every personal claim of hers, awoke a little spark in Lady Markland's breast. A little while ago she would herself have said (nay, this morning she would have said it) that she had no life but in him, that for her there was no future save Geoff's future. Even now it seemed guilt in her that she should have calculations of her own.

And as for saying anything to him on the subject, how could she do it? It was impossible. Had he been a young man, with some acquaintance with life, she thought it would not have been so hard; or had he been a mere child, to whom she could have said that Theo was to be his new papa. But ten; a judge and a critic; a creature who knew so much and so little. Half a dozen times she cleared her throat to begin, to lead the conversation back to Theo, to make some attempt at disclosure: but another look at his face chilled the words on her lips. She could not do it: how could she ever do it? They went out and had a long drive together; they strolled about the park afterwards before dinner, the boy hanging as was his habit upon her arm, pressed close to her, talking—about everything in heaven and earth: but never loosening that claim which was supreme, that proprietorship in her which she had never contested till now, never herself doubted. Geoff meant to be very good to his mother, her protector, her support, as soon as he should be big enough. She was to be his chief companion, always with him, his alone, all his, as she was now. Any other reading of life was not possible to him. He felt sure there was something about Theo which he had not been told, some story which he would get mamma to tell him sooner or later, but never that this story could interfere with himself and his mother; that was impossible, beyond the range of the boy's wildest misgivings.

As for Lady Markland, she was more than silenced, she was overawed by this certainty. She let him run on, her own thoughts drifting away, pulled up now and then by an importunate, repeated question, then wandering again, but not far, only to this impossibility of making Geoff understand. How should she convey to him the first germ of the fact that mother and son are not one; that they separate and part in the course of nature; that a woman in the flower of her life does not necessarily centre every wish in the progress of a little boy? How to tell him this, how to find a language which could express it, in which such a horrible fact could be told! To herself it was terrible, a thing foreign to all her tenets, to all her principles. Even now that she had done it and bound herself for ever, and raised this wall between herself and her child, between herself and her past life, it was terrible to her. If she had ever been certain of anything in her life, it had been that such a step was impossible. Marriage, for her who was already married; a new life to come in place of the old; a state of affairs in which Geoff should no longer be first, in which, in fact, it would be better, an ease to her, that Geoff should be away! Oh, horrible thought! an ease to her to be without Geoff! She had lived for him, she had said and felt that he was everything to her, the sole object of her love and her life. And now he was an embarrassment, and it would be well for her if he could be got away.

In this confusion of mind mingled with impulses to flight, with impulses of going and throwing herself on Theo's mercy, begging him to give her up, for she could not do it, the day passed. Geoff clung to her and talked, talked incessantly all the day through, giving her his opinions about Theo as well as about everything else; and she listened hearing some things—that most distinctly as it may be believed—but not all, nor near all; weary, was it possible? of her own child; of the ceaseless voice in her ears. She was conscious of urging him to go to bed, as she would not have thought of doing in other circumstances; urging him against his will, telling him that he was getting later and later, that it made him pale and nervous, that he must go—all because she was anxious to escape, because she had promised to meet——Could a woman sink into lower humiliation, a woman, a mother, not a foolish girl? At last she could escape breathlessly, tying a black veil over her head; stealing out, saying a nervous word to Soames about the beautiful moonlight. Even Soames had to see her humiliation. She had to linger, as if she were looking at the moonlight, while Soames stood upon the steps—and with shame and confusion to cross the space before the door, which was all one flood of light marked only by her little shadow, small and clinging to her feet. She could have wished that there should never be moonlight more, so shamed and mortified and humiliated did she feel. The darkness would have been better; the darkness would have hidden her at least. In this condition of shame and pain she went along, gliding into what shadow the young trees could throw, brushing against the bushes underneath. And then suddenly, all in a moment, there was calm; ah, more than calm, a refuge from all trouble, a sudden escape from herself and all things that were oppressing her; without any word said, a sudden meeting in the shade of the trees, and two where there had been but one,—a young lover, and a woman who, Heaven help her, was young too, and could still drop her burden off her shoulders and for a moment forget everything, except the arm that supported her, and the whisper close to her ear, and the melting of all her bonds, the melting of her very being into his, the heavenly ease and forgetfulness, the *Vita Nuova* never known before.

It seemed not herself all laden with shame, but another woman, who raised her head, and said to him, shaking as it were her bondage from her: "This is not becoming for you and me. Let us go in. Whatever we have to encounter together, we must not do it in secret. I must not linger about here, Theo, like one of my maids."

"Yet stay a moment," he said. Perhaps the maids have the best of it. The sweet air of the night, the magical light so near them, the contact and close vicinity, almost unseen of each other, added an ethereal atmosphere to the everlasting, always continued tale.

> 'Twas partly love and partly fear,
> And partly 'twas a bashful art,
>   That I might rather feel than see
> The swelling of her heart.

After a time, they emerged into the moonlight, slowly moving towards the house, she leaning upon his arm, he stooping over her, a suggestive posture. Soames upon the doorsteps could not believe his eyes. He would have shut up before now, if he had not seen my lady go out. To admire the moonlight! it did not seem to Soames a very sensible occupation; but when he saw her coming back, not alone, wonder and horror crept over him. He watched them with his mouth open, as well as his eyes, and when he went downstairs and told Black, who had made the horses comfortable for the night, to go and bring out Mr. Warrender's horse, a shock ran through the entire house. After all! but then it was possible that he had always intended to come back and ride his horse home.

Black walked about (very unwillingly and altogether

indifferent to the beauty of the moonlight) for nearly an hour before Warrender came out. The young man's aspect then was very unlike that of the morning. Happiness beamed from him as he walked, and Lady Markland came out to the door to see him start, and called good-night as he rode away. "Good-night, till to-morrow," he said, turning back as long as he could see her, which was a tempting of providence on the part of a man who was not a great rider, and with a big horse like the black, and so fresh, and irritated to be taken out of the stable at that hour of the night. The servants exchanged looks as my lady walked back with eyes that shone as they had never shone before, and something of that glory about her, that dazzling and mist of self-absorption which belongs to no other condition of the mind. She went back into the room and shut the door, and sat down where she had been sitting, and delivered herself over to those visions which are more enthralling than the reality; those mingled recollections and anticipations which are the elixir of love. She had forgotten all about herself; herself as she was before that last meeting. Her age, her gravity, the falseness of the position, the terrible Geoff, all floated away from her thoughts. They were filled only with what *he* had been saying and doing, as if she had been that "fresh girl" of whom she had spoken to him. She forgot that she was not that girl. She forgot that she was four years (magnified this morning into a hundred) and a whole life in advance of Theo. She thought only—nay, poor lady, assailed after her time by this love-fever, taking it late and not lightly! she thought not at all, but surrendered herself to that overwhelming wave of emotion which, more than almost anything else, has the power of filling up all the vacant places of life. Her troublous thoughts, her shame, her sense of all the difficulties in her way, went from her in that new existence. They were all there unchanged, but for the moment she thought of them no more.

It was some time after this, when she went upstairs with her candle through the stilled and darkened house, the light in her hand showing still that confused sweet shining in her eyes, the smile that lurked about the corners of her mouth. A faint sound made her look up as she went towards the gallery upon which all the bedrooms opened. Standing by the banister, looking down into the dark hall, was Geoff, a little white figure, his colourless hair ruffled by much tossing on his bed, his eyes dazzled by the light. "Geoff!" She stood still and her heart seemed to stop beating. To see him there was as if a curtain had suddenly fallen, shutting out all the sweet prospects before her, showing nothing but darkness and danger instead.

"Geoff! Is it you out of bed at this hour?"

"Yes, it is me," he said, in a querulous tone; "there is no one else so little in the house; of course it is me."

"You are shivering with cold; have you——" Her breath seemed to go from her as she came up to him and put her arm round him. "Have you been here long, Geoff?"

"I couldn't sleep," said the child, "and I heard a noise. I saw Theo. Has Theo been back here with you? What did Theo want here so late at night?"

He did not look at her, but stared into the candle with eyes opened to twice their size.

"Come into my room," she said. "You are so cold; you are shivering. Oh, Geoff! if you make yourself ill, what shall I do?"

He let her lead him into her room, wrap him in a fur cloak, and kneel down beside him to chafe his feet with her hands; this helped her in the dreadful crisis which had come so suddenly, which she had feared beyond anything else in the world. "You must have been about a long time or you could not have got so cold, Geoff."

"Yes, I have been about a long time. I thought you would come up directly, after Theo went away." He looked at her very gravely as she knelt with her face on a level with his. He had filled the place of a judge before, without knowing it; but now Geoff was consciously a judge, and interrogating—one who was too much like a criminal, who avoided the looks of that representative of offended law. "Theo stayed a long time," he said, "and then he rode away. I suppose he came to get his horse." How he looked at her! Her eyes were upon his feet, stretched out on the sofa, which she was rubbing; but his eyes burned into her, through her downcast eyelids, making punctures in her very brain.

"He did come for his horse." She could hardly hear the words she was saying, for the tumult of her heart in her ears; "but that was not all, Geoff."

For a long minute no more was said; it seemed like an hour. The mother went on rubbing the child's feet mechanically, then bent down upon them and kissed them. No Magdalen was ever more bowed with shame and trouble. Her voice was choked; she could not speak a word in her own defence. It had been happiness, but oh, what a price to pay!

At last Geoff said, with great gravity, "Theo was always very fond of you."

"I think so, Geoff," she answered, faltering.

"And now you are fond of him."

She could say nothing. She put her head down upon the little white feet and kissed them, with what humility, with what compunction! her eyes dry and her cheeks blazing with shame.

"It's not anything wrong, mamma?"

"No, Geoff, oh no, my darling! they say not: if only you don't mind."

The brave little eyes blinked and twinkled to get rid of unwelcome tears. He put his hand upon her head and stroked it, as if it had been she that was the child. "I do mind," he said. She thought, as she felt the little hand upon her head, that the boy was about to call upon her for a supreme sacrifice; but for a moment there was nothing more. Afterwards he repulsed her a little, very slightly, but yet it was a repulse. "I suppose," he said, "it cannot be helped, mamma? My feet are quite warm now, and I'll go to bed."

"Geoff, is that all you have got to say to me? It can make no difference, my darling, no difference. Oh, Geoff, my own boy, you will always be my first——"

Would he, could he be her first thought? She paused, conscience-stricken, raising for the first time her eyes to his. But a child does not catch such an unconscious admission. He took no notice of it. His chief object, for the moment, was not to cry, which he felt would be beneath his dignity. His little heart was all forlorn. He had no clear idea of what it was, or of what was going to happen, but only a vague certainty that mamma and Theo were to stand more and more together, and that he was "out of it." He could not talk of grown-up things like them; he would be sent to play as he had been this morning. He who had been companion, counsellor, everything to her, he would be sent to play. The dreary future seemed all summed up in that. He slid out of her arms with his little bare feet on the carpet, flinging the fur cloak from him. "I was a little cold because the door was open, but I'm quite warm now, and I'm sleepy too. And it's long, long past bedtime, don't you think, mamma? I wonder if I was ever as late before?"

He looked at her when he asked that question, and suddenly before them both, a little vague and confused to the child, to her clear as if yesterday, came the picture of that night when Geoff and she had watched together, he at her feet, curled into her dress, while his father lay dying. Oh, *he* had no right to reproach her, no right! and yet the pale, awful face on the pillow, living, yet already wrapt in the majesty of death, rose up before her. She gave a great cry and clasped Geoff in her arms. She was still kneeling, and his slight little white figure swayed and trembled with the sudden weight. To have that face like a spectre rise up before her, and Geoff's countenance averted, his little eyes twitching to keep in the tears, was there anything in the world worth that? Magdalen! ah, worse than Magdalen! for she poured out her tears for what was past, whereas all this shame was the price at which she was going to buy happiness to come.

And yet it was nothing wrong.

CHAPTER XXIX.

Mrs. Warrender and Chatty left the Warren in the end of the week in which these events had taken place. They had a farewell visit from the rector and Mrs. Wilberforce, which no doubt was prompted by kindness, yet had other motives as well. The Warren looked its worst on the morning when this visit was paid. It was a gray day, no sun visible, the rain falling by intervals, the sky all neutral tinted, melting in the gray distance into indefinite levels of damp soil and shivering willows,—that is, where there was a horizon visible at all. But in the Warren there was no horizon, nothing but patches of whitish gray seen among the branches of the trees, upon which the rain kept up such an endless, dismal patter as became unendurable after a time—a continual dropping, the water dripping off the long branches, drizzling through the leaves with incessant monotonous downfall. The Wilberforces came picking their way through the little pools which alternated with dry patches along all the approaches to the house, their wet umbrellas making a moving glimmer of reflection in the damp atmosphere. Inside, the rooms were all dark, as if it had been twilight. Boxes stood about in the hall, packed and ready, and there were those little signs of neglect in the usual garnishing of the rooms which is so apt to occur when there is a departure. Chatty, with her hat on, stood arranging a few very wet flowers in a solitary vase, as if by way of keeping up appearances, the usual decorations of this kind being all cleared away. "Theo is so little at home," she said, by way of explanation, "he would get no good of them." Afterwards when she thought of it, Chatty was sorry that she had mentioned her brother at all.

"Ah, Theo! We have been hearing wonderful things of Theo," said Mrs. Wilberforce, as Mrs. Warrender approached from the drawing-room to meet them and bid them enter. "I have never been so surprised in my life; and yet I don't know why I should be surprised. Of course it makes his conduct all quite reasonable when we look back upon it in that light."

"Who speaks of conduct that is reasonable?" said Mrs. Warrender. "It is kinder than reason to come and see us this melancholy day: for it is very discouraging to leave home under such skies."

"But you don't need to leave in such a hurry, surely. Theo would never press you: and besides, I suppose with a larger house so close at hand they would not live here."

"There is nobody going to live here that I know of, except Theo," said his mother. ("Let me take off your cloak," cried Chatty;) "notwithstanding the packing and all the fuss the servants love to make, we may surely have some tea. I ought to ask you to come and sit down by the fire. Though it is June, a fire seems the only comfortable thing one can think of." Mrs. Warrender was full of suppressed excitement, and talked against time that her visitors might not insist upon the one topic of which she was determined nothing should be said. But the rector's wife was not one whom it was easy to balk.

"A fire would be cosy," she said; "but I suppose now the Warren will be made to look very different. With all the will in the world to change, it does need a new start, doesn't it, a new beginning, to make a real change in a house?"

This volley was ineffective from the fact that it called forth no remark. As Mrs. Warrender had no answer to make, she took refuge in that which is the most complete of all—silence: and left her adversary to watch, as it were, the smoke of her own guns, dispersing vaguely into the heavy air.

"We are going to London, first," Mrs. Warrender said. "No, not for the season, it is too late; but if any little simple gaieties should fall in Chatty's way——"

"Little simple gaieties are scarcely appropriate to London in June," said the rector, with a laugh.

"No, if we were to be received into the world of fashion, Chatty and I—but that doesn't seem very likely. We all talk about London as if we were going to plunge into a vortex. Our vortex means two or three people in Kensington, and one little bit of a house in Mayfair."

"That might be quite enough to set you going," said Mrs. Wilberforce. "It only depends upon whom the people are; though now, I hear that in London there are no invitations more sought after, than to the rich parvenu houses,—people that never were heard of till they grew rich; and then they have nothing to do but get a grand house in Belgravia, and let it be known how much money they have. Money is everything, alas, now."

"It always was a good deal, my dear," observed the rector mildly.

"Never in my time, Herbert! Mamma would no more have let us go to such houses! It is just one of those signs of the time which you insist on ignoring, but which one day—— This new connection will be a great thing for Chatty, dear Mrs. Warrender. It is such a nice thing for a girl to come out under good auspices."

"Poor Chatty, we cannot say she is coming out," said her mother, "and the Thynnes, I have always understood, were dull people, not fashionable at all."

"Oh, you don't think for a moment that I meant the Thynnes! She has been very quiet, to be sure; but now, of course, with a young husband—and I am sure Chatty does not look more than nineteen; I always say she is the youngest looking girl of her age. And as she has never been presented, what is she but a girl coming out? But I do think I would wait till she had her sister-in-law to go out with. It may be a self-denial for a mother, but it gives a girl such an advantage!"

"But Chatty is not going to have a husband either young or old," said Mrs. Warrender, with a laugh which was a little forced. "Ah, here is the tea, I wish we had a fire too, Joseph, though it is against rules."

"I'll light you a fire, mum," said Joseph, "in a minute. None of us would mind the trouble, seeing as it's only for once, and the family going away."

"That is very good of you not to mind," said his mistress, laughing. "Light it, then, it will make us more cheerful before we go."

"Ah, Joseph," said the rector's wife, "you may well be kind to your good old mistress, who has always been so considerate to you. For new lords, new laws, you know, and when the new lady comes——"

Joseph, who was on his knees lighting the fire, turned round with the freedom of an old servant. "There ain't no new ladies but in folks' imagination," he said. "The Warren ain't a place for nothing new."

"Joseph!" cried his mistress sharply; but she was glad of the assistance thus afforded to her. And there was a little interval during which Mrs. Wilberforce was occupied with her tea. She was cold and damp, and the steaming cup was pleasant to see; but she was not to be kept in silence even by this much-needed refreshment. "I should think," she resumed, "that the boy would be the chief difficulty. A step-mother is a difficult position; but a step-father, and one so young as dear Theo!"

"Step-fathering succeeds better than step-mothering," said the rector, "so far as my experience goes. Men, my dear, are not so exacting; they are more easily satisfied."

"What nonsense, Herbert! They are not brought so much in contact with the children, perhaps, you mean; they are not called on to interfere so much. But how a mother could trust her children's future to a second husband—— For my part I would rather die."

"Let us hope you will never need to do so, my dear," said the rector, at which little pleasantry Mrs. Warrender was glad to laugh.

"Happily none of us are in danger," she said. "Chatty must take the warning to heart and beware of fascinating widowers. Is it true about the Elms—that the house is empty and every one gone?"

"Thank heaven! it is quite true; gone like a bubble burst, clean swept out, and not a vestige left."

"As every such place must go sooner or later," said Mrs. Wilberforce. "That sort of thing may last for a time, but sooner or later——"

"I think," said the rector, "that our friend Cavendish had, perhaps, something to do with it. It appears that it is an uncle of his who bought the house when it was sold three years ago, and these people wanted something done to the drainage, I suppose. I advised Dick to persuade his uncle to do nothing, hoping that the nuisance—for, I suppose, however wicked you are, you may have a nose like other people—might drive them out; and so it has done apparently," Mr. Wilberforce said, with some complacency, looking like a man who deserved well of his kind.

"They might have caught fever, too, like other people. I wonder if that is moral, to neglect the drains of the wicked?"

"No," said Mrs. Wilberforce firmly; "they have not noses like other people. How should they, people living in that way? The sense of smell is essentially a belonging of the better classes. Servants never smell anything. We all know that. My cook sniffs and looks me in the face and says, 'I don't get anything, m'm,' when it is enough to knock you down! And persons of *that* description living in the midst of every evil—! Not that I believe in all that fuss about drains," she added, after a moment. "We never had any drains in the old times, and who ever heard of typhoid fever *then*?"

"But if they had been made very ill?" said Chatty, who, up to this time, had not spoken. "I don't think surely Mr. Cavendish would have done that."

She was a little moved by this new view. Chatty was not interested in general about what was said, but now and then a personal question would rouse her. She thought of the woman with the blue eyes, so wide open and red with crying, and then of Dick with his laugh which it always made her cheerful to think of. Chatty had in her mind no possible link of connection between these two: but the absence of any power of comprehending the abstract in her made her lay hold all the more keenly of the personal, and the thought of Dick in the act of letting in poisonous gases upon that unhappy creature filled her with horror. She was indignant at so false an accusation. "Mr. Cavendish," she repeated with a little energy, "never would have done that."

"It is all a freak of those scientific men," said Mrs. Wilberforce. "Look at the poor people, they can do a great deal more, and support a great deal more, than we can: yet they live among bad smells. I think they rather like them. I am sure my nursery is on my mind night and day, if there is the least little whiff of anything; but the children are as strong as little ponies—and where is the drainage there?"

With this triumphant argument she suddenly rose, declaring that she knew the brougham was at the door, and that Mrs. Warrender would be late for the train. She kissed and blessed both the ladies as she took leave of them. "Come back soon, and don't forget us," she said to Chatty; while to Mrs. Warrender she gave a little friendly pat on the shoulder. "You won't say anything, not even to true friends like Herbert and me? but a secret like that can't be kept, and though you mayn't think so, everybody knows."

"Do you think that is true, mamma?" Chatty asked when the wet umbrellas had again gone glimmering through the shrubberies and under the trees, and the travellers were left alone.

"That everybody knows? It is very likely. There is no such thing as a secret in a little world like ours; everybody knows everything. But still they cannot say that they have it by authority from you and me. It is time enough to talk of it when it is a fact, if it is to be."

"But you have not any doubt of it, mamma?"

"I have doubt of everything till it is done; even," she said, with a smile as the wheels of the brougham cut the gravel and came round with a little commotion to the door, "of our going away: though I allow that it seems very like it now."

They did go away, at last, leaving the Warren very solitary, damp, and gray, under the rain,—a melancholy place enough for Theo to return to. But he was not in a state of mind to think of that or of any of his home surroundings grave or gay. Chatty put her head out of the window to look behind her at the melancholy yet dear old house, with tears in her innocent eyes, but Mrs. Warrender, feeling that at last she had shaken herself free from that bondage, notwithstanding the anxiety in her heart for her son, had no feeling to spare for the leave-taking. She waved her hand to Mrs. Bagley at the shop, who was standing out at her door with a shawl over her cap to see the ladies go by. Lizzie stood behind her in the doorway saying nothing, while her grandmother curtsied and waved her hand and called out her wishes for a good journey, and a happy return. Naturally Chatty's eyes sought those of the girl, who looked after her with a sort of blank longing as if she too would fain have gone out into the world. Lizzie's eyes seemed to pursue her as they drove past,—poor Lizzie, who had other things in her mind, Chatty began to think, beside the fashion books; and then there came the tall red mass of the Elms, with all its windows shut up, and that air of mystery which its encircling wall and still more its recent history conferred upon it. The two ladies looked out upon it, as they drove past, almost with awe.

"Mamma," said Chatty, "I never told you. I saw the—the lady, just when she was going away."

"What lady?" asked Mrs. Warrender, with surprise.

"I don't think," said Chatty, with a certain solemnity, "that she was any older, perhaps not so old as I. It made my heart sick. Oh, dear mother, must there not be some explanation, some dreadful, dreadful fate, when it happens that one so young——"

"Sometimes it may be so—but these are mysteries which you, at your age, Chatty, have no need to go into."

"At my age—which is about the same as hers," said Chatty; "and—oh, mamma, I wanted in my heart to stop her, to bring her to you. She had been crying—she had such innocent-looking, distracted eyes—and Lizzie said——"

"Lizzie! what had Lizzie to do with it?"

"I promised to tell no one, but you are not any one, you are the same as myself. Lizzie says she knew her long ago, that she is the same as a child still, not responsible for what she is doing—fond of toys and sweets like a child."

"My dear, I am sorry that Lizzie should have kept up such a friend. I believe there are some poor souls that if an innocent girl were to do what you say, stop them and bring them to her mother, might be saved, Chatty. I do believe that: but not—not that kind."

The tears by this time were falling fast from Chatty's eyes. "I wonder," she said, "if I shall ever see her again."

"Never, I hope; for you could do nothing for her. Shut the window, my dear, the rain is coming in. Poor Theo, how wet he will get coming home! I wonder if he will have the thought to change everything now that there is no occasion to dress, now that we are away."

"Joseph will give him no peace till he does," said Chatty, happily diverted, as her mother had intended, from sadder thoughts. "And don't you think she will make him stay to dinner on such a day? Don't you think she must care a great deal for him, mamma?"

"She must care for him or she would not have listened to him. Poor Theo!" said the mother, with a sigh.

"But he cares very much for her: and he is happy," said Chatty, with a certain timidity, a half question; for to her inexperience there were very serious drawbacks, though perhaps not such as might have occurred to a more reasonable person. Mrs. Warrender had to change this subject, too, which Chatty showed a disposition to push too far, by making an inquiry into the number of their bags and parcels, and reminding her daughter that they were drawing near the station. It was a very forlorn little station, wet and dismal, with a few men lounging about, the collars of their coats up to their ears, and Mrs. Warrender's maid standing by her pile of boxes, having arrived before them. It had been an event long looked for, much talked of, of late, but it was not a cheerful going away.

But the rain had gone off by the time they reached town, and a June day has a power of recovering itself, such as youth only possesses. But no, that is an error, as Mrs. Warrender proved. She had been leaning back in her corner very quiet, saying little, yet with an intense sense of relief and deliverance. She came in to London with as delightful a consciousness of novelty and freedom as any boy coming to seek his fortune. Chatty's feelings were all very mild in comparison with her mother's. She was greatly pleased to see the clouds clear off, and the humid sweetness of the skies, which even the breath of the great city did not obscure. "After all, Theo will have a nice evening for his drive home," she said, unexcited. Though it was all very agreeable, Chatty did not know of anything that might await her in town. She knew more or less, she believed, what awaited her,—a few parties, a play or two, the Row in the morning, the pictures, a pleasant little glimpse of the outside of that fashionable life which was said to be "such a whirl," which she had no expectation, nor any desire to see much of. There was no likelihood that she and her mother would be drawn into that whirl. If all the people they knew asked them to dinner, or even to a dance, which was not to be thought of, there would still be no extravagant gaiety in that. Driving from the railway to Half Moon Street was as pleasant as anything—to a girl of very highly raised expectations, it might have been the best of all: but Chatty did not anticipate too much, and would not be easily disappointed. She neither expected nor was afraid of any great thing that might be coming to her. Her quiet heart seemed beyond the reach of any touch of fate.

CHAPTER XXX.

On the mantelpiece of the little lodging-house drawing-room in Half Moon Street, supported against the gilt group that decorated the timepiece, was a note containing an invitation. "Why, here is the whirl beginning already," Mrs. Warrender said. "Don't you feel that you are in the vortex, Chatty?" Her mother laughed, but was a little excited even by this mild matter; but Chatty did not feel any excitement. To the elder woman, the mere sense of the population about her, the hurry in the street, the commotion in the air, was an excitement. She would have liked to go out at once, to walk about, to get into a hansom like a man, and drive through the streets, and see the lights and the glimmer of the shops, and the crowds of people. To be within reach of all that movement and rapidity went into her veins like wine. After the solitude and silence of so many years,—nothing but the rustle of the leaves, the patter of the rain, the birds or the winds in the branches, and the measured voices indoors, to vary the quiet,—the roar of Piccadilly mingling with everything was a sort of music to this woman. To many others, perhaps the majority, the birds and breezes would be the thing to long for; but Mrs. Warrender was one of the people who love a town and all that seems like a larger life in the collection together of many human lives. Whether it is so or not is another question, or if the massing together of a multitude of littles ever can make a greatness. It seems to do so, which is enough for most people; and though the accustomed soul is aware that no desert can be more lone than London, to the unaccustomed its very murmur sounds like a general consent of humanity to go forth and do more than in any other circumstances. It is the constitution of the ear which determines what it hears. For Chatty took the commotion rather the other way. She said, "One can't hear one's self speak," and wanted to close the windows. But Mrs. Warrender liked the very noise.

The dinner to which they were invited was in Curzon Street, in a house which was small in reality, but made the most of every inch of its space, and which was clothed and curtained and decorated in a manner which made the country people open their eyes. The party was very small, their hostess said; but it would have been a large party at the Warren, where all the rooms were twice as big. Chatty was a little fluttered by her first party in London; but this did not appear in her aspect, which was always composed and simple, not demanding any one's regard, yet giving to people who were *blasé* or tired of much attraction (as sometimes happens) a sense of repose and relief. She must have been more excited, however, than was at all usual with her; for though she thought she had remarked everybody in the dim drawing-room,—where the ladies in their pretty toilets and the men in their black coats stood about in a perplexing manner, chiefly against the light, which made it difficult to distinguish them, instead of sitting down all round the room, which in the country would have seemed the natural way,—it proved that there was one very startling exception, one individual, at least, whom she had not remarked. She went down to dinner with a gentleman, whose name of course she did not make out, and whose appearance, she thought, was exactly the same as that of half the gentlemen in the procession down the narrow staircase. Chatty, indeed, made disparaging reflections to herself as to society in general, on this score; the thought flashing through her mind that in the country there was more difference between even one curate and another (usually considered the most indistinguishable class), than between these men of Mayfair. She was a little bewildered, too, by the appearance of the dining-room, for at that period the *diner à la Russe* was just beginning to establish itself in England, and a thicket of flowers upon the table was novel to Chatty, filling her first with admiration, then with a little doubt whether it would not be better to see the people more distinctly on the other side. Dinner had gone on a little way, and her companion had begun to put the usual questions to her about where she had been, and where she was going, questions to which Chatty, who had been nowhere, and had not as yet one other invitation (which feels a little humiliating when you hear of all the great things that are going on), could make but little reply, when in one of the pauses of the conversation, she was suddenly aware of a laugh, which made her start slightly, and opened up an entirely new interest in this as yet not very exciting company. It was like the opening of a window to Chatty, it seemed to let in pure air, new light. And yet it was only a laugh, no more. She looked about her with a little eagerness: and then it was that she began to find the flowers and the ferns, which had filled her with enthusiasm a moment before, to be rather in the way.

"I suppose you go to the Row every morning," said her entertainer. "Don't you find that always the first thought when one comes to town? You ride, of course. Oh, why not in the Row? there is nothing alarming about it. A little practice, that is all that is wanted; to know how to keep your horse in hand. But you hunt? then you are all right——"

"Oh no, we never hunted." It struck Chatty with a little surprise to be talked to as if she had a stud at her command. Should she tell him that this was a mistake; that there were only two horses beside Theo's, and that Minnie and she had once had a pony between them—which was very different from hunting, or having nerve to ride in the Row? Chatty found afterwards that horses and carriages, and unbounded opportunities for amusing yourself, and a familiar acquaintance with the entire peerage, were always taken for granted in conversation whenever you dined out; but at first she was unacquainted with this peculiarity and did not feel quite easy in her mind about allowing it to be supposed that she was so much greater a person. Her little hesitations, however, as to how she should reply and the pauses she made when she heard that laugh arrested the current of her companion's talk, and made it necessary for her, to her own alarm, to originate a small observation which, as often happens to a shy speaker, occurred just at the time when there was a momentary lull in the general talk. What she said was, "Do you ride often in the Row?" in a voice which though very soft was quite audible. Chatty retired into herself with the sensation of having said something very ridiculous when she caught a glance or two of amusement, and heard a suppressed titter from somebody on the other side of the fashionable young man to whom she had addressed this very innocent question. She thought it was at her they were laughing, whereas the fact was that Chatty was supposed by those who heard her to be a satirist of more than usual audacity, putting a coxcomb to deserved but ruthless shame. Naturally she knew nothing of this, and blushed crimson at her evidently foolish remark, and retired in great confusion into herself, not conscious even of the stumbling reply. She was almost immediately conscious, however, of a face which suddenly appeared on the other side of the table round the corner of a bouquet of waving ferns, lit up with smiles of pleasure and eager recognition. "Oh, Mr. Cavendish! then it was you," she said, unawares; but the tumult of the conversation had arisen again, and it seemed very doubtful whether her exclamation could have reached his ear.

When the gentlemen came upstairs, Chatty endeavoured to be looking very naturally the other way; not to look as if she expected him; but Dick found his way to her immediately. "I can't think how I missed you before. I should have tried hard for the pleasure of taking you down, had I known you were here," he said, with that look of interest which was the natural expression in his eyes when he addressed a woman. "When did you come to town, and where are you? I do not know anything that has been going on, I have heard nothing of you all for so long. There must be quite a budget of news."

Chatty faltered a little, feeling that Mr. Cavendish had never been so intimate in the family as these questions seemed to imply.

"The Wilberforces were quite well when we left," she said, with the honesty of her nature, for to be sure it was the Wilberforces rather than the Warrenders who were his friends.

"Oh, never mind the Wilberforces," he said, "tell me something about you."

"There is something to tell about us, for a wonder," said Chatty. "My sister Minnie is married: but perhaps you would hear of that."

"I think I saw it in the papers, and was very glad——" here he stopped and did not finish his sentence. A more experienced person than Chatty would have perceived that he meant to express his satisfaction that it was not she: but Chatty had no such insight.

"Yes, he has a curacy quite close, for the time: and he will have an excellent living, and it is a very nice marriage. We came to town for a little change, mamma and I."

"That is delightful news. And Theo? I have not heard from Theo for ages. Is he left behind by himself?"

"Oh! Theo is very well. Theo is—— Oh, I did not mean to say anything about that."

Chatty did not know why she was so completely off her guard with Dick Cavendish. She had almost told him everything before she was aware.

"Not in any trouble, I hope. Don't let me put indiscreet questions."

"It is not that. There is nothing indiscreet, only I forgot that we had not meant to say anything."

"I am so very sorry," cried Cavendish. "You must not think I would ask anything you don't wish to tell me."

"But I should like to tell you," said Chatty, "only I don't know what mamma will say. I will tell her it came out before I knew: and you must not say anything about it, Mr. Cavendish."

"Not a syllable, not even to your mother. It shall be something between you and me."

The way in which this was said made Chatty's eyes droop

for a moment: but what a pleasure it was to tell him! She could not understand herself. She was not given to chatter about what happened in the family, and Dick was not so intimate with Theo that he had a right to know; but still it was delightful to tell him. "We don't know whether to be glad or sorry," she said. "It is that perhaps Theo, after a while, is going to marry."

"That is always interesting," said Dick; but he took the revelation calmly. "What a lucky fellow! No need to wait upon fortune like the rest of us. To marry—whom? Do I know the lady? I hope she is all that can be desired."

"Oh, Mr. Cavendish, that is just the question. There is mamma coming, perhaps she will tell you herself, which would be so much better than if you heard it from me."

Mrs. Warrender came up at this moment very glad to see him, and quite willing to disclose their number in Half Moon Street, and to grant a gracious permission that he should call and be "of use," as he offered to be. "I am not a gentleman at large, like Warrender, I am a toiling slave, spending all my time in Lincoln's Inn. But in the evening I can spare a little time—and occasionally at other moments," he added, with a laugh, "when I try. A sufficient motive is the great thing. And of course you will want to go to the play, and the opera, and all that is going on."

"Not too much," said Mrs. Warrender. "The air of London is almost enough at first, but come, and we shall see."

She said nothing, however, about Theo, nor was there any chance of saying more. But when Cavendish took Chatty downstairs to put her in the carriage (only a cab, but that is natural to country people in town), he hazarded a whisper as they went downstairs, "Remember there is still something to tell me." "Oh yes," she replied, "but mamma herself, I am sure——" "No," he said, "she has nothing to do with it. It is between you and me." This little conference made her wonderfully bright and smiling when she took her place beside her mother. She did not say anything for a time, but when the cab turned into Piccadilly, with its long lines of lights,—an illumination which is not very magnificent now, and was still less magnificent then, but very new and fine to Chatty, accustomed to little more guidance through the dark than that which is given by the light of a lantern or the oil lamp in Mrs. Bagley's shop,—she suddenly said, "Well! London is very pleasant," as if that was a fact of which she was the first discoverer.

"Is it not?" said her mother, who was far more disinterested and had not had her judgment biassed by any whisper on the stairs. "I am very glad that you like it, Chatty. That will make my pleasure complete."

"Oh, who could help liking it, mamma?" She blushed a little as she said this, but the night was kind and covered it; and how could Mrs. Warrender divine that this gentle enthusiasm related to the discovery of what Chatty called a friend among so many strangers, and not to the mere locality in which this meeting had taken place? Who could help liking it? To be talked to *like that*, with eyes that said more than even the words, with that sudden look of pleasure, with the delightful little mystery of a special confidence between them, and with the prospect of meetings hereafter,—who could tell how many?—of going to the play. Chatty laughed under her breath with pleasure, at the thought. It was a most admirable idea to come to London. After all, whatever Minnie might say, there was nobody for understanding how to make people happy like mamma!

Dick's sensations were not so innocent nor so sweet. He walked home to his chambers, smoking his cigar, and chewing the cud of fancy, which was more bitter than sweet. What right had he to bend over that simple girl, to lay himself out to please her, to speak low in her ear? Dick knew unfortunately too well what was apt to come of such a beginning. Without being more of a coxcomb than was inevitable, he was aware that he had a way of pleasing women. And he had a perception that Chatty was ready to be pleased, and that he himself wished—oh, very much, if he dared—to please her. In these circumstances it was perfectly evident that he should peremptorily take himself out of all possibility of seeing Chatty. But this was utterly contrary to the way in which he had greeted her, and in which he had immediately flung himself into the affairs of the family. It was his occupation while he walked home to defend and excuse himself for this to himself. In the first place, which was perfectly true, he had not known at all that the Warrenders were to be of the party; he had thus fallen into the snare quite innocently, without any fault of his. Had he known, he might have found an excuse and kept away. But then he asked himself, why in the name of heaven should he have kept away? Was he so captivating a person that it would be dangerous to Miss Warrender to meet him—once; or such a fool as to be unable to meet a young lady whom he admired—once: without harm coming to it? To be sure he had gone farther: he had thrown himself, as it were, at the feet of the ladies, with enthusiasm, and had made absurd offers of himself to be "of use." There could be no doubt that in the circumstances this was mad enough, and culpable too; but it was done without premeditation, by impulse, as he was too apt to act, especially in such matters; and it could be put a stop to. He was pledged to call, it was true; but that might be once, and no more. And then there was the play, the opera, to which he had pledged himself to attend them; once there could not do much harm, either. Indeed, so long as he kept, which he ought to do always, full control over himself, what harm could it at all do to be civil to Theo Warrender's mother and sister, who were, so to speak, after a sort, old friends? He was not such an ass (he said to himself) as to think that Chatty was at his disposal if he should lift up his finger; and there was her mother to take care of her; and they were not people to be asking each other what he "meant," as two experienced women of society might do. Both mother and daughter were very innocent; they would not think he meant anything except kindness. And if he could not take care of himself, it was a pity! Thus in the course of his reflections Dick found means to persuade himself that there was nothing culpable in pursuing the way which was pleasant, which he wanted to pursue; a result which unfortunately very often follows upon reflection. The best way in such an emergency is not to reflect, but to turn and fly at once. But that, he said to himself, not without some complaisance, would be impulse, which he had just concluded to be a very bad thing. It was impulse which had got him into the scrape, he must trust to something more stable to get him out.

In the course of his walking, and, indeed, before these thoughts had gone very far, he found himself at the corner of Half Moon Street, and turned along with the simple purpose of seeing which was No. 22. There were lights in several windows, and he lingered a moment wondering which might be Chatty's. Then with a stamp of his foot, and a laugh of utter self-ridicule, which astounded the passing cabmen (for in any circumstances he was not surely such a confounded sentimental ass as *that*), he turned on his heel and went straight home without lingering anywhere. It was hard upon him that he should be such a fool; that he should not be able to restrain himself from making idiotic advances, which he could never follow out, and for a mere impulse place himself at the mercy of fate! But he would not be led by impulse now in turning his back. It should be reason that should be his guide; reason and reflection and a calm working out of the problem, how far and no farther he could with safety go.

And yet if it had been so that he could have availed himself of the anxiety of his family to get "a nice girl" to take an interest in him! Where could there be a nicer girl than Chatty? There were prettier girls, and as for beauty, that was not a thing to be spoken of at all in the matter. Beauty is rare, and it is often (in Dick's opinion) attended by qualities not so agreeable. It was often inanimate, he thought, apt to rest upon its natural laurels, to think it did enough when it consented to look beautiful. He did not go in, himself, for the sublime. But to see the light come over Chatty's face as if the sun had suddenly broken out in the sky; to see the pleased surprise in her eyes as she lifted them quickly, without any affectation, in all the sweetness of nature. She was not clever either; all that she said was very simple. She was easily pleased, not looking out for wit as some girls do, or insisting upon much brilliancy in conversation. In short, if he had been writing a poem or a song about her (with much secret derision he recognised that to be the sort of thing of which in the circumstances foolish persons were capable), the chief thing that it occurred to him any one could say would be that she was Chatty. And quite enough too! he added, to himself, with a curious warmth under his waistcoat, which was pleasant. Wasn't there a song that went like that? Though this was fair, and that was something else, and a third was so-and-so, yet none of them was Mary Something-or-other. He was aware that the verse was not very correctly quoted, but that was the gist of it; and a very sensible fellow, too, was the man who wrote it, whoever he might be.

With this admirable conclusion, showing how much reason and reflection had done for him, Dick Cavendish wound up the evening—and naturally called at 22 Half Moon Street next day.

CHAPTER XXXI.

Dick Cavendish called at Half Moon Street next day: and found the ladies just returned from a walk, and a little tired and very glad to see a friendly face, which his was in the most eminent degree. They had been out shopping, that inevitable occupation of women, and they had been making calls, and informing their few acquaintances of their arrival. Mrs. Benson, at whose house the dinner had been, was one of the few old friends with whom Mrs. Warrender was in habits of correspondence, and thus had known of their coming beforehand. Dick found himself received with the greatest cordiality by Mrs. Warrender, and by Chatty with an air of modest satisfaction which was very sweet. Then Mrs. Warrender was desirous to have a little guidance in their movements, and took so sincerely his offer to be of use that Dick found no means at all of getting out of it. Indeed, when it came to that, he was by no means so sure that it was so necessary to get out of it, as when he had begun his reflections on the subject. He even proposed—why not?—that they should all go to the play that very evening, there being nothing else on hand. In those days the theatre was not so popular an institution as at present, and it was not necessary to engage places for weeks in advance. This sudden rush, however, was too much for the inexperienced country lady. "We are not going to be so prodigal as that," she said, "it would deprive us of all the pleasure of thinking about it; and as everything is more delightful in anticipation than in reality——"

"Oh, mamma!" said Chatty, shocked by this pessimistic view.

"And what am I to do with myself all the evening?" said Dick, with mock dismay, "after anticipating this pleasure all day? If anticipation is the best part of it, you will allow that disappointment after is doubly——"

"If you have nothing better to do, stay and dine with us," Mrs. Warrender said. This proposal made Chatty look up with pleasure, and then look down again lest she should show, more than was expedient, how glad she was. And Dick, who had reflected and decided that to call once and to go to the theatre once could do no harm, accepted with enthusiasm, without even pausing to ask himself whether to dine with them once might be added without further harm to his roll of permissions. The dinner was a very commonplace, lodging-house dinner, and Chatty got out her muslin work afterwards, and had a quiet industrious evening, very much like her evenings at home. She was like a picture of domestic happiness impersonified, as she sat in the light of the lamp with her head bent, the movement of her arm making a soft rustle as she worked. She wore a muslin gown after the fashion of the time, which was not in itself a beautiful fashion, but pretty enough for the moment, and her hair, which was light brown, fell in little curls over her soft cheek. She looked up now and then, while the others talked, turning from one to another, sometimes saying a word, most frequently giving only a smile or look of assent. Let us talk as we will of highly educated women and of mental equality and a great many other fine things: but as a matter of fact, this gentle auditor and sympathiser, intelligent enough to understand without taking much part, is a more largely accepted symbol of what the woman ought to be, than anything more prominent and individual. Just so Eve sat and listened when Adam discoursed with the angel, putting by in her mind various questions to ask when that celestial but rather long-winded visitor was gone. Perhaps this picture is not quite harmonious with the few facts in our possession in respect to our first mother, and does scant justice to that original-minded woman: but the type has seized hold upon the imagination of mankind. Dick thought of it vaguely, as he looked (having secured a position in which he could do so without observation) at this impersonation of the woman's part.

He thought if another fellow should look in for a talk, which was his irreverent way of describing to himself the visit of the angel, it would be highly agreeable to have her there listening, and to clear up the knotty points for her when they should be alone. He had little doubt that Eve would have an opinion of her own, very favourable to *his* way of stating the subject, and would not mind criticising the other fellow, with a keen eye for any little point of possible ridicule. He kept thinking this as he talked to Mrs. Warrender, and also that the little cluster of curls was pretty, and the bend of her head, and, indeed, everything about her; not striking, perhaps, or out of the common, but most soothing and sweet.

And next evening, having had those pleasures of anticipation which Mrs. Warrender thought so much of, he went with them to the play, and spent an exceedingly pleasant evening, pointing out such people as he knew (who were anybody) to Mrs. Warrender between the acts, and enjoying the sight of Chatty's absorption in the play, which made it twice as interesting to himself. The play was one in which there was a great deal of pretty love-making along with melodramatic situations of an exciting kind. The actors, except one, were not of sufficient reputation to interest any reader save those with a special inclination to the study of the stage. But though the performance was not on the very highest level, there was a great deal in it that thrilled this young man and woman sitting next to each other, and already vaguely inclined towards each other in that first chapter of mutual attraction which is, perhaps, in its vagueness and irresponsibility, the most delightful of all. Dick would have laughed at the idea of feeling himself somehow mixed up with the lover on the stage, who was not only a good actor, but a much handsomer fellow than he was; but Chatty had no such feeling, and with a blush and quiver felt herself wooed in that romantic wooing, with a half sense that the lights should be lowered and nobody should see, and at the same time an enchantment in the sight which only that sense of a personal share in it could have given.

After this beginning Dick's reflections went to the wind.

He felt injured when he found that, not knowing their other friends in town, he had no invitation to accompany them, when those persons did their duty by their country acquaintances, and asked them, one to dinner, another—oh, happiness to Chatty—to a dance. But it did not turn out unmingled happiness for Chatty after all, though she got a new dress for it, in which she looked prettier (her mother thought, who was no flattering mother) than she had ever done in her life. Mrs. Warrender saw the awakening in Chatty's face which gave to her simple good looks a something higher, a touch of finer development; but the mother neither deceived herself as to the cause of this, nor was at all alarmed by it. Dick was a quite suitable match for Chatty; he was well connected, he was not poor, he was taking up his profession, if somewhat late, yet with good prospects. If there had been escapades in his youth, these were happily over, and as his wild oats had been sown on the other side of the Atlantic, no one knew anything about them. Why, then, should she be alarmed to see that Chatty opened like a flower to the rising of this light which in Dick, too, was so evident as to be unmistakable? In such circumstances as these the course of true love would be the better of a little obstacle or two; the only difficulty was that it might run too smooth. Mrs. Warrender thought that, perhaps, it was well to permit such a little fret in the current as this dance proved to be. She could have got Dick an invitation had she pleased, but was hard-hearted and refrained. And Chatty did not enjoy it. She said (with truth) that there was very little room for dancing; that to sit outside upon the stairs with a gentleman you didn't know, among a great many other girls and men whom you didn't know, was not her idea of a hall; and that if this was the London way, she liked a dance in the country much better. The time when she did enjoy it was next day, when she gave her impressions of it to Dick, who exulted as having not been there secretly over Mrs. Warrender, who would not have him asked. Chatty grew witty in the excitement of her little revenge on society, and on fate which had drifted her into that strange country, without the ever-ready aid to which she had grown accustomed of "some one she knew." "Yes, I danced," she said, "now and then, as much as we could. It was not Lady Ascot's fault, mamma; she introduced a great many gentlemen to me, but sometimes I could not catch their names, and when I did, how was I to remember which was Mr. Herbert and which was Mr. Sidney, when I had never seen either of them before? and gentlemen," she said, with a little glance (almost saucy: Chatty had developed so much) at Dick, "are so like each other in London."

At which Dick laughed, not without, gratification, with a secret consciousness that though this little arrow was apparently levelled at him, he was the exception to the rule, the one man who was recognisable in any crowd. "Yes," he said, "we should wear little labels with our names. I have heard that suggested before."

"They put down initials on my programme. I don't know what half of them mean: and I suppose they came and looked for me when the dance was going to begin, or perhaps in the middle of the dance, or towards the end; they didn't seem to be very particular," proceeded Chatty, with a certain exhilaration in the success of her description. "And how were they to find me among such a lot of girls? I saw two or three prowling about looking for me."

"And never made the smallest sign?"

"Oh, it is not the right thing for a girl to make any sign, is it, mamma? One can't say, Here I am! If they don't manage to find you, you must just put up with it, though you may see them prowling all the time. It is tiresome when you want very much to dance; but when you are indifferent——"

"The pleasures of society are all for the indifferent," said Dick; "everything comes to you, so the wise people say, when you don't care for it: but my brothers, who are dancing men, don't know how malicious ladies are, who make fun of their prowling. I shall remember it next time when I can't find my partner, and imagine her laughing at me in a corner."

"The amusement is after," said Chatty, with candour.

"I think it funny now when I think of it, but it seemed stupid at the time. I don't think I shall care to go to a dance in London again."

But as she said these words there escaped a mutual glance from two pairs of eyes, one of which said in the twitching of an eyelash, "Unless I am there!" while the other, taken unawares, gave an answer in a soft flash, "Ah, if you were there!" But there was nothing said: and Mrs. Warrender, though full of observation, never noticed this telegraphic, or shall we say heliographic, communication at all.

This little hindrance only made them better friends. They made expeditions to Richmond, where Dick took the ladies out on the river; to Windsor and Eton, where Theo and he had both been to school. Long before now he had been told the secret about Theo, which in the meantime had become less and less of a secret, though even now it was not formally made known. Lady Markland! Dick had been startled by the news, though he declared afterwards that he could not tell why: for that it was the most natural thing in the world. Had not they been thrown together in all kinds of ways; had not Theo been inevitably brought into her society, almost compelled to see her constantly?

"The compulsion was of his own making," Mrs. Warrender said. "Perhaps Lady Markland, with more experience, should have perceived what it was leading to."

"It is so difficult to tell what anything is leading to, especially in such matters. What may be but a mutual attraction one day becomes a bond that never can be broken the next."

Dick's voice changed while he was speaking. Perhaps he was not aware himself of the additional gravity in it, but his audience was instantly aware of it. That was the evening they had gone to Richmond; the softest summer evening, twilight just falling; Chatty, very silent, absorbed (as appeared) in the responsibilities of steering; the conversation going on entirely between her mother and Dick, who sat facing them, pulling long, slow, meditative strokes. Even when one is absorbed by the responsibilities of the steerage, one can enter into all the lights and shades of a conversation kept up by two other people, almost better than they can do themselves.

"That is true in some cases. Not in Theo's, I think. It seems to me that he gave himself over from the first. I am not sure that I think her a very attractive woman."

"Oh yes, mamma!" from Chatty, in an undertone.

"I am not talking of looks. She has a good deal of power about her, she will not be easily swayed; and after having suffered a great deal in her first marriage I think she has very quickly developed the power of acting for herself which some women never attain."

"So much the better," said Dick. "Theo doesn't want a puppet of a wife."

"But he wants a wife who will give in to him," said Mrs. Warrender slightly shaking her head.

"I suppose we all do that, in theory: then glide into domestic servitude and like it, and find it the best for us."

"Let us hope you will do that," she said, with a smile; "but not Theo, I fear. He has been used to be made much of. The only boy, they say, is always spoiled. You have brothers, Mr. Cavendish,— and he has a temper which is a little difficult."

"Oh, mamma," from Chatty again. "Theo is always kind."

"That does not make much difference, my dear. When a young man is accustomed to be given in to, it is easy to be kind. But when he meets for the first time one who will not give in, who will hold her own—I do not blame her for that: she is in a different position from a young girl."

"And how is it all to be settled?" asked Dick; "where are they to live? how about the child?"

"All these questions make my heart sink. He is not in the least prepared to meet them. Her name even; she will of course keep her name."

"That always seems a little absurd; that a woman should

keep her own name, as they do more or less everywhere but in England—yes; well, a Frenchwoman says *née* So-and-so; an Italian does something still more distinct than that, I am not quite clear how she does it. That's quite reasonable I think: for why should she wipe out her own individuality altogether when she marries? But to keep one husband's name when you are married to another——"

"It is because of the charm of the title. I suppose when a woman has been once called my lady, she objects to come down from those heights. But I think if I were a man, I should not like it, and Theo will not like it. At the same time there is her son, you know, to be considered. I don't like complications in marriages. They bring enough trouble without that."

"Trouble!" said Dick, in a tone of lively protest, which was a little fictitious. And Chatty, though she did not say anything, gave her mother a glance.

"Yes, trouble. It breaks as many ties as it makes. How much shall I see of Theo, do you think, when this marriage takes place? and yet by nature you would say I had some right to him. Oh, I do not complain. It is the course of nature. And Minnie is gone; she is entering into all the interests of the Thynnes, by this time: and a most bigoted Thynne she will be, if there are any special opinions in the family. I don't know them well enough to know. Fancy giving up one's child to become bigoted to another family, whom one doesn't even know!"

"It seems a little hard, certainly. The ordinary view is that mothers are happy when their daughters marry."

"Which is also true in its way: for the mother has a way of being older than her daughter, Mr. Cavendish, and knows she cannot live for ever; beside, marriage being the best thing for a woman, as most people think, it should be the mother's duty to do everything she can to secure it for her daughter. Yes, I go as far as that—in words," Mrs. Warrender added, with a little laugh.

"But not for her son?"

"I don't say that: no, not at all. I should rejoice in Theo's marriage, but for the complications, which I think he is not the right person to get through, with comfort. You, now, I think," she added, cheerfully, "might marry Lady——Anybody, with a family of children, and make it succeed."

"Thank you very much for the compliment. I don't mean to try that mode of success," he said quickly.

"Neither did Theo mean it until he was brought in contact with Lady Markland: and who can tell but you too—Oh yes, marriage almost always makes trouble; it breaks as well as unites; it is very serious; it is like the measles when it gets into a family." Mrs. Warrender felt that the conversation was getting much too significant, and broke off with a laugh. "The evening is delightful, but I think we should turn homewards. It will be quite late before we get back to town."

Dick obeyed without the protest he would have made half an hour before. He resumed the talk when he was walking up with the ladies to the hotel, where they had left their carriage. "One laughs, I don't know why," he said, "but it is very serious in a number of ways. A man when he is in love doesn't ask himself whether he's the sort of man to make a girl happy. There are some things, you know, which a man has to give up too. Generally, if he hesitates, it seems a sort of treason; and often he cannot tell the reason why. Now Theo will have a number of sacrifices to make."

"He is like Jacob, he will think nothing of them for the love he bears to Rachel," said Theo's mother. "I wish that were all."

"But I wish I could make you see it from a man's point of view." Dick did not himself know what he meant by this confused speech. He wanted to make some sort of plea for himself, but how, or in what words, he did not know. She paused for a moment expecting more, and Chatty, on the other side of her mother, felt a little puncture of pain, she could scarcely tell why. "There are some things which a man has to give up too." What did he mean by that? A little vague offence which flew away, a little pain which did not, a sort of needle point, which she kept feeling all the rest of the evening, came to Chatty from this conversation. And Mrs. Warrender paused, thinking he was going to say more. But he said no more, and when he had handed them into the carriage, broke out into an entirely new subject, and was very gay and amusing all the way home.

The two ladies did not say a syllable to each other on this subject, neither had they said anything to each other about Dick, generally, except that he was very nice, that it was kind of him to take so much trouble, and so forth. Whether experienced mothers do discuss with their daughters what So-and-so meant, or whether he meant anything, as Dick supposed, is a question I am not prepared to enter into. But Mrs. Warrender had said nothing to Chatty on the subject, and did not now: though it cannot be said that she did not ponder it much in her heart.

CHAPTER XXXII.

The ladies were in town three weeks, which brought them from June into July, when London began to grow hot and dusty, and the season to approach its close. They were just about to leave town, though whether to continue their dissipations by going to the seaside, or to return to Highcombe and put their future residence in order, they had not as yet made up their minds. Cavendish gave his vote for the seaside. "Of course you mean to consult me, and give great weight to my opinion," he said. "What I advise is the sea, and I will tell you why: I am obliged to go to Portsmouth about some business. If you were at the Isle of Wight, say, or Southsea——"

"That would be very pleasant: but we must not allow ourselves to be tempted, not even by your company," said Mrs. Warrender, who began to fear there might be enough of this. "We are going home to set our house in order, and to see if, perhaps, Theo has need of us. And then the Thynnes are coming home."

"Is it Miss Warrender who has developed into the Thynnes?"

"Indeed it is; that is how everybody inquires for her now. I have got quite used to the name. That is one of the drawbacks of marrying one's daughters, which I was telling you of. One's Minnie becomes in a moment the Eustace Thynnes!"

They were not a smiling party that evening, and Mrs. Warrender's little pleasantry fell flat. It flew, perhaps, across the mind of all, that Chatty might be changed, in a similar way, into the Cavendishes. Dick grew hot and cold when the suggestion flashed through him. Then it was that he recollected how guilty he had been, and how little his reflections had served him. He who had determined to call but once, to go with them once to the play, had carried out his resolution so far that the once had been always. And now the time of recompense was coming. The fool's paradise was to be emptied of its tenants. He went away very gloomy, asking himself many troubled questions. It was not that he had been unaware, as time went on, what it was that went along with it,—a whole little drama of simple pleasure, of days and evenings spent together, of talks and expeditions. Innocent? Ah, more than innocent, the best and sweetest thing in his life, if—— But that little monosyllable makes all the difference. It was coming to an end now, they were going away; and Dick had to let them go, without any conclusion to this pretty play in which he had played his part so successfully. Oh, he was not the first man who had done it! not the first who had worn a lover's looks and used all a lover's assiduities, and then—nothing more. Perhaps that was one of the worst features in his behaviour to himself. To think that he should be classed with the men who are said to have been amusing themselves! and Chatty placed in the position of the victim, on whose behalf people were sorry or indignant! When he thought that there were some who might presume to pity her, and who would say of himself that he had behaved ill, the shock came upon him with as much force as if he had never thought of it before; although he had thought of it, and reflected upon how to draw out of the intercourse which was so pleasant, before he gave himself up to it, with an abandon which he could not account for, which seemed now like desperation. Desperation was no excuse. He saw the guilt of it fully, without self-deception, only when he had done all the harm that was possible, had yielded to every temptation, and now found it impossible to go any further. To repent in these circumstances is not uncommon; there is nothing original in it. Thousands of men have done it before him,—repented when they could sin no more. For a moment it flashed across his mind to go and throw himself on Mrs. Warrender's mercy and tell her all, and make what miserable excuse he could for himself. Was it better to do that, to part for ever from Chatty, or to let them think badly of him, to have it supposed that he had trifled or amused himself, or whatever miserable words the gossips chose to use, and yet leave a door open by which he might some time, perhaps, approach her again? Some time! after she had forgotten him, after his unworthiness had been proved to her, and some other fellow, some happier man who had never been exposed to such a fate as had fallen upon him, some smug Pharisee (this fling at the supposed rival of the future was very natural and harmed nobody) had cut him out of all place in her heart! It was so likely that Chatty would go on waiting for him, thinking of him, for years perhaps, the coxcomb that he was!

"I said very suddenly that we must go home," said Mrs. Warrender, after he had left them. "You did not think me hard, Chatty? It seemed to me the best."

"Oh no, mamma," said Chatty, with a slight faltering.

"We have seen a great deal of Mr. Cavendish, and he has been very nice, but I did not like the idea of going to the Isle of Wight."

"Oh no, mamma," Chatty repeated, with more firmness. "I did not wish it at all."

"I am very glad you think with me, my dear. He has been very nice; he has made us enjoy our time in town much more than we should have done. But of course, that cannot last for ever, and I do really think now that we should go home."

"I have always thought so," said Chatty. She was rather pale, and there was a sort of new-born dignity about her, with which her mother felt that she was unacquainted. "It has been very pleasant, but I am quite ready. And then Minnie will be coming back as you said."

"Yes." Then Mrs. Warrender burst into a laugh which might as well have been a fit of crying. "But you must prepare yourself to see not Minnie, but the Eustace Thynnes," she said. And then the mother and daughter kissed each other and retired to their respective rooms, where Chatty was a long time going to bed. She sat and thought, with her pretty hair about her shoulders, going over a great many things, recalling a great many simple little scenes and words said,—which were but words after all,—

and then of a sudden the tears came, and she sat and cried very quietly, even in her solitude making as little fuss as possible, with an ache of wonder at the trouble that had come upon her, and a keen pang of shame at the thought that she had expected more than was coming, more perhaps than had ever been intended. A man is not ashamed of loving when he is not loved, however angry he may be with himself or the woman who has beguiled him; but the sharpest smart in a girl's heart is the shame of having given what was not asked for, what was not wanted. When those tears had relieved her heart, Chatty put up her hair very neatly for the night, just as she always did, and after a while slept,— much better than Dick.

He came next day, however, for a final visit, and the day after to see them away, without any apparent breach in the confidence and friendship with which they regarded each other. There might be, perhaps, a faint almost imperceptible difference in Chatty, a little dignity like that which her mother had discovered in her, something that was not altogether the simple girl, younger than her years, whom Mrs. Warrender had brought to town. On the very last morning of all, Dick had also a look which was not very easy to be interpreted. While they were on their way to the station he began suddenly to talk of Underwood and the Wilberforces, as if he had forgotten them all this time, and now suddenly remembered that there were such people in the world. "Did I ever tell you," he said, "that one of the houses in the parish belongs to an uncle of mine, who bought it merely as an investment, and let it?"

"We were talking of that," said Mrs. Warrender. "Mr. Wilberforce hoped you had persuaded your uncle to leave the drainage alone in order to make a nuisance and drive undesirable tenants away."

He laughed in a hurried, breathless way, then said quickly, "Is it true that the people who were there are gone?"

"Quite true. They seem to have melted away without any one knowing, in a single night They were not desirable people."

"So I heard; and gone without leaving any sign?"

"Have they not paid their rent?" said Mrs. Warrender.

"Oh, I don't mean to say that. I know nothing about that. My uncle——" and here he stopped, with an embarrassment which, though Mrs. Warrender was an unsuspicious woman, attracted her notice. "I mean," said Cavendish, perceiving this, and putting force upon himself, "he will of course be glad to get rid of people who apparently could do his property no good."

And after this his spirits seemed to rise a little. He told them that he had some friends near Highcombe, who sometimes in the autumn offered him a few days' shooting. If he got such an invitation this autumn might he come? "It is quite a handy distance from London, just the Saturday-to-Monday distance," he added, looking at Mrs. Warrender with an expression which meant a great deal, which had in it a question, a supplication. And she was so imprudent a woman! and no shadow of Minnie at hand to restrain her. It was on her very lips to give the invitation he asked. Some good angel of a class corresponding in the celestial world to that of Minnie in this, only stopped her in time, and gave a little obliqueness to the response.

"I hope we shall see you often," she said, which was pleasant but discouraging, and then began to talk about the Eustace Thynnes, who were at present of great use to her as a diversion to any more embarrassing subject of conversation. Chatty scarcely spoke during this drive, which seemed to her the last they should take together. The streets flying behind them, the scenes of the brief drama falling back into distance, the tranquillity of home before, and all this exciting episode of life becoming as if it had never been, occupied her mind. She had settled all that in her evening meditation. It was all over; this was what she said to herself. She must not allow even to her own heart any thought of renewal, any idea that the break was temporary. Chatty was aware that she had received all his overtures, all his amiabilities (which was what it seemed to come to) with great and unconcealed pleasure. To think that he had nothing but civility in his mind all the time gave a blow to her pride, which was mortal. She did not wear her pride upon her sleeve, though she had worn her heart upon it. Her nature indeed was full of the truest humility; but there was a latent pride which, when it was reached, vibrated through all her being. No more, she was saying to herself. Oh, never more. She had been deceived, though most likely he had never wished to deceive her. It was she who had deceived herself; but that was not possible, ever again.

"We have not thanked you half enough," said Mrs. Warrender, as he stood at the door of the railway carriage. "I will tell Theo that you have been everything to us. If you are as good to all the mothers and sisters of all your old schoolfellows——"

"You do me a great wrong," he said, "as if I thought of you as the mother of——" His eyes strayed to Chatty, who met them with a smile which was quite steady. She was a little pale, but that was all. "Some time," he added hastily, holding Mrs. Warrender's hand, "I may be able to explain myself a little better than that."

"Shall I say if you are as kind to all forlorn ladies astray in London?"

Dick's face clouded over as if (she thought) he were about to cry. Men don't cry in England, but there is a kind of mortification, humiliation, a sense of being persistently misunderstood, and of having no possibility of mending matters, which is so insupportable that the lip must quiver under it, even when garnished with a moustache. "I hope you don't really think that of me," he cried. "Don't! there is no time to tell you how very different—But surely you know—something more than that——"

The train was in motion already and Chatty had shaken hands with him before. She received the last look of his eyes, half indignant, appealing, though in words it was to her mother he was speaking; but made no sign. And it was only Mrs. Warrender who looked out of the window and waved her hand to him, as he was left behind. Chatty—Chatty who was so gentle, so little apt to take anything upon her, even to judge for herself, was it possible that on this point she was less soft-hearted than her mother? This thought went through him like an arrow as he stood and saw the carriages glide away in a long curving line. She was gone and he was left behind. She was gone, was it in resentment, was it in disdain? thinking of him in his true aspect as a false lover, believing him to have worn a false semblance, justly despising him for an attempt to play upon her. Was this possible? He thought (with that oblique sort of literary tendency of his) of Hamlet with the recorder. Can you play upon this pipe?—and yet you think you can play upon me! As a matter of fact there could nothing have been found in heaven or earth less like Hamlet than Chatty Warrender; but a lover has strange misperceptions. The steady soft glance, the faint smile, not like the usual warm beaming of her simple face, seemed to him to express a faculty of seeing through and through him which is not always given to the greatest philosophers. And he stood there humiliated to the very dust by this mild creature, whom he had loved in spite of himself, to whom even in loving her he had attributed no higher gifts, perhaps had even been tenderly disrespectful of as not clever. Was she the one to see through him now?

If she only knew! but when Dick, feeling sadly injured and wounded, came to this thought, it so stung him that he turned round on the moment, and, neglecting all the seductions of waiting cabmen, walked quickly, furiously, to Lincoln's Inn, which he had been sadly neglecting. If she knew everything! it appeared to Dick that Chatty's clear dove's eyes (to which he all at once had attributed an insight and perception altogether above them) would slay him with the disdainful dart which pierces through and through subterfuge and falsehood. That he should have ventured, knowing what he knew, to approach her at all with the semblance of love: that he should have dared,—oh, he knew, well he knew, how, once the light of clear truth was let down upon it, his conduct would appear,—not the mere trifler who had amused himself and meant no more, not the fool of society, who made a woman think he loved her, and "behaved badly," and left her *planté là*. What were these contemptible images to the truth! He shrank into himself as he pursued these thoughts and skulked along. He felt like a man exposed and ashamed, a man whom true men would avoid. "Put in every honest hand a whip,"—ah no, that was not wanted. Chatty's eyes, dove's eyes, too gentle to wound, eyes that knew not how to look unkindly, to conceal a sentiment, to veil a falsehood—one look from Chatty's eyes would be enough.

Chatty knew nothing of the tragic terror which had come upon him at the mere apprehension of this look of hers. She had no thought of any tragedy, except that unknown to men which often becomes the central fact in a life such as hers; the tragedy of an unfinished chapter in life, the no-ending of an episode which had promised to be the drama in which almost every human creature figures herself (or himself) as the chief actor, one time or other. The drama indeed had existed, it had run almost all its course, for the time it lasted it had been more absorbing than anything else in the world. The greatest historical events beside it had been but secondary. Big London, the greatest city in the world, had served only as a little bosquet of evergreens in a village garden might have done, as the background and scene for it. But it had no end; the time of the action was accomplished, the curtain had fallen, and the lights had been put out, but the comedy had come to no conclusion. Comedy-tragedy; it does not matter much which words you use. The scenes had all died away in incompleteness, and there had been no end. To many a gentle life such as that of Chatty might be, this is all that ever happens beyond the level of the ordinary and common. It was with a touch of insight altogether beyond her usual intellectual capacity that she realised this as she travelled very quietly with her mother from London to Highcombe, not a very long way. Mrs. Warrender was very silent too. She had meant the visit to town to be one of pleasure merely,—pleasure for herself, change after the long monotony, and pleasure to her child who had never known anything but that monotony. It was not, this little epoch of time only three weeks long, to count for anything. It was to be a holiday and no more. And lo! with that inexplicableness, that unforeseenness which is so curious a quality of human life, it had become a turning point of existence, the pivot perhaps upon which Chatty's being might hang. Mrs. Warrender was not so decided as Chatty. She saw nothing final in the parting. She was able to imagine that secondary causes, something about money, some family arrangements that would have to be made, had prevented any further step on Dick's part. To her the drama indeed was not ended: the curtain had only fallen legitimately upon the first act without prejudice to those which were to follow. She did not talk, for Chatty's silence, her unusual dignity, her retirement into herself, had produced a great effect upon her mother; but her mind was not moved as Chatty's was, and she was able to think with pleasure of the new home awaiting them, and of what they were to find there. The Eustace Thynnes! she said to herself, with a laugh, thanking Providence within herself that there had been no Minnie to inspect the progress of the relations between Dick and Chatty, and probably to deliver her opinion very freely on that subject and on her mother's responsibility. Then there was the more serious chapter of Theo and his affairs which must have progressed in the meantime. Mrs. Warrender caught herself up with a little fright as she thought of the agitation and doubt which wrapped the future of both her children. It was a wonderful relief to turn to the only point from which there was any amusement to be had, the visit of the Eustace Thynnes.

CHAPTER XXXIII.

The return of the Warrenders to their home was not the usual calm delight of settling again into one's well-known place. The house at Highcombe was altogether new to their experiences, and meant a life in every way different, as well as different surroundings. It was a tall red brick house, with a flight of steps up to the door, and lines of small, straight, twinkling windows facing immediately into the street, between which and the house there was no interval even of a grass plot or area. The garden extended to the right with a long stretch of high wall, but the house had been built at a period when people had less objection to a street than in later times. The rooms within were of a good size but not very high; some of them were panelled to the ceiling with an old-fashioned idea of comfort and warmth. The drawing-room was one of these, a large oblong room to the front with a smaller one divided from it by folding-doors, which looked out upon the garden. It possessed, as its great distinction, a pretty marble mantelpiece, which some one of a previous generation had brought from Italy. It is sad to be obliged to confess that the panelling here had been painted, a warm white, like the colour of a French salon, with old and dim pictures of no particular merit let in here and there,—pictures which would have been more in keeping with the oak of the original than with the present colour of the walls. The house had been built by a Warrender, in the end of the seventeenth century, and though it had been occupied by strangers often, and let to all sorts of people, a considerable amount of the furniture, and all the decorations, still belonged to that period. The time had not come for the due appreciation of these relics of ancestral taste. Chatty thought them all old-fashioned, and would gladly have replaced them by fresh chairs and tables from the upholsterers: but this was an expense not to be thought of, and, perhaps, even to eyes untrained in any rules of art, there was something harmonious in the combination. Something harmonious, too, with Chatty's feelings was in the air of old tranquillity and long established use and wont. The stillness of the house was as the stillness of ages. Human creatures had come and gone, as the days went and came, sunshine coming in at one moment, darkness falling the next, nothing altering the calm routine, the established order. Pains and fevers and heartbreaks, and death itself, would disappear and leave no sign, and all remain the same in the quaint rose-scented room. The quiet overawed Chatty, and yet was congenial. She felt herself to have come "home" to it, with all illusions over. It was not just an ordinary coming back after a holiday,—it was a return, a settling down for life.

It would be difficult to explain how it was that this conviction had taken hold of her so strongly. It was but a month since she had left the Warren with her mother, with some gentle anticipations of pleasure, but none that were exaggerated or excessive. All that was likely to happen, as far as she knew, was that dinner party at Mrs. Benson's, and a play or two, and a problematical hall. This was all that the "vortex" meant about which her mother had laughed; she had not any idea at that time that the vortex would mean Dick Cavendish. But now that she fully understood what it meant, and now that it was all over, and her agitated little bark had come out of it, and had got upon the smooth calm waters again, there had come to Chatty a very different conception both of the present and the past. All the old quiet routine of existence seemed to her now a preface to that moment of real life. She had been working up to it vaguely without knowing it. And now it had ended, and this was the Afterwards. She had come back— after. These words had to her an absolute meaning. Perhaps it was want of imagination which made it so impossible for her to carry forward her thoughts to any possible repetition, any sequel of what had been; or perhaps some communication, unspoken, unintended, from the mind of Cavendish had affected hers and given a certainty of conclusion, of the impossibility of further development. However that might be, her mind was entirely made up on this subject. She had lived (for three weeks), and it was over. And now existence was all Afterwards. She found scarcely any time for her habitual occupations while she was in London, but now there would be time for everything. Afterwards is long, when one is only twenty-four, and it requires a great deal of muslin work and benevolence to fill it up in a way that will be satisfactory to the soul; but still, to ladies in the country it is a very well known state, and has to be faced, and lived through all the same. To a great many people life is all afternoon, though not in the sense imagined by the poet: not the lotus-eating drowsiness and content, but a course of little hours that lead to nothing, that have no particular motive except that mild duty which means doing enough trimming for your new set of petticoats and carrying a pudding or a little port wine to the poor girl who is in a consumption in the lane behind your house. This was the Afterwards of Chatty's time, and she settled down to it, knowing it to be the course of nature. Nowadays, matters have improved: there is always lawn tennis and often ambulance lectures, and far more active parish work. But even in those passive days it could be supported, and Chatty made up her mind to it with a great, but silent courage. But it made her very quiet, she who was quiet by nature. The land where it is always afternoon chills at first and subdues all lively sentiments. The sense of having no particular interest, took possession of her mind as if it had been an absorbing interest, and drew a veil between her and the other concerns of life.

This was not at all the case with Mrs. Warrender, who came home with all the agreeable sensations of a new beginning, ready to take up new lines of existence, and to make a cheerful centre of life for herself and all who surrounded her. If any woman should feel with justice that she has reached the Afterwards, and has done with her active career, it should be the woman who has just settled down after her husband's death to the humbler house provided for her widowhood apart from all her old occupations and responsibilities. But in reality there was no such sentiment in her mind. "You'll in your girls again be courted." She had hanging about her the pleasant reflection of that wooing, never put into words, with which Dick Cavendish had filled the atmosphere, and which had produced upon the chief object of it so very different an effect; and she had the less pleasurable excitement of Theo's circumstances, and of all that was going on at Markland, a romance in which her interest was almost painful, to stimulate her thoughts. The Eustace Thynnes did not count for much, for their love-making had been very mild and regular, but still, perhaps, they aided in the general quickening of life. She had three different histories thus going on around her, and she was placed in a new atmosphere, in which she had to play a part of her own. When Chatty and she sat down together in the new drawing-room for the first time with their work and their plans, Mrs. Warrender's talk was of their new neighbours and the capabilities of the place. "The rector is not a stupid man," she said, in a reflective tone. The proposition was one which gently startled Chatty. She lifted her mild eyes from her work, with a surprised look.

"It would be very sad for us if he was stupid," she said.

"And Mrs. Barham still less so. What I am thinking of is society, not edification. Then there is Colonel Travers, whom we used to see occasionally at home, the brother, you know, of ——. An old soldier is always a pleasant element in a little place. The majority will of course be women like ourselves, Chatty."

"Yes, mamma, there are always a great many ladies about Highcombe."

Mrs. Warrender gave forth a little sigh. "In a country neighbourhood we swamp everything," she said; "it is a pity. Too many people of one class are always monotonous: but we must struggle against it, Chatty."

"Dear mamma, isn't ladies' society the best for us? Minnie

always said so. She said it was a dreadful thing for a girl to think of gentlemen."

"Minnie always was an oracle. To think of gentlemen whom you were likely to fall in love with, and marry, perhaps—but I don't think there are many of that class here."

"Oh no," said Chatty, returning to her work, "at least I hope not."

"I am not at all of your opinion, my dear. I should like a number of them; and nice girls too. I should not wish to keep all these dangerous personages for you."

"Mamma!" said Chatty, with a soft reproachful glance. It seemed a desecration to her to think that ever again—that ever another——

"That gives a little zest to all the middle-aged talks. It amuses other people to see a little romance going on. You were always rather shocked at your light-minded mother, Chatty."

"Mamma! it might be perhaps very sad for—for those most concerned, though it amused you."

"I hope not, my darling. You take things too seriously. There is, to be sure, a painful story now and then, but very rarely. You must not think that men are deceivers ever, as the song says."

"Oh no," said Chatty, elevating her head with simple pride, though without meeting her mother's eyes, "that is not what I would say. But why talk of such things at all? why put romances, as you call them, into people's heads? People may be kind and friendly without anything more."

Mrs. Warrender here paused to study the gentle countenance which was half hidden from her, bending over the muslin work, and for the first time gained a little glimpse into what was going on in Chatty's heart. The mother had long known that her own being was an undiscovered country for her children; but it was new to her and a startling discovery that perhaps this innocent creature, so close to her, had also a little sanctuary of her own, into which the eyes most near to her had never looked. She marked the little signs of meaning quite unusual to her composed and gentle child—the slight quiver which was in Chatty's bent head, the determined devotion to her work which kept her face unseen—with a curious confusion in her mind. She had felt sure that Dick Cavendish had made a difference in life to Chatty; but she had not thought of this in any but a hopeful and cheerful way. She was more startled now than she dared say. Had there been any explanation between them which she had not been told of? Was there any obstacle she did not know? Her mind was thrown into great bewilderment, too great to permit of any exercise of her judgment suddenly upon the little mystery—if mystery there was.

"I did not mean to enter into such deep questions," she said, in a tone which she felt to be apologetic. "I meant only a little society to keep us going. Though we did not go out very much in London, still there was just enough to make the blank more evident if we see nobody here."

Chatty's heart protested against this view: for her part she would have liked that life which had lasted three weeks to remain as it was, unlike anything else in her experience, a thing which was over, and could return no more. Had she not been saying to herself that all that remained to her was the Afterwards, the long gray twilight upon which no other sun would rise? In her lack of imagination, the only imagination she had known became more absolute than any reality, a thing which once left behind would never be renewed again. She felt a certain scorn of the attempt to make feeble imitations of it, or even to make up for that light which never was on sea or shore, by any little artificial illuminations. A sort of gentle fury, a wild passion of resistance, rose within her at the thought of making up for it. She did not wish to make up for it: the blank could not be made less evident whatever any one might do or say. But all this Chatty shut up in her own heart. She made no reply, but bent her head more and more over her muslin work, and worked faster and faster, with the tears collecting, which she never would consent to shed, hot and salt behind her eyes.

Mrs. Warrender was silent too. She was confounded by the new phase of feeling, imperfectly revealed to her, and filled with wonder, and self-reproach, and sympathy. Had she been to blame to leave her child exposed to an influence which had proved too much for her peace of mind?—that was the well-worn conventional phrase, and it was the only one that seemed to answer the occasion, too much for her peace of mind! The mother, casting stealthy glances at her daughter, so sedulously, nervously busy, could only grope at a comprehension of what was in Chatty's mind. She thought it was the uncertainty, the excitement of suspense, and all that feverish commotion which sometimes arises in a woman's mind when the romance of her life comes to a sudden pause and silence follows the constant interchange of words and looks, and the doubt whether anything more will ever follow, or whether the pause is to be for ever, turns all the sweeter meditations into a whirl of confusion and anxiety and shame. A mother is so near that the reflection of her child's sentiments gets into her mind, but very often with such prismatic changes, and oblique catchings of the light, that even sympathy goes wrong. Mrs. Warrender thus caught from Chatty the representation of an agitated soul in which there was all the sensitive shame of a love that is given unsought, mingled with a tender indignation against the offender who perhaps had never meant—But the mother on this point took a different view, and there rose up in her mind on the moment, a hundred cheerful, hopeful plans to bring him back and to set all right. Naturally there was not a word said on the subject, which was far too delicate for words; but this was how Mrs. Warrender followed, as she believed, with an intensity which was full of tenderness, the current of her daughter's thoughts.

And yet these were not Chatty's thoughts at all. If she felt any excitement it was against those plans for cheering her, and the idea that any little contrivances of society could ever take the place of what was past—conjoined with a sort of jealousy of that past, lest any one should interfere with it, or attempt to blur the perfect outline of it as a thing which had been, and could be no more, nor any copy of it. This was what the soul most near her own did not divine. They sat together in the silence of the summer parlour, the cool sweet room full of flowers, with the July sun shut out, but the warm air coming in, so full of mutual love and sympathy, and yet with but so disturbed and confused an apprehension each of each. After some time had passed thus, without any disturbance, nothing but the softened sounds of morning traffic in the quiet street, a slow cart passing, an occasional carriage, the voices of the children just freed from school, there came the quick sound of a horse's hoofs, a pause before the door, and then the bell echoing into the silence of the house.

"That must be Theo," cried Mrs. Warrender. "I was sure he would come to-day. Chatty, after luncheon, will you leave us a little, my dear? Not that we have any secrets from you: but he will speak more freely, if he is alone with me."

"I should have known that, mamma, without being told."

"Dear Chatty, you must not be displeased. You know many things more than I had ever thought."

"Displeased, mamma!"

"Hush, Chatty, here is my poor boy."

Her poor boy! the triumphant lover, the young man at the height of his joy and pride. They both rose to meet him, eager, watching to take the tone which should be most in harmony with his. But Mrs. Warrender had a pity in her heart for Theo which she did not feel for Chatty—perhaps because in her daughter's case her sympathy was more complete.

CHAPTER XXXIV.

Warrender met his mother and sister with a face somewhat cloudy, which, however, he did his best to clear as he came in, in response to their pleasure at the sight of him. It did not become him in his position to look otherwise than blessed: but a man has less power of recognising and adapting himself to this necessity than a woman. He did his best, however, to take an interest in the house, to have all its conveniencies pointed out to him, and the beauty of the view over the garden, and the coolness of the drawing-room in which they sat. What pleased him still more, however, or at least called forth a warmer response, was the discovery of some inconveniencies which had already been remarked. "I am very glad you told me," he said. "I must have everything put right for you, mother. A thing that can be put right by bricks and mortar is so easy a matter."

"It is the easiest way, perhaps, of setting things right," she said, not without an anxious glance; "but even bricks and mortar are apt to lead you further than you think. You remember Mr. Briggs, in *Punch*?"

"They will not lead me too far," said Theo. "I am all in the way of renovation and restoration. You should see—or rather, you should not see, for I am afraid you would be shocked—our own house——"

"What are you doing? No, I should not be shocked. I never was a devotee of the Warren. I always thought there were a great many improvements I could make."

"Oh, mamma!"

"You must remember, Chatty, I was not born to it, like you. What are you doing? Are you building? Your letters are not very explicit, my dear."

"You shall see. I cannot describe. I have not the gift." Here the cloud came again over Theo's face, the cloud which he had pushed back on his entrance as if it had been a veil. "We have let in a little light at all events," he said, "that will always be something to the good. Now, mother, let me have some lunch; for I cannot stay above an hour or so. I have to see Longstaffe. There has been a great deal to do."

"Mr. Longstaffe, I am sure, will not give you any trouble that he can help."

"He is giving me a great deal of trouble," said the young man, with lowering brows. Then he cleared up again with an effort. "You have not told me anything about your doings in town."

"Oh, we did a great deal in town." Here Mrs. Warrender paused for a moment, feeling that neither did the auditor care to hear, nor the person concerned in those doings care to have them told. Between these two, her words were arrested. Chatty's head was more than ever bent over her muslin, and Theo had walked to the window, and was looking out with the air of a man whose thoughts were miles away. No one said anything more for a full minute, when he suddenly came back, so to speak, and said, with a sort of smile:—

"So you were very gay?" as if in the meantime she had been pouring forth an account of many gaieties into his ear. So far as Theo was concerned, it was evidently quite unnecessary to say any more, but there was now the other silent listener to think of, who desired that not a word should be said, yet would be equally keen to note and put a meaning to the absence of remark. Between the two, the part of Mrs. Warrender was a hard one. She said, which, perhaps, was the last thing she ought to have said: "We saw a great deal of your friend Mr. Cavendish."

"Ah, Dick! yes, he's about town I suppose—pretending to do law, and doing society. Mother, if you want me to stay to luncheon——"

"I will go and see after it," said Chatty. She gave her mother a look, as she put down her work. A look—what did it mean, a reproach for having mentioned him? an entreaty to ask more about him? Mrs. Warrender could not tell. When they were left alone, her son's restlessness increased. He felt, it was evident, the dangers of being left with her *tête-à-tête*.

"I hope you didn't see too much of him," he said hastily, as if picking up something to defend himself. "Cavendish is a fellow with a story, and no one knows exactly what it is."

"I am sure he is honourable and good," said Mrs. Warrender, and then she cried, "Theo! don't keep me in this suspense—there is something amiss."

He came at once, and sat down opposite to her, gazing at her across the little table. "Yes," he said with defiance, "you have made up your mind to that beforehand. I could see it in your eyes. What should be amiss?"

"Theo, you do me wrong. I had made up my mind to nothing beforehand—but I am very anxious. I know there must be difficulties. What are your negotiations with Mr. Longstaffe? Is it about settlements?—is it——"

"Longstaffe is an old fool, mother: that is about what it is."

"No, my dear. I am sure he is a kind friend, who has your interests at heart."

"Whose interests?" he said, with a harsh laugh. "You must remember there are two sides to the question. I should say that the interests of a husband and wife were identical, but that is not the view taken by those wretched little pettifogging country lawyers."

"Dear Theo, it is never, I believe, the view taken by the law. They have to provide against the possibility of everything that is bad—they must suppose that it is possible for every man to turn out a domestic tyrant."

"Every man!" he said, with a smile of scorn: "do you think I should be careful about that? They may bind me down as much as they please. I have held out my hands to them ready for the fetters. What I do grudge," he went on, as if, the floodgates once opened, the stream could not be restrained, "is all that they are trying to impose upon her, giving her the appearance of feelings entirely contrary to her nature—making her out to be under the sway of—— That's what I can't tolerate. If I knew her less, I might imagine—but thank God, I am sure on that point," he added, with a sharpness in his voice which did not breathe conviction to his mother's ear.

She laid her hand upon his arm, soothing him. "You must remember, that in the circumstances a woman is not her own mistress. Oh, Theo, that was always the difficulty I feared. You are so sensitive, so ready to start aside like a restive horse, so intolerant of anything that seems less than perfect."

"Am I so, mother?" He gathered her hand into his, and laid down his head upon it, kissing it tremulously. "God bless you for saying so. My own mother says it—a fastidious fool, always looking out for faults, putting meanings to everything—starting at a touch, like a restive horse."

How it was that she understood him, and perceived that to put his faults in the clearest light was the best thing she could do for him, it would be hard to tell. She laid her other hand upon his bent head. "Yes, my dear, yes, my dear! that was always your fault. If your taste was offended, if anything jarred—though it might be no more than was absolutely essential, no more than common necessity required."

"Mother, you do me more good than words can say. Yes, I know, I know—I never have friends for that cause. I have always wanted more, more——"

"More than any one could give," she said softly. "Those whom you love should be above humanity, Theo: their feet should not tread the ground at all. I have always been afraid, not knowing how you would take it when necessary commonplaces came in."

"I wonder," he said, raising his head, "whether mothers are always as perfect comforters as you are. That was what I wanted: but nobody in the world could have said it but you."

"Because," she said, carrying out her rôle unhesitatingly, though to her own surprise and without knowing why, "only your mother could know your faults, without there being the smallest possibility that any fault could ever stand between you and me."

His eyes had the look of being strained and hot, yet there seemed a little moisture in the corners, a moisture which corresponded with the slight quiver in his lip, rather than with the light in his eyes. He held her hand still in his and caressed it almost unconsciously. "I am not like you in that," he said. Alas no! he was not like her in that: though the accusation of being fastidious, fantastic, intolerant of the usual conditions of humanity, was, for the moment, the happiest thing that could be said to him, yet a fault! a fault would stand between him and whosoever was guilty of it, mother even—love still more. A fault: he was determined that she should be perfect, the woman whom he had chosen. To keep her perfect he was glad to seize at that suggestion of personal blame, to acknowledge that he himself was impatient of every condition, intolerant even of the bonds of humanity. But if there ever should arise the time when the goddess should be taken from her pedestal, when the woman should be found fallible like all women, heaven preserve poor Theo then. The thought went through Mrs. Warrender's mind like a knife. What would become of him? He had given himself up so unreservedly to his love, he had sacrificed his own fastidious temper in the first place, had borne the remarks of the county, had supported Geoff, had allowed himself to be laughed at and blamed. But now if he should chance to discover that the woman for whom he had done all this was not in herself a piece of perfection——His mother felt her very heart sink at the thought. No one was perfect enough to satisfy Theo; no one was perfect at all so far as her own experience went. And when he made this terrible discovery, what would he do?

In the meantime they went to luncheon, and there was talk of the repairs wanted in the house, and of what Theo was doing "at home." He was very unwilling, however, to speak of "home," or of what he had begun to do there. He told them indeed of the trees that had been cut down, over which Chatty made many exclamations, mourning for them; but even Chatty was not vigorous in her lamentations. They sat and talked, not interested in anything they were saying, the mother seated between them, watching each, herself scarcely able to keep up the thread of coherent conversation, making now and then incursions on either side from which she was obliged to retreat hurriedly; referring now to some London experience which Chatty's extreme dignity and silence showed she did not want to be mentioned, or to something on the other side from which Theo withdrew with still more distinct reluctance to be put under discussion. It was not till this uncomfortable meal was over that Theo made any further communication about his own affairs. He was on his way to the door, whither his mother had followed him, when he turned round as if accidentally. "By the bye," he said, "I forgot to tell you. *She* will be here presently, mother. She wanted to lose no time in seeing you."

"Lady Markland!" said Mrs. Warrender, with a little start.

He fixed his eyes upon her severely. "Who else? She is coming about three. I shall come back, and go home with her."

"Theo, before I meet your future wife—— You have never given me any details. Oh, tell me what has happened and what is going to happen. Don't leave me to meet her in ignorance of everything."

"What is it you want to know?" he said, with his sombre air, setting his back against the wall. "You know all that I know."

"Which is no more than that she has accepted you, Theo."

"Well, what more would you have? That is how it stands now, and may for months for anything I can tell."

"I should have thought it would have been better to get everything settled quickly. Why should there be any delay?"

"Ah, why? You must ask that of Mr. Longstaffe," he said, and turned away.

Mrs. Warrender was much fluttered by the announcement of this visit. She had expected no doubt to meet Lady Markland very soon, to pay her perhaps a solemn visit, to receive her so to speak as a member of the family, which had been an alarming thought. For Lady Markland, though always grateful to her, and on one or two occasions offering something that looked like a close, confidential friendship, had been always a great lady in the opinion of the squire's wife, a more important person than herself, intimacy with whom would carry embarrassments with it. She had not been even, like other people in her position, familiarly known in the society of the county. Her seclusion during her husband's lifetime, the almost hermit life she led, the pity she had called forth, the position as of one apart from the world which she had maintained, all united to place Lady Markland out of the common circle on a little eminence of her own. She had been very cordial especially on the last evening they had spent together, the summer night when she had come to fetch Geoff. But still they had never been altogether at their ease with Lady Markland. Mrs. Warrender went back into the drawing-room, and looked round upon it with eyes more critical than when she had regarded it in relation to herself, wondering if Lady Markland would think it a homely place, a residence unworthy her future husband's mother. She made some little changes in it instinctively, put away the work on which she had been engaged, and looked at Chatty's little workbox with an inclination to put that too out of the way. The rooms at Markland were not so fine as to make such precautions necessary; yet there was a faded splendour about them very different from the limitation and comfortable prim neatness of this. When she had done all that it was possible to do, she sat down to wait for her visitor, trying to read though she could not give much attention to what she read. "Lady Markland is to be here at three," she said to Chatty, who was slightly startled for a moment, but much less than her mother, taking a strip of muslin out of her box, and beginning to work at it as if this was the business of life and nothing else could excite her more. The blinds were all drawn down for the sunshine, and the light came in green and cool though everything was blazing out-of-doors. These lowered blinds made it impossible to see the arrival though Mrs. Warrender heard it acutely—every prance of the horses, every word Lady Markland said. It seemed a long time before, through the many passages of the old-fashioned house, the visitor appeared. She made a slight pause on the threshold, apparently waiting for an invitation, for a special reception. Mrs. Warrender, with her heart beating, had risen, and stood with her hands clasped in tremulous expectation. They looked at each other for a moment across the parlour maid, who did not know how to get out of the room from between the two ladies, neither of whom advanced towards the other. Then Mrs. Warrender went hurriedly forward with extended hands.

"Theo told me you were coming. I am very glad to see you." They took each other's hands, and Mrs. Warrender bent forward to give the kiss of welcome. They were two equal powers, meeting on debatable ground, fulfilling all the necessary courtesies. Not like this should Theo's mother have met his wife. It should have been a young creature whom she could have taken into her arms, who would have flung herself upon the breast of his mother, or at her knees, like a child of her own. Instead of this, they were two equal powers, if, indeed, Lady Markland were not the principal, the one to give and not receive. Mrs. Warrender felt herself almost younger, less imposing altogether than the new member of the family, to whom it should have been her part to extend a tender patronage, to draw close to her, and set at her ease. Things were better when this difficult first moment was over. It was suitable and natural that Lady Markland should give to Chatty that kiss of peace—and then they all seated themselves in a little circle. "You have just arrived," Lady Markland said.

"Yesterday. We have scarcely settled down."

"And you enjoyed your stay in town? Chatty at least —Chatty must have enjoyed it." Lady Markland turned to her with a soft smile.

"Oh yes, very much," said Chatty, almost under her breath.

And then there was a brief pause, after which, "I hope Geoff is quite well," Mrs. Warrender said.

"Quite well, and I was to bring you his love." Lady Markland hesitated a little, and said, "I should like if I might—to consult you about Geoff."

"Surely," Mrs. Warrender replied, and again there was a pause.

In former times, Chatty would not have perceived the embarrassment of her two companions: but she had learned to divine since her three weeks' experience. She rose up quietly. "I think, mamma, you will be able to talk better if I go away."

"I don't know, my dear," said Mrs. Warrender, with a slight tremulousness. Lady Markland did not say anything. She retained the advantage of the position, not denying that she wished it, and Chatty accordingly, putting down her work, went away. Mrs. Warrender felt the solemnity of the interview more and more; but she did not know what to say.

Presently Lady Markland took the initiative. She rose and approached nearer to Mrs. Warrender's side. "I want you to tell me," she said, herself growing for the first time a little tremulous, "if you dislike this very much—for Theo."

"Dislike it! oh, how can you think so? His happiness is all I desire, and if you——"

"If I can make him happy? that is a dreadful question, Mrs. Warrender. How can any one tell that? I hope so; but if I should deceive myself——"

"That was not what I meant: there is no happiness for him, but that which you can give: if you think him good enough—that was what I was going to say."

"Good enough! Theo? Oh then, you do not know what he is, though he is your son; and so far I am better than you are."

"Lady Markland, you are better in a great many ways. It is this that frightens me. In some things you are so much above any pretensions of his. He has so little experience, he is not rich, nor even is he clever (though he is very clever) according to the ways of the world. I seem to be disparaging my boy. It is not that, Lady Markland."

"No; do you think I don't understand? I am too old for him; I am not the kind of woman you would have chosen, or even that he would have chosen, had he been in his right senses."

"It is folly to say that you are old. You are not old; you are a woman that any man might be proud to love. And his love—has been a wonder to me to see," said his mother, her voice faltering, her eyes filling. "I have never known such adoration as that."

"Ah, has it not!" cried the woman who was the object of it, a sudden melting and ineffable change coming over her face. "That was what gave me the courage," she said, after a moment's pause. "How could I refuse? It is not often, is it, that a man—that a woman"—here her voice died away in a confusion and agitation which melted all Mrs. Warrender's reluctance. She found herself with her arms round the great lady, comforting her, holding her head against her own breast. They shed some tears together, and kissed each other, and for a moment came so close that all secondary matters that could divide them seemed to fade away.

"But now," said Lady Markland, after this little interval, "he is worried and disturbed again, by all the lawyers think it right to do. I should like to spare him all that, but I am helpless in their hands. Oh, dear Mrs. Warrender, you will understand. There are so many things that make it more difficult. There is—Geoff."

Mrs. Warrender pressed her hands and gave her a look full of sympathy; but she said nothing. She did not make a cheerful protest that all these things were without importance, and that Geoff was no drawback, as perhaps it was hoped she might do. Lady Markland drew back a little, discouraged—waiting for some word of cheer which did not come.

"You know," she said, her voice trembling, "what my boy has been to me: everything! until this new light that I never dreamed of, that I never had hoped for, or thought of. You know how we lived together, he and I. He was my companion, more than a child, sharing every thought. You know——"

"Lady Markland, you have had a great deal of trouble, but how much with it—a child like that, and then——"

"And then—Theo! Was there ever a woman so blessed—or so—— Oh, help me to know what I am to do between them! You can understand better than any of the young ones. Don't you see," said Lady Markland, with a smile in which there was a kind of despair, "that though I am not old, as you say, I am on your level rather than on his, that *you* can understand better than he?"

If it were possible that a woman who is a mother could cease to be that in the first place and become a friend, first of all a sympathiser in the very difficulties that overwhelm her son, that miracle was accomplished then. The woman whom she had with difficulty accepted as Theo's future wife became, for a moment, nearer to her in this flood of sympathy than Theo himself. The woman's pangs and hindrances were closer to her experience than the man's. To him, in the heat of his young passion, nothing was worth considering that interfered with the perfect accomplishment of his love. But to her—the young woman, who had to piece on the present to the past, who though she might have abandoned father and mother could never abandon her child—the other woman's heart went out with a pang of fellow-feeling. Mrs. Warrender, like most women, had an instinctive repugnance to the idea of a second marriage at all, but that being determined and beyond the reach of change, her heart ached for the dilemma which was more painful than any which enters into the possibilities of younger life. As Lady Markland leant towards her, claiming her sympathy, her face full of sentiments so conflicting, the joy of love and yet the anguish of it, and all the contrariety of a heart torn in two, the youthfulness, when all was said, of this expressive countenance, the recollection that, after all, this woman who claimed to be on her own level was not too old to be her child, seized upon Mrs. Warrender. Nothing that is direct and simple can be so poignant as those complications in which right and wrong and all the duties of human life are so confused that no sharply cut division is possible. What was she to do? She would owe all her heart to her husband, and what was to remain for her child? Geoff had upon her the first claim of nature; her love, her care, were his right—but then Theo? The old mother took the young one into her arms, with an ache of sympathy. "Oh, my dear, what can I say to you? We must leave it to Providence. Things come round when we do not think too much of them, but do our best."

How poor a panacea, how slight a support! and yet in how many cases all that one human creature can say to another! To do our best and to think as little as possible, and things will come round! The absolute mind scorns the mild consolation. To Theo it would have been an irritation, a wrong, but Theo's betrothed received it with humbler consciousness. The sympathy calmed her, and that so moderate, so humble, voucher of experience that things come round. Was it really so? was nothing so bad as it appeared? was it true that the way opened before you little by little in treading it, as she who had gone on so much farther on the path went on to say? Lady Markland regained her composure as she listened.

"You are speaking to me like a true mother," she said. "I have never known what that was. Help me, only help me! even to know that you understand me is so much—and do not blame me."

"Dear Lady Markland——"

"I have a name," she said, with a smile which was full of pain, as if marking another subject of trouble, "which is my own, which cannot be made any question of. Will you call me Frances? It would please him. They say it would be unusual, unreasonable, a thing which is never done—to give up—— Is that Theo? Dear Mrs. Warrender, I shall be far happier, now that I know I have a friend in you."

She grasped his mother's hands with a hurried gesture, and an anxious, imploring look. Then gave a hasty glance into the glass, and recovered in a moment her air of gentle dignity, her smile. It was this that met Theo when he came in eager, yet doubtful, his eyes finding her out, with a rapid question, the instant that he entered. Whatever her troubles might be, none of them were made apparent to him.

CHAPTER XXXV.

Next day Mr. Longstaffe called upon Mrs. Warrender, nominally about the alterations that had to be made in her house, but really with objects much more important. He made notes scrupulously of what she wanted, and hoped that she would not allow anything to be neglected that was necessary for her comfort. When these necessary preliminaries were over, there was a pause. He remained silent with an expectant air, waiting to be questioned, and though she had resolved if possible to refrain from doing so, the restriction was more than her faculties could bear.

"My son tells me," she said, as indifferently as possible, "that there is a great deal going on between him and you."

"Naturally," cried Mr. Longstaffe, with a certain heat of indignation. "He is making a marriage which is not at all a common kind of marriage, and yet he would have liked it to be without any settlements at all."

"He could not wish anything that was not satisfactory to Lady Markland."

"Do you think so? then I must undeceive you. He would have liked Lady Markland to give herself to him absolutely with no precautions, no restrictions."

"Mr. Longstaffe, Theo is very much in love. He has always been very sensitive: he cannot bear (I suppose) mixing up business matters, which he hates, with——"

"It is all very well for him to hate business, though between you and me, if you will allow me to say so, I think it very silly. Ladies may entertain such sentiments, but a man ought to know better. If you will believe me, he wants to marry her as if she were sixteen and had not a penny! To make her Mrs. Theodore

Warrender and take her home to his own house!"

"What should he do else? is not that the natural thing that every man wishes to do?"

"Yes, if he marries a girl of sixteen without a penny, as I said. Mrs. Warrender, I know you are full of sense. Perhaps you will be able to put it before him in a better light. When a man marries a lady, with an established position of her own like Lady Markland, and a great many responsibilities, especially when she is a sort of queen mother and has a whole noble family to be accountable to——"

"I do not wonder that Theo should be impatient, Mr. Longstaffe; all this must be terrible to him, in the midst of his—— Why should not they marry first, and then these things will arrange themselves?"

"Marry first! and leave her altogether unsecured."

"I hope you know that my son is a man of honour, Mr. Longstaffe."

"My dear madam, we have nothing to do with men of honour in the law. I felt sure that you would understand at least. Suppose we had left Miss Minnie dependent upon the honour (though I don't doubt it at all) of the Thynne family."

"I don't mean in respect to money," said Mrs. Warrender, with a slight flush. "He will not interfere with her money, of that I am certain."

"No: only with herself; and she has been left the control of everything; and she must be free to administer her son's property and look after his interests. If you will allow me to say it, Mrs. Warrender, Lady Markland is a much better man of business than Theo."

Mr. Longstaffe had known Theo all his life, and had never addressed him otherwise than by that name, but it seemed an over-familiarity, a want of respect, even a sign of contempt in the position in which Theo now stood. She replied with a little offence:—

"That is very possible. He has had little experience, and he is a scholar, not a person of business. But why should the marriage be delayed? This is the worst moment for them both. I know my son, Mr. Longstaffe. All this frets him beyond description now; but when the uncertainty is over, and all these negotiations, everything will come round. He will never interfere or prevent her from doing what is necessary for her son. When they are once married all will go well."

This was a long speech for Mrs. Warrender, and she made it with interruptions, with trepidation, not quite so sure perhaps of her own argument as she had thought she was. The lawyer looked at her with a kind of respectful contempt.

"There may be a certain justice in what you say, that this is the worst moment: but I for one could never agree to anything so unbusiness-like as you seem to suggest. Marriage first, and business afterwards—no, no—and then there is the little boy. You would not have him sent off to nurse while his mother goes upon her honeymoon. Poor little fellow, so devoted as she was to him before!"

"A second marriage," said Mrs. Warrender, subdued, "can never be so simple, so easy, as one in which there are no complications."

"They are better, if they so abide," said Mr. Longstaffe. "I agree with St. Paul for my part. But it would be hard upon a young woman, poor thing, that made such a failure in her first. If Theo were not so restive, if you could get him to take things a little more easy—— Dear me, of course I trust in his honour; no one doubts that. But he will lead her a pretty dance; whether it will be better for her to have a good crotchety high-tempered young fellow who adores her, or a rough young scamp who neglected her——"

"There can be no comparison between the two."

"No," said Mr. Longstaffe ruefully, but perhaps his judgment did not lean to Theo's side.

"And why should not they live at the Warren?" she asked. "It is not a fine house, but it is a good house, and with the improvements Theo is making——"

"My dear lady, to me the Warren is a delightful little place, or at least it could be made delightful. But Markland—Markland is a very different matter. To change the one for the other would be—well it would be, you won't deny, something like a sacrifice. And why should she? when Markland is all ready, wanting no alteration, an excellent house, and in the middle of the property which she has to manage, whereas the Warren——"

"I have lived in the Warren all my life," said Mrs. Warrender, with a little natural indignation. It wounded her sore that he should talk of it patronisingly as "a delightful little place." She was not in any way devoted to the Warren; still this patronage, this unfavourable comparison irritated her, and she began to range herself with more warmth upon her own side. "I can see no reason why my son's wife should not live there."

"But there are reasons why Lady Markland should not live there."

Mrs. Warrender's eyes shot forth fire. She no longer wondered that Theo was driven to the verge of distraction. Oh that he had loved some young creature on his own level, some girl who would have gone sweetly to his home with him and glorified the old life! His mother had wept over and soothed the woman of his choice only yesterday, entering into all the difficulties that beset her path, and pledging her own assistance to overcome them; but now she was all in arms in behalf of her boy, whose individuality was to be crushed among them, who was to be made into an appendage to Lady Markland, and have no place of his own. Instead of giving her assistance to tame Theo, she felt herself take fire in his defence.

"You are very right, no doubt, to consider Lady Markland in the first place," she said, "but I don't think we can argue the question further, for to me my son must be the first."

"It is the right way," said the lawyer, "but when a young man lifts his eyes——"

"We will say no more on the subject," she said quickly. And Mr. Longstaffe was too judicious to do anything else than resume the question about the garden palings, and then to bow himself out. He turned, indeed, at the door to express his regrets that he had not brought her to his way of thinking, that he lost her valuable help, upon which he had calculated: but this did not conciliate Mrs. Warrender. She had no carriage at her orders, or she would have gone to the Warren at once, with the impulsiveness of her nature, to see what Theo was doing, what he was thinking of. But Theo was at Markland, alternating between the Paradiso and the Inferno, between the sweetness of his betrothed's company and all the hard conditions of his happiness, and the Warren was in the hands of a set of leisurely country tradespeople, who if Theo had meant to carry his bride there must have postponed that happiness for a year or two—not much wonder, perhaps, since they were left by the young master to dawdle on their own way.

Mrs. Warrender, however, had another and a surprising visitor on this same day. The ladies were sitting together in their usual way, in the heat of the afternoon, waiting until it should be cool enough for their walk, when the parlour maid, not used, perhaps, to such visitors, opened the door with a little excitement, and announced, "Lord Markland." Mrs. Warrender rose quickly to her feet, with a low cry, and a sudden wild imagination such as will dart across a troubled mind. Lord Markland! had he never died then, was it all a dream, had he come back to stop it in time? A small voice interrupted this flash of thought, and brought her back to herself with a giddy sense of the ridiculous and a sensation of shame quite out of proportion to the momentary illusion. "It is only me, Geoff: but I thought when she asked me my name, I was obliged to give my right name." He seemed smaller than ever, as he came across the room twitching his face as his habit was, and paler, or rather grayer, with scanty locks and little twinkling eyes. "Did you think it was some one else?" he said.

"Of course it could be no one but you. I was startled for the moment, not thinking of you by that title. And have you come all this way alone—without any——"

"Oh, you were thinking of that other time. There is a great deal of difference since that other time. It is nearly a year since—and now I do a great many things by myself," said the boy, looking at her keenly. "I am let to go wherever I please."

"Because you are now old enough to take care of yourself," said Mrs. Warrender, "with the help of Black."

"Yes," said Geoff, "how did you know? I have got Black. But there is more in it than that. Would mamma have ruined me, if she had kept on always coddling me, Mrs. Warrender? that is what the servants say."

"My dear, one never allows the servants to say things of that kind. You should understand your mother's meaning much better than they can do."

"I see a great deal of the servants now," said Geoff—then he corrected himself with a look of sudden recollection—"that is, I am afraid I disobey mamma, Mrs. Warrender. I am rather fond of the servants, they are more amusing than other people. I go to the stables often when I know I oughtn't. To know you oughtn't, and yet to do it, is very bad, don't you think?"

"I am afraid it is, Geoff. Don't you have any lessons now?"

"They say this is holiday time," said the boy. "Of course I am glad of the holidays, but it is a little stupid too, not having any one to play with—but I may come out a great deal more than I used to. And that is a great advantage, isn't it? I read too, chiefly stories; but a whole day is a very long time, don't you think so? I did not say where I was coming this afternoon, in case the pony might get tired, or Black turn cross, or something, but it appears Black likes to come to Highcombe, he has friends here." The boy had come close to Mrs. Warrender's work-table, and was lifting up and putting down again the reels of silk, the thimbles and scissors. He went on with his occupation for some time very gravely, his back turned to the light. At length he said, "I want you to tell me one thing. They say Warrender is coming to live at our house."

"I am afraid it is true, Geoff."

"Don't you like it, then?" said the boy. "I thought if you did not like it you would not let it be."

"My dear, my son Theo is a man. I cannot tell him what he must do as your mother does to you. And if I do not like it, it is because he has a good house of his own."

"Ah, the Warren!" said Geoff: then he added, pulling all the reels about in the work-table, and without raising his eyes to her face, "If he is coming, I wish he would come, Mrs. Warrender, then perhaps I should go to school. Don't you think school is a good thing for a boy?"

"Everybody says so, Geoff."

"Yes, I know—it is in all the books. Mrs. Warrender, if—Warrender is coming to live with us, will you be a sort of grandmother to me?"

This startled her very much. She looked at the odd child with a sensation almost of alarm.

"Because," he continued, "I never had one, and I could come and talk to you when things were bad."

"I hope you will never have any experience of things being bad, Geoff."

He gave a glance at her face, his hands still busy among the threads and needles.

"Oh no, never, perhaps—but, Mrs. Warrender, if—Warrender is coming to Markland to live, *I* wish he would do it now, directly. Then it would be settled what was going to be done with me—and—and other things." Geoff's face twitched more than ever, and she understood that the reason why he did not look at her was because his little eyelids were swollen with involuntary tears. "There are a lot of things—that perhaps would get—settled then," he said.

"Geoff," she said, putting her arm round him, "I am afraid you don't like it any more than I do, my poor boy."

Geoff would not yield to the demoralising influence of this caress. He held himself away from her, swaying backwards, resisting the pressure of her arm. His eyelids grew bigger and bigger, his mouth twitched and quivered. "Oh, it is not that," he said, with a quiver in his voice, "if mamma likes it. I am only little, I am rather backward, I am not—company enough for mamma."

"That must be one of the things that the servants say. You must not listen, Geoff, to what the servants say."

"But it is quite true. Mamma knows just exactly what is best. I used to be the one that was always with her—and now it is Warrender. He can talk of lots of things—things I don't understand. For I tell you I am very backward, I don't know half, nor so much as half, what some boys do at my age."

"That is a pity, perhaps; but it does not matter, Geoff, to your— to the people who are fond of you, my dear."

"Oh yes, it does," cried the boy; "don't hold me, please! I am a little beast, I am not grateful to people nor anything! the best thing for me will just be to be sent to school." Here Geoff turned his back upon her abruptly, forced thereto by the necessity of getting rid of those tears. When he had thus relieved himself, and cleared his throat of the climbing sorrow that threatened to shake his voice, he came back and stood once more by her table. The great effort of swallowing down all that emotion had made him pale, and left the strained look which the passage of a sudden storm leaves both upon the human countenance and the sky. "They say it's very jolly at Eton," he resumed suddenly, taking up with his hot little nervous fingers Mrs. Warrender's piece of work.

But at this point Geoff's confidences were interrupted by the entrance of visitors, who not only meant to make themselves agreeable to Mrs. Warrender on her first arrival at Highcombe, but who were very eager to find out all that they could about the marriage of Theo, if it really was going to take place, and when, and everything about it. It added immensely to the excitement, but little to the information acquired, when in answer to the first question Mrs. Warrender indicated to her visitors that the little boy standing at her side, and contemplating them with his hands in his pockets, was little Lord Markland. "Oh, the boy," they said under their breath, and stopped their questioning most unwillingly, all but the elder lady, who got Mrs. Warrender into a corner, and carried on the interrogatory. Was she quite pleased? but of course she was pleased. The difference of age was so little that it did not matter, and though the Markland family were known not to be rich, yet to be sure it was a very nice position. And such a fine character, not a woman that was very popular, but quite above criticism. "There never was a whisper against her—oh, never a whisper! and that is a great thing to say." Geoff did not hear, and probably would not have understood, these comments. He still stood by the work-table, taking the reels of silk out of their places and putting them back again with the gravity of a man who has something very important in hand. He seemed altogether absorbed in this simple occupation, bending over it with eyebrows contracted over his eyes, and every sign of earnestness. "What a curious thing for a boy to take pleasure in: but I suppose being always with his mother has rather spoiled him. It will be so good for the child to have a man in the house," said the lady who was interviewing Mrs. Warrender. There was a little group of the younger ladies round Chatty, talking about the parish and the current amusements, and hoping that she would join the archery club, and that she loved croquet. The conversation was very animated on that side, one voice echoing another, although the replies of Chatty were mild. Geoff had all the centre of the room to himself, and stood there as on a stage, putting the reel of red silk into the square which was intended for the blue, and arranging the colours in squares and parallels. He was much absorbed in it, and yet he did not know what he was doing. His little bosom swelled high with thought, his heart was wrung with the poignancy of love rejected—of loss and change. It was not that he was jealous; the sensations which he experienced had little bitterness or anger in them. Presently he turned round and said, "I think I shall go home, Mrs. Warrender," with a disagreeable consciousness that everybody paused and looked at him, when his small voice broke the murmur of the feminine conversation. But what did that matter to Geoff? He had much to occupy him, too much to leave him free to think how people looked, or what they said.

CHAPTER XXXVI.

Geoff's heart was full. He pondered all the way home, neglecting all the blandishments of Black's conversation, who had visited a friend or two in Highcombe, and was full of cheerfulness and very loquacious. Geoff let him talk, but paid no attention. He himself had gone to Mrs. Warrender, whom he liked, with the hope of disburdening from his little bosom some of the perilous stuff which weighed upon his soul. He had wanted to *sfogarsi*, as the Italians say, to relieve a heart too full to go on any longer: but Geoff found, as so many others have found before him, that the relief thus obtained but made continued silence more intolerable. He could not shut up the doors again which had thus been forced open. The sensation which overwhelmed him was one which most people at one time or another have felt,—that the circumstances amid which he was placed had become insupportable, that life could no longer go on, under such conditions,—a situation terrible to the maturest man or woman, but what word can describe it in the heart of a child? In his mother was summed up all love and reliance, all faith and admiration for Geoff. She had been as the sun to him. She had been as God, the only known and visible representative of all love and authority, the one unchangeable, ever right, ever true. And now she had changed, and all life was out of gear. His heart was sick, not because he was wronged, but because everything had gone wrong. He did not doubt his mother's love, he was not clear enough in his thoughts to doubt anything, or to put the case into any arrangement of words. He felt only that he could not bear it, that anything would be better than the present condition of affairs. Geoff's heart filled and his eyes, and there came a constriction of his throat when he realised the little picture of himself wandering about with nobody to care for him, no lessons; for the first time in his life forbidden to dart into his mother's room at any moment, with a rush against the door, in full certainty that there could never be a time when she did not want him. Self-pity is very strong and very simple in a child, and to see, as it were, a little picture in his mind of a little boy, shut out from his mother, and wanted by no one, was more poignant still than the reality. The world was out of joint: and Geoff felt with Hamlet that there was nobody but he to set it right. The water came into his eyes, as he rode along, but except what he could get rid of by winking violently, he left it to the breeze to dry, no hand brushing it off, not even a little knuckle piteously unabsorbent, would he employ to show to Black that he was crying. Crying! no, he would not cry, what could that do for him? But something would have to be done, or said; once the little floodgates had been burst open they could not close any more.

Geoff pondered long, though with much confusion in his thoughts. He was very magnanimous: not even in his inmost soul did he blame his mother, being still young enough to believe that unhappy events come of themselves and not by anybody's fault. To think that she liked Theo better than himself made his heart swell, but rather with a dreadful sense of fatality than with blame. And then he was a little backward boy, not knowing things like Theo, whom, by the way, he no longer called Theo, having shrunk involuntarily, unawares, out of that familiarity as soon as matters had grown serious. As he thought it all over, Geoff's very heart was rent. His mother had cried when she took him into her arms, he remembered that she had kissed his cold feet, that she had looked as if she were begging his pardon, kneeling by his side on that terrible night when he had come dimly to an understanding of what it all meant. Geoff, like Hamlet, in his little way felt that nothing that could be done could ever undo that night. It was there, a fact which no after resolution could change. No vengeance could have put back the world to what it was before Hamlet's mother had married her brother-in-law, and the soft Ophelia turned into an innocent traitor, and all grown false: neither could anything undo to little Geoff the dreadful revolution of heaven and earth through which his little life had gone. All the world was out of joint, and what could he do to mend it, a little boy of ten—a backward little boy, not knowing half so much as many at his age? His little bosom swelled, his eyes grew wet, and that strange sensation came in his throat. But he kept on riding a little in front of Black so that nothing could be seen.

Lady Markland was in the avenue as he rode up to the gate. Geoff knew very well that she had walked as far as the gate with Warrender, whom he had seen taking the road to the right, the short way across the fields. But when he saw his mother he got down from his pony, and walked home with her. "Where have you been?" she cried. "I was getting very anxious; you must not go those long rides by yourself."

"I had Black," said Geoff, "and you said I should have to be independent, to be able to take care of myself."

"Did I say so, dear? Perhaps it is true: but still you know how nervous I am, how anxious I grow."

Geoff looked his mother in the face like an accusing angel, not severely, but with all the angelic regret and tenderness of one who cannot be deceived, yet would fain blot out the fault with a tear. "Poor mamma!" he said, clasping her arm in his old childish way.

"Why do you call me poor mamma? Geoff, some one has been saying something to you, your face is not like the face of my own boy."

She was seized with sudden alarm, with a wild desire to justify herself, and the sudden wrath with which a conscious culprit takes advantage of the suggestion that ill tongues alone or evil representations have come between her and those whom she has wronged. The child on his side took no notice of this. He had gone so much further; beyond the sphere in which there are accusations or defences—indeed he was too young for anything of the kind. "Mamma," he said clasping her arm, "I think I should like to go to school. Don't you think it would be better for me to go to school?"

"To school!" she cried, "do you want to leave me, Geoff?" in a tone of sudden dismay.

"They say a boy ought to go to school, and they say it's very jolly at Eton, and I'm very backward, don't you know—Warrender says so."

"Geoff! he has never said it to me."

"But if it is true, mamma! There is no difference between me and a girl staying at home: and there I should have other fellows to play with. You had better send me. I should like it."

She gave him an anxious look, which Geoff did not lift his eyes to meet, then with a sigh, "If you think you would like it, Geoff. To be sure it is what would have to be sooner or later." Here she made a hurried breathless pause, as if her thoughts went quicker than she could follow. "But now it is July, and you could not go before Michaelmas," she said.

Was she sorry he could not go at once, though she had exclaimed at the first suggestion that he wanted to leave her? Geoff was too young to ask himself this question, but there was a vague sensation in his mind of something like it, and of a mingled satisfaction and disappointment in his mother's tone.

"Warrender says there are fellows who prepare you for Eton," the boy said, holding his breath hard that he might not betray himself. "He is sure to know somebody. Send me now."

"You are very anxious to leave me," she cried in a tone of piteous excitement and misery. "Why, why should you wish it so much?" Then she paused and cried suddenly, "Is it Mr. Warrender who has put this in your mind?"

"I don't know nothing about Warrender," said Geoff, blinking his eyes to keep the tears away. "I never spoke to Warrender. He said that when he was not thinking about me."

And then she clasped her arms about him suddenly in a transport of pain and trouble and relief. "Oh, Geoff, Geoff," she cried, "why, why do you want to leave me?" The boy could not but sob, pressed closely against her, feeling her heart swell as his own was doing, but neither did he make any attempt to answer, nor did she look for any reply.

CHAPTER XXXVII.

Various scenes to which Markland was all unaccustomed had been taking place in these days, alternations of rapture and gloom on the part of Warrender, of shrinking and eagerness on the part of Lady Markland, which made their intercourse one of perpetual vicissitude. From the quiet of her seclusion she had been roused into all the storms of passion, and though this was sweetened by the absolute devotion of the young man who adored her, there were yet moments in which she felt like Geoff that the position was becoming insupportable. Everything in her life was turned upside down by this new element in it, which came between her and her child, between her and her business, the work to which she had so lately made up her mind to devote herself as to the great object of her existence. All that was suspended now. When Theo was with her, he would not brook, nor did she desire, any interruption; and when he was not with her the bewildering thoughts that would rush upon her, the questions in her mind as to what she ought to do, whether it might not even now be better for everybody to break, if it was possible, those engagements which brought so much agitation, which hindered everything, which disturbed even the bond between herself and her child, would sometimes almost destroy her moral balance altogether. And then her young lover would arrive, and all the miseries and difficulties would be forgotten, and it would seem as if earthly conditions and circumstances had rolled away, and there were but these two in a new life, a new world, where no troubles were. Then Lady Markland would say to herself that it was the transition only that was painful, that they were all in a false position, but that afterwards, when the preliminaries were over and all accomplished, everything would be well. When she was his, and he hers, beyond drawing back or doubt, beyond the possibility of separation, then all that was over-anxious, over-sensitive in Theo would settle down in the sober certainty of happiness secured, and Geoff, who was so young, would reconcile himself to that which would so soon appear the only natural condition of life, and the new would seem as good, nay, better than the old. She trembled herself upon the verge of the new, fearing any change and shrinking from it as is natural for a woman, and yet in her heart felt that it would be better this great change should come and be accomplished rather than to look forward to it, to go through all its drawbacks, and pay its penalties every day.

A few days after these incidents Theo came to Markland one morning with brows more than usually cloudy. He had been annoyed about his house, the improvements about which had been going on very slowly: one of his tradespeople worse than another, the builder waiting for the architect, the carpenter for the builder, the new furniture and decorations naturally lagging behind all. And to make these things more easy to bear he had met Mrs. Wilberforce, who had told him that she wondered to see so much money being spent at the Warren, as she heard his home was to be at Markland, and so natural, as it was so much better a house: and that she had heard little Lord Markland was going to school immediately, which no doubt was the best thing that could be done, and would leave his mother free. After this he had rushed to Markland in hot impetuosity. "I am never told," he cried. "I do not wish to exact anything, but if you have made up your mind about Geoff, I think I might have heard it from yourself."

"Dear Theo!" Lady Markland said, and that was all.

Then he threw himself at her feet in sudden compunction, "I am a brute," he said. "I come to you with my idiotic stories and you listen to me with that sweet patience of yours, and never reprove me. Tell me I am a fool and not worthy of your trust; I am so, I am so! but it is because I can't bear this state of affairs—

to be everything and yet nothing, to know that you are mine, and yet have a stranger informing me what you are going to do."

"No stranger need inform you, Theo. Geoff has asked me to send him to school. I can't tell how any one could know. He wishes to go—directly. He is not happy either. Oh, Theo, I think I make everybody unhappy instead of——"

"Not you," he cried, "not you, those men with their idiotic delays. Geoff is wise, wiser than they are. Let us follow his example, dearest. You don't distrust me; you know that whatever is best for you, even what they think best, all their ridiculous conditions, I will carry out. Don't you know, that the less my hands are bound, the more I should accept the fetters, all, as much as they please, that they think needful for you—but not as conditions of having you. That is what I cannot bear."

"You have me," she said, smiling upon him with a smile very close upon tears, "you know, without any conditions at all."

"Then let it be so," he cried. "Oh let it be so—directly, as Geoff wishes: dear little Geoff, wise Geoff—let him be our example."

"Theo—oh, try to love my boy!"

"I will make him my model, if you will take his example, directly, directly! The child is wise, he knows better than any of us. Darling, let us take his example, let us cut this knot. When the uncertainty is over, all these difficulties will melt away."

"He *is* wise, Theo—you don't know how right you are. Oh, my boy! and I am taking so little thought of him. I felt my heart leap when he asked to go away. Can you believe it? My own boy, my only one! I was glad, and I hate myself for it, though it was for you."

"All that," he said, eagerly addressing himself with all the arts he knew to comfort and reassure her, "is this state of miserable delay. We are in the transition from one to another. What good can we do to keep hanging on, to keep the whole county in talk, to make Geoff unhappy? He goes by instinct and he sees it—my own love, let us do so too. Let us do it—without a word to any one, my dearest!"

"Oh, Theo," she cried, "if you will but promise me to love my boy."

In the distracted state in which she was, this no-argument of Geoff's little example went to her heart. It seemed to bring him somehow into the decision, to make it look like a concession to Geoff, a carrying out of his wishes, and at the same time a supreme plea with Theo for love and understanding of Geoff. Yet it was with falterings and sinkings of soul indescribable that Lady Markland went through the two following days. They were days wonderful, not to be ever forgotten. Theo did not appear, he had gone away, she said, for a little while upon business, and Geoff and she were left alone. They went back into all the old habitudes as if nothing were changed; and the house fell again into a strange calm, a quietness almost unnatural. There were no lessons, no business, nothing to be done, but only an abandonment to that pleasure of being together which had been so long broken. He went with her for her drives, and she went with him for his walk. She called for Geoff whenever he disappeared for a moment, as if she could not bear him away from her side. They were as they had been before Theo existed for them, when they were all in all to each other. Alas, they were, yet were not, as they had been. When they drove through the fair country where the sheaves were standing in the fields and everything aglow with the mirth of harvest, they were both lost in long reveries, only calling themselves back by intervals, with a recollection of the necessity of saying something to each other. When they walked, though Geoff still clung to his mother's arm, his thoughts as well as hers were away. They discovered in this moment of close reunion that they had lost each other. Not only did the mother no longer belong to the child, but the child even, driven from her side he knew not how, was lost to the mother; they had set out unconsciously each upon a new and separate way. Geoff was not grieved, scarcely even startled, when she told him on the second evening that she was going to town next day —for shopping, she said. He did not ask to be taken with her, nor thought of asking; it appeared to Geoff that he had known all along that she would go. Lady Markland proposed to him that he should pay Mrs. Warrender a visit, and he consented, not asking why. He drove in with her to the station at Highcombe, where Chatty met him, and took leave of his mother, strangely, in a curious, dreamy way, as if he were not sure what he was doing. To be sure it was a parting of little importance. She was going to town, to do some shopping, and in less than a week she was to be back. It had never happened before, which gave the incident a distinguishing character, that was all. But she seated herself on the other side of the railway carriage and did not keep him in her eye till she could see him no more. And though she cried under her veil some tears which were salt and bitter, yet in her heart there was a feeling of relief—of relief to have parted with her boy! Could such a thing be possible? Geoff on his side went back with Chatty very quietly, saying little. He sat down in a corner of the drawing-room, with a book, his face twitching more than usual, his eyes puckered up tight: but afterwards became, as Chatty said, "very companionable," which was indeed the chief quality of this little forsaken boy.

It was not till nearly a week after that Lady Markland came back. She arrived suddenly, one evening, with Theo, unexpected, unannounced. Dinner was over, and they had all gone into the garden in the warm summer twilight when these unlooked-for visitors came. Lady Markland was clad from head to foot in gray, the colour of the twilight, she who had been for so long all black. Theo followed her closely, in light attire also, and with a face all alight with happiness, more bright than in all his life his face had ever been before. He took Geoff by the shoulders with a sort of tender roughness, which was almost like an embrace. "Is that you, my old boy?" he said, with an unsteady laugh, pushing him into his mother's arms. And then there was some crying and kissing, and Geoff heard it said that they had thought it better so, to avoid all fuss and trouble, and that it had taken place in town five days ago. To him no further explanations were made, but he seemed to understand it as well as the most grown-up person among them all.

This sudden step, which put all the power in Theo's hands to thwart the lawyers and regulate matters at his own pleasure, made him at once completely subservient to them, accepting everything which he had struggled against before. He took up his abode at Markland with his wife without so much as a protest; from thence he found it an amusement to watch the slow progress of the works at the Warren, riding over two or three times a week, sometimes accompanied by Geoff on his pony, sometimes by Geoff's mother, who it appeared could ride very well too. And when they went into society it was as Lady Markland and Mr. Warrender. Even on this point, without a word, Theo had given in.

There was, of course, a great outcry in the county about this almost runaway marriage. It was not dignified for Lady Markland, people said; but there were some good-natured souls who said they did not wonder, for that a widow's wedding was not a pretty spectacle like a young girl's, and of course there were always embarrassments, especially with a child so old as Geoff. What could his mother have done with him, had he been present at the wedding, and he must have been present at the wedding, if it had been performed in the ordinary way. Poor little Geoff! If only the new husband would be good to him, everybody said.

CHAPTER XXXVIII.

"Of course it was perfectly right. No one could say that I was in any way infatuated about Lady Markland, never from the first: but I quite approve of that. Why should she call herself Mrs. Theodore Warrender, when she has the title of a viscountess? If it had been a trumpery little baronetcy," said Minnie, strong in her new honours, "that would have been quite a different matter; but why should one give up one's precedency, and all that? I should not at all like to have Mrs. Wilberforce, for instance, or any other person of her class, walk out of a room before me—now."

"Nor me, I suppose," Mrs. Warrender said, with a smile.

"Oh, you! that is different of course," said the Hon. Mrs. Eustace Thynne; but though she was good enough to say this, it was very evident that even for her mother Minnie had no idea of waiving her rights. "When a thing is understood it is so much easier," she added, "every one must see that. Besides it was not her fault," said Minnie triumphantly, "that her first husband died."

"It was her fault that she married again, surely."

"Oh, what do you know about it, Chatty? An unmarried girl can't really have any experience on that subject. Well, to be sure it was her own doing marrying again: but a lady of any rank *never* gives up her title on marrying a commoner. A baronet's wife, as I say,—but then a baronet is only a commoner himself."

"You seem to have thoroughly studied the subject, Minnie."

"Yes, I have studied it; marrying into a noble family naturally changes one's ideas. And the Thynnes are very particular. You should have seen my mother-in-law arranging the dinner-party she asked to meet us. *I* went first of course as the bride, but there was Lady Highcourt and Lady Grandmaison, both countesses, and the creation within twenty years of each other. Eustace said nobody but his mother could have recollected without looking it up that the Grandmaisons date from 1425 and the Highcourts only from 1450—not the very oldest nobility either of them," said Minnie, with a grand air. "The Thynnebroods date from 1395."

"But then," said Mrs. Warrender, much amused, shooting a bow at a venture, "their descent counts in the female line."

Upon which a deep blush, a wave of trouble and shame, passed over Minnie's countenance. "Only in one case," she cried, "only once; and that you will allow is not much in five hundred years."

This bridal pair had arrived on their visit only the day before: they had taken a long holiday, and had been visiting many friends. It was now about two months since their marriage, and the gowns in Minnie's trousseau began to lose their obtrusive newness: nor can it be said that her sentiments were new. They were only modified a little by her present *milieu*. "I suppose," she said, after an interval, "that Lady Markland will come to see me as soon as she knows I am here. Shall they have any one there for the shooting this year? Eustace quite looks forward to a day now and then. There is the Warren at least, which poor dear papa never preserved, but which I hope Theo—Eustace says that Theo will really be failing in his duty if he does not preserve."

"I know nothing about their plans or their visitors. Theo is very unlikely to think of a party of sportsmen, who were never much in his way."

Chatty in the meantime had gone out of the room about her flowers, which were always her morning's occupation. When she closed the door, Minnie, who had been waiting eagerly, leaned forward to her mother. "As for being in his way, Theo has no right to be selfish, mamma. He ought to think of Chatty. *She* ought to think of Chatty. I shall not have nearly so good an opinion of her, if she does not take a little trouble and do something for Chatty now she is going out again and has it in her power."

"For Chatty—but Chatty does not shoot!"

"You never will understand, mamma," said Mrs. Eustace Thynne with gentle exasperation. "Chatty ought to be thought of now. I am sure I never was; if it had not been for Eustace coming to Pierrepoint, I should have been Miss Warrender all my life: and so will Chatty be Miss Warrender all her life, if no one comes to the rescue. Of course it should lie with me in the first place: but except neighbouring clergymen, we are likely to see so few people just at present. To be sure I have married a clergyman myself: but Eustace was quite an exceptional case, and clergymen as a rule can scarcely be called eligible: so there is nothing for it but that Lady Markland should interfere."

"For Chatty? I beg your pardon, my dear. You are much wiser than I am; but in the present case I think Chatty's mother is sufficient for all needs."

"That was always your way, mamma, to take one up at a word without thinking. Don't you remark Chatty, how awfully quiet she is? Eustace remarked it the very first day. He is very quick to see a thing, and he has a lot of sisters of his own. He said to me, Either Chatty has had a disappointment or she is just bored to death staying at home. I think very likely it is my marriage that has done it, for of course there could have been no disappointment," Minnie added calmly. "Seeing both me and Theo happy, she naturally asks herself, Am I always to sit here like an old person with mamma?"

Mrs. Warrender felt the prick, but only smiled. "I don't think she asks herself that question: but in any case I am afraid she must just be left, however dull it may be, with mamma."

"Oh, I hope you will be reasonable," said Minnie, "I hope you will not stand in poor Chatty's way. It is time she saw somebody, and that people saw her. She is twenty-four. She has not much time to lose, Eustace says."

"My dear Minnie, I don't object to what you say about your sister—that is, I allow you have a right to speak: but Eustace is quite a different matter. We will leave him out of the question. What he may think or say about Chatty is of no consequence to me; in short, I think it is very bad taste, if you will allow me to say so——"

"Mamma!" Minnie rose up to much more than her full height, which was by no means great. "Is it possible that you would teach your own daughter to disregard what her husband says?"

The righteous indignation, the lofty tone, the moral superiority of Minnie's attitude gave her mother a kind of painful amusement. She said nothing, but went to the writing-table at the other side of the room. Everything was very peaceful around and about, no possibility of any real disturbance in the calm well-being of the family so far as any ordinary eye could see: Theo gone with his bride into a sphere a little above that which belonged to him by nature; Minnie with her husband in all the proud consciousness of virtuous bliss; Chatty quiet and gentle among her flowers; a soft atmosphere of sunshine and prosperity, shaded by blinds at the windows, by little diversities and contrarieties in the spirit, from being excessive and dazzling, was all about. In the midst of the calm Minnie's little theories of the new-made wife made a diverting incident in the foreground. Mrs. Warrender looked at her across the writing-table, with a smile in her eyes.

"I knew," cried Minnie, "that you had many ways of thinking I did not go in with—but to throw any doubt upon a woman's duty to her husband! Oh, mamma, that is what I never expected. Eustace is of course the first in all the world to me, what he says is always of consequence. He is not one to say a word that he has not weighed, and if he takes an interest in his sister-in-law, it is because he thinks it his duty to me."

"That is all very well, my dear," said Mrs. Warrender, with some impatience, "and no doubt it is a great matter for Chatty to have a sister so correct as yourself, and a brother-in-law to take an interest in her. But as long as I live I am the first authority about Chatty, and Eustace is not the first in the world to me. Chatty——"

"Were you calling me, mamma?"

Chatty was coming in with a tall vase of flowers held in both hands. The great campanulas, with their lavish, magnificent bells, flung up a flowery hedge between her face and the eyes of the others. It was not that she had anything to conceal, but undeniably, Chatty felt herself on a lower level of being, subdued by Minnie's presence. There is often in young married persons a pride in their new happiness, an ostentation of superiority in their twofold existence, which is apt to produce this effect upon the spectators. Minnie and her husband stood between the two ladies, neither of whom possessed husbands, as the possessors of conscious greatness stand between those who have fallen and those who have never attained. And Chatty, who had no confidence to give, whose little story was all locked in her own bosom, had been fretted by her sister's questions, and by Mr. Eustace Thynne's repeated references to the fact that she "looked pale."

"No, my dear. We were talking of you, that was all. Minnie is anxious that you should see—a little more of the world."

"Mamma, be correct at least. I said that it would be a duty for myself if I had any opportunity, and for Frances—"

"Do you mean Lady Markland?"

"Well, she is Frances, I hope, to her husband's sisters. I said it was Frances' duty, now that she is going into society, to take you about and introduce you to people. A little while ago," said Minnie with dignity, "mamma was all for gadding about; and now she finds fault when I say the simplest things, all because I said that Eustace—of course Eustace takes an interest in Chatty: next to his own sisters of course he naturally takes an interest in you."

Chatty placed her tall vase in the corner which she had chosen for it, in silence. She expressed no thanks for the interest Eustace took in her. Neither did Mrs. Warrender say anything further. The chill of this ingratitude had upon Minnie a contrary effect to that which might have been anticipated. She grew very hot and red.

"I don't know what you all mean," she cried; "it is what we have never met with yet, all the places we have been. Everybody has been grateful to Eustace for his good advice. They have all liked to know what he thought. 'Try and find out what Eustace thinks' is what has been said—and now my own mother and sister——" Here words failed and she wiped away a few angry tears.

At this Chatty's tender heart was touched. She went to her sister and gave her a gentle kiss. "Dear Minnie, I am sure you are very kind, and if there was anything to take an interest about——But mamma and I have just settled down. We want nothing, we are quite happy." Chatty looked across the room at her mother, which was natural enough, but then Mrs. Warrender observed that the girl's eyes went farther, that they went beyond anything that was visible within those white panelled walls. "Oh, quite happy," Chatty repeated very softly, with that look into the distance, which only her mother saw.

"That is all very well for the present—but you don't suppose you will always be quite satisfied and happy with mamma. That is exactly what Eustace says. I never knew anybody take so little interest in her girls as mamma does. You will be thrown among the little people here—a curate in Highcombe, or somebody's son who lives in the town. Mamma, you may say what you please, but to have a little nobody out of a country town for a brother-in-law, a person probably with no connections, no standing, no——" Minnie paused out of mere incapacity to build up the climax higher.

It is not solely characteristic of women that a small domestic controversy should excite them beyond every other: but perhaps only a woman could have felt the high swelling in her breast of that desire to cast down and utterly confound Minnie and all her pretensions by the mention of a name—and the contrariety of not being able to do it, and the secret exultation in the thought of one day cutting her down, down to the ground, with the announcement. While she was musing her heart turned to Cavendish—a relation within well-authenticated lines of the duke, very different from the small nobility of the Thynnes, who on their side were not at all related to the greater family of the name. Mrs. Warrender's heart rose with this thought so that it was almost impossible for her to keep silence, to look at Minnie and not overwhelm her. But she did refrain, and the consciousness that she had this unanswerable retort behind kept her, as nothing else could, from losing her temper. She smiled with a sense of the humour of the situation, though with a little irritation too.

"It will be very sad, my dear, if Chatty provides Eustace with an unsuitable brother-in-law; but we must not look so far ahead. There is no aspirant for the moment who can give your husband any uneasiness. Perhaps he would like a list of the ineligible young men in the neighbourhood? there are not very many, from all I can hear."

"Oh, mamma, I never knew any one so unsympathetic as you are," said Minnie, with an angry flush of colour. Chatty had not stayed to defend herself. She had hurried away out of reach of the warfare. No desire to crush her sister with a name was in Chatty's mind. It had seemed to her profane to speak of such a possibility at all. She realised so fully that everything was over, that all idea of change in her life was at an end for ever, that she heard with a little shiver, but with no warm personal feeling, the end of this discussion. She shrank, indeed, from the idea of being talked over—but then, she reflected, Minnie would be sure to do that, Minnie could not be expected to understand. While Mrs. Warrender began to write her letters Chatty went softly in and out of the room in her many comings and goings about the flowers. She had them on a table in the hall, with a great jug of fresh water and a basket to put all the litter, the clippings of stalks and unnecessary leafage in, and all her pots and vases ready. She was very tidy in all her ways. It was not a very important piece of business, and yet all the sweet orderly spirit of domestic life was in Chatty's movements. There are many people who would have been far more pleased and touched to see her at this simple work than had she been reading Greek, notwithstanding that the Greek, too, is excellent; but it was not Chatty's way.

Mrs. Warrender sat at her writing-table with a little thrill of excitement and opposition in her. She saw the angry flush on Minnie's face, and watched without seeming to watch her as she rose suddenly and left the room, almost throwing down the little spindle-legged table beside her. Just outside the door Mrs. Warrender heard Chatty's calm voice say to her sister, "Will you have these for your room, Minnie?" evidently offering her some of her flowers. (It was a pretty blue and white china pot, with a sweet smelling nosegay of mignonette and a few of the late China roses, sweet enough to scent the whole place.) "Oh, thanks, I don't like flowers in my room, Eustace thinks they are not healthy," said Minnie, in tones that were still full of displeasure, the only interruption to the prevailing calm. Mrs. Warrender was not a wise woman. She was pleased that she and the child who was left to her were having the better of the little fray. "Eustace thinks"—Minnie might quote him as much as she pleased, she would never get her mother to quail before these words. A man may be Honourable and Reverend both, and yet not be strong enough to tyrannise over his mother-in-law and lay down the law in her house. This is a condition of affairs quite different from the fashionable view, and then, Mrs. Warrender was in her own house, and quite independent of her son-in-law. She had a malicious pleasure in the thought of his discomfiture. Cavendish! She imagined to herself how they would open their eyes, and tasted in advance the pleasure of the letter which she should write to Minnie, disclosing all that would happen. It seemed to her that she knew very well what would happen. The young man was honourable and honest, and Chatty was most fit and suitable, a bride whom no parents could object to. As for mysterious restraining influences, Mrs. Warrender believed in no such things. She had not lived in a world where they exist, and she felt as sure of Dick Cavendish as of herself—that is to say, *almost* as sure.

All this might have been very well and done no harm, but in the energy of her angry, excited, exasperated, exhilarated mood, it occurred to Mrs. Warrender to take such a step as she had never done before nor thought herself capable of doing. To make overtures of any sort to a man who had shown a disposition to be her daughter's lover, yet had not said anything or committed himself in any way, would, twenty-four hours before, have seemed to her impossible. It would have seemed to her inconsistent with Chatty's dignity and her own. But opposition and a desire to have the better of one's domestic and intimate opponents is very strong, and tempts people to the most equivocal proceedings. Mrs. Warrender did not wait to think, but took out a fresh sheet of paper and dipped her pen in the ink with that impulsiveness which was characteristic of her. A note or two had already passed between Dick Cavendish and herself, so that it was not so extraordinary a proceeding as it seemed. This was what she wrote:—

Dear Mr. Cavendish—Is it worth while coming to us only from Saturday to Monday as your modesty suggests? I fear Chatty and I in our quietness would scarcely repay the long journey. But Minnie is with us (with her husband), and she was always a much more practical person than her mother. She has just been suggesting to me that Theo has now the command of covers more interesting from the sportsman point of view than our old thicket at the Warren. If, therefore, you really feel inclined to come down for a few days, there will, it appears, be a real inducement—something more in a young man's way than the tea-parties at Highcombe. So bring your gun, and let it be from Monday to Saturday instead of the other way.

We think of our brief campaign in town with great pleasure, and a strong sense of obligation to you who did so much for the pleasure of it. Most truly yours,

M. WARRENDER.

She sent this epistle off with great satisfaction, yet a little sense of guilt, that same evening, taking particular care to give it to the parlour maid with her own hand, lest Chatty should see the address. It was already September, and the time of the partridges had begun.

CHAPTER XXXIX.

When the ladies left London, Dick Cavendish had felt himself something like a wreck upon the shore. The season was very near its end, and invitations no longer came in dozens. To be sure there were a great many other wrecks whose society made life tolerable; but he felt himself out of heart, out of temper, seized by that sudden disgust with life in general which is often the result of the departure of one person who has given it a special interest. It was a strong effect to be produced by Chatty's unpretending personality, but it affected him more than if she had been in herself a more striking personage. For it was not so much that her presence made a blank in any of the gay scenes that still remained, but that she suggested another kind of scene altogether. He felt that to say it was a bore to go out was no longer that easy fiction which it usually is. It *was* a bore to go out into those aimless assemblies where not to go was a social mistake, yet to go was weariness of the flesh and spirit. In the midst of them his thoughts would turn to the little group in Half Moon Street which had made the commonplace drawing-room of the lodging-house into a home. Chatty over her muslin work—he laughed to himself when he thought of it. It was not lovely; there was no poetry about it; the little scissors and sharp pointed blade that made the little holes; the patient labour that sewed them round. So far as he was aware there was not much use in the work, and no prettiness at all; a lover might linger over an embroidery frame, and rave of seeing the flowers grow under her hand; but the little checkered pattern of holes—there was nothing at all delightful in that. Yet he thought of it, which was amazing, and laughed at himself, then thought of it again. He was not what could be called of the domestic order of man. He had "knocked about," he had seen all sorts of things and people, and to think that his heart should be caught by Chatty and her muslin work! He was himself astonished and amused, but so it was. He could not take kindly to anything now that she was gone, and even in the rapidity of the last expiring efforts of the season, he felt himself yawn and think of quite another scene: of a little house to go home to, and say what a bore it was, while Chatty took out her muslin work. He was so far gone that he scrawled patterns for that muslin work over his blotting books, arrangements of little holes, in squares, in rounds, in diagonal formations, in the shape of primitive leaf and berry, at which he would laugh all by himself and blush, and fling them into the fire—which did not, however, by any means, withdraw the significance from these simple attempts at ornamental art.

This would have been simple indeed had it been all. All the Cavendishes, small and great, even the highest divinities of the name, would have stooped from their high estate to express their pleasure that Dick had found the "nice girl" who was to settle him and make him everything a Cavendish should be. Ah, had that been but all! Dick was no coxcomb; but he had read so much in Chatty's modest eyes as warranted him in believing that he would not woo in vain. Though he could still laugh, being of that nature of man, his heart, in fact, was overwhelmed with a weight of trouble such as might have made the strongest cry out. But crying out was not in his constitution. He went about his occupations, his work, which, now that Chatty was gone, had few interruptions, chewing the cud of the bitterest fancy and the most painful thought. He walked about the streets, turning it over and over in his mind. He thought of it even when he made the patterns of the holes and laughed at them, tossing them into the fire. Underneath all his lightest as well as his most serious occupations ran this dark and stern current. The arrival of Mrs. Warrender's note made it still darker and more urgent, carrying him away upon its tide. It was not the first letter he had received from her. He had insisted upon hearing whether their journey home had been a pleasant one, how they had liked their new house, and many other trivial things, and he had asked for that invitation from Saturday to Monday, which now was reversed and turned into an almost-week, from Monday to Saturday. He did not know whether he meant or not to go: but anyhow the invitation, the power of going if he pleased, was sweet to him. He kept it by him as an anticipation, a sweetmeat which took the bitter taste of life out of his mouth.

But this letter was more formal, more business-like, than anything that had gone before. To go to see the woman whom you think of most in the world, that is a vague thing which other engagements may push aside; but an invitation to go for the partridges is business and has to be answered. Dick got it at his club, where he was lingering though it was September, making little runs into the country, but avoiding his home, where he knew many questions would be put to him about what he was going to do. It is a sad thing when there is nobody who cares what you are going to do—but this is not the view of the matter most apparent to young men. Dick very much disliked the question. It was not one to which he could give any reply. He was going to do—nothing, unless life and feeling should be too much for him and he should be driven into doing what would be a villainy—yes a villainy, though probably no harm would ever come of it; most probably, almost certainly, no harm would come of it—and yet it would be a villainy. These were the thoughts that were with him wherever he went or came. And after he got Mrs. Warrender's letter they grew harder and harder, more and more urgent. It was this which took him one day to the rooms of an old gentleman who had not Dick's reasons for staying in town, but others which were perhaps as weighty, which were that he was fond of his corner in the club, and not of much else. His corner in the club, his walk along the streets, his cosy rooms, and the few old fogies, like himself, sharp as so many needles, giving their old opinions upon the events of the time with a humour sharpened by many an experience of the past: who counted every day only half a day when it was spent out of town. This old gentleman was a lawyer of very high repute, though he had retired from all active practice. He was a man who was supposed to know every case that had ever been on the registers of justice. He had refused the Bench, and he might even have been, if he would, Attorney-General, but to all these responsibilities he preferred freedom and his corner at the club. To him Dick went with a countenance fresh and fair, which contrasted with the parchment of the old lawyer's face, but a heart like a piece of lead lying in his breast, weighing down every impulse, which also contrasted strongly, though no one could see it, with the tough piece of mechanism screwed up to a very level pitch and now seldom out of order, which fulfilled the same organic functions under the old gentleman's coat.

"What, Dick! what ill wind—it must be an ill wind—sends you here in September? You ought to be among the partridges, my boy."

"It is an ill wind," said Dick.

"No need to tell me that: but judging by your complexion nothing of a tremendous character. Money? or love?"

"Well, sir, it is not really my own business at all. As for my complexion, that don't matter. I don't show outside."

"Some men don't," said the old lawyer laconically; "but if the trouble is not your own that is easy to understand."

At this Dick gave a short laugh. He wanted it to be believed that the trouble was not his own, and yet he did not quite care to be supposed indifferent to it.

"It's an old story," he said. "It is something that happened to— Tom Wyld, an old crony of mine out on the other side."

"I suppose you mean in America. No more slang than you can help, please. It's admirably expressive sometimes, I allow: but not being used to it in my youth I have some difficulty in following. Well, about Tom Wyld—one of the old judge's sons or grandsons, I suppose."

Dick's complexion heightened a little.

"Oh, not any one you ever heard of—a fellow I picked up—out

there."

"Oh, a fellow you picked up out there?"

"It was in one of the new States far West; not the sort of place for nicety of any sort, sir, to tell the truth. Judge Lynch and not much else, in the way of law."

"Works very well I don't doubt—simplifies business immensely," said the old lawyer, nodding his head.

"Makes business, too—lots of it. Well, sir, my friend met with a girl there." Dick seemed to have great difficulty in getting this out. He stammered and his healthy complexion grew now pale, now red.

"Most likely—they generally do, both in novels and out of them," the old gentleman said. "You had better tell me your story straight off. I shall interrupt you no more."

"Well, sir, the girl was very young, very pretty, I might say beautiful—not like anything he had ever met before. Without training, but he thought at her pliable age it was so easy to remedy that." (The old lawyer shook his head with a groan but said nothing.) "She had never seen anything but the rough people about, and knew only their manners and ways. Everything went on well enough for a little while after they were married."

"Good Lord, they were married!"

"What else?" said Dick, turning scarlet. "He respected her as every man must respect the woman he—the woman he—thinks he loves."

"I am glad you have the sense to see that he only thought he——Well, and what was the end of it, Mr. Dick?"

"The end of it was—what you have foreseen, sir," said Dick, bowing his head. "The fellow is my friend, that's to say Tom did all he could. I don't think he was without patience with her. After, when she left him for good, or rather for bad, bad as could be, he did everything he could to help her. He offered, not to take her back, that was not possible, but to provide for her and—and all that. She had all the savage virtues as well as faults. She was honourable in her way. She would take nothing from him.

She even made out what she called a paper, poor thing, to set him free. She would not take her freedom herself and leave him bound, she said. And then she disappeared."

"Leaving him the paper?"

"Yes," said Dick, with a faint smile, "leaving him the paper. He found it on his table. That is six years ago. He has never seen her since. He came home soon, feeling—I can't tell you how he felt."

"As if life were not much worth living, according to the slang of the day."

"Well, sir," said Dick, "he's a droll sort of a fellow. He—seemed to get over it somehow. It took a vast deal out of him, but yet he got over it in a kind of a way. He came back among his own people; and what have they been doing since ever he came back but imploring him to marry! It would settle him they all said, if he could get some nice girl: and they have done nothing but throw nice girls in his way—some of the nicest girls in England, I believe,—one——"

"Good Lord!" said the old man, "you don't mean to say this unlucky young fellow has fallen in love again?"

Dick shook his head with a rueful air, in which it was impossible not to see a touch of the comic, notwithstanding his despair. "This is precisely why he wants your opinion, that is, some one's opinion—for of course he has not the honour of knowing you."

"Hasn't he? Ah! I began to think I remembered something about your Tom—or was it Dick—Wyld? Tom Wyld—I think I have heard the name."

"If you should meet him in society," cried Dick, growing very red, "don't for heaven's sake make any allusion to this. I ought not to have mentioned his name."

"Well, get on with the story," said the old man. "He thinks, perhaps, he is free to make love to the other girl and marry—because of that precious paper."

"He is not such a fool as that: I, even," said Dick, faltering, "know law enough to warn him that would be folly. But you know, sir, in some of the wild States, like the one he lived in, divorce is the easiest thing in the world."

"Well: and he thinks he can get a divorce? He had better do it then without more ado. I suppose the evidence—is sufficient?"

Dick gave vent to a hoarse, nervous laugh. "Sufficient—for twenty divorces," he said, then he added quickly: "But that's not the question."

"Why, what is the question then? He should be very thankful to be able to manage it so easily instead of being dragged through the mud for everybody to gloat over in London. What does the fellow want?" said the old man peevishly. "Many a man would be glad to find so easy a way."

Dick's embarrassment was great, he changed colour, he could not keep still, his voice grew husky and broken. "I don't say that I agree with him, but this is what he thinks. It's easy enough: but he would have to summon her by the newspapers to answer for herself, which she wouldn't do. And who can tell what hands that newspaper might fall into? He says that nobody knows anything about it here; no one has the slightest suspicion that he ever was married or had any entanglement. And she, poor soul, to do her justice, would never put forth a claim. She never would molest him, of that he is sure. He thinks——"

"You take a great deal of interest in your friend's cause, Dick!" For Dick had paused with parted lips, unable to say any more.

"I do. It's a case that has been very interesting to me. He asks why he should take any notice of it at all—a thing done when he was scarcely of age, thousands of miles away, a mistake—an utter failure—a—ah!"—Dick had been speaking very rapidly against time to get out what he had to say before he was interrupted— "you don't see it in that point of view."

"Do you mean to say, sir," said the old gentleman, "that you contemplate betraying a woman by a fictitious marriage, making her children illegitimate and herself a—I can't suppose that you have any real intention of that."

Dick, who had got up in his excitement, here sat down

suddenly as if his strength had failed him, with an exclamation of horror and alarm.

"You don't see that? Why, what else would it be? so long as there is a Mrs.—what do you call her?—living—living and undivorced, the union of that woman's husband with another woman could be nothing but a fictitious marriage. There is a still uglier word by which it could be called."

"You forget," said Dick, "that Mrs. Wyld—neither bears that name nor lays any claim to it. She put it aside long ago when she went upon her own course. It was nothing to her. She is not of the kind that try to keep up appearances or—anything of that sort. I'll do her that justice, she never meant to give the—the—unfortunate fellow any trouble. She didn't even want to stand in his way. She told him he should neither hear of her nor see her again. She is honest, though she is—— She has been to him as if she did not exist for years."

"Why does that matter," cried the old gentleman, "so long as she does exist? There are women who are mad and never can be otherwise—but that does not give their husbands a right to marry again. Divorce her, since you are sure you can do so, and be thankful you have that remedy. I suppose this woman is—not a lady."

"No." Dick spoke in a very low voice. He was quite cowed and subdued, looking at his old friend with furtive looks of trouble. Though he spoke carefully as if the case were not his own, yet he did not attempt to correct the elder man who at once assumed it to be so. He was so blanched and tremulous, nothing but the red of his lips showing out of his colourless face, and all the lines drawn with inward suffering, that he too might have been an old man. He added in the same low tones: "A man who is divorced would be a sort of monster to them. They would never permit—she would never listen."

"You mean—the other? well, that is possible. There is a prejudice, and a just prejudice. So you think on the whole that to do a young lady—for I suppose the second is in your own class—a real, an unspeakable injury would be better than to shock her prejudices? If that is how you of the new generation confuse what's right and wrong——"

Dick made no reply. He was not capable of self-defence, or even of understanding the indignation he had called forth. He continued as if only half conscious. "It need never be known. There is not a creature who knows of it. She sent me her marriage lines. She has nothing to prove that there ever was anything— and she would not want to prove anything. She is as if she were dead."

"Come, sir," said the lawyer, "rouse yourself, Dick; she is not dead, and for every honourable man that must be enough. Don't bewilder yourself with sophistries. Why should you want to marry—again? You have had enough of it, I should think; or else divorce her, since you can. You may be able to do that secretly as well as the marriage. Why not?"

Dick said nothing, but shook his head. He was so completely cast down that he had not a word to say for himself. How he could have supposed that a dispassionate man could have taken his side and seen with his eyes in such a matter, it is hard to say. He had thought of it so much that all the lines had got blurred to him, and right and wrong had come to seem relative terms. "What harm would it do?" he said to himself, scarcely aware he was speaking aloud. "No one would be wronged, and they would never know. How could they know? it would be impossible. Whereas, on the other side, there must be a great scandal and raking up of everything, and betrayal—to every one." He shuddered as he spoke.

"Whereas, on the other side," said the old lawyer, "there would be a betrayal—very much more serious. Suppose you were to die, and that then it were to be found out (in the long run everything is found out) that your wife was not your wife, and her children—— Come, Dick, you never can have contemplated a blackguard act like that to an unsuspecting girl!"

"Sir!" cried Dick, starting to his feet. But he could not maintain that resentful attitude. He sank down in the chair again, and said with a groan, "What am I to do?"

"There is only one thing for you to do: but it is very clear. Either explain the real circumstances to the young lady or her friends— or without any explanation give up seeing her. In any case it is evident that the connection must be cut at once. Of course if she knows the true state of the case, and that you are a married man, she will do that. And if you shrink from explanations, *you* must do it without an hour's delay."

Dick made no reply. He sat for a time with his head in his hands: and then rose up with a dazed look, as if he scarcely knew what he was about. "Good-bye," he said, "and thank you. I'll—tell Tom—what you said."

"Do," said the old lawyer, getting up. He took Dick's hand and wrung it in his own with a pressure that, though the thin old fingers had but little force, was painful in its energy. "You don't ask my silence, but I'll promise it you—except in one contingency," and here he wrung Dick's hand again. "Should I hear of any marriage—after what you have said, I shall certainly think it my duty to interfere."

When Dick came out the day seemed to have grown dark to him; the sky was all covered with threads of black; he could scarcely see his way.

CHAPTER XL.

Nevertheless Dick went down to Highcombe on the following Saturday. There are two ways in which advice can work: one by convincing the man who receives it to abandon his own evil way, and adopt the good way set before him, which of course is the object of all good advice, although but rarely attained to; the other is to make him far more hotly and determinedly bent upon his own way, with a sort of personal opposition to the adviser, and angry sense that he has not properly understood the subject, or entered into those subtle reasons below the surface which make a certain course of action, not generally desirable, perhaps, the only one that can be appropriately adopted in this particular case. This was the effect produced upon Dick. He spent the intervening time in turning it over and over in his mind, as he had already done so often, until all the outlines were blurred. For a long time he had been able to put that early, fatal, mad marriage out of his mind altogether, finding himself actually able to forget it; so that if any one had suddenly accused him of being, as his old friend said, a married man, he would have, on the first shock, indignantly denied the imputation. It had lasted so short a time, it had ended in such miserable disaster! Scarcely a week had passed before he had discovered the horror and folly of what he had done. He had not, like many men, laid the blame upon the unhappy creature who had led him into these toils. She was no unhappy creature, but one of those butterfly-women without any soul, to whom there are no distinctions of right and wrong. He discovered afterwards that if he had not himself been honourable, it was not she who would have insisted upon the bond of marriage, and whether she had ever intended to be bound by it he could not tell. Her easy, artless independence of all moral laws had been a revelation to the young man such as arrested his very life, and filled him with almost awe in the midst of his misery, disgust, and horror. Without any soul, or heart, or shame, or sense that better was required from her—this was what she was. All the evil elements of corrupt civilisation and savage freedom seemed to have got mixed in her blood: half of the worst of the old world, half of the rudest and wildest of the new. She had been a captivating wonder to the young Englishman, accustomed to all the domestic bonds and decorums, when he saw her first, a fresh wild-flower, as he thought, with the purity as well as the savagery of primitive nature. But afterwards it seemed an uncertain matter whether she had ever known what purity was, or whether those links which bound him to her had not bound other men even before his day. She had flung in his face those marriage lines which women of the lower classes generally hold in such reverence, and had laughed and assured him that they were so much waste paper, and that as she did not mean to be bound by them, neither need he; and then she had disappeared, and for years he had not known that she existed. The awful discovery that she was in the neighbourhood of his friends, and that he himself might by chance meet her any moment on the common road, had turned him to stone. Lizzie Hampson had been her maid during the brief period in which she was his wife, and had loved and clung to her, the subject of a fascination not uncommon between women, after every other trace of that episode in her life had passed away. Dick Cavendish had not for years thought of that miserable episode in his until he had by chance recognised Lizzie at Underwood. He had even lent himself with no serious purpose, yet with a light heart, to that scheme of his family and friends about the nice girl who was to convert him into a steady member of society. No doubt the moment it had become serious he must have felt himself brought face to face with the burdens and hindrances of his previous career, even had he not seen Lizzie Hampson. This reminder of what had been, however, came at the exact crisis when Chatty

Warrender had (as his errant imagination always pictured her) pushed open lightly the door of his heart and walked in with the bowl of roses in her hands: and hence all the tumults and storms which had suddenly seized again upon a life almost forgetful of any cause for these tempests. He knew what he ought to have done then. He ought to have flown from Chatty and every other "nice girl," as indeed he had done at once, to do him justice. But who could have foreseen that meeting in London, who provided against the necessity of "paying a little attention" to the mother and sister of his friend? And now here was this invitation, which meant—what did it mean?

It meant at least that Mrs. Warrender did not object to the continuance of that intercourse, that perhaps Chatty herself—perhaps Chatty—— His pulses had been beating hotly enough before: but when this thought came, the mingling of a delicious sort of intoxicating pleasure with the misery was more than he could bear. When he got home to his rooms he opened the despatch box which had accompanied him through all his wanderings, and which, he suddenly recollected, should "anything happen to him," held all the indications of a secret in his life without any explanation of it, and went over its contents. He was interrupted in the midst of this by a chance and inopportune visitor, no less than a younger brother, who pulled the papers about, and cried, "Hallo, what's this?" with the unjustifiable freedom of a near relation, bringing Dick's heart into his mouth, and furnishing him with a dreadful example of what might be, were a touch of more authority laid upon those scattered *débris* of his life. A young brother could be sent away, or otherwise disposed of, but there might come those who could not be sent away. When he was alone again, he found the few papers connected with his secret amid many others of no consequence, and it gave Dick a curious thrill, half of amusement, to think of the spring of astonished interest with which some problematical person who might examine these papers after his death would come upon this little trace of something so different from the tame relics of every day. There was the letter which she had left behind her setting him free, as the lawless creature intended; there was the marriage certificate and some little jumble of mementos which somehow, without any will of his, had got associated with the more important papers. Dick looked over the bundle as if through the eyes of that man who would go through them after his death, finding out this appalling mystery. The man would be delighted, though it might not be a pleasant discovery—it might (Dick went on imagining to himself) throw a horrible doubt, as old What's-his-name said, upon the standing of his widow, upon the rights of his child—but the man who found it would be delighted. It would come so unexpectedly amid all these uninteresting letters and records of expenditure. It would brighten them up with the zest of a story, of a discovery; it would add an interest to all the lawyer's investigations into his estate. All the men about would meet and shake their heads over it, putting two and two together, making out what it meant. Probably they would advertise cautiously (which was what Dick himself, as a budding lawyer, would recommend in the circumstances) for *her*, poor creature, sure to be dead and buried long before that. They would consult together whether it was necessary to inform poor Mrs. Cavendish until they had something more definite to say. Dick, looking down the vale of years, saw, or thought he saw, with a curious quiver of his heart between pleasure and pity, Chatty in a widow's cap, shedding tears at the sound of his name, absolutely obtuse and incapable of understanding how any dishonour could have come to her by him. They would think her stupid, Dick believed, with a tear stealing to the corner of his eye. Yes, she would be blank with a holy stupidity, God bless her, idiotic, if you like, my fine gentleman, in that—not capable of understanding dishonour. It was with a sort of grim pleasure that he got up after this and lighted a candle, which shone strangely yellow and smoky in the clear September sunshine. "I'll balk them," he said to himself, with fierce satisfaction, as if those respectable imaginary executors of his had been ill-natured gossips bent on exposing him. And he burnt the papers one by one at his candle, watching the last fibre of each fade away in redness and then in blackness, disappearing into nothing.

And then he packed his portmanteau and went down to Highcombe. There are some people who will think this inconceivable, but then these good persons perhaps have never had a strong overpowering inclination to fight against, never been pressed and even menaced by an urgent adviser, never recognised that necessity of doing one thing which seems to throw the troubled mind into the arms of the other. And then below all these contentions Dick had a stubborn, strong determination to conduct this matter his own way. He had decided in his mind that it was the best way. If there had been any latent doubt on the subject before he consulted his old friend, that had been dissipated by the interview and by all the old gentleman's cogent reasoning on the other side. Dick felt that he had taken the bit in his teeth and would be guided by no man. It *was* the best way, there was no risk in it, no wrong in it—certainly no wrong. He had not dealt even harshly with that wretched creature. He knew that he had been kind, that he had tried every way to reclaim her, and she had freed him from every law, human or divine. He could get a divorce anywhere, that he knew; and after all a divorce was but the legal affirmation of that severance which had been made by nature, ay, and by God. Even the pure law of Christianity permitted it for that one cause. Therefore there was no wrong. And to spare publicity was merciful, merciful to her as well as to himself.

Thus he reasoned, growing more certain on each repetition, and packed his portmanteau. But yet he did not take Mrs. Warrender's invitation in all its fulness. There was a little salve for any possible prick of conscience in this. Instead of from Monday to Saturday, as she said, he kept to the original proposal and went from Saturday to Monday. There was something in that; it was a self-denial, a self-restraint—he felt that it was something to the other side of the account.

The Eustace Thynnes were still at Highcombe when he arrived, and Mrs. Warrender had a little foretaste of the gratification which she proposed to herself in announcing to Minnie at some future period the name of her brother-in-law, in perceiving how deeply Minnie was impressed by the visitor, and the evident but very delicately indicated devotion with which he regarded Chatty, a thing which took the young married lady altogether by surprise and gave her much thought. As for Chatty herself, it was with the sensation of one reluctantly awaked out of a dream, that she suffered herself once more to glide into the brighter life which seemed to come and go with Cavendish, an attendant atmosphere. The dream, indeed, had not been happy, but there had been a dim and not unsweet tranquillity in it—a calm which was congenial to Chatty's nature. Besides that she was still young enough to feel a luxury in that soft languor of disappointment and failure against which she had never rebelled, which she had accepted as her lot. Was it possible that it was not to be her lot after all? Was there something before her brighter, more beautiful, after all? not an agitated happiness, more excitement than bliss, like that of Theo, not the sort of copartnery of superior natures laying down the law to all surroundings, like Minnie and her Eustace: but something much more lovely, the true ideal, that which poetry was full of—was it possible that to herself, Chatty, the simplest and youngest (she was older than Theo it was true, but that did not seem to count somehow now that Theo was a man and married), this beautiful lot was to come? She was very shy to accept the thought, holding back with a gentle modesty, trying not to see how Dick's thoughts and looks turned to her— an attitude that was perfect in its conformity with her nature and looks, and filled Dick with tender admiration mingled with a little alarm, such as he had not heretofore felt, but which touched Minnie with astonishment and indignation. "She can't be going to refuse Mr. Cavendish," she said afterwards to the partner of all her thoughts. "It would be very surprising," said Eustace. "Oh, it must not be allowed for a moment," Minnie cried.

On the first evening, which was Saturday, Lady Markland and Theo came to dinner: she very sweet, and friendly and gracious to every one, he full of cloudy bliss, with all his nerves on the surface, ready to be wounded by any chance touch. The differing characteristics of the family thus assembled together might have given an observer much amusement, so full was each of his and her special little circle of wishes and interests: but time does not permit us to linger upon that little society. Lady Markland attached herself most to the mother, with a curious fellow-feeling which touched yet alarmed Mrs. Warrender. "I am more on your level than on theirs," she whispered. "My dear, that is nonsense, Minnie is as old as you are," Mrs. Warrender said. But then Minnie had never been anything but a young lady until she married Eustace, and Lady Markland—ah, nothing could alter the fact that Lady Markland had already lived a life with which Theo had nothing to do. In the midst of this family party Chatty and her affairs were a little thrown into the background. She fulfilled all the modest little offices of the young lady of the house, made the tea and served it sweetly, brought her mother's work and footstool, did everything that was wanted. Dick could not talk to her much, indeed talking was not Chatty's strong point; but he followed her about with his eyes, and took the advantage of all her simple ministrations, in which she shone much more than in talk.

But the Sunday morning was the best. The Rev. Eustace took the duty by special request of the vicar in the chief church of Highcombe, and Dick went with the mother and daughter to a humble little old church standing a little out of the town, with its little inclosure round it full of those rural graves where one cannot help thinking the inmates must sleep sounder than anywhere else. Here, as it was very near, they were in the habit of attending, and Chatty, though she was not a great musician, played the organ, as so many young ladies in country places do. When the little green curtain that veiled the organ loft was drawn aside for a moment Dick had a glimpse of her, looking out her music before she began, with a chubby-faced boy who was to "blow" for her at her hand: and this foolish lover thought of Luca della Robbia's friezes, and the white vision of Florentine singers and players on the lute. The puffy-cheeked boy was just like one of those sturdy Tuscan urchins, but the maiden was of finer ware, like a madonna. So Dick thought: although Chatty had never called forth such fine imaginations before. They all walked home together very peacefully in a tender quiet, which lasted until the Eustace Thynnes came back with their remarks upon everybody. And in the afternoon Dick told Mrs. Warrender that he must go over and see Wilberforce at Underwood. There were various things he had to talk to Wilberforce about, and he would be back to dinner, which was late on Sunday to leave time for the evening church-going. Chatty had her Sunday-school, so it was as well for him to go. He set out walking, having first engaged the people at the Plough Inn to send a dog-cart to bring him back. It was a very quiet unexciting road, rather dusty, with here and there a break through the fields. His mind was full of a hundred things to think of; his business was not with Wilberforce, but with Lizzie Hampson, whom he must see, and ask—what was he to ask? He could scarcely make out to himself. But she was the sole custodian of this secret, and he must know how she could be silenced, or if it would be necessary to silence her, to keep her from interfering. The walk, though it was six long miles, was not long enough for him to decide what he should say. He went round the longest way, passing the Elms in order to see if the house was still empty, with a chill terror in his heart of seeing some trace of those inhabitants whose presence had been an insult to him. But all was shut up, cold and silent; he knew that they were gone, and yet it was a relief to him when he saw with his eyes that this was so. Then he paused and looked down the little path opening by a rustic gate into the wood, which led to the Warren. It was a footpath free to the villagers, and he saw one or two people at long intervals passing along, for the road led by the farther side of the pond and was a favourite Sunday walk.

Dick thought he would like to see what changes Warrender had made and also the spot where he had seen Chatty if not for the first time, yet the first time with the vision which identified her among all women. He went along, lingering to note the trees that had been cut down and the improvements made, and his mind had so completely abandoned its former course of thought for another, that when Lizzie Hampson came out of the little wood, and met him, he started as if he had not known she was here. There was nobody else in sight, and he had time enough as she approached him to recover the former thread of his musings. She did not recognise him until they were close to each other: then she showed the same reluctance to speak to him which she had done before, and after a hasty glance round as if looking for a way of escape, cast down her eyes and head evidently with the intention of hurrying past as if she had not seen him. He saw through the momentary conflict of thought, and kept his eyes upon her. "I am glad that I have met you," he said; "I wanted to see you," standing in front of her so that she could not escape.

"But I don't want to see you, sir," Lizzie said, respectfully enough.

"That may be: but still—I have some questions to ask you. Will you come with me towards the house? We shall be less interrupted there."

"If I must, I'd rather hear you here, sir," said Lizzie. "I won't have the folks say that I talk with a gentleman in out-of-the-way places. It's better on the common road."

"As you please," said Dick. "You know what the subject is. I want to know——"

"What, sir? You said as I was to let you know when trouble came. Now no trouble's come, and there's no need, nor ever will be. She would never take help from you."

"Why? She has done me harm enough," he said.

"She never says anything different. She will never take help from you. She will never hear of you, nor you of her. Never, never. Consider her as if she were dead, sir—that's all her desire."

"I might have done that before I saw you. But now——"

"You don't mean," said Lizzie, with a sudden eager gleam of curiosity, "that you—that after all that's come and gone——?" The look that passed over his face, a flush of indignation, a slight shudder of disgust, gave her the answer to her unspoken question. She drew herself together again, quickly, suddenly catching her breath. "I can't think," she said, "what questions there can be."

"There is this," he said: "I had almost forgotten her existence— till I saw you: but now that is not possible. Look here, I may have to try and get a divorce—you know what that means—out there, not here: and she must have warning. Will you let her know?"

The girl started a little, the word frightened her. "Oh, sir," she cried, "you wouldn't punish her, you wouldn't put her in prison or that? Oh, don't, sir. She would die—and you know she's not fit to die."

"You mistake," said Dick; "there is no question of punishment, only to be free of each other—as if indeed, as you say, she were dead to me."

"And so she is," cried Lizzie earnestly. "She never will have her name named to you, that's what she says, never if she should be ever so—— She's given you your freedom as she's taken hers, and never, never shall you hear word of her more: that is what she says."

"Yet she is in England, for all she says."

"Did she ever pass you her word not to come to England? But I don't say as she's in England now. Oh, it was an ill wind, sir," cried Lizzie with vehemence, "that brought you here!"

"It may be so," Dick said, with a gravity that went beyond any conscious intention of regret he had. "There is but one thing now, and that is that I must be free. Let her know that I must take proceedings for divorce. I have no way of reaching her but through you."

"Sir, there is somebody coming," said Lizzie; "pass on as if you had been asking me the way. I'll let her know. I'll never open my lips to you more nor to any one, about her, but I'll do what you say. That's the way to the house," she added, turning, pointing out the path that led away from the side of the pond towards the Warren. He followed the indication without another word, and in a minute stood in the peaceful shadow of the deserted house. It came upon him chill, but wholesome, life reviving after the agitation of that brief encounter. Divorce—it was a bad word to breathe in such an honest place—a bad blasphemous word, worse than an oath. He had not meant to say it, nor thought of it before this meeting: but now he seemed to be pledged to this step involuntarily, unwillingly; was it by some good angel, something that was working in Chatty's interests and for her sweet sake?

CHAPTER XLI.

Dick went back to town on the Monday, having taken no decisive step, nor said any decisive words. All that he had done was to make it apparent that the matter was not to end there, as had seemed likely when they parted in London. Chatty now saw that it was not to be so. The thing was not to drop into the mere blank of unfulfilledness, but was to be brought to her decision, to yea or nay. This conviction, and the company of Dick in a relation which could not but be new, since it was no longer accidental, but of the utmost gravity in her life, gave a new turn altogether to her existence. The change in her was too subtle for the general eye. Even Minnie, sharp as she was, could make nothing more of it than that Chatty was "more alive looking," a conclusion which, like most things nowadays, she declared to come from Eustace. Mrs. Warrender entered with more sympathy into her daughter's life, veiled not so much by intention as by instinctive modesty and reserve from her as from all others: but even she did not know what was in Chatty's mind, the slow rising of an intense light which illuminated her as the sun lights up a fertile plain,— the low land drinking in every ray, unconscious of shadow,— making few dramatic effects, but receiving the radiance at every point. Chatty herself felt like that low-lying land. The new life suffused her altogether, drawing forth few reflections, but flooding the surface of her being, and warming her nature through and through. It was to be hers, then,—not as Minnie, not as Theo had it,—but like Shakespeare, like poetry, like that which maidens dream.

Dick went back to town. When he had gone to his old friend for advice his mind had revolted against that advice and determined upon his own way; but the short interview with Lizzie Hampson had changed everything. He had not meant to speak to her on the subject; and what did it matter though he had spoken to her for a twelvemonth? She could not have understood him or his desire. She thought he meant to punish the poor, lost creature, perhaps to put her in prison. The word divorce had terrified her. And yet he now felt as if he had committed himself to that procedure, and it must be carried out. Yet a strange reluctance to take the first steps retarded him. Even to an unknown advocate in the far West a man is reluctant to allow that his name has been dishonoured. The publicity of an investigation before a tribunal, even when three or four thousand miles away, is horrible to think of,—although less horrible than had the wrong and misery taken place nearer home. But after six years, and over a great ocean and the greater part of a continent, how futile it seemed to stir up all those long-settled sediments again! He wrote and rewrote a letter to a lawyer whose name he remembered, to whom he had done one or two slight services, in the distant State which was the scene of his brief and miserable story. But he had not yet satisfied himself with this letter when there occurred an interruption which put everything of the kind out of his thoughts.

This was the receipt of a communication in black borders so portentous that Dick, always alive to the comic side of everything, was moved for the moment to a profane laugh. "No mourning could ever be so deep as this looks," he said to himself, and opened the gloomy missive with little thought. It could, he believed, only convey to him information of the death of some one whom he knew little, and for whom he cared less. But the first glance effectually changed his aspect. His face grew colourless, the paper fell out of his hands. "Good God!" he said. It was no profane exclamation. What was this? a direct interposition of heaven in his behalf, a miracle such as is supposed never to happen nowadays? The first effect was to take breath and strength from him. He sat with his under jaw fallen, his face livid as if with dismay. His heart seemed to stand still; awe, as if an execution had been performed before his eyes, came over him. He felt as if he had a hand in it, as if some action of his had brought doom upon the sufferer. A cold perspiration came out on his forehead. Had he wished her death in the midst of her sins, poor, miserable woman? Had he set the powers of fate to work against her, he, arrogant in his virtue and the happiness that lay within his reach? Compunction was the first thought. It seemed to him that he had done it. Had he a right to do it, to cut off her time of repentance, to push her beyond the range of hope?

After this, however, he picked up the letter again with trembling hands, and read it. It was from a man who described himself as the head of a circus company in Liverpool, with whom Emma Altamont had been performing. She had died in consequence of a fall two days before. "She directed me with her last breath to write to you, to say that you would know her under another name, which she was not going to soil by naming it even on her deathbed, but that you would know. She died very penitent, and leaving her love to all friends. She was very well liked in the company, though she joined it not so very long ago. A few things that she left behind she requested you to have the choice of, if you cared for any keepsake to remember her by, and sent you her forgiveness freely, as she hoped to be forgiven by you. The funeral is to be on Sunday, at two o'clock; and I think she would have taken it kind as a mark of respect if she had thought you would come. I leave that to your own sense of what is best."

This was the letter which fell like a bomb into Dick's life. It was long before he could command himself enough to understand anything but the first startling fact. She was dead. In his heart, by his thoughts, had he killed her? was it his fault? He did not go beyond this horrible idea for some long minutes. Then there suddenly seized upon him a flood of gladness, a sensation of guilty joy. God had stepped in to set the matter straight. The miracle which we all hope for, which never seems impossible in our own case, had been wrought. All lesser ways of making wrong right were unnecessary now. All was over, the pain of retrospection, the painful expedients of law, the danger of publicity, all over.

The choice of her poor little leavings for a token to remember her by! Dick shuddered at the thought. To remember her by! when to forget her was all that he wished.

It was long before he could do anything save think, in confused whirls of recollection, and painful flashes of memory, seeing before his hot eyes a hundred phantasmal scenes. But at last he roused himself to a consideration of what he ought to do. Prudence seemed to suggest an immediate journey to Liverpool, to satisfy himself personally that all was effectually winded up and concluded in this miserable account; but a dread, a repugnance, which he could not overcome, held him back. He could not take part by act or word in anything that concerned her again; not even, poor creature, in her funeral; not from any enmity or hatred to her, poor unfortunate one, but because of the horror, the instinctive shrinking, which he could not overcome. Dick determined, however, to send the man who had charge of his chambers, a man half servant, half clerk, in whom he could fully trust. It was Friday when he received the letter. He sent him down next day to Liverpool with instructions to represent him at the funeral, to offer money if necessary to defray its expenses, to let no "respect" be spared. She would have liked "respect" in this way. It would have given her pleasure to think that she was to have a fine funeral. Dick gave his man the fullest instructions. "She was connected with—friends of mine," Dick said, "who would wish everything to be respectably done, though they cannot themselves take any part." "I understand, sir," said the man, who put the most natural interpretation upon the strange commission, and did not believe in any fiction about Dick's "friends." Dick called him back when he had reached the door. "You can see the things of which this person writes, and choose some small thing without value, the smaller the better, to send as he proposes to—the people she belongs to." This seemed the last precaution of prudence to make assurance sure.

After this, three days of tumultuous silence till the messenger came back. He came bringing a description of the funeral, a photograph of "the poor young lady," and a little ring—a ring which Dick himself had given her, so long, so long ago. The sight of these relics had an effect upon him impossible to describe. He had to keep his countenance somehow till the man had been dismissed. The photograph was taken in fancy dress, in one of the circus costumes, and was full of all manner of dreadful accessories; the stage smile, the made-up beauty, the tortured hair: but there was no difficulty in recognising it. A trembling like palsy seized upon him as he gazed at it: then he lit his taper once more, and with a prayer upon his quivering lips burnt it. The ring he twisted up in paper, and carried out with him in his hand till he reached the muddy, dark-flowing river, where he dropped it in. Thus all relics and vestiges of her, poor creature, God forgive her! were vanished and put out of sight for evermore.

Next day Dick Cavendish, a new man, went once more to Highcombe. He was not quite the light-hearted fellow he had been. There was a little emotion about him, a liquid look in the eyes, a faint quiver about the mouth, which Chatty, when she lifted her soft eyes with a little start of surprise and consciousness to greet him, perceived at once and set down to their true cause. Ah yes, it was their true cause. Here he was, come to offer himself with a past full of the recollections we know, with a life which had been all but ruined in times gone by, to the whitest soul he had ever met with, a woman who was innocence and purity personified; who would perhaps, if she knew, shrink from him, refuse the hand which she would think a soiled one. Dick had all this in his mind, and it showed in his countenance, which was full of feeling, but feeling of which Chatty understood nothing. He found her alone by the merest chance. Everything seemed to work for him in this season of fortune. No inquisitive sister, no intrusive brother-in-law, not even the mother with her inquiring eyes was here to interrupt. The jar with the big campanulas stood in the corner; the mignonettes breathed softly an atmosphere of fragrance; her muslin work was in Chatty's hand.

Well, he had not a great deal to say. It had all been said by his eyes in the first moment, so that the formal words were but a repetition. The muslin work dropped after a few seconds, and Chatty's hands were transferred to his to be caressed and kissed and whispered over. He had loved her ever since that day when she had lightly pushed open the door of the faded drawing-room at the Warren and walked in with her bowl of roses. "That was the door of my heart," Dick said. "You had come in before I knew. I can smell the roses still, and I shall ask Theo for that bowl for a wedding present. And you, my Chatty, and you?"

Mrs. Warrender had her little triumph that afternoon. She said, with the most delicate politeness: "I hope, Minnie, that Eustace after all will be able to tolerate his new brother-in-law." Minnie gave her mother a look of such astonishment as proved that the fine edge of the sarcasm was lost.

"To tolerate—a Cavendish! I can't think what you mean, mamma! Eustace is not an ignorant goose, though you seem to think so; nor am I."

"I am glad your Honours are pleased," said the ironical mother, with a laugh. Minnie stared and repeated the speech to Eustace, who was not very clear either about its meaning. But "Depend upon it, dear, your mother meant to be nasty," he said, which was quite true.

After this, all was commotion in the house. Dick, though he had been an uncertain lover, was very urgent now. He made a brief explanation to Mrs. Warrender that his proposal had not been made at the time they parted in London, "only because of an entanglement of early youth," which made her look grave. "I do not inquire what you mean," she said, "but I hope at least that it is entirely concluded." "Entirely," he replied with fervour; "nor am I to blame as you think, nor has it had any existence for six years. I was young then." "Very young, poor boy!" she said with her old indulgent smile. He made the same brief explanation to Chatty, but Chatty had no understanding whatever of what the words meant and took no notice. If she thought of it at all she thought it was something about money, to her a matter of the most complete indifference. And so everything became bustle and commotion, and the preparations for the wedding were put in hand at once. The atmosphere was full of congratulations, of blushes and wreathed smiles. "Marriage is certainly contagious; when it once begins in a family, one never knows where it will stop," the neighbours said: and some thought Mrs. Warrender much to be felicitated on getting all her young people settled; and some, much to be condoled with on losing her last girl just as she had settled down. But these last were in the minority, for to get rid of your daughters is a well understood advantage, which commends itself to the meanest capacity.

It was arranged for the convenience of everybody that the wedding was to take place in London. Dick's relations were legion, and to stow them away in the Dower house at Highcombe, or even to find room to give them a sandwich and a glass of wine, let alone a breakfast, after the ceremony, was impossible. Dick himself was particularly urgent about this particular, he could not have told why, whether from a foreboding of disturbance or some other incomprehensible reason. But as for disturbance, there was no possibility of that. Every evil thing that could have interfered had been exorcised and lost its power. There was nothing in his way; nothing to alarm or trouble, but only general approval and the satisfaction of everybody concerned.

CHAPTER XLII.

Lizzie Hampson heard, like everybody in the village, of what was about to happen. Miss Chatty was going to be married. At first all that was known was that the bridegroom was a gentleman from London, which in those days was a description imposing to rustics. He was a gentleman who had once been visiting at the Rectory, who had been seen in the rector's pew at church, and walking about the village, and on the road to the Warren. Many of the village gossips remembered, or thought they remembered, to have seen him, and they said to each other, with a natural enjoyment of a love story which never fails in women, that no doubt that was when "it was all made up." It gave many of them a great deal of pleasure to think that before Miss Minnie had ever seen "that parson," her more popular sister had also had a lover, though he hadn't spoken till after, being mayhap a shy gentleman, as is seen often and often. He was a fair-haired gentleman and very pleasant spoken. What his name was nobody cared so much; the villagers found it more easy to recollect him by the colour of his hair than by his name. It was some time before Lizzie identified the gentleman whom Miss Chatty was about to marry. She had a small part of the trousseau to prepare, one or two morning dresses to make, a commission which made her proud and happy, and gave her honour in the sight of her friends and detractors, a thing dear to all. And then at the very last Lizzie discovered who the bridegroom was. The discovery affected her very greatly. It was the occasion of innumerable self-arguments, carried on in the absolute seclusion of a mind occupied by matters, its acquaintance with which is unknown. Old Mrs. Bagley talked about the marriage to every one who came into the shop. It was, she said, almost as if it was a child of her own.

Thus Lizzie heard—all that there was to hear: and her mind grew more perplexed as time went on. She had the strange ignorances and the still more strange beliefs common to her kind. She put her faith in those popular glosses of the law, at which the better instructed laugh, but which are to the poor and unlearned like the canons of faith. It was the very eve of the wedding before her growing anxiety forced her to action. When Mr. Wilberforce was told that a young woman wanted to see him, he was arranging with his wife the train by which they were to go up to town to the wedding, not without comments on the oddness of the proceeding, which Mrs. Wilberforce thought was but another of the many signs of the times—which severed all bonds, and made a nasty big hotel better than your own house. The rector was in the habit of taking his wife's comments very calmly, for he himself was not so much alarmed about our national progress to destruction as she was. But yet he had his own opinion on the subject, and thought it was undignified on the part of Mrs. Warrender not to have her daughter married at home. He was only to be the second in importance in point of view of the ceremony itself, having no more to do than to assist a bishop who was of the Cavendish clan: whereas he felt himself quite man enough to have married Chatty out of hand without any assistance at all. However, to assist a bishop in the capacity of the parish clergyman of the bride was a position not without dignity, and he felt that he had, on the whole, little to complain of. He went into his study to speak to the young woman when that little consultation was over. Lizzie was seated, as they always were, upon the edge of one of the chairs. He was surprised to see her, though he could scarcely have said why.

"Oh, Lizzie! I am sorry to have kept you waiting: but I had something to do for Mrs. Wilberforce," the rector said.

"It doesn't matter, sir. I came to ask your advice, if I may make so bold."

"Certainly, certainly, Lizzie—anything that I can do."

"It isn't for me, sir, it's for a friend," she said, with the same device which Dick had employed, but in her case with more appropriateness. "I want to ask you, sir, about marriages. Oh, it's very serious, sir, there's nothing to smile about."

"I will not smile then, Lizzie. I shall be as serious as you please."

"It's just this, sir. When a man has been married and has had his wife run away from him and hasn't seen her nor heard of her for years—for six or seven years—he's free to marry again?"

"Do you think so? I should not like to affirm so much as that."

"But what I want you to tell me," said Lizzie, running on very quickly and taking no notice of his interruption, "is whether, if it could be proved that he *had* heard of her though he hadn't seen her, if that would make any difference?"

"I have no doubt it would make all the difference in the world. Even your first statement is doubtful, I fear. I don't think seven years is a sacred period that would justify a second marriage."

"I didn't say seven, sir, for certain. Six or seven."

"That is of little importance. The presumption is, that if he has heard nothing of her for a long period she must be dead; but of course, if he has heard of her existence——"

"But dead to him, oh, dead to him!" cried Lizzie, "leading a dreadful life, not a woman he could ever touch, or so much as look at again."

"I am afraid," said the rector, shaking his head, "though it is a very hard case for him, that there is nothing to be done. He should try and get a divorce—but that is a serious business. I don't know what else there is in his power."

"Would he be punished for it, sir?"

"It is not so much the punishment to him. In a hard case like this, the circumstances would be very much taken into consideration. Very likely it would be only a nominal punishment. The fatal consequences are not to the man, but to the woman—— I mean the second wife."

"But she knows nothing about it, sir. Why should she be punished? It's no doing of hers. She don't know."

"Then, my good girl, you should warn her. Though she knows nothing about it, and is quite innocent, it is upon her chiefly that the consequences will fall. She will not be his wife at all; her children, if she has any, will be illegitimate. She will have no claim upon him, if he should happen to be a bad fellow. In short, if she was married, even as Miss Warrender is going to be to-morrow, by a bishop, Lizzie, it would be simply no marriage at all."

Lizzie uttered a wild exclamation, clasping her hands—and said, "Oh, sir, is there anything that a woman that wishes her well could do?"

"There is only one thing you can do: to warn her before it is too late. Tell her she must break it off if it were at the last moment— if it were at the very altar. She must not be allowed to sacrifice herself in ignorance. I'll see her myself, if that will do any good."

"She's going to be married to-morrow," cried Lizzie breathlessly. "Oh, sir, don't deceive me! there's not a creature that knows about it, not one—and she the least of all. Oh, Mr. Wilberforce, how could any judge or jury, or any one, have the heart to punish *her*?"

"Neither judge nor jury, my poor girl: but the law which says a man must not marry another woman while his first wife is living. There are many even who will not allow of a divorce in any circumstances; but I am not so sure of that. Tell me who this poor girl is, and I will do my best to warn her while there is time."

Lizzie rose up and sat down again, in nervous excitement She made a hall of her handkerchief and pressed it alternately to each of her wet eyes. "Oh, I don't know what to do. I don't know what to do!" she cried.

"If there is anything that can be done to-night," he said,— "Quick, Lizzie, there is no time to lose, for I must leave early to-morrow for Miss Warrender's marriage."

"And there's not another train leaves to-night," cried Lizzie; then she made an effort to compose herself, and a curtsy, rising from her seat. "I must do it myself, sir, thank you all the same," she said, and went away tottering and unsteady in her great trouble: yet only half believing him after all. For how, oh how, ye heavens, could the law punish one that meant no harm and knew no evil? a question which minds more enlightened than that of Lizzie have often asked in vain.

CHAPTER XLIII.

Lizzie had a tiresome argument with her grandmother that night, who could not understand why she should be so bent on going into Highcombe by the first train. To see Miss Chatty married, that was reasonable enough; but Miss Chatty would not be married till eleven at the earliest, perhaps later. Mrs. Bagley knew that gentlefolks ran it almost too late, as late as was possible, which was the fashion, or else because they didn't like to get up so early as poor folks,—and why should Lizzie start by the seven o'clock train? But Lizzie was determined and got her way, declaring that she would stay up all night and do her work before she started sooner than not go. It would not have mattered much had she done so, for there was no sleep for Lizzie that night. She had not any certainty of being right to support her in what she was going to do. She thought of disturbing all the wedding preparations, stopping the bride with her veil on and the orange blossoms in her hair, and all the guests assembled— for what? because of—one who made no claim, who would never make any claim, who had not been heard of for more than six years. That was the flaw which disturbed Lizzie. It was not quite out seven years. Had that mystic period been accomplished she felt that she could have left Chatty to the protection of God. But at the outside it was only six and a half, and he *had* heard of her through Lizzie herself—though she inwardly resolved that no inducement on earth would make her appear before judge and jury to tell that. No! she would rather fly than tell it. And then her mind came back to the picture of the bride in her glistening white silk or satin, with the veil over her head, and the orange blossoms—to stop all that, to turn away the carriages from the door, and set herself up as knowing better than a gentleman like

Mr. Cavendish, and perhaps making a fool of herself, and not being believed or listened to after all!

These thoughts tormented Lizzie all through the night: she got up very early, while it was still dark, and lighted the fire, and put everything straight for her grandmother, and made herself a cup of tea, which she needed much to settle her agitated nerves. Old Mrs. Bagley got up, too, disturbed by the sound of some one stirring, not without grumbling at being awoke so early. Lizzie came and kissed her before she went away. "Oh, Granny, say God bless you!" she cried; "for I'm all shaking and trembling, and I don't know what may come to me to-day." "Lord bless the child!" said Mrs. Bagley, "what's a-coming to her? A body would think as it's you as is going to be married to-day; but God bless you's easy said, and meant from the 'art, and never comes amiss; and God bless Miss Chatty too, the dear, and give her a happy weddin' and a happy life." Lizzie felt that she could not say Amen. It seemed to choke her, when she tried to utter that word, for it was little happiness poor Miss Chatty would have, if she did what she was going to do. She hurried to the station, which was a long walk in the fresh morning, feeling the air chill and sharp. It was a long way to the station, and then the railway made a round, so that an active person would have found it almost as quick to walk straight to Highcombe, and it was between eight and nine when Lizzie at last found herself before the door of Mrs. Warrender's house. She thought it looked wonderfully quiet for the morning of a wedding, the shutters still closed over the drawing-room windows. But it would be vain to attempt to describe her dismay when she heard the explanation of this tranquillity. Not here, but in London! Didn't she know? the housemaid said, who was a girl from Underwood. She thought everybody had known. And Lizzie had the sickening consciousness that had she inquired a little more closely she might have discovered for herself, and saved herself this trouble. She was taken in by the sympathising housemaid to have a second cup of tea at least, if not breakfast, and to hear all about the preparations and the dresses, which

Betsey, though sadly disappointed to miss the glories of the wedding, had yet seen, and could describe. And there was not a train to London till nearly ten. She asked herself in her dismay whether it was worth going then, whether perhaps it were not Providence that had stopped her; but then, with a returning obstinacy of purpose, determined that she would not be beaten, that whatever hindered she would not be kept back.

She got to London just at the hour when the wedding party were to leave for church, and found them gone when she arrived at the house. Lizzie's habits did not consist with taking cabs. She had toiled along from the station, hot and weary, on foot. "If you want to catch them up you had better take an 'ansom," said one of the white-neckclothed men who were busy preparing the wedding breakfast. Lizzie scarcely knew what a hansom was; but she submitted to be put into one, and to get with much difficulty a shilling out of her purse to pay it. The sudden whirl, the jar and noise, the difficult getting out and in, the struggle to pursue that shilling into a corner of her purse among the pennies and sixpences, aided in confusing her brain utterly. She rushed up the steps of the church, which were crowded with idlers, not knowing what she did. The organ was pealing through the place, making a little storm of sound under the gallery, as she rushed in desperate, meeting the fine procession, the bride in all that glory which Lizzie had dreamt of, which she had been so reluctant to spoil; her white dress rustling over the red cloth that had been laid down in the aisle, her white veil flowing over her modest countenance, her arm in that of her bridegroom; all whiteness, peace, and sweet emotion, joy touched with trembling and a thousand soft regrets. Chatty came along slowly, her soft eyes cast down, her soul floating in that ecstasy which is full of awe and solemn thoughts. Dick's eyes were upon her, and the eyes of all, but hers saw nothing save the wonderful event that had come to pass, the boundary between the old and the new upon which she stood. And Lizzie had forgotten everything that could be called reason or coherence in her thoughts. She forgot her doubts, her scruples, her sense of the misery she might make, her uncertainty as to whether it might be needful at all. At this moment of bewildering excitement she had but one idea. She fell down upon her knees before them in the aisle, and caught at Chatty's white dress and the folds of her floating veil. "Oh, Miss Chatty, stop, stop, leave go of his arm: for he is married already, and his wife is living." She lifted her eyes, and there appeared round her a floating sea of horror-stricken faces, faces that she knew in the foreground, and floating farther off, as if in the air, in the distance, one she knew still better. Lizzie gave a shriek which rang through the church. "His wife is living, and she is HERE."

CHAPTER XLIV.

The wedding morning had been confusing and full of many occupations, as wedding mornings always are. Chatty, left in the quiet of her room, had received innumerable little visits: from her mother, who came and came again, with a cheerful front, but her heart very low, merely to look at her, to give her a kiss in passing, to make sure that she was still there: and from Minnie, very busy, wanting to have a finger in everything, to alter her dress at the last moment, and the way in which her veil was put on. "For it is quite different from mine," Minnie cried, "and it stands to reason that there cannot be *two* ways of putting on a veil." Then there would come a young sister of Dick's, very shy, very anxious to make friends, admiring Chatty and her orange blossoms, with that sense of probable future occurrences in her own life of the same description which makes sympathy so warm. Then Mrs. Wilberforce, who though disapproving much of the wedding in London, was yet mollified by her husband's share in it, and association with the bishop; and Lady Markland, who gave the bride a kiss of tender sympathy and said nothing to her, which Chatty felt to be the kindest of all. Minnie, on the other hand, had a great inclination from the depths of her own experience to give her sister advice. "You must remember, Chatty, that a man is not just like one of us. When you are travelling you must be sure to recollect that—they can't do with a bun or a cup of coffee or that sort of thing, they must always have something substantial to eat. You see they take so much more out of themselves than we do. And they like you to be ready to the minute, though you have often got to wait for them—and——"

"But, dear Minnie, men are not all alike," said Mrs. Wilberforce, "no more than women are. Don't you think you had better leave her to find out for herself? She will learn soon enough," she added with a sigh, softly shaking her head, as though the experience could not but be melancholy when it came; "men, like everything else, are changing every day. The chivalry one used to meet with is quite gone—but what can you expect in these times?"

"I don't like this puffing at all," said Minnie; "if I were you, I would have it taken off. Oh, I am not at all of your opinion about the times. We are Liberal on both sides. The Thynnes have always gone in for progress and advancement; and when you think how much everything has improved——"

"If you call it improvement!" said Mrs. Wilberforce with something like a groan; but whether this was in reference to things in general, or to the removal of the tulle puffing over which Minnie was holding her hand, it would be difficult to say.

And thus the morning went by. Chatty took it all very sweetly, responding with smiles to every one, feeling the hours pass like a dream until it was time to go into the dream chariot, and be carried away to the fulfilment of the dream. In the large, dull, London drawing-room below, meanwhile, guests were assembling, guests in rustling garments of many-coloured silk, with bonnets which were enough to drive any ordinary mortal out of her senses, a little tulle tossed up with flowers or feathers into the most perfect little crown for a fair head, a little velvet with nodding plumes that made the wearer at once into a duchess. The duchess herself was present, but she was dowdy, as duchesses have a right to be. And then the arrivals, the carriages that came gleaming up, the horses that pranced and curved their beautiful necks, as highbred as the ladies! Geoff, who had come with his mother, posted himself at one of the windows inside the filmy white curtains to watch the people coming. He suddenly called out "mother" when it was almost time to start, and the brougham was already waiting at the door for the bridegroom. Lady Markland was standing close by the window talking to Dick, who, as bridegrooms often are, was agitated and required support and encouragement. "What is it, Geoff?" she asked in the midst of what she was saying, without turning from her companion.

"Oh, look here. I say, there is the lady that was at the big house at Underwood, the lady that picked me up the day I ran away—the one that was at the Elms. Look, mamma. Ah, you're just too late," cried Geoff, "you are always too late. She's gone now."

It was Dick and not Lady Markland who came forward to the window. "The lady who was at the Elms?" he said, and Geoff, looking up, saw a face that was like ashes looking not at him, but out of the window, with wide staring eyes.

"Look there—just going away—in a big veil—don't you see her? but I saw her face quite plain—the same lady that took me up beside her on the big tall phaeton. I did not like her much," the boy added in an undertone.

"I think"—in a still lower voice, almost a whisper—"you are mistaken, Geoff; that lady is dead."

"I saw her all the same," said the boy.

And here some of the jocular persons who make weddings more dreadful than they need to be came forward and touched Dick on the arm. "Come along, old fellow," he said; "no skulking, it's too late to draw back. The bridegroom's carriage stops the way."

There are resolute people in the world, who can look as they please, who can receive a mortal blow, and smile all the time, or worse, look gravely self-possessed, as if nothing had ever happened to them, or could happen to the end of time. Dick Cavendish was not of this heroic kind, but yet he managed to make himself look as a bridegroom ought, as he went through the little crowd and made his way downstairs. He said to himself it was not possible; had not her death been certified beyond doubt, had not Saunders attended the funeral and brought that photograph and the poor little ring? Was the certainty of all these facts to be shaken by the random recollection of a foolish child; or a chance resemblance which that child might imagine in a passer-by? He said to himself that there could be no greater folly than to pay any attention to such a piece of absurdity. But as he went out, and all the way along as he drove, hearing without paying any attention to the occasional remarks of his best man, who was with him, his eyes were searching among the wayfarers, the little crowd round the door, the other little crowd round the church. Just as he stepped inside the portico, turning round for a last look, he saw something approaching in a hansom—something rather than some one, a gray veil covering an unseen face. Was it some woman peacefully going about her own business, or was it——? He went in, feeling the faces in the church turn round to look at him, wondering if his face was like the face of a man who was going to marry Chatty, or of one who was standing by the side of a grave? When he got up to the altar and took his place to wait for his bride there was a moment of silence, during which no intrusive fool could talk to him. And in the quiet he stood and closed his eyes and felt himself—oh, not here at the altar, waiting for Chatty in her orange flowers, but by the side of the dark pit into which the coffin was descending, straining his eyes to see through the lid if indeed the other was there. But then again, with an effort, he shook his miserable nightmare off. It was not possible he could be deceived. What motive could any one have to deceive him? Saunders had seen her buried, and had brought the photograph and that ring. The ring was conclusive; unless a horrible trick had been played upon him there was no room for doubt, and to whose interest could it be to play him a trick of this dreadful kind?

And then came the little rustle and thrill of the arriving train. And something white came up, a succession of whitenesses streaming one after the other, with no sound but the delicate rustle, that soft touch upon the air that might almost have been wings. They stood together, both but half conscious of what was going on round them: Chatty, sweetly wrapped in a maze of soft-coming fancies of wonder and pleasure and awe and regret; while he, touched to the heart by her presence, yet only half conscious of it, went through the whole in a kind of trance, mingling the words spoken with interlinings of unspeakable dumb reasonings, self-assurances, self-exhortations. Nobody knew anything about all this. The ceremony went on, just as such ceremonies go on every day in the year. The priest said the words and paused while they were repeated; by one voice firmly and strongly, by the other low and unassured, yet clear. And then there was the flutter of tension relieved, the gathering round of the little crowd, the little procession to the vestry, where everything was signed, the kissings and good wishes. Dick had no mother, but his elder sister was there, who kissed him in her place, and his younger sister, who was a bridesmaid, and hung about Chatty with all a girl's enthusiasm. What could be more simple, more natural and true? There was no shadow there of any dread, but everything happy, honest, pure. He recovered his soul a little in the midst of that group; though when Geoff with his little sharp face, in which there always seemed more knowledge than belonged to his age, caught his eye, a slight shiver ran over him. He felt as if Geoff knew all about it; and might, for anything he could tell, have some horrible secret to bring forth.

And then they set out again, the husband with his wife on his arm, to go away. The touch of Chatty's hand on his arm seemed to restore his confidence. She was his, in spite of all that Fate could do—in spite of everything, he thought. They walked together, he feeling more and more the pride and triumph of the moment, she moving softly, still in her dream, yet beginning too to feel the reality, past the altar where they had knelt a little while before, going down the aisle, facing the spectators who still lingered well pleased to see the bride. And then in a moment the blow fell. Some one seemed to rise up before them, out of the ground, out of the vacancy, forming before his horror-stricken eyes. And then there rose that cry which everybody could hear—which paralysed the bridal procession and brought the clergyman startled out of the vestry, and thrilled the careless lookers-on. "He has a wife living. She is living, and she is here!" Had he heard these words before in a dream? Had he known all along that he would hear them, ringing in his ears on his wedding day? "His wife is living—and she is here!"

"What is it? what is it?" cried the wedding guests, crowding upon each other, those who were nearest at least, while those at the end of the procession paused with the smile on their lips to stare and wonder at the sudden disturbance. Chatty was the most self-possessed of all. She said softly: "Lizzie, Lizzie! Something has happened to her," and put out her disengaged hand in its white glove to raise her from her knees.

"Miss Chatty, it's you that something has happened to—Oh stop, oh stop! there she is! Don't—don't let Miss Chatty go away with him, don't let her go away with him!" Lizzie cried.

"The woman is mad!" said some one behind. And so it might have been thought; when suddenly those immediately following who had closed up behind Chatty heard the bridegroom's voice, extremely agitated, yet with a nervous firmness, say audibly: "It is not true. Lizzie, the woman you speak of is dead. I know for certain that she is dead."

"Look there!" the intruder cried.

And he turned round in the sight of them all, the bride half turning too with the voluntary impulse, and saw behind the sea of anxious wondering faces another, which seemed to float in a mist of horror, from under the half-lifted cloud of a gray veil. He saw this face; and the rest of the wedding guests saw his, blanched with dread and misery, and knew every one that the marriage was stopped, and Chatty no wife, and he a dishonoured man.

Her eyes had followed his, she had not looked at him, but still held his arm, giving him a support he was incapable of giving her. The face in the background was not unknown to Chatty. She remembered it well, and with what a compunction of pity she had looked at it when she met that poor creature on the road at home, and wanted in her heart to take the lost one to her mother. She did not understand at all what was going on about her, nor what Mrs. Warrender meant, who came closely up behind, and took hold of her arm, detaching her from Dick. "Chatty, let us get home, my darling. Come, come with me. Theo will take us home," the mother said.

Then Chatty, turning round wondering, saw her bridegroom's face. She looking at him earnestly for the moment, holding his arm tighter, and then said with a strange, troubled, yet clear voice: "Dick—what does it mean? Dick!"

"Come home, come home, my dearest," cried Mrs. Warrender, trying to separate them.

"Come back to the vestry, Cavendish," cried Theo with threatening tones; and then arose a loud murmur of other suggestions, a tumult most unusual, horrifying, yet exciting to the spectators who closed around. The clergyman came out still in his surplice, hurrying towards the spot "Whatever the interruption is," he said, "don't stay there, for Heaven's sake. Come back if you will, or go home, but don't let us have a disturbance in the church."

"Chatty, go with my mother. For God's sake, Frances, get them all away."

"I will not leave Dick," said Chatty in her soft voice, "until I know what it is." She who was so yielding and so simple, she turned round with her own impulse the unhappy young man whose arm she held, and who seemed for the moment incapable of any action of his own, and led him back towards the place from which they had come. The horror had not penetrated sufficiently into Chatty's mind to do more than pale a little the soft colour in her face. She had grown very serious, looking straight before her, taking no notice of anything. They all followed like so many sheep in her train, the ladies crowding together, Dick's sister at his other hand, Mrs. Warrender close behind, Lizzie carried along with them, now crying bitterly and wringing her hands, utterly cowed by finding herself in the midst of this perfumed and rustling crowd, amid which her flushed and tear-stained face and humble dress showed to such strange disadvantage. Unnoticed by the rest, Geoff, who had wriggled out of the mass, pursued down the farther aisle a hurrying flying figure and stopped her, holding her fast.

In the vestry Chatty began to fail a little. She relinquished Dick's arm, and stood trembling, supporting herself by the table. "I want him," she said, faltering a little, "mamma, to tell me—what it means. There is something—to find out. Dick," with a tremulous smile, "you have concealed something. It is not that I don't trust you,—but tell me"—Then, still smiling, she murmured, "Lizzie—and that—that poor—girl."

Dick had collected himself "My darling," he said, "I have done wrong. I have concealed what you ought to have known. Warrender, stop before you speak. I married when I was a boy. I declare upon my soul that I had every assurance the woman was dead. My clerk saw her buried, he brought me the certificate, and her portrait, and her ring. I had no reason, no reason at all, to doubt, I have no reason now," he said, with a sudden recovery of courage, "except what this girl says,—who has no way of knowing, while my information is sure. It is sure—quite sure. Chatty! can you think I would have brought you here to—to——The woman is dead."

"Mr. Cavendish!" cried Lizzie loudly. "You saw her—as well as I."

He looked at her for a moment, his face grew once more gray as ashes, he trembled where he stood. "It must have been—an illusion," he said.

Here Warrender caught Lizzie somewhat roughly by the arm. "If this woman is here, find her," he cried peremptorily, pushing her to the door before him. The church was still full of excited spectators whom the vergers were endeavouring to get rid of. In the aisle stood Geoff with some one veiled and muffled to the eyes. The boy was standing in front of her, like a little dog who has been set to watch. She could not move a step without a movement on his part. He gave to Warrender a sort of invitation with a nod of his little head. "I've got her here," he said; then whispering, "It is the lady—the lady that ran you over, that picked me up,—the lady at the Elms."

"At the Elms!" There rushed over Theo's mind a recollection of Dick's visit to the village, of his hurried departure, of agitation unnoticed at the time. "I must ask you to step into the vestry," he said.

"Oh, Mr. Warrender, I know you, though you don't know me; don't ask me to do that. What, among all those nicely dressed people, and me so!—oh no, please do not ask me, please don't ask me! What good could I do? It seems to me I've done harm, but I meant none. I thought I'd just come and have a peep after hearing so much about you all, and knowing him so long."

"Will you tell me who you are, and what is your connection with Cavendish? Come, and let us know before his face."

"Oh, my connection with—Dear, dear! is it necessary to go into that—a thing of an age ago? Oh, Lord, Lizzie, let me alone, will you! it's all your doing. Why couldn't you let things alone?"

"Whatever you have to say, it had better be said before us all," said Warrender sternly, for various members of the bridal party had straggled out, and were listening from the vestry door. He took her by the arm and led her into the room. "What is your relation to that man?" he said, keeping his hand upon her arm.

The wedding guests made a circle round, the clergyman in his white surplice among the ladies' gay dresses, the white figure of Chatty leaning with her hand on the table, her mother's anxious face close behind her. Poor Dick in his spruce wedding clothes, with his ghostly face, stood drawing back a little, staring with eyes that seemed to sink deeper in their sockets as he gazed. He had never looked upon that face since he parted with her in utter disgust and misery six years before. She came in, almost forced into the inclosure of all those fine people gazing at her, with all her meretricious graces, not an imposing sinner, a creature ready to cry and falter, yet trying to set up against the stare of the ladies the piteous impudence of her kind.

"What are you to that man?" Theo asked.

"Oh,—what should I be to him? a gentleman doesn't ask such

questions. I—I—have been the same to him as I've been—you know well enough," she added, with a horrible little laugh that echoed all about, and made a stir among the people round.

"Are you his wife?"

She shuddered, and began to cry. "I—I'm nobody's wife. I've been—a number of things. I like my freedom—I——" She stopped hysterical, overcome by the extraordinary circumstances, and the audience which listened and looked at her with hungry ears and eyes.

Dick put out his arms as if to wave the crowd away. What were all these spectators doing here, looking on at his agony? He spoke in a hoarse and husky voice. "Why did you deceive me? why did you pretend you were dead, and lead me to this?"

"Because I've nothing to do with you, and I don't want nothing to do with you," she cried; "because I've been dead to you these long years; because I'm not a bad, cruel woman. I wanted to leave you free. He's free for me," she said, turning to Warrender. "It's not I that wants to bind him. If I made believe it was me that died, where was the wrong? I wanted to set him free. That's not deceiving him, it was for his good, that he might feel he was free."

"Answer, woman. Are you his wife?"

"What right have you to call me a woman? His wife? How can you tell whether I wasn't married before ever I set eyes upon him?" she cried, with a hysterical laugh. "They don't think so much of that where I came from. There! I hope you've had enough of me now. Lizzie, you fool, you spoil-sport, you hateful creature, give me hold of your arm, and let's go away. We've done you harm, Mr. Cavendish, instead of doing you good, but that is no fault of mine."

There was a pause as she went out of the vestry, holding Lizzie's arm, whose sobs were audible all the way down the aisle. It did not last long, but it was as the silence of death. Then Dick spoke.

"You see how it is. I married her when I was a boy. She deserted me in a very short time, and I have never seen her from that day to this, nearly seven years ago. Six weeks since

I received information that she was dead. She tells you it was a trick, a device,—but I—had every reason to believe it. God knows I wanted to believe it! but I thought I spared no pains. Then I went to Chatty, whom I had long loved." Here he paused to regain his voice, which had become almost inaudible. "I thought all was right. Don't you believe me?" he cried hoarsely, holding out his hands in appeal. At first his little sister was the only one who responded. She threw herself weeping upon one of his outstretched arms and clasped it. Chatty had been put into a chair, where she sat now very pale, under the white mist of the veil, beginning to realise what it was that had happened. When she heard the anguish in Dick's voice, she suddenly rose to her feet, taking them all by surprise. Instinctively the party had separated into two factions, his side and her side. The group about Chatty started when she moved, and Theo seized hold almost roughly of her elbow. But Chatty did not seem sensible of this clutch. She went forward to the bridegroom so disastrously taken from her, and took his other hand in hers. "I believe you— with all my heart," Chatty said. "I blame you for nothing, oh, for nothing. I am sorry—for us both."

"Take her away, mother. The carriage has come round to the vestry door. Chatty! This is no longer any place for you."

Chatty looked round upon her faction, who were encircling her with dark or miserable looks. "We are very unfortunate," she said, "but we have done nothing that is wrong."

"Chatty, O Chatty, my darling, come away. You cannot stay any longer here."

"What, without a word to Dick, mother! Speak to him. He is the most to be pitied. We never thought we should have to say good-bye again." Here she paused and the tears came. She repeated in a voice that went to the hearts of all the staring, excited spectators, "I am sorry—for us both."

"God bless you, Chatty! God bless you, my own love! And must we part so?" cried poor Dick, falling down upon his knees, and sobbing over the hands which held his. He was altogether broken down. He knew there was nothing to be said to him, or for him. He was without help or hope. For a moment even Warrender, who was the most severe, could say nothing in sight of this lamentable scene,—the bride and her bridegroom, who had been pronounced man and wife half-an-hour before, and now were parting,—perhaps for ever,—two people between whom there was now no bond, whose duty would be to keep apart. Chatty stooped over him, whom she must see no more, her white veil fell over him covering them both, she laid her pale cheek against his. "It is not our fault. We are very unfortunate. We must have patience," she said.

He kept on kneeling there, following her with his eyes, while her brother and her mother led her away, then with a groan covered his face with his hands. Was this the end?

CHAPTER XLV.

After this extraordinary and terrible event there were a great many conferences and explanations, which did little good as may be understood. Dick's life—the part of it which had passed during his absence, the wanderyear which had brought such painful consequences—was laid entirely open, both to his own family and all the Warrenders. There was nothing in it to be ashamed of—still he had wanted to keep that episode to himself, and the consequence, of course, was that every detail became known. He had thrown himself into the wild, disorderly population on the edge of civilisation: people who lived out of reach of law, and so long as they were not liable to the tribunal of Judge Lynch, did no harm in the eyes of the community. There he had fallen in love, being clean and of pure mind, and disposed to think everybody like himself, and married in haste—a girl whom his tiresome proprieties had wearied at once, and who did not in the most rudimentary way comprehend what to him was the foundation of life. He shuddered, but could give no coherent account of that time. She left him, inclosing him her "marriage lines" and a paper declaring him to be free. And from that time until she had been brought face to face with him in the vestry he had never seen her again. His old father, whom Dick had been anxious to spare from any annoyance, and who was too old to be present at the wedding, had to be called forth from his retirement to hear the whole story; his eldest brother, who was abroad, hurried home, to know what was meant by the paragraphs in the papers, and what it was all about. No particular of bitterness was spared to the unfortunate young man; the particulars of his conduct were discussed at every dinner-party. Had there been collusion? had he known all the time that the woman was not dead? Society did not quite understand the want of accordance with conventional rules that had been shown by everybody concerned. The wicked wife ought to have planned this villainous trick as a way of vengeance against him: whereas it was evident that she had meant only kindness, abandoned creature as she was. And the poor bride, the unfortunate Miss Warrender, should with all her family have sworn everlasting feud with him, whereas it was known that Chatty took his part, and would say nothing but that they were very unfortunate both. Women should not act like this, they should fly at each other's throats, they should tear each other to pieces.

But if Chatty (backed up by her mother, it was said) showed undue indulgence, this was not the case with her brother and sister. Theo's keen temper had taken up and resented the whole matter almost with violence. He had not only treated Cavendish, and the Cavendishes generally, who were more important than the individual Dick, with harsh contumely and enmity, refusing to hear any excuse, and taking the occurrence as an insult to himself: but he had quarrelled with his mother, who was disposed to forgive, and with still more vehemence with Chatty, who made no pretence of any wrath, but believed Dick's story fully, and would not hear anything against him. Chatty had a soft obstinacy about her which nobody had known till now. She had not broken down, nor hidden herself from her family, nor taken any shame to herself. She had even received him, against the advice of everybody, in a long interview, hearing everything over again, and fully, from his own lips, and had kissed him (it was whispered) at parting, while her mother and his sister looking on could do nothing but cry. There began after a while to be many people who sympathised with these two unhappy lovers—who were not so unhappy either, because they understood and had faith in each other. But Theo made an open quarrel with his mother and sister after this meeting. He was furious against both of them, and even against his wife when it became known that she had gone to see and sympathise with them. Warrender declared that he would consider any man his enemy who spoke to him of Cavendish. He was furious with everything and everybody concerned. He said that he had been covered with shame, though how no one could tell. Lady Markland, who also was on the side of Dick, was helpless to restrain her young husband. She too, poor lady, began to feel that her lot was not one of unmixed good, nor her bed of roses. Though the force of events had carried Theo over all the first drawbacks to their marriage, he had never recovered the bitterness and exasperation which these had given. He had not forgiven her, though he adored her, for being still Lady Markland, and though he lived at Markland with her, yet it was under a perpetual protest, to which in moments of excitement he sometimes gave utterance, but which even in silence she was always conscious of. His smouldering discontent burst forth on the occasion given him by this *mariage manqué*. The rage that filled him was not called forth by Dick Cavendish alone. It was the outflow of all the discontents and annoyances of his life.

And Minnie's outraged virtue was almost more rampant still. That Eustace should have any connection with a scandal which had even got into the newspapers, that a girl who was his sister-in-law should have got herself talked about, was to Minnie a wrong which blazed up to heaven. "For myself, I should not have minded," she said, "at least, however much I minded I should have said as little as possible; but when I think that Eustace has been made a gazing-stock to all the world through me—oh, you may think it extravagant, but I don't. Of course, he has been made a gazing-stock. 'Brother-in-law to *that* Miss Warrender, you know'—that is how people talk, as if it could possibly be his fault. I am sure he bears it like an angel. All he has ever said, even to me, is, 'Minnie, I wish we had looked into things a little more beforehand,' and what could I say? I could only say you were all so headstrong, you would have your own way."

"Next time he says so, you will perhaps refer him to me, Minnie. I think I shall be able to answer Mr. Thynne!"

"Oh," cried Minnie, "by making a quarrel! I know your way of answering, mamma. I tell Eustace if I had been at home it never, never could have happened. I never cared about that man from the first. There was always something in the look of his eyes: I told Eustace before anything happened—something about the corner of his eyes. I did not like it when I heard you had seen so much of him in town. And Eustace said then, 'I hope your mother has made all the necessary inquiries.' I did not like to say: 'Oh, mamma never makes any inquiries!' but I am sure I might have said so. And this is what it has come to! Chatty's ruin,—yes, it is Chatty's ruin, whatever you may say. Who will ever look at her,—a girl who has been married and yet isn't married? She will never find any one. She will just have to live with you, like two old cats in a little country town, as Eustace says."

"If Mr. Thynne calls your mother an old cat, you should have better taste than to repeat it," said Mrs. Warrender; "I hope he is not so vulgar, Minnie, nor you so heartless."

"Vulgar! Eustace! The Thynnes are just the best bred people in the world. I don't know what you mean. A couple of old ladies living in a little place, and gossiping about everything,—everybody has the same opinion. And this is just what it comes to, when no attention is paid. And they say you have actually let him come here, let Chatty meet him, to take away every scrap of respect that people might have had. He never heard of such a mistake, Eustace says, it shows such a want of knowledge of the world."

"This is going too far, Minnie; understand, once for all, that what Eustace Thynne says is not of the least importance to me, and that I think his comments most inappropriate. Poor Dick is going off to California to-morrow. He is going to get his divorce."

Minnie gave a scream which made the thinly built London house ring, and clasped her hands. "A DIVORCE!" she cried; "it only wanted this. Eustace said that was what it would come to. And you would let your daughter marry a man who has been divorced!"

Minnie spoke in such a tone of injured majesty that Mrs.

Warrender was almost cowed, for it cannot be denied that this speech struck an echo in her own heart. The word was a word of shame. She did not know how to answer; that her Chatty, her child who had come so much more close to her of late, should be placed in any position which was not of good report, that the shadow of any stain should be upon her simple head, was grievous beyond all description to her mother. And she was far from being an emancipated woman. She had all the prejudices, all the diffidences of her age and position. Her own heart cried out against this expedient with a horror which she had done her best to overcome. For the first time she faltered and hesitated as she replied—

"There can be no hard-and-fast rule; our Lord did not do it, and how can we? It is odious to me as much as to any one. But what would you have him do? He cannot take that wretched creature, that poor unhappy girl."

"You mean that shameless, horrible thing, that abandoned——"

"There must be some good in her," said Mrs. Warrender, with a shudder. "She had tried to do what she could to set him free. It was not her fault if it proved more than useless. I can't prolong this discussion, Minnie. Eustace and you can please yourselves by making out your fellow-creatures to be as bad as possible. To me it is almost more terrible to see the good in them that might, if things had gone differently—— But that is enough. I am going to take Chatty away."

"Away! where are you going to take her? For goodness' sake don't: they will think you are going after him—they will say——"

"I am glad you have the grace to stop. I am going to take her abroad. If she can be amused a little and delivered from herself—— At all events," said Mrs. Warrender, "we shall be free from the stare of the world, which we never did anything to attract."

"Going away?" Minnie repeated. "Oh, I think, and I am sure Eustace would say, that you ought not to go away. You should live it down. Of course people will blame *you*, they must, I did myself:

but after all that is far better than to be at a place abroad where everybody would say, Oh, do you know who that is? that is Mrs. Warrender, whose eldest daughter married one of the Thynnes, whose youngest was the heroine of *that* story, you know about the marriage. Oh, mamma, this is exactly what Eustace said he was afraid you would do. For goodness' sake don't! stay at home and live it down. We shall all stand by you," said Minnie. "I am sure Frances will do her very best, and though Eustace is a clergyman and ought always to show an example, yet in the case of such near relations—we——"

Mrs. Warrender only turned her back upon these generous promises, walking away without any answer or remark. She was too angry to say anything: and to think that there was a germ of reality in it all, a need of some one to stand by them, a possibility that Chatty might be a subject for evil tongues, made Chatty's mother half beside herself. It seemed more than she could bear. But Chatty took it all very quietly. She was absorbed in the story, more entertaining than any romance, which was her own story. No thought of what divorce was, or of anything connected with it, disturbed her mind. What Dick had to do seemed to her natural: perhaps anything he had done in the present extraordinary crisis would have seemed to her natural. He was going to put things right. She did not think much for the moment what the means of doing so were, nor what in the meantime her own position was. She had no desire to make any mystery of it, to conceal herself, or what had happened. There was no shame in it so far as Chatty knew. There was a dreadful, miserable mistake. She was "very sorry for us both," but for herself less than for Dick, who had suffered, she said to herself, far more than she, for though he had done no wrong, he had to bear all the penalties of having done wrong, whereas in her own case there was no question of blame. Chatty was so much absorbed in Dick that she did not seem to have time to realise her own position. She did not think of herself as the chief sufferer. She fell back into the calm of the ordinary life without a murmur, saying little about it. With her own hands she packed up all the new dresses, the wealth of the pretty trousseau. She was a little pale, and yet she smiled. "I wonder if I shall ever have any need for these," she said, smoothing down the silken folds of the dresses with a tender touch.

"I hope so, my dear, when poor Dick comes back."

Then Chatty's smile gave way to a sigh. "They say human life is so uncertain, mamma, but I never realised it till now. You cannot tell what a day may bring forth. But it very, very seldom happens, surely, that there are such changes as this. I never heard of one before."

"No, my darling, it is very rare: but oh, what a blessing, Chatty, that it was found out at once, before you had gone away!"

"Yes, I suppose it was a blessing; perhaps it would have been wrong, but I should never have left him, mamma, had we gone away."

"Oh, do not let us think of that; you were mercifully saved, Chatty."

"On my wedding day! I never heard that such a thing ever happened to a girl before. The real blessing is that Dick had done nothing wrong. That comforts me most of all."

"I don't know, Chatty. He ought perhaps to have taken better care: at all events he ought to have let people know that he was a—that he was not an unmarried man."

Chatty trembled a little at these words. She did not like him to be blamed, but so far as this was concerned she could not deny that he was in the wrong. It was the foundation of all. Had it been known that he was or had been married, she would not have given him her love. But at this Chatty flushed deep, and felt that it was a cruel suggestion. To find that she was not married was an endless pain to her, which still she could scarcely understand. But not to have loved him! Poor Dick! To have done him that wrong over and above all the rest, he who had been so much wronged and injured! No, no, neither for him nor for herself could it be anything but profane to wish that. Not to have loved him! Chatty's life seemed all to sink into gray at the thought.

"At all events," she said, returning to those easier outsides of things in which the greatest events have a humble covering, and looking again at her pretty gowns, "they can wait, poor things, to see what will happen. If it should so be, as that it never comes right——"

"Oh, Chatty, my poor dear."

"Life seems so uncertain," said Chatty, in her new-born wisdom. "It is so impossible to tell what may happen, or what a day may bring forth. I think I never can be very sure of anything now. And if it never should come right, they shall just stay in the boxes, mother. I could not have the heart to wear them." She put her hand over them caressingly, and patted and pressed them down into the corners. "It seems a little sad to see them there, doesn't it, mamma, and I in my old gray frock?" The tears were in her eyes, but she looked up at Mrs. Warrender with a little soft laugh at herself, and at the little tragedy, or at least the suspended drama, laid up with something that was half pathetic, half ludicrous, in the wedding clothes.

Chatty suffered herself to be taken abroad without any very strong opinion of her own. She would have been content to adopt Minnie's way, to go back to Highcombe and "live it down," though indeed she was unconscious of scandal, or of the necessity of living down anything. There were some aspects of the case in which she would have preferred that,—to live on quietly day by day, looking for news of him, expecting what was to come. But there was much to be said on the other hand for her mother's plan, and Chatty now, as at all times, was glad to do what pleased her mother. They went off accordingly when the early November gales were blowing, not on any very original plan, to places where a great many people go, to the Riviera, where the roses were still blowing with a sort of soft patience which was like Chatty. And thus strangely out of nature, without any habitual cold, or frost, or rain, or anything like what they were used to, that winter which had begun with such very different intentions glided quietly away. Of course they met people now and then who knew their story, but there were also many who did not know: ladies from the country, such as abound on the Riviera, who fortunately did not think a knowledge of London gossip essential to salvation, and who thought Miss Warrender must be delicate, her colour changed so from white to red. But as it is a sort of duty to be delicate on the Riviera and robust persons are looked down upon, they did very well, and the days, so monotonous, so bright, with so little in them, glided harmlessly away. Dick wrote not very often, but yet now and then, which was a thing Minnie had protested against, but then, mamma, Mrs. Eustace Thynne said, *had* always "her own ways of thinking," and if she permitted it, what could any one say?

CHAPTER XLVI.

Mrs. Warrender and her daughter came home in the early summer, having lingered longer than they intended in the South. They had lingered for one thing, because a long and strange interruption had occurred in the letters from America. Dick had made them aware of his arrival there, and of the beginning of his necessary business, into the details of which naturally he did not enter. He had told them of his long journey, which was not then so rapid as now, but meant long travelling in primitive ways by waggons and on horseback, and also that he had found greater delays and more trouble than he expected. In the spring he was still lingering, investigating matters which he did not explain, but which he said might very likely facilitate what he had to do and make the conclusion more fortunate than he had anticipated. And then there came a pause. They waited, expecting the usual communication, but it did not come; they waited longer, thinking it might have been delayed by accident, and finally returned home with hearts heavier than those with which they went away. Theo came to meet them at the station, when they arrived in London. He was there with his wife in the beginning of the season. Mrs. Warrender's anxious looks, withdrawn for the moment from Chatty, fell with little more satisfaction upon her son. He was pale and thin, with that fretted look as of constant irritation which is almost more painful to look at than the indications of sorrow. He put aside with a little impatience her inquiries about himself. "I am well enough,—what should be the matter with me? I never was an invalid that I know of."

"You are not looking well, Theo. You are very thin. London does not agree with you, I fear, and the late nights."

"I am a delicate plant to be incapable of late nights," he said, with a harsh laugh.

"And how is Frances? I hope she does not do too much: and——"

"Come, mother, spare me the catalogue. Lady Markland is quite well, and my Lord Markland, for I suppose it was he who was meant by your and——"

"Geoff, poor little fellow! he is at school, I suppose."

"Not a bit of it," said Warrender, with an ugly smile. "He is delicate, you know. He has had measles or something, and has come home to his mother to be nursed. There's a little too much of Geoff, mother; let us be free of him here, at least. You are going to your old rooms?"

"Yes. I thought it might be a little painful: but Chatty made no objection. She said indeed she would like it."

"Is she dwelling on that matter still?"

"Still, Theo! I don't suppose she will ever cease to dwell on it till it comes all right."

"Which is very unlikely, mother. I don't give my opinion on the subject of divorce. It's an ugly thing, however you take it; but a man who goes to seek a divorce avowedly, with the intention of marrying again—— That is generally the motive, I believe, at the bottom, but few are so bold as to put it frankly on evidence."

"Theo! you forget Dick's position, which is so very peculiar. Could any one blame him? What could he do otherwise? I hope I am not lax—and I hate the very name of divorce as much as any one can: but what could he do?"

"He could put up with it, I suppose, as other men have had to do—and be thankful it is no worse."

"You are hard, Theo. I am sure it is not Frances that has taught you to be so hard. Do you think that Chatty's life destroyed, as well as his own, is so little? and no laws human or divine could bind him to—I don't think I am lax," Mrs. Warrender cried, with the poignant consciousness of a woman who has always known herself to be even superstitiously bound to every cause of modesty, and who finds herself suddenly assailed as a champion of the immoral. Her middle-aged countenance flushed with annoyance and shame.

"No, I don't suppose you are lax," said Theo: but the lines in his careworn forehead did not melt, and Chatty, who had been directing the maid about the luggage, now came forward and stopped the conversation. Warrender put his mother and sister into a cab, and promised to "come round" and see them in the evening. After he had shut the door, he came back and asked suddenly: "By the way, I suppose you have the last news of Cavendish. How is he?"

"We have no news. Why do you ask? is he ill?"

"Oh, you don't know then?" said Warrender. "I was wondering. He is down with fever, but getting better, I believe, getting better," he added hurriedly, as Chatty uttered a tremulous cry. "They wrote to his people. We were wondering whether you might not have heard."

"And no one thought it worth while to let us know!"

"Lady Horton thought if you did not know it was better to say nothing: and that if you did it was unnecessary—besides, they are like me, they think it is monstrous that a man should go off with an avowed intention—they think in any case it is better to drop it altogether."

"Theo," said Chatty, in her soft voice, "can we hear exactly how he is?"

"He is better, he is going on well, he will get all right. But if you should see Lady Horton——"

Lady Horton was Dick's elder and married sister, she who had stood by him on the day that was to have been his wedding-day.

"I think we had better drive on now," Chatty said. And when Theo's somewhat astonished face had disappeared from the window, and they were rattling along over the stones, she suddenly said, "Do you think it should have been—dropped altogether? Why should it be dropped altogether? I seem to be a little bewildered—I don't —understand. Oh, mamma, I had a presentiment that he was ill—ill and alone, and so far away."

"He is getting better, dear; he would think it best not to write to make us anxious; probably he has been waiting on day by day. I will go to Lady Horton to-morrow."

"And Lady Horton thinks it should be dropped altogether," said Chatty, in a musing reflective tone. "She thinks it is monstrous—what is monstrous? I don't—seem to understand."

"Let us not think of it till we get home, till we have a little calm and—time."

"As if one could stop thinking till there is time!" said Chatty, with a faint smile. "But I feel that this is a new light. I must think. What must be dropped? Am not I married to him, mother?"

"Oh, my darling, if it had not been for that woman——"

"But that woman—my thoughts are all very confused. I don't understand it: perhaps he is not married to me—but I have always considered that I—— The first thing, however, is his health, mother. We must see at once about that."

"Yes, dear; but there is nothing alarming in it, from what Theo says."

The rest of the drive was in silence. They rattled along the London streets in all the brightness of the May evening, meeting people in carriages going out to dinner, and the steady stream of passengers on foot, coming from the parks, coming from the hundred amusements of the new season. Chatty saw them all without seeing them; her mind was taken up by a new strain of thought. She had taken it for granted that all was natural, that Dick was doing the thing that it was right to do: and now she suddenly found herself in an atmosphere of uncertainty to which she was unaccustomed, and in which, for the moment, all her faculties seemed paralysed. Was it monstrous? Ought it to have been dropped? She was so much bewildered that she could not tell what to say.

Theo and his wife both "came round" in the evening; she with a fragile look as of impaired health, and an air of watching anxiety which it was painful to see. She seemed to have one eye upon Theo always, whatever she was doing, to see that he was pleased, or at least not displeased. It had been her idea to go to Lady Horton's on the way and bring the last news of Dick. Much better, going on quite well, will soon be allowed to communicate with his friends, was the bulletin which Lady Markland took Chatty aside to give.

"He has not been able to write himself all the time. The people who have taken care of him—rough people, but very kind, from all that can be presumed—found his father's address, and sent him word. Otherwise for six or seven weeks there has been nothing from himself."

This gave Chatty a little consolation. "Theo says—it is all wrong, that it ought to be dropped," she said.

"Theo has become severe in his judgments, Chatty."

"Has he? he was always a little severe. He got angry"—Chatty did not observe the look of recognition in Lady Markland's face, as of a fact *connu*. She went on slowly: "I wish that you would give me your opinion. I thought for a long time I was the first person to be thought of, and that Dick must do everything that could be done to set us right. But now it seems that is not the right view. Mamma hesitates,—she will not speak. Oh, will you tell me what you think——!"

"About," said Lady Markland, faltering, "the divorce?"

"I don't seem to know what it means; that poor creature—do people think she is—anything to him?"

"She is his wife, my dear."

"His—wife! But then I—am married to him."

"Dear Chatty, not except in form, a form which her appearance broke at once."

Chatty began to tremble, as if with cold. "I shall always feel that I am married to him. He may not be bound, but I am bound—till death do ye part."

"My dear, all that was made as if it never had been said by the appearance of the—wife."

Chatty shivered again, though the evening was warm. "That

cannot be," she cried. "He may not be bound, but I am bound. I promised. It is an oath before God."

"Oh, Chatty, it was all, all made an end of when that woman appeared. You are not bound, you are free; and I hope, dear, when a little time has passed——"

Chatty put up her hand with a cry. "Don't!" she said. "And do you mean that he is bound to her?—oh, I am sorry for her, I am sorry for her,—to one who has forsaken him and gone so far, so very far astray, to one who has done things that cannot be borne, and not to me—by the same words, the same words—which have no meaning to her, for she has left him, she has never held by him, never; and not to me, who said them with all my heart, and meant them with all my heart, and am bound by them for ever and ever?" She paused a little, and the flush of vehemence on her cheek and of light in her eye calmed down. "It is not just," she said.

"Dear Chatty, it is very hard, harder than can be said."

"It is not just," said Chatty once more, her soft face falling into lines in which Lady Markland saw a reflection of those which made Theo's countenance so severe.

"So far as that goes, the law will release him. It would do so even here. I do not think there is any doubt of that,—though Theo says,—but I feel sure there is not any doubt."

"And though the law does release him," said Chatty, "and he comes back, you will all say to me it must be dropped, that it is not right, that he is divorced, that I must not marry him, though I have married him. I know now what will happen. There will be Minnie and Theo,—and even mamma will hesitate, and her voice will tremble. And I don't know if I will have strength to hold out," she cried, with a sudden burst of tears. "I have never struggled or fought for myself. Perhaps I may be a coward. I may not have the strength. If they are all against me, and no one to stand by me, perhaps I may be unjust too, and sacrifice him—and myself."

This burst of almost inaudible passion from a creature so

tranquil and passive took Lady Markland altogether by surprise. Chatty, so soft, so simple, so yielding, driven by cruel fate into a position so terrible, feeling everything at stake, not only her happiness but the life already spoiled and wasted of the man she loved, feeling too that on herself would depend the decision of all that was to follow, and yet seized by a prophetical terror, a fear which was tragic, lest her own habit of submission should still overwhelm all the personal impulse, and sweep away her very life. The girl's face, moved out of all its gentle softness into the gravity almost stern which this consciousness brought, was a strange sight.

"I do not count for much," said Lady Markland. "I cannot expect you to think much of me, if your own sister, and your brother, and even your mother, as you fear, are against you: but I will not be against you, Chatty. So far as I can I will stand by you, if that will do you any good."

"Oh yes, it will do me good," cried Chatty, clasping her hands; "it does me good already to talk to you. You know I am not clever, I don't go deep down into things," she added after a moment. "Minnie always said I was on the surface: but I never thought until to-day, I never thought—I have just been going on, supposing it was all right, that Dick could set it all right. And now it has burst upon me. Perhaps after all mamma will be on my side, and perhaps you will make Theo——" here she paused instinctively, and looked at her sister-in-law, feeling in the haste and rush of her own awakened spirit a sudden insight of which she had not been capable before.

Lady Markland shook her head. She was a little sad, a little overcast, not so assured in her gentle dignity, slightly nervous and restless, which was unlike her. "You must not calculate on that," she said. "Theo—has his own way of looking at things. It is right he should. We would not wish him to be influenced by—by any one."

"But you are not—any one."

"No, indeed. I am no one, in that point of view. I am his wife, and ought to take my views from him, not he his from me; and besides," she said, with a little laugh, "I am, after all, not like an old acqu—not like one he has known all his life, but comparatively new, and a stranger to his ways of thinking—to any of his ways of thinking—and only learning how he will look at this and that; you don't realise how that operates even when people are married. Theo has very distinct views—which is what he ought to have. The pity is that—I have lived so much alone—I have too. It is a great deal better to be blank," she said, laughing again. Her laugh was slightly nervous too, and it seemed to be intended for Theo, whose conversation with his mother had now paused, and who was occasionally glancing, not without suspicion, at his wife and sister in the corner. Did she laugh to make him think that there was nothing serious in their talk? She called to him to join them, making room upon the sofa. "Chatty is tired," she said, "and out of spirits. I want to try and amuse her a little, Theo, before Mrs. Warrender takes her away."

"Amusement is the last thing we were thinking of," he said, coming forward with a sort of surly opposition, as if it came natural to him to go against what she said. "My opinion is that she should go down to the country at once, and not show at all in town this season. I don't think it would be pleasant for any of us. There has been talk enough."

"There has been no talk that Chatty need care for," said Lady Markland quietly; "don't think so, pray don't think so. Who could say anything of her? People are bad enough in London, but not so bad as that."

"Nevertheless, mother," said Theo, "I think you and I understand each other. Chatty and you have been enjoying yourselves abroad. You never cared for town. It would be much better in every sense that you should go home quietly now."

"We intended nothing else," said Mrs. Warrender, with a slight irritation, "though I confess I see no reason. But we need not discuss that over again. In the end of the week——"

"But this is only Monday. You cannot have anything to keep

you here for days. I think you should go to-morrow. A day's rest is surely enough."

"We have some people to see, Theo."

"If I were you I would see nobody. You will be sure to meet with something unpleasant. Take Chatty home, that is far the best thing you can do. Frances would say the same if she had not that unfortunate desire to please everybody, to say what is agreeable, which makes women so untrustworthy. But my advice is, take Chatty home. In the circumstances it is the only thing to do."

Chatty rose from where she had been seated by Lady Markland's side. "Am I to be hidden away?" she said, her pale face flushing nervously. "Have I done anything wrong?"

"How silly to ask such questions. You know well enough what I mean. You have been talked about. My mother has more experience; she can tell you. A girl who has been talked about is always at a disadvantage. She had much better keep quite quiet until the story has all died away."

"Mother," cried Chatty, holding out her hands, "take me away then to-night, this moment, from this horrible place, where the people have so little heart and so little sense."

CHAPTER XLVII.

"What was Chatty saying to you? I rely upon your good sense, Frances, not to encourage her in this sentimental folly."

"Is it sentimental folly? I think it is very true feeling, Theo."

"Perhaps these are interchangeable terms," he said, with the angry smile she knew so well; "but without discussing that matter I am determined that this business shall go no farther. A sister of mine waiting for a married man till he shall be divorced! the very thought makes my blood boil."

"Surely that is an unnecessarily strong statement. The circumstances must be taken into consideration."

"I will take no circumstances into consideration. It is a thing which must not be. The Cavendishes see it in precisely the same light, and my mother,—even my mother begins to hear reason."

Lady Markland made no reply. They were walking home, as their house was close at hand, a house taken for the season, in which there was not the room and space of the country, nor its active interests, and which she, having come there with much hope in the change, would already have been glad to exchange for Markland, or the Warren, or almost any other place in the world. He walked more quickly than suited her and she required all her breath to keep up with him; besides that she was silenced by what he said to her, and did not know how to reply.

"You say nothing," he continued after a moment, "from which I conclude that you are antagonistic and mean to throw your influence the other way."

"Not antagonistic: but I cannot help feeling very much for Chatty, whose heart is so much in it, more perhaps than you think."

"Chatty's heart doesn't trouble me much," he said carelessly.

"Chatty will always obey whatever impulse is nearest and most continuous, if she is not backed up on the other side."

"I don't believe you realise the strength of her feelings, Theo. That is what she is afraid of, not to be strong enough to hold out."

"Oh! So you have been over that ground with her already!"

"She spoke to me. She was glad of the opportunity to relieve her mind."

"And you promised to stand by her?" he said.

Lady Markland had been a woman full of dignity and composure. She was so still to all outward appearance, and the darkness concealed the flush that rose to her face; But it could not conceal the slight tremor with which she replied after a pause: "I promised not to be against her at least."

A flood of angry words rose to Theo's lips, the blood mounted to his head. He had taken the bias so fatal between married people of supposing when his wife disagreed with him that she did it on purpose, not because she herself thought so, but because it was opposition. Perhaps this was because of that inherent contempt for women which is a settled principle in the minds of so many men, perhaps because he had been used to a narrow mind and opinions cut and dry in the case of his sister, perhaps even because of his hot adoration and faith in Lady Markland as perfect. To continue perfect in his eyes, after their marriage, she would have needed to agree always with him, to think his thoughts. He exacted this accord with all the susceptibility of a fastidious nature, which would be content with no forced agreement, and divined in a moment when an effort was required to conform her opinions to his. He would not tolerate such an effort. He would have had her agree with him by instinct, by nature, not even by desire to please him, much less by policy. He could not endure to think of either of these means of procuring what he wanted. What he wanted was the perfect agreement of a nature which arrived at the same conclusions as his by the same means, which responded before he spoke, which was always ready to anticipate, to give him the exquisite satisfaction of feeling he was right by a perpetual seconding of all his decisions and anticipation of his thoughts. Had he married a young creature like Chatty, ready to take the impress of his more active mind, he might have found other drawbacks in her to irritate his *amour propre*, and probably would have despised her judgment in consequence of her perpetual agreement with him. But the fact was that he was jealous of his wife, not in the ordinary vulgar way, for which there was no possibility, but for every year of additional age, and every experience, and all the life she had led apart from him. He could not endure to think that she had formed the most of her ideas before she knew him: the thought of her past was horrible to him. A suspicion that she was thinking of that, that her mind was going back to something which he did not know, awoke a sort of madness in his brain. All this she knew by painful intuition now, as at first by discoveries which startled her very soul, and seemed to disturb the pillars of the world. She was aware of the forced control he kept over himself, not to burst forth upon her, and she would have fled morally, and brought herself round to his ideas and sworn eternal faith to him, if it would have done any good. But she knew very well that his uneasy nature would not be satisfied with that.

"I might have divined," he said, after a long pause, during which they went quickly along, he increasing his pace unawares, she losing her breath in keeping up with him, "that you would see this matter differently. But I must ask, at least, that you won't circumvent us, and neutralise all our plans. The only thing for Chatty to do is to drop it altogether, to receive no more letters, to cut the whole concern. It is a disreputable business altogether. It is better she should never marry at all than marry in that way."

"I feel sure, Theo, that except in this way she will never marry at all—if you think that matters."

"If I think that matters! It is not very flattering to me that you should think it doesn't matter," he said.

And then they reached their house, and he followed her into the drawing-room, where one dim lamp was burning, and the room had a deserted look. Perhaps that last speech had been a little unkind. Compunction visited him not unfrequently. He seated himself at the little table on which the lamp was standing, as she took off her hat and recovered her breath. "Since we are at home, and alone for once in a way," he said, more graciously, "which happens seldom enough, I'll read to you for an hour, if you like, Frances; that is, if you have no letters to write."

There was a little irony in the last words, for Lady Markland had, if the truth must be told, a foible that way, and liked, as so many women do, the idea of having a large correspondence, and took pleasure in keeping it up. She answered eagerly that she had no letters to write (though not without a glance at her table where one lay unfinished) and would like his reading above everything: which was so far true that it was a sign of peace, and an occupation which he enjoyed. She got her work while he got the book, not without a horrible sense that Geoff, always wakeful, would have heard her come in, and would call for her, nor without a longing desire to go to him, if only for a moment, which was what she had intended to do. Perhaps it was to prevent this that Theo had been so ready with his offer, and so sensitive was he to every impression that the poor lady felt a thrill of terror lest her half-formed intention, or Geoff's waking, might thrill through the atmosphere to her husband's mind, and make him fling down the book with impatience. She got her work with a nervous haste, which it seemed he must divine, and seated herself opposite to him. "Now, I am ready," she said.

Poor Lady Markland! He had not read a page—a page to which she gave the most painful attention, trying not to think that the door might open any moment, and the nurse appear begging her to speak a word to Lord Markland—when a faint cry reached her ears. It was faint and far away, but she knew what it was. It was the cry of "Mamma," from Geoff's bed, only given forth, she knew, after much tossing and turning, and which a year ago she would have heard from any corner of the house and flown to answer. She started when she heard it, but she had been so much

425

on the alert, and prepared for some interruption of the kind, that she hoped Theo did not see the little instinctive movement "Mamma!" She sat with a nervous thrill upon her, taking no notice, trying to listen, seeing in the dark the little sleepless boy tossing upon his uneasy pillow, and calling in vain for his mother, but resisting all the impulses both of heart and habit. If only Theo might not hear! After a while, however, Theo's ear caught the sound. "What's that?" he said sharply, stopping and looking at her across the table. Alas! the repressed agitation in her smile told its own story to Theo. He knew that she pretended to listen, that she knew very well what it was. "*That*" she said, faltering. "What? Oh! it sounds like Geoff calling—some one."

"He is calling *you*; and you are dying to be with him, to rush upstairs and coax and kiss him to sleep. You are ruining the boy."

"No, Theo. It is probably nurse he is calling. He sleeps so badly," she said, with a broken voice, for the appeals to mamma came quicker, and she felt as if the child was dragging at her very heart-strings.

"He would have slept better, had he been paid less attention to; but don't let me keep you from your boy," he said, throwing down the book on the table. She made an attempt at an appeal.

"Theo! please don't go away. I will run for a moment, and see what is the matter."

"You can do what you please about that: but you are ruining the boy," said Warrender. And then he began to hum a tune, which showed that he had reached a white heat of exasperation, and left the room. She sat motionless till she heard the street door closed loudly. Her heart seemed to stand still: yet was there, was it possible, a certain relief in the sound? She stole upstairs noiselessly and into Geoff's room and threw herself down by the bedside. "Oh, Geoff, what is the matter?" she asked: though her heart had dragged her so, there was in her tone a tender exasperation too.

"I can't sleep," the boy said, clinging to her, with his arms round her neck.

"But you must try to sleep—for my sake. Don't toss about, but lie quite still, that is far the best way."

"I did," said Geoff, "and said all the poetry I knew, and did the multiplication table twice. I wanted you. I kept quiet as long as I could—but I wanted you so."

"But you must not want me. You are too big to want your mother."

"I shall never be too big, I want you always," said Geoff, murmuring in the dark, with his little arms clinging close round her neck.

"Oh, Geoff, my dearest boy! but for my sake you must content yourself—for my sake."

"Was he angry?" the child asked, and in the cover of the darkness he clenched his little hands and contracted his brows; all of which she guessed, though she saw not.

"That is not a question to ask," she said. "You must never speak to me so; and remember, Geoff,—they say I am spoiling you—I will never come when you call me after to-night."

But Lady Markland's heart was very heavy as she went downstairs. She had put her child away from her; and she sat alone in the large still drawing-room all the evening, hearing the carriages come and go outside, and hansoms dashing up which she hoped might be coming to her own door. But Theo did not come back. This was one of many evenings which she spent alone, in disgrace, not knowing how to get her pardon, feeling guilty, yet having done nothing. Her second venture had not brought her very much additional happiness so far.

CHAPTER XLVIII.

"Two little girls. He came over to tell us yesterday. Poor Theo! He is pleased, of course, but I think half ashamed too. It seems a little ridiculous to have twins, and the first."

"I can't think how you can say it is ridiculous. It is very interesting. But nowadays people seem to be ashamed of having children at all. It used to be thought the strength of a country, and doing your duty to the state. But people have different notions now."

"Well," said the rector, "I should have thought Theo would be pleased; for he likes to be original in everything, and two little girls are as unlike as possible to one little boy."

Mrs. Warrender's eyes shot forth a gleam, half of humorous acquiescence, half of irritation, that Mr. Wilberforce should have divined her son's state of mind. She had come to the Warren with Chatty for a few weeks, for what they called "change," though the change of a six miles' journey was not much. The Warren bore a very different aspect now from that which it had borne in former days. It was light and cheerful; some new rooms had been built, which broke the commonplace outlines of the respectable house. It was newly furnished with furniture as unlike as possible to the mahogany catafalques. Only the hall, which had been old-fashioned and harmonious, in which Chatty was attending to the flowers, was the same; and so far as that went, it might have been the very same day on which Dick Cavendish had paid his first visit, when Chatty with her bowl of roses had walked in, as he said, into his heart. There were still roses of the second bloom, with the heat of July in their fervent heart, and she stood at the table arranging them, changed, indeed, but not so changed as to affect the indifferent spectator, to whom she still seemed a part of the background, a figure passive though sweet, with no immediate vocation in life. Old Joseph, too, was in the depths of the hall, just visible, doing something,—something that was not of the least urgency or importance, but which kept him about and hearing all that passed. He and his old wife were in charge of the Warren, in the present changed days, and though they both half resented the fact that the young master had abandoned his own house, they were yet more than half pleased to have this tranquillity and ease at the end of their long service. To do them justice, they had been glad to receive their old mistress and her daughter, welcoming them as visitors with a sense of hospitality, and declaring that they did not mind the trouble, notwithstanding that Joseph's health was bad, and late dinners had always been an affliction to his wife.

"I hope," Mrs. Warrender said, "that the two little girls will soon make their own welcome, as babies have a way of doing—and make everybody certain that they are much sweeter than any one little boy."

This was how Theo's mother took the sting out of the rector's speech, which was not intended to have any sting, and was only a stray gleam of insight out of a confused realisation of the state of affairs; but it was so true that it was difficult to believe it was that, and no more. The Wilberforces had come to inquire, not only for Lady Markland and her babies, but into many other things, could they have found the opportunity. But Chatty's presence stopped even Mrs. Wilberforce's mouth. And when they went in to inspect all the improvements and the new decorations and furniture, Chatty came after them, and followed everywhere, which seemed very strange to the rector's wife. Did she mean to prevent them from talking? Was that her purpose? She took little part in the conversation. She was more silent than she had ever been, though she had never been given to much talk; and yet she came with them wherever they went, putting an effectual stop to the questions that quivered on the very edge of Mrs. Wilberforce's lips. Nor had the rector the sense, which he might so easily have had, to engage her in talk, to occupy her attention, and leave his wife free to speak. Anybody but a man would have had the sense to have done so, but a man is an unteachable creature, and never will divine the things that are required of him which cannot be told him in plain words. Accordingly, the whole party strolled from one room to another, commenting upon the new arrangements without a possibility of any enlightenment as to the real state of affairs. Mrs. Wilberforce was very indignant with her husband as they left,—an indignation that seemed very uncalled for to this injured man.

"What you could have done? Why, you could have talked to Chatty. You could have interested her on some subject or another, about where they were abroad, or about the parish, or—— Dear me, there are always plenty of subjects. When you knew how anxious I was to find out all about it! Dick Cavendish is a great deal more a friend of yours than he was of theirs until this unfortunate business came about, and it seems very strange that we should know nothing. Why, I don't know even what to call her,—whether she is still Miss Warrender, or what she is."

"You would not call her Miss Warrender in any case," said the rector, with a little self-assertion. "And you know that is nonsense, for the moment the other wife was proved to be living, poor Chatty's marriage was as if it had not been."

"Well, that is what I cannot understand, Herbert: to be married just like anybody else, and the ring put on, and everything (by the way, I did notice that she does not wear her ring), and that it is as if it had not been. Bigamy one can understand: but how it should mean nothing! And do you mean to say she could marry somebody else, the same as if it had never happened?"

"To-morrow if she likes,—and I wish she would, poor Chatty! It would be the best way of cutting the knot."

"Then I can tell you one thing that all your superior information would never teach you," cried Mrs. Wilberforce, —"*that she never will!* You may take my word for it, Chatty has far too much principle. What! be married to one man in church, and then go and be married to another! Never, Herbert! Oh, you may tell me the ceremony is nothing, and that they must have nothing to say to each other, and all that: it may be quite true, but that Chatty will ever marry any one else is not true. She will never do it. For anything I can tell, or you can tell, she may never see Dick Cavendish again. But she will never marry any one else. It is very hard to be sure of anything nowadays, when all the landmarks are being changed, and the country going headlong to—— But if I know anything, I hope I know Chatty Warrender, and *that*, you may be sure, she will never do."

This flood of eloquence silenced the rector, and indeed he had no objection to make: for he was aware of all those sacred prejudices that live in the hearts of ladies in the country, and he thought it very likely that Chatty would feel herself bound for ever by what was no bond at all.

In the meantime there had been only one letter from Dick, a short and hasty one, telling that he was better, explaining that he had not been able to let them know of his illness, and announcing that he was off again as soon as he should be able to move upon his search. Chatty and her mother wondered over this, without communicating its contents to any one. His search!—what did his search mean? There was no search wanted for those proceedings which he had declared were so easy and so certain at that far end of the world. Evidently they had not been so easy, and the words that he used were very strange to the ladies. He had no doubt, he said, of his success. Doubt! he had spoken of it before he went away as a thing which only required asking for, to have; and the idea that there was no doubt at once gave embodiment and force to the doubt which had never existed. Mrs. Warrender joined the forces of the opposing party from the moment she had read this letter. After a day or two of great depression and seriousness, she had taken Chatty into her arms and advised her to give up the lover, the husband, who was no husband, and perhaps an unfaithful lover. "I said nothing at first," Mrs. Warrender had said with tears. "I stood by him when there was so much against

him. I believed every word he said,—notwithstanding everything.
But now, my darling,—oh, Chatty, now! He was to be gone for
three months at the outside, and now it is eight: and he was quite
sure of being able to do his business at once. But now he says
he has no doubt, and that he is off on his search. His search for
what? Oh, my dearest, I am most reluctant to say it, but I fear
Theo is right. To think of a man trying, and perhaps trying in
vain, to get a divorce in order to marry *you!* Chatty, it is a thing
that cannot be; it is impossible, it is disreputable. A divorced man
is bad enough,—you know how Minnie spoke even of that,—but
a man who is trying for a divorce with the object—— Chatty, my
darling, it is a thing which cannot be."

Chatty was not a girl of many words, nor did she commit
herself to argument: she would enter into no controversy with
her mother. She said only that she was married to Dick. Perhaps
he was not married to her: that might be: and she might never
see him again: but she was bound for ever. And in the meantime,
until they knew all the circumstances, how could they discuss
the matter? When Dick returned and gave them the necessary
information, then it would be time enough. In the meantime
she had nothing to say. And nothing more could be got from
her. Minnie came and quoted Eustace: but Chatty only walked
out of the room, leaving her sister in possession of the field, but
without any of the satisfaction of a victory. And Theo came, but
he contented himself with talking to his mother. Something
of natural diffidence or feeling prevented him from assailing
Chatty in the stronghold of that modest determination which
they all called obstinacy.

Theo came and made his mother miserable, almost
commanding her to use her authority, declaring that it would
be her fault if this farce went on,—this disreputable farce he
called it; while poor Mrs. Warrender, now as much opposed
to it as he, had to bear the brunt of his objurgations until she
was driven to make a stand upon the very arguments which she
most disapproved. In the midst of all this Chatty stood firm. If

she wept, it was in the solitude of her own chamber, from which even her mother was shut out; if she ever wavered or broke down, it was in secret. Externally, to the view of the world, she was perfectly calm and cheerful, fulfilling all her little duties with the composure of one who has never known what tragedy means. A hundred eager eyes had been upon her, but no one had been able to tell how Chatty "bore it." She said nothing to anybody. It was thought that she held her head a little higher than usual and was less disposed for society: but then she had never loved society. She arranged her flowers, she took her walks, she carried beef-tea and port wine to the sick people. She even sat down daily at the usual hour and took out her muslin work, a height of tranquillity to which it was indeed difficult to reach. But what woman could do, Chatty would do, and she had accomplished even that. There are many in the world who must act and cannot sit still, but there are also some who, recognising action to be impossible, can wait with the whole passive force of their being, until that passiveness becomes almost sublime. Chatty was of this kind. Presumably she did not torment herself hour by hour and day by day, as her mother did, by continual re-arguments of the whole question, but if she did, she kept the process altogether to herself.

There had been one interview, indeed, which had tried her very much, and that had taken place a day or two after her arrival at the Warren, when she had met Lizzie Hampson on the road. Lizzie had shrunk from the young lady in whose life she had interfered with such extraordinary effect, but Chatty had insisted on speaking to her, and had called her almost imperiously. "Why do you run away? Do you think I am angry with you?" she said.

"Oh, Miss Chatty!" The girl had no breath or courage to say more.

"You did right, I believe," Chatty said. "It would have been better if you had come and told me quietly at home, before—anything had happened. But I do not blame you. I think you did right."

"I never knew till the last minute that it would hurt you so!"

Lizzie cried. "I knew it might be bad for the gentleman, and that he could be tried and put in prison; but she would never, never have done that. She wanted him to be free. It was only when I knew, Miss Chatty, what it would do to you—and then it was too late. I went to Highcombe, but you had gone from there; and then when I got to London——"

A flush came over Chatty's face, as all the extraordinary scene came back to her. "It seems strange that it should be you who were mixed up with all," she said. "Things happen very strangely, I think, in life; one can never tell—If you have no objection, I should like you to tell me something of—. I saw her—do you remember? here, on this very road: and you told me—ah! that to put such people in penitentiaries would not do; that they wanted to enjoy themselves. Do you remember? It seemed very strange to me then. And to think that——" This moved Chatty more than all the rest had done. Her soft face grew crimson, her eyes filled with tears.

"To think that she—oh, Miss Chatty, I feel as if I ought to go down on my knees and ask you to forgive me for ever having anything to do with her."

"That was no fault of yours, I think," said Chatty very softly. "It can have been nobody's fault. It is just because—it has happened so: that makes it harder and harder: none of us meant any harm—except perhaps——"

"Miss Chatty, she didn't mean any harm to you. She meant no harm to any one. She was never brought up to care for what was good. She was brought up just to please her fancy. Oh, the like of you can't understand, if you were to be told ever so: nor should I if I hadn't seen it. They make a sort of principle of that, just to please their fancy. We're taught here that to please ourselves is mostly wrong: but not there. It's their religion in a kind of a way, out in these wild places, just to do whatever they like; and then when you come to grief, if you are plucky and take it cheerful—— The very words sound dreadful, here where everything is so different," Lizzie said, with a shudder, looking round her, as if there might be ears in the trees.

Chatty did not ask any further questions. She walked along very gravely, with her head bent. "It makes one's heart ache," she said. There was an ease in speaking to this girl who had played so strange a part in her life, who knew her trouble as no one else did. "It makes one's heart ache," she repeated. She was not thinking of herself. "And where is she now? Do you hear of her? Do you know what has become of her?"

"Only one thing can become of her," said Lizzie. "She'll fall lower and lower. Oh, you don't think a poor creature can fall any lower, I know," for Chatty had looked at her with wonder, shaking her head; "but lower and lower in her dreadful way. One day there," said Lizzie philosophically, but sadly, pointing to the high wall of the Elms, "with her fine dresses and her horses and carriages: and the next in dirt and misery. And then she'll die, perhaps in the hospital. Oh, she'll not be long in anybody's way. They die soon, and then they are done with, and everybody is glad of it—" the girl cried, with a burst of sudden tears.

Chatty stopped suddenly upon the road. They were opposite to the gate from which so often the woman they were discussing had driven forth in her short-lived finery; a stillness as of death had fallen on the uninhabited house, and all was tranquil on the country road, stretching on one side across the tranquil fields, on the other towards the clustering houses of the village and the low spire which pointed to heaven. "Lizzie," she said, "if it is never put right,—and perhaps it will never be put right, for who can tell?— if you will come with me who know so much about it, we will go and be missionaries to these poor girls. I will tell them my story, and how I am married but have no husband, and how three lives are all ruined,—all ruined for ever. And we will tell them that love is not like that; that it is faithful and true: and that women should never be like that—that women should be—oh, I do not believe it, I do not believe it! Of her own free will no woman could ever be like that!" Chatty cried, like Desdemona, suddenly clenching her soft hands in a passion of indignation and pity.

"We will go and tell them, Lizzie!"

"Oh, Miss Chatty! They know it all, every word," Lizzie cried.

CHAPTER XLIX.

Two little girls are as unlike as anything can be to one little boy. This gave Warrender a sort of angry satisfaction in the ridiculous incident which had happened in his life. For it is a ridiculous incident. When a man is hardened to it, when he has had several children and is habituated to the paternal honours, it may be amusing and interesting and all the rest. But scarcely a year after his marriage, when he was not quite four-and-twenty, to be the father of twins! He felt sometimes as if it was the result of a conspiracy to make him ridiculous. The neighbouring potentates, when he met them, laughed as they congratulated him. "If you are going to continue like this, you will be a patriarch before you know where you are," one of them said. It was a joke to the entire country round about. Twins! He felt scarcely any of the stirrings of tenderness in his heart which are supposed to move a young father, when he looked at the two little yawning, gaping morsels of humanity. If there had been but one, perhaps!—but two! He was the laughing-stock of the neighbourhood, he felt. The sight of his wife, pale and smiling, touched his heart indeed. But even this sight was not without its pangs. For alas! she knew all about this position which was so novel to him. She understood the babies and their wants, as it was natural a mother who was already experienced in motherhood should. And finally she was so far carried away by the privileges and the expansion of the moment as to ask him—him! the last authority to be consulted on such a subject—whether Geoff was delighted to hear of his little sisters. Geoff's little sisters! The thought of that boy having anything to do with them, any relationship to claim with *his* children clouded Warrender's face. He turned it away, and Lady Markland, in the sweet enthusiasm of the moment, fortunately did not perceive that change. She thought in her tender folly that this would make everything right; that Geoff, as the brother of his little girls, would be something nearer to Theo, claiming a more favourable consideration. She preserved this hope for some time, notwithstanding a great many signs to the contrary. Even Theo's dark face, when he found Geoff one day in his mother's room, looking with great interest at the children, did not alarm the mother, who was determined not to part with her illusion. "Do you think it right to have a boy of Geoff's age here in your room?" he said. "Oh, Theo, my own boy!—what harm can it do?" she had said, so foolishly, forgetting that Geoff's crime in the eyes of his young stepfather was exactly this, that he was her own boy.

Thus the circumstance which every one concerned hoped was to make the most favourable change in the position did only intensify its difficulties. Geoff naturally was more thrown into the society of his stepfather during his mother's seclusion, and Geoff was very full of the new event and new relationships, and was no wiser than his mother so far as this was concerned. When they lunched together the boy was so far forgetful of former experiences as to ply Theo with questions, as he had not done since the days when the young man was his tutor, and everything was on so different a footing. Geoff's excitement made him forget all the prudence he had acquired. His "I say, Warrender," over and over repeated drove Theo to heights of exasperation indescribable. Everything about Geoff was offensive to his stepfather: his ugly little face, the nervous grimaces which he still made, the familiarity of his address, but above all the questions which it was impossible to silence. Lady Markland averted them more or less when she was present, and Geoff had learnt prudence to some extent, but in his excitement he remembered these precautions no more.

"I say, Warrender! shall you take mamma away? Nurse says she must go for a change. I think Markland is always the nicest place going, don't you?"

"No, I prefer the Warren, as you know."

"Oh!" Geoff could scarcely keep out of his voice the wondering contempt with which he received this suggestion: but here his natural insight prevailed, and a sort of sympathetic genius which the little fellow possessed. "To be sure, I like the Warren very much indeed," he said. "I suppose what makes me like Markland best is being born here."

"And I was born there," Theo said.

"Yes, I know. I wonder which the babies will like best. They are born here, like me; I hope they will like Markland. It will be fun seeing them run about, both the same size, and so like. They say twins are always so like. Shall we have to tie a red ribbon round one and a blue ribbon round the other, as people do?"

To this question the father of the babies vouchsafed no reply.

"Nurse says they are not a bit like me," Geoff continued, in a tone of regret.

"Like you! Why should they be like you?" said Warrender, with a flush of indignation.

"But why not, Warrender? Brothers and sisters are alike often. You and Chatty are a little alike. When I am at Oxford, if they come to see me, I shall like fellows to say, 'Oh, I saw your sisters, Markland.'"

"Your sisters!" Theo could scarcely contain his disgust, all the more that he saw the old butler keeping an eye upon him with a sort of severity. The servants in the house, Theo thought, all took part with Geoff, and looked to him as their future master. He continued hastily: "I can only hope they will prefer the Warren, as I do, for that will be their home."

"Oh!" cried Geoff again, opening round eyes. "But if it isn't our home, how can it be theirs? They don't want a home all to themselves."

"I think they do," said Theo shortly.

The boy gave him a furtive glance, and thought it wise to change the subject. "Mrs. Warrender is there now. Oh, I say! she will be granny to the babies. I should like to call her granny too. Will she let me, do you think, Warrender? She is always so kind to me."

"I should advise you not to try."

"Why, Warrender? Would she be angry? She is always very kind. I went to see her once, as soon as she came home, and she was awfully kind, and understood what I wanted." Geoff paused here, suddenly catching himself up, and remembering with a forlorn sense that he had gone a long way beyond that in his little life, the experiences which were sufficiently painful, of that day.

"It requires a very wise person to do that," said Warrender, with an angry smile.

"Yes, to understand you quite right even when you don't say anything. I say, Warrender, if mamma has to go away for a change, when shall we go?"

"We!" said Warrender significantly. "Are you also in want of a change?"

The boy looked up at him suddenly, with a hasty flush. The tears came to his brave little eyes. He was over-powered by the sudden suggestion, and could not find a word to say.

"Markland is the best change for you, after Eton," said Theo. "You don't want to travel with a nursery, I suppose."

Geoff felt something rise in his throat. Why, it was his own nursery, he wanted to say. It was his own family. Where should he go but where they went? But the words were stopped on his lips, and his magnanimous little heart swelled high. Oh, if he could but fly to his mother!—but to her he had learnt never now to fly.

"Wherever we may go," said Warrender coldly, "I think you had much better spend your holidays here;" and he got up from the table, leaving Geoff in a tumult of feelings which words can scarcely describe. He had suffered a great deal during the past year, and had said little. A sort of preternatural consciousness that he must keep his own secret, that he must betray nothing to his mother, had come upon him. He sat now silent, his little face twitching and working, a sudden new, unlooked-for horror stealing over him, that he was to be separated from his mother;

that he was to be left behind while they went away. It did not seem possible, and yet, with all the rapidity of a child's imagination, Geoff's mind flashed over what might happen,—he to be left alone here, while *they* went away. He saw his mother go smiling into the carriage, thinking of the babies, in their little white hoods, little dolls—oh no, dear little helpless creatures, to whom the boy's heart went out; his little babies as well as his mother's. But of course she would think of them. She must think of them. And Geoff would be left behind, with no one, nobody to speak to, the great rooms all empty, only the servants about. He remembered what it had been when his mother was married; but then he had the hope that she would come back to him, that all would be well: and now he knew that never, never, as of old, could he have her back. Geoff did not budge from the table for some time after, but sat with his elbows on it and his head in his hands, in the attitude which he had so often been scolded for, with nobody to scold him or take any notice. He thought to himself that he might put his elbows on the table as much as he liked, and nobody would care. But this thought only made the position more terrible. It was only the return of the servants to clear the table, and the old butler's question, "What's the matter, Master Geoff?" that roused him. The butler's tone was far too sympathetic. He was an old servant, and the only one in the house who did not call poor little Geoff My lord. But the boy was not going to accept sympathy. He sprang up from the table with a "Nothing's the matter. I'm going out for a ride," and hurried towards the stables, which were now his resource more and more.

This knowledge rankled in Geoff's heart through all the time of his mother's convalescence. He was very brave, very magnanimous, without knowing that he was either. That he would not vex his mother was the determination of his soul. She was very sweet, sweeter than ever, but pale, and her hands so thin that you could see the light through them. Though he anticipated with a dull anguish the time when she should go away, when Warrender would take her away, leaving him behind, Geoff resolved that he would say nothing about it, that he would not make her unhappy. He would bear it; one could bear anything when one tried, even spending the holidays by one's self. But his heart sank at the thought. Supposing she were to stay a month away,—that was four weeks; it was thirty days,—and he alone, all alone in Markland. And when she came back it would be time for him to go to school. Sometimes he felt as if he must cry out when he thought of this; but he would not say a word, he would not complain; he would bear it rather than vex mamma. When she came downstairs she was so pale. She began to walk about a little, but only with Warrender's arm. She drove out, but the babies had to be with her in the carriage; there was no room for Geoff. He twisted his poor little face out of shape altogether in the effort to get rid of the scalding tears, but he would not betray the state of his mind; nothing, he vowed to himself, should make him worry mamma.

One day he rode over to the Warren, pondering upon what Theo had said, that the Warren must be liked best by the babies, because it was their home. Would it ever really be their home? Would Warrender be so hard as that, to take away mamma and the babies for good, and leave a fellow all alone in Markland, because it was Geoff's and not his own? Geoff's little gray face was as serious as that of a man of eighty, and almost as full of wrinkles. He thought and thought what he could do to please Warrender. Though his heart rose against this interloper, this destroyer of his home, Geoff was wise, and knew that to keep his mother he must please her husband. What could he do? Not like him,—that was impossible. Riding along, now slowly, now quickly, rather at the pony's will than at his own, Geoff, with loose reins in his hands and a slouch in his shoulders which was the despair of Black, pondered the subject till his little mind was all in confusion. What could he do to please Warrender? He would be good to the babies, by nature, and because he liked the two funny little things, but that would not please Warrender. He would do almost anything Warrender chose to tell him, but that wouldn't please him. What was there, then, that would? He did not know what he could do. He rode very carelessly, almost as much at the mercy of the pony as on the occasion when Theo picked him from under the wheels of the high phaeton; but either the pony was more wise, or Geoff stronger, for there was no question now of being thrown. When he came in sight of the little gate of the Warren, he saw some one standing there, at sight of whom he quickened his pace. He knew the general aspect of the man's figure though he could not see his face, and this welcome new excitement made the heart jump up again in Geoff's breast. He hurried along in a sudden cloud of dust, and threw himself off the pony like a little acrobat. "Mr. Cavendish!" cried Geoff, "have you come back?" with a glow of pleasure which drove all his troubles away.

It was Dick, very brown, very thin, a little wild in his aspect and dress. "Hallo, Geoff!" he replied. "Yes, I have come back. Didn't they expect me to come back?"

"Oh, I don't know. I think they wondered."

"That's how it is in this world," said the other; "nobody trusts you: as soon as you are out of sight—oh, I don't say you're out of mind—but nobody trusts you. They think that perhaps, after all, you were a villain all the time."

To this, naturally, Geoff had no reply to make, but he said, "Are you going in that way, Mr. Cavendish?" Upon which Dick burst into a loud laugh, which Geoff knew meant anything but laughing.

"What do you think, Geoff?" he said. "My wife's inside, and they've locked me out here. That's a joke, isn't it?"

"I don't think it's any joke. And Chatty wants you so. Come round to the other door."

"Are you sure of that?" said Dick. "Here's that fellow been here,—that Thynne fellow,—and tells me——" Then he paused and looked at the boy, with another laugh. "You're a queer confidant for a poor vagabond, little Geoff."

"Is it because I'm little?" cried Geoff. "But though I am little there are a heap of things I know. I know they are all against you except Chatty. Come along and see Chatty. I want to go to her this moment and tell her——"

"I thought," said Cavendish, "I'd wait for her here. I don't want to make a mummy of that fellow, my brother-in-law, don't you know, the first moment. Tell Chatty—tell my wife, Geoff—that I am waiting for her here."

Geoff did not wait for another word, but clambered on to his pony again and was off like the wind, round by the village to the other gate. Meantime Dick stood and leaned upon the wooden paling. His face was sharp and thin with illness, with eagerness and suspense, his complexion browned and paled out of its healthful English tints. But this was not because he was weak any longer, or in diminished health. He was worn by incessant travelling, by anxiety and the fluctuation of hope and fear; but the great tension had strung his nerves and strengthened his vitality, though it had worn off every superfluous particle of flesh. A keen anxiety mingled with indignation was in his eyes as he looked across the gate which the clergyman had fastened against him,—indignation, yet also a smile. From the moment when Geoff's little voice had broken upon his angry reverie, Dick had begun to recover himself. "Chatty wants you so." It was only a child that spoke. But a child does not flatter or deceive, and this was true. What Eustace Thynne thought, what anybody thought, was of little consequence. Chatty! The simple name brought a softening glow to Dick's eye. Would she come and open to him? Would she reverse the judgment of the family by her own act, or would it be he who must emancipate Chatty? He waited with something of his old gaiety rising in his mind. The position was ludicrous. They had shut him out, but it could not be for long.

Geoff galloped his pony to the gate, and up the little avenue, which was still very shady and green, though so much of the wood had been cut. He threw himself off and flung the reins to the gardener's boy, who stood gazing open-mouthed at the little lord's headlong race. The doors were not open, as usual, but Geoff knew that the drawing-room windows were seldom fastened in the summer weather. He darted along round the corner of the house, and fell against one of the windows, pushing it open. In the drawing-room there seemed a number of people assembled, whom he saw vaguely without paying any attention. Mr. and Mrs. Thynne, Warrender, in a group, talking with their heads together, Mrs. Warrender standing between them and the tranquil figure of Chatty, who sat at work at the other end of the room, taking no part in the consultation of the others, paying no heed to them. Chatty showed an almost ostentation of disregard, of separation from the others, in her isolated place and the work with which she was busy. She looked up when Geoff came stumbling through the window, with a little alarm, but she did not look as if she expected any one, as if she had heard who was so near at hand. The boy was covered with dust and hot with haste, his forehead bathed in perspiration. He called out to her almost before he was in the room: "Chatty! Mr. Cavendish is outside at the gate. They will not let him come in. He sent me to tell you."

Chatty rose to her feet, and the group in the end of the room scattered and crowded to the window. Theo seized his stepson by the collar, half choking the boy. "You confounded imp!" he cried, "what business is that of yours?"

"Geoff, where, where?" Chatty rushed to the child and caught his hand. He struggled in Theo's grasp, in a desperate, nervous anguish, fearing he could not tell what,—that he would be strangled, that Chatty would be put in some sort of prison. The strangling was in progress now; he called out in haste, that he might get it out before his breath was gone—

"Oh, run, Chatty! The little gate in the road—the wooden gate." She seemed to flash past his eyes,—his eyes which were turning in his head, with the pressure and the shaking of Warrender's arm. Then the child felt himself suddenly pitched forward and fell, stunned for the moment, and thinking, before consciousness failed him, that all was over, and that he was killed indeed—yet scarcely sorry, for Chatty had his message and he had fulfilled his commission before he died.

Chatty flew along the shady paths, a line of whiteness fluttering through sunshine and shadow. She called out her lover's name as she approached the gate. She had neither fear nor doubt in her mind. She did not know what news he was going to bring her, what conclusion was to be put to the story. She called to him as soon as he was within hearing, asking no questions, taking no precautions. "Dick, Dick!" Behind her, but at some distance, Minnie too fluttered along, inspired by virtuous indignation, which is only less swift than love and happiness. The gentlemen remained behind, even Eustace perceiving that the matter had now passed beyond their hands. This is one of the points in which men have the advantage over women. They have a practical sense of the point at which opposition becomes impossible. And Warrender had the additional knowledge that he had done that in his fury which at his leisure it would be difficult to account for. Mrs. Warrender, who had not been informed of the crisis, nor known upon what matter her children were consulting, was too much horrified by what had happened to Geoff to think even of Chatty. She raised the boy up and put him on a sofa, and bathed his forehead, her own heart aching and bleeding, while Warrender stood dumbly by, looking at his handiwork, his passion still hot in him, and a half frenzy of dislike and repugnance in his mind.

CHAPTER L.

"Dick!" Curiously enough Dick had not thought till then that even a high gate may be vaulted by a man whose heart has leaped it before him, and who is in perfect training, and knows no fear. He had been more discouraged by Eustace Thynne than any authority on the part of that poor creature at all warranted, and his heart had failed him still more when he thought that perhaps Chatty might have been talked over, and might stand by him no longer. She was his wife, but what if her heart had given him up! But when a man hears the voice he loves best in the world calling him, everything takes a different aspect. "Dick!" Her voice came first faint, so that he scarcely believed it; then nearer and nearer, giving life to the silent world. The thin brown face of the vagabond, as he had called himself, grew crimson with a flush of happiness and new life. He could not wait until she came; his soul flew to meet her in a great revulsion of confidence and joy. The gate was high, but he was eager and she was coming. He put his sinewy, thin hands upon it, and was over in a moment. And there she came, flying, fluttering, her light dress making a line of whiteness under the trees. She did not stop to ask a question, but ran straight to him, into his arms. "Dick, Dick!" and "Chatty, my darling, at last!"—that was all they said.

Minnie did not run so fast. She had not the same inducement; for opposition, though very nearly as swift, has not quite the same impetus as love. She only came up to them when these first greetings were over, and when, to the consciousness of both, life had taken up its threads again exactly where they had broken off. Chatty did not ask any questions,—his presence was answer enough to all questions; but indeed she did not think of any. Everything else went out of her mind except that he was there.

"Mr. Cavendish!" Minnie came up breathless, putting her hand to her side. "Oh, Chatty, you are shameless! Do you know what you are doing? It was his duty—to satisfy us first. Mr. Cavendish, if she is lost to—all sense of shame——"

Panting, she had got up to them, and was pulling Chatty away from him by her arm.

"There is no shame in the matter," he said. "But, Chatty, your sister is right, and I must explain everything to your relatives at once. There is no time to lose, for the train leaves at six, and I want to take you away with me. If you can be ready."

"Yes, Dick, I can be ready. I am ready, whenever you please."

He pressed her arm, which she had placed within his, with a look that said everything there was to say. But Minnie replied with a scream. "Take her away! What right have you to take her away? Eustace will never consent, and my mother—oh, even my mother will not hear of that. If you were a hundred times divorced,—which it is a shame to think of,—you can't take her away like that; you will have to be married again."

"I am sorry to push past you, Mrs. Thynne. It is your husband's fault, who stopped my entrance in the natural way. But we have no time to lose." He looked back, waving his hand to Minnie, whose wrath took away the little breath she had left. "I am not a divorced man," he said. Mrs. Eustace looked after them with feelings indescribable. They went hurrying along, the two figures melting into one, swift, straight, carried as by a wind of triumph. What did he mean? It was horrible to Minnie that she could not go so fast, that she had to wait and take breath. With a pang of angry disappointment she felt at once that they were on the winning side, and that they must inevitably reach the Warren before she could, and that thus she would not hear what Dick had to say. It may here be added that Minnie had, like Chatty, the most perfect confidence that all was right. She no more believed that Dick would have been there had the end of his mission been unsatisfactory than she believed that night was day. She would not have owned this for the world, and she was vexed and mortified by the conviction, but yet at the bottom of her heart, being not at all so bad as she wished to believe she was, felt a sense of consolation and relief, which made it at once easier and more tantalising to have to wait.

Foolish Chatty held Dick's arm fast, and kept up a murmur of happiness. "Oh, Dick, are you sure it is you? Have you come at last? Are you well now? And I that could not go to you, that did not know, that had no one to ask! Oh, Dick, didn't you want me when you were ill? Oh, Dick! oh, Dick!" After all, his mere name was the most satisfactory thing to say. And as he hurried her along, almost flying over the woodland path, Chatty too was soon out of breath, and ended in a blissful incapacity to say or do anything except to be carried along with him in his eager progress towards the tribunal which he had to face.

Eustace Thynne opposed his entrance, but quite ineffectually, at the drawing-room door. Dick with his left hand was more than a match for the Reverend Eustace. Warrender stood in the middle of the room, with his head towards the sofa, over which his mother was bending, though his eyes turned to the new-comers as they entered. He made a step towards them as if to stop them, but a movement on the sofa drew him back again as by some fascination. It was Geoff, who struggled up with a little pale gray face and a cut on his forehead, like a little ghost. His sharp voice piped forth all at once in the silence: "I told her, Mr. Cavendish. I gave her your message. Oh, I'm all right, I'm all right. But I told Chatty. I—I did what you said."

"Mr. Cavendish!" cried Mrs. Warrender, turning from the child. She was trembling with the excitement of these hurrying events, though the sick terror she had been seized with in respect to Geoff was passing away. "Mr. Cavendish, my son is right in this,—that before you saw Chatty we should have had an account of you, he and I."

"I should have said so too, in other circumstances," said Dick holding Chatty's arm closely within his own. "If my presence or my touch could harm her, even with the most formal fool,"—he flashed a look at Eustace, angrily, which glowed over the pale parson like a passing lamp, but left him quite unconscious. "As it is, you have a right to the fullest explanation, but not to keep my wife from me for a moment."

"She is not your wife," cried Warrender. "Leave him, Chatty. Even in the best of circumstances she cannot be your wife."

"Chatty, do not move. I have as full a right to hold her here as you have, or any married man. Mrs. Warrender, I don't want to get angry. I will tell you my story at once. On our wedding-day, when that terrible interruption occurred, the poor creature whom I then thought, whom I then believed, to have been——"

"You mean Mrs. Cavendish, your lawful wife."

"Poor girl, do not call her by that name; she never bore it. She did not mean to do any harm. There was no sanctity to her in that or any other tie."

Chatty pressed his arm more closely in sympathy. "Oh, Dick, I know, I know."

"She meant no harm, from her point of view. She scarcely meant to deceive me. Mrs. Warrender, it was a fiction all through. There has been no need of any divorce. She was already married when—she made believe to marry me. The delusion was mine alone. I hunted the man over half the continent. I did not dare to tell you what I was doing, lest it should prove to be a false hope. But at last I found him, and I have all the evidence. I have never had any wife but Chatty. She forgives me what was done in folly so long ago, before I ever saw her. There was no marriage. What was done was a mere idle form, in deference to my prejudices," he said, with a short laugh of excitement. "I was a fool, it appears, all through; but it was not as a wise man that Chatty married me," he said, turning to her. "Our marriage is as true as ever marriage was. I have no wife but Chatty. Mrs. Warrender, I have all the evidence. Don't you believe me? Surely you must believe me!" Dick cried.

His voice was interrupted by a shrill little outburst from the sofa behind. "Hurrah! Hurrah!" cried little Geoff before Dick had ended. "Chatty, it was me that brought the first news! Chatty, are you happy now?"

Mrs. Warrender, in the act of going forward to the pair who stood before her awaiting her judgment, turned with a thrill of anxious terror. "Oh, hush, hush!" she cried, putting herself before the boy.

Theo, too, had turned round with a suppressed but passionate exclamation, clenching his hands. "Mother, I can think of nothing till that imp is out of the way."

"He shall go, Theo. Speak to them, speak to them!" cried the mother anxiously, bending over the sofa, with an indescribable tumult in her heart. She had to leave her own child's fate at its crisis to look after and protect this child who was none of hers, who was the stumbling-block in her son's way. And yet her heart condemned her son, and took part with the little intruder. Thus Chatty for the moment was left to stand alone before her husband's judge, but was not aware of it, thought nothing of it, in her confidence and joy. Warrender stood looking darkly after them till his mother had taken his stepson out of the room. The pause, perhaps, was useful in calming the excitement of all. When the door closed Theo turned round, mastering himself with an effort. Geoff had diverted the rush of hasty temper which was natural to him. He looked upon the new-comer less severely.

"We can have no interest," he said, "but that your story should be true. But it cannot rest on your word, Cavendish. You have been deceived once; you may be deceived again. My mother is no judge of points of law, and she is favourable, too favourable, to you. You had better come with us into another room, and let us see what proofs you have of what you say."

"That is quite just," said Dick. "I'd like you to kiss that little beggar for me, Chatty; he knows what it is to stand by a man in trouble. It is all right, Warrender. Of course it is the interest of all of us that there should be no mistake. Send for Wilberforce, who will be impartial; and if you could have Longstaffe too——"

Minnie came in, out of breath, at this stage of the affairs.

451

"What does he say, Eustace,—oh, what does he say? Are you sure it is true? What has he got to say? And what does he mean about Mr. Longstaffe and Mr. Wilberforce? Aren't you good enough for him? Can't you judge without Wilberforce? Wilberforce," she cried, with professional contempt for another clergyman, "is nothing so very wonderful; and he is *his* friend and will be sure to be on his side. Why can't Eustace do?"

Mrs. Warrender, with her anxious face, had now come back again alone. She went up to Dick, holding out both her hands. "God bless you!" she said. "I believe you, dear Dick, every word you say. But everything must be made as clear as daylight both for her sake and your own."

"I know it, dear mother," he replied. "I am quite ready. I should be the first to ask for a full examination. Take care of my Chatty while I show my papers. I want to take my wife away with me. I cannot be parted from her again."

"Oh, Dick! oh, Dick!" The mother, like the daughter, could find no other words to say.

Little Geoff found himself alone in Mrs. Warrender's room. She had taken him there with much kindness and many tender words, and made a little nest for him upon the sofa. "Lie down and try to go to sleep," she said, stooping to kiss him, a caress which half pleased, half irritated, Geoff. But he obeyed, for his head was still aching and dazed with the suddenness and strangeness of all that had passed. To lie down and try to sleep was not so hard for him as for most children of his age, and for the first moment no movement of revolt was in him. He lay down in the silence, not unwilling to rest his head on a soft pillow. But the fire of excitement was in Geoff's veins, and a restlessness of energy and activity which after a minute or two forebade all possibility of rest. Something had happened to him which had never happened before. He had not been quite clear what it was at first; whether it was the wonder of Dick's return or of his own part in it,—the fact that he had been the messenger and had discharged his trust. But presently it all came to him, as he lay quietly with his aching head pressed against the cool pillow. Geoff had encountered many new experiences in the last two years of his life, but he had not known at any time what personal violence was. Everybody round him had made much of him; his delicate health had always been in the thoughts of those who were about him, and perhaps the rank to which he was so indifferent, of which he was scarcely conscious. Till Theo had appeared upon the scene, Geoff had been the central figure in his own little world. Since that time, the boy had suffered with a magnanimity which few men could have equalled a gradual deposition from most of the things he prized most. He was no longer first; he had partially lost the mother who for so long had been his companion and playfellow as well as the chief object in his existence. Many humiliations had come to the keen feelings and sensitive heart of the little dethroned boy. Many a complaint and reproach had been on his lips, though none had got utterance. But now a deeper indignity still had befallen him. As Geoff lay in the room to which he had been banished to be out of Warrender's sight, all this swept across his little soul like a tempest. He remembered the suffocating sensation in his throat, the red mist in his eyes, the feeling that he had but a moment left in which to deliver his message; and then the giddy whirl of movement as he was flung away like a rag or a stone, the crash in his ears, the sharp blow which brought back his scattered faculties for a moment, only to banish them again in the momentary unconsciousness which brought all the tingling and thrilling into his ears of which he had not yet got free. How had all this come about? It was Warrender who had seized him, who had flung him upon the floor, who had—had he? tried to kill him? had he tried to kill him? Was that what Warrender meant? A wild flood of feeling, resentment, terror, desire for revenge, swept through Geoff's mind. Warrender, to whom already he owed so much; Warrender, who had taken his mother from him, and his home, and everything he cared for in the world,—Warrender now wanted to kill him! If mamma knew! Mamma had not ceased to care for her boy. Even now that the babies had come she still loved Geoff,—and if she knew! The boy jumped up from his couch. He was pale and trembling, and the cut on his forehead showed doubly from the total absence of colour in his little gray face; but he got himself a great draught of water, and, restored by that and by the rush of rage that swelled all his veins, he flew downstairs, past Joseph in the hall, who gave an outcry of astonishment, to where the gardener's boy was still holding his pony outside. Geoff, scarcely able to stand, what with the shock and what with the emotion, clambered up upon the pony, and turned its head homewards. The pony was well pleased to find himself in that way, and obeyed with enthusiasm his little master's impulse. The small steed and rider flew along the road to Markland. Geoff had no cap; he was dusty, as if he had been for days on the road; and as he flew by, the cottagers came out to the doors to look, and said to each other that the little lord must be mad, that he would have an accident like his father. He went on thus, with scarcely a pause, till he reached the gates of Markland, wrath and pain carrying him on at a swifter rate even than the pony, eager for sympathy and for revenge.

Something stayed this headlong race all at once. It was when he came within sight of the avenue, which was so bare, which had no trees except at distant intervals. There he saw a speck upon the way, a slowly moving figure which he recognised at once. It was his mother, coming down, as was her wont, to meet—whom? Her husband. Geoff's hot heart, all blazing with childish rage, sank into a shivering calm at the sight of her. In a moment he turned from heat to cold, from headlong passion to the chill of thought and self-sacrifice. Mamma! She it was now who was "delicate," as he had been all his life. It might make her ill; it would make her miserable. What! she who had been everything to him,—was he now going to seize upon her as Theo had seized him, and shake her and hurt her, he, her own boy? The child drew up his unwilling pony with a sudden force which almost carried him over its head. No, he could not do that. He would not. He would rather be shaken, strangled, thrown down, anything in the world, rather than hurt mamma. His little heart swelled with a new spring of impassioned emotion. He would bear it for her sake; he would bear anything, he did not mind what, rather. He would never, he cried to himself, with a rush of scalding tears to his eyes, hurt *her*. He turned the pony's head round with a force of passion which that astonished animal could not resist, to give himself, after the wild rush of his flight homeward, a little time to think. And he thought, knitting his little brows, twitching his little face, his heart aching, his little body, even, all strained with the effort. No! whatever he did, whatever he had to bear, he would not hurt mamma.

CHAPTER LI.

Warrender had a long conference with Dick Cavendish in the old library at the Warren. Mr. Wilberforce, who had been sent for, came at once, full of curiosity and excitement; and though Mr. Longstaffe could not be had, the experience of the two clergymen, who knew all about marriage registers and the proofs that were necessary, was of use in this curious family crisis. It was all very important both to Chatty and to the family in general, and Theo did his utmost to keep his attention to it, but his thoughts were elsewhere. He was glad to be released, when all was done that could be done by the little family commission. The result was a kind of compromise. No one had any moral doubt that Dick was right, but some higher sanction seemed to be necessary before he could be allowed to take Chatty away. The ladies had to be called in to soothe and subdue his impetuosity, to get him to consent to delay. Warrender scarcely waited to see how it was settled. The impatience within him was not to be controlled. His heart was at Markland, hot with anger and anxiety, while he was forced to remain here and talk of other things. Yes, to be sure, Chatty's good name, her happiness,—if she considered that her happiness lay in that,—were important. It was important for Cavendish too, if any one cared what was important for Cavendish: but good heavens! not so important,—could any one suppose so for a moment?—as what had happened, what might be happening, elsewhere. Old Joseph had stopped him as he went through the hall to tell him that the little lord had run off and got on his pony, and had gone home. He had gone home. It was a relief for one thing, for Theo had felt that it would be impossible for him to carry that little demon back with him in the dog-cart, as it would have been his duty to do. But in another—how could he tell what might be happening while he was kept there, amid maddening delays and hesitations, looking over Dick Cavendish's papers? What could Dick Cavendish's papers matter? A few days sooner or later, what could it matter to Dick Cavendish? Whereas to himself— That boy might be lying senseless on the road, for anything he knew; or, what was worse, he might have got home and told his story. And the sting was that he had a story to tell.

Warrender knew that he had done what he ought not to have done. He had treated the child with a violence which he knew to be unmanly. He had thrown him down, and stunned, and might have killed him. He did not deny to himself what he had done. He would not deny it to her,—and he fully expected that she would meet him with upbraidings, with anger. With anger! when it was he who was the injured person,—he, her husband, whose privacy was constantly disturbed and all his rights invaded by her son. He turned this over and over in his mind, adding to the accumulation of his wrongs, till they mounted to a height which was beyond bearing. The fire blazed higher and higher as he kept on throwing in fuel to the flames. It must come to some decision, he said to himself. It was contrary not only to his happiness, but to his dignity, his just position, to let it go on, to be tormented perpetually by this little Mordecai at the gate, this child who was made of more importance than he was, who had to be thought of, and have his wishes consulted, and the supposed necessities of his delicate health made so much of. Geoff's generosities, the constant sacrifices of which he was conscious, were all lost upon his stepfather. He knew nothing of the restraint the child put on himself, or of the wistful pain with which Lady Markland looked on, divining more than she knew. All that was a sealed book to Theo. From his side of the question Geoff was an offence on every point. Why should he be called upon to endure that interloper always in sight,—never to feel master in his own house? To be sure, Markland was not his house, but Geoff's; but that was only a grievance the more, for he had not wished to live in Markland, while his own house stood ready for his own family, with plenty of room for his wife and children. There grew upon Warrender's mind a great resolution, or, rather, there started up in his thoughts, like the prophet's gourd, a determination, that this unendurable condition of affairs should exist no longer. Why should he be bound to Geoff, in whose presence he felt he was not capable of doing himself justice, who turned him the wrong way invariably, and made him look like a hot-tempered fool, which he was not? No, he would not endure it longer. Frances must be brought to see that for the sake of her son her husband was not always to be sacrificed. It should not continue. The little girls must not grow up to see their father put in the second place, to think him an irritable tyrant. No, it must not continue, not for a day.

And there occurred to Theo, when he approached the gate of Markland, something like the same experience which had befallen Geoff. He saw going slowly along the bare avenue two figures, clinging closely together,—as he had seen them a hundred times, though never without jealousy, when he had no right to interfere. For a long time these walks had been intermitted, and he had almost forgotten the irritation of the past in this respect. But now it all surged back with an exasperation entirely out of proportion to the offence. For the offence was no more than this: that Lady Markland was walking slowly along, with Geoff clinging with both hands to her arm, clasping it, with his head almost on her shoulder, with a sort of proprietorship which made the spectator frantic. He stopped the dog-cart and sprang down, flinging the reins to the groom outside of the gate. The sight brought his resolution, his rage, the fierce passion within him, to a climax. Yes, he had been anticipated; that was clear. The story of all that had passed had been poured into his wife's ear. She would meet him with reproaches, perhaps with tears, pointing to the cut on her son's forehead. There came into Theo's mind a maddening recollection that he himself had been cut on the forehead for Geoff; but no one, not *she* at least, would remember that now. She would meet him furious, like a tigress for her cub; or, worse, she would meet him magnanimous, forgiving him, telling him that she knew it must have been an accident—whereas it was no accident. He would make no pretence; he would allow that he had done it, he would allow that he had meant to do it; he would make no further pretences, and tolerate no pretences from this day.

In his anger he was as swift and light as a deer. Their backs were turned towards him, and they were too much absorbed in their talk to hear his approach. He was close to them, on Lady Markland's other side, before they heard anything. The mother and son looked up simultaneously, and started as if they were but one being. At the sight of him she gave a faint cry,—"Theo!"—and he unclasped her arm and slid from her in a moment: which, though it was what he wished, made the fire burn still higher in Warrender's heart.

"So," he said, with the harsh laugh of excited temper, "he has been telling you his story. I knew he would."

"He has been telling me no story, Theo," said Lady Markland. "Oh yes, he has been telling me that Mr. Cavendish——"

"Confound Mr. Cavendish! I am speaking of your boy, Lady Markland. He has been telling you about the cut on his forehead."

She looked from the man to the child, growing pale. "He fell," she said faltering. "But he says it does not hurt."

"The little liar!" cried Theo, in his excitement. "Why didn't you tell your mother the truth?"

"Warrender!" said little Geoff, in a tone which conveyed such a warning as Theo would not have taken from any man in the excited state of his mind. The child was red with sudden indignation, but still he held fast to his part.

"Geoff, run away home!" cried his mother, trembling. "Nurse will bathe it for you: and papa,"—she had ventured to call her young husband by this name since the birth of the babies,—"will give me his arm."

"I tell you he is a little liar," said Theo again. "He did not fall. I threw him down. He thrust himself into the midst of my family affairs, a meddling little fool, and I caught hold of him and threw him out of the way. It is best that you should know the truth."

They stood all three in the middle of the bare road, the afternoon sun throwing its level light into their eyes,—looking at each other, confronting each other, standing apart.

"Theo," said Lady Markland, "I am sure you did not mean to hurt him. It was—an accident, after all. And Geoff, I am sure, never meant to interfere. But, indeed, you must not use such words of my boy."

"What words would you like me to use? He is the pest of my existence. I want you to understand this once for all. I cannot go on in this way, met at every turn by a rival, an antagonist. Yes, he is my rival in your heart, he is my opponent in everything. I cannot turn round at my own table, in my own house, without his little grinning face——" Here Theo stopped, with a still harsher laugh. The startled faces of the mother and son, the glance they gave at each other like a mutual consultation, the glow of indignation that overcame Lady Markland's paleness, were all apparent to him in a flash of meaning. "Oh, I know what you will say!" he cried. "It is not my house; it is Geoff's. A woman has no right to subject her husband to such a humiliation. Get your things together, Frances, and come with me to my own house. I am in a false position here. I will have it no longer. Let him have what is his right. I am resolved that he and I shall not sleep again under the same roof."

"Theo, you cannot mean what you say. You can't be so—— If Geoff has done anything wrong, he will beg your pardon. Oh, what is it, what is it?" She did not ask her son for his version of the story with her lips, but she did with her eyes, which exasperated Theo more and more.

"It does not matter what it is," he said. "It is not any temporary business, to be got over with an apology. It is just this, that you won't face what is inevitable. And it is inevitable. You must choose between him and me."

Geoff had been overwhelmed by this sudden storm. He was so young to play the hero's part. He was not above crying when such a tempest burst upon him, and had hard ado to keep back his tears. But when he met his mother's anguished imploring look, Geoff felt in his little forlorn heart a courage which was more than man. "Warrender," he said, biting his lips to keep them from quivering,—"Warrender, I say. As soon as the holidays are over, I—I'll go to school. I'll—be out of the way."

"Oh, Geoff!" Lady Markland said, with a heartrending cry.

"It's—it's right enough, mamma; it's—quite right. I'm too old. I'm too—Warrender, I'll be going back to school in about six weeks." Alas, the holidays were just begun. "Won't that do?" said little Geoff, with horrible twitchings of his face, intended to keep back the tears.

His mother went up to him, and kissed him passionately, and put him away with her hand. "Go," she said. "Geoff, go, and wait for me in your room. We must talk—alone; we must talk alone. Go. Go."

Geoff would have given much to throw himself into her arms, to support and to be supported by her: but the child was moved beyond himself. He obeyed her without a word, turning his back upon the combat, though he would fain have stood by her in it. Warrender had taken no part in this; he had made no response to Geoff's appeal. He was walking up and down with all the signs of impatience, pale with passion and opposition. He paused, however, as the boy went away, a solitary forlorn little figure stealing along the avenue in silence, too dutiful even to look back. Lady Markland stood, too, and looked after him, with a pang of compunction, of compassion, of heart-yearning, which it would be impossible to put into words. Her boy! who had been her chief, almost only companion for years; who was more dear—was he more dear?—than any one; who was her very own, all her own, with no feeling in his mind or experience in his little consciousness that was not all hers,—and this man bade her send him away, separate from her child: this—man. It is not safe for a union when one of the parties thinks of the other as that man. All at once a light had flashed up in Lady Markland's heart. She had been made very soft, very submissive, by her marriage. She had married a young man, younger than herself. She had seemed to herself ever since to be asking pardon of him and of the world for doing so. But now his violence had called her back to herself. She had not been too soft or submissive in the old days. She had been a woman with a marked character, not always yielding. The temporary seemed suddenly to disappear out of her life, and the original came back. She stood for a moment looking after her child, and then, being feeble of body, though waking up to such force of mind, she went to a bench which stood on the edge of the road, and sat down there. "If this is as you say, it is better that we should understand each other," she said.

Her tone had changed. From the anxiety to soften and smooth everything, the constant strain of deprecation and apology which had become habitual to her, she had suddenly emerged into a composure which was ominous, which was almost tragic. Even the act of sitting down, which was due to her weakness, made her appear as if taking a high position, assuming an almost judicial place. She did not intend it so, but this was the effect it produced upon Warrender, stinging him more deeply still. He felt that he was judged, that his wife had thrown off the yoke which he had made so heavy, and that his chance of bringing her back to her subjection, and of forcing her into the new and sudden decision which he called for, was small. This conviction increased his fury, but it also made him restrain the outward signs of it. He went after her, and stood in front of the bench of which she had made a sort of judicial throne.

"You are right in that," he said. "Things have gone too far to return to their old level. I must have my house to myself, and for that reason it must be my own. I wish you to come with me to the Warren,—the children and you."

"Your mother and your sisters are there," she said, fixing upon him a steady look.

"What does that matter? There is room, I hope, at all times for the master of the house."

"You ask me," she said, "to turn all my life upside down, to change my habits and arrangements, at a moment's notice. But you have not told me why. Have you told me? You have said that my little boy of twelve has offended you, and that you knocked him down. Is that why I must change my house, and all my life?"

The slow steadiness of her tone made him frantic; that, more than the deliberate way in which she was putting him in the wrong.

"I have told you," he cried, "that I am in a false position altogether, and that I will not bear it any longer! You ought to see that I am in a false position. As for your little boy—of twelve——"

"What of him?" she asked, growing very pale, and rising again from her seat.

"Only this one thing, Frances: that you can't serve God and mammon, you know; you can't keep both. You must choose between him and me."

"Choose!" She sat down again suddenly, as if her strength had failed her. "Choose! between Geoff, my little Geoff—my boy—my baby—Geoff——"

There was a kind of ridicule in her voice, a ridicule which was tragic, which was full of passion, which sounded like a scoff at something preposterous, as well as an indignant protest.

"Your scorn does not make it different. Yes, Geoff, who is all that: and me—between him and me."

For a moment they gazed at each other, having arrived at that decisive point, in a duel of the kind, when neither antagonist can find a word more to say. Lady Markland was very pale. She had been brought in a moment from her ease and quiet, when she expected no harm, to what might be the most momentous decision. She was still feeble, her nerves strained and weak from the long tension at which they had been held. She had clasped her hands together, and the fingers quivered. Her eyes seemed to grow larger and more luminous as she looked at him. "Theo," she said with a long breath. "Theo! do you know—what you are saying? Do you mean—all that—all that?"

He thought he was going to get an easy, an unlooked-for victory; he congratulated himself with a swift flash of premature triumph that he had pushed matters to a crisis, that he had been so firm. "Yes," he cried, "I mean it all! We can't go on longer as we are. You must choose between him and me."

She kept looking at him, still without relaxing from that fixed gaze. "Do you know what you are asking?" she said again. "That I should give up my child,—my first-born child, my little delicate boy, who has never been parted from me. Was it ever heard of that a mother was asked to give up her child?"

"They have done it," he said,—"you must know that,—when a higher claim came in."

"Is there any higher claim? Every other is at our own choice, but this is nature. God made it. It cannot change. There may be other—other"—she faltered, her voice grew choked,—"but only one mother," she said.

"Other—other?" he cried. "What? To me there has been but one, as you know. I have put all my chances in one. God made it? Has not God made you and me one?—whom God has joined together—"

"Oh, Theo." She got up and came towards him, holding out her hands. "One, to bear each other's burdens, to help each other; not to go against nature, to abandon what is the first of duties. Theo! oh, help me; do not make it impossible, do not rend me in two! What can I say to you? Theo!" She tottered in her weakness; her limbs were not strong enough to support her. But Warrender made no forward step. He did not take the hands she held out to him. He had to be firm. It was now or never, he said to himself.

"If we are ever to live happily together the sacrifice must be made. I don't want to hurt you, Frances. If I seem harsh, it is for our good, the good of both of us. Make up your mind. Can any one doubt what is your first duty? It is to me. It is I that must settle what our life is to be. It is you who must yield and obey. Are you not my wife? Spare yourself farther pain, and me," he went on, with all the absolute and cruel sincerity of youth.

He made it up in his own mind that this was the right thing to do, and steeled himself to resist the appeal of her weakness, to see her flutter back to the hard bench, and drop down there, unsupported, unaided. It was for the best, it was for her good, to put things on a right footing at once and for always. After this, never a harsh word, never an opposition, more.

Her husband thus having her to himself, standing before her, magisterial, coldly setting down what her duty was, enforcing obedience,—he who little more than a year ago—— She wavered back to her bare seat alone, and sat there, looking up at him till his peroration came to an end. In these few minutes many things flew through Lady Markland's thoughts,—unspeakable offence, revolt against the unlovely duty presented to her, a sudden fierce indignation against him who had thus thrust himself into her life and claimed to command it. At that moment, after all the agitation he had made her suffer, and before the sacrifice he thus demanded of her, she could scarcely believe that she too had loved him, that she had been happy in his love. It seemed to her that he had forced himself upon her, taken advantage of her loneliness, compelled her to put herself in his power. It had been all adoration, boundless devotion, help, and service. And now it was command. Oh, had he but said this before! Had he bidden her then choose between her child and him, before— And as she looked at him a wild ridicule added itself to these other thoughts. To see him standing making his speech, thinking he could coerce like that a woman like herself, thinking in his youthfulness that he could sway any woman's heart like that, and cut off the ties that vexed him, and settle everything for the good of both! Heaven! to see him lifting up his authoritative head, making his decision, expecting her to obey! Spare yourself, and me! That she should refuse did not enter into his mind. She might struggle for a time, but to what use? Spare yourself, and me! She could not help a faint smile, painful enough, bitter enough, curving her lips.

"You speak at your ease," she cried, when his voice stopped. "It is easy to make up your mind for another. What if I should refuse—to obey, as you say? A wife's obedience, since you appeal to that, is not like a servant's obedience or a child's. It must be within reason and within nature. Suppose that I should refuse."

He had grown cool and calm in the force of his authority. The crimson flushed to his face and the fire to his eye at her words. "Refuse—and I have my alternative!" he cried. "I will never enter your house again nor interfere in your concerns more."

Again they contemplated each other in a deadly pause, like antagonists before they close for the last struggle. Then Lady Markland spoke.

"Theo, I have done all that a woman could do to please you, and satisfy you,—all, and more than all. I will not desert my little boy."

"You prefer Geoff to me?"

"There is no preferring; it is altogether different. I will not give up my child."

"Then you give up your husband?"

They looked at each other again,—she deadly pale, he crimson with passion, both quivering with the strain of this struggle; her eyes mutely refusing to yield, accepting the alternative, though she said no more. And not another word was said. He turned on his heel, and walked back down the avenue, with quick, swinging steps, without ever turning his head. She watched him till he was out of sight, till he was out of hearing, till the gate swung behind him, and he was gone. She did not know how she was to get back to the house, over that long stretch of road, without any one to help her, and thought with a sickening and failing of her heart of the long way. But in this great, sudden, unlooked-for revolution of her life she felt no weakness nor failing. The revulsion was all the greater after the long self-restraint. For the first time after so long an interval she was again herself.

CHAPTER LII.

That night Lady Markland did not close her eyes. The strength of resistance, of indignation, of self-assertion, failed her, as was inevitable in the long and slow hours, during which she looked out, at first with a certainty, then with a hope, that Theo would come back. He must come back, she said to herself, even if all were over, which seemed impossible, impossible!—all in an hour or two, in one afternoon, when she thought no evil. Still the most prosaic of considerations, the least important, his clothes, if nothing more, must bring him back. She went on saying this to herself, till from a half scorn which was in it at first it came to a kind of despair. He must come back, at all events, for his clothes! She could scarcely bear Geoff all the afternoon, though it was for him all this misery was. She never could, nor would, give up her child: but his society was intolerable to her for the moment; and she felt that if Theo came and found them together he might think—he would have a certain right to think. It was a relief to her when at last Geoff went to bed, silenced in all his questions, chilled, terrified, yet still heroically restraining himself, and making up his mind that he was to be sent away. After this she felt a kind of relief, a freedom in being left to herself, in wandering about the rooms and looking out in succession at every window that commanded the avenue. When the hour came to shut up the house she gave the butler an elaborate explanation; how Mr. Warrender had been obliged to return to the Warren about some business, how it was possible that he might not come back that night; in fact, she did not expect him that night, but still he might return. It was not necessary that any one should sit up, oh no, not necessary at all. She would hear him if he came, or he could let himself in. "But I really do not expect him to-night. He

467

has—business," she said, with a smile, which the butler thought not at all like my lady. She was not given to explanations in an ordinary way. She was very kind and considerate; but she was always a great lady, and not expansive to her servants. She smiled in a strange conciliatory way, as if begging him to believe her, and explained, to make it all right. The butler was not deceived. When was any butler ever deceived by such pretences? He knew better,—he knew that something had happened. He told the company downstairs that he made no doubt there had been a row, and most likely about Master Geoff, and that they might make up their minds to see rare changes. They were all making their comments upon this in the servants' hall, while Lady Markland, standing at the window, looked out with a sort of desperation, shaping the figure of Theo a hundred times in the distance, scarcely able to restrain the impulse to go out and look for him; saying to herself, no longer scornfully, but with the profoundest tragic gravity, that he must come back, if only for his clothes! It was a dim summer night, the sky veiled with clouds, and after midnight fitfully lit by the gleam of a waning moon. She went from window to window noiselessly, thinking that now one, now another, had the most perfect command of the avenue; hearing a hundred sounds of footsteps, even of distant wheels and horses' hoofs, which seemed to beat upon the ground far off, and never came to anything; then when the dawn began to be blue in the sky, threw herself upon her bed and hid her face, knowing that all was over, and that he would come back no more.

Scarcely less was the consternation in the Warren when Theo, pale and silent, wrapped in silence as in a cloak, making no reply to the questions asked, ordering his old room to be made ready without any explanation, came back to the already excited house. Dick and Chatty and all their affairs were forgotten in the extraordinary new event. "Oh, Theo, what has happened," Mrs. Warrender cried, "what has happened? Are you not going home?"

"This is my home, I suppose," he said, "unless you have any objections," which closed her mouth. She thought there must have been a quarrel, and that Lady Markland had resented Theo's treatment of Geoff, which his mother immediately began to justify to herself; saying that of course he did not mean to hurt the child, but that a person put in charge of the children of another, in any case, must have some power of correcting them when they wanted correction, and with great wonder and indignation at his wife had yet a wondering question in her mind—what would she herself have done if any one had corrected Theo so when he was a boy? She did all she could to urge him to return, sitting up till very late, keeping the groom awake for possible orders. "Frances will be very anxious," she said to her son. "She has no reason to be anxious; she knows where I am." "Oh, Theo, don't let it come to a quarrel," Mrs. Warrender urged imploringly, with tears in her eyes. Her attitude put him in mind of his wife's attitude as she stood holding out her hands, and was intolerable to him. "Goodnight, mother. I am going to bed," he said. Mrs. Warrender was as restless as Lady Markland. She had come and listened to his breathing outside his door, and seen that his light was out, and that he had actually gone to bed, as he said, before she would allow herself to be convinced. It was a quarrel, then; and what was to come of it,—what was to come of it? Lady Markland was very yielding and gentle, but Theo! Theo was not yielding. Mrs. Warrender, too, lay down when it was nearly morning, as miserable as could be.

And yet none of them, not even the chief actors, who were both at the pitch of desperation, really believed that what this meant was a breach which should last for years. Even they would not have believed it had it been put to them. That it should not all come right was incredible. But as a matter of fact it did not come right. Lady Markland was not by nature the yielding and anxious woman whom for this year of troubled wedlock she had appeared; and everybody knew that Theo was neither persuadable nor reasonable, but had the hottest temper, the most rigid will, of his own, and that ingenuity in finding himself in the right which gives a fatal character to every quarrel. Lady Markland was willing to make any concession but the one which he required, the abandonment of Geoff. But he would make no concession; he stood upon his rights. With all the fervour and absolutism of inexperience he stood fast. No, nothing less than everything, nothing but entire submission, nothing but obedience. Alarmed and anxious friends gathered to the fray, as was inevitable, and everything was made worse. The result was that within a few weeks Theo Warrender had gone off with a burning sense of injury and wrong, to travel he did not much care where, to forget himself he did not much care how; and Lady Markland, feeling as if she had awakened suddenly from a strange dream, a dream full of fever and unrest, of fugitive happiness but lasting trouble, came to herself all alone with the two little babies, in a strange solitude which was no longer natural, and with Geoff. She had chosen, who could say wrongly?—and yet in a way which set wrong all the circumstances of her life.

This was how for the moment her second venture came to an end. Theo went forth upon the world for that Wanderyear in which so much of the superfluous vigour of life is so often expended, which it would have been so well for everybody he had taken before: and stormed about the world for a time, no one knowing what volcanoes were exploding in his soul. How much he gathered of better wisdom it is not within the limits of this history to say.

The happy ones were Dick and Chatty, who began their life together as if there had been no cloud upon it. He had fully lived out his Wanderyear, and had paid dearly for the follies, which had been done with no evil meaning on his part, but in all honour and good intention, bitterly foolish though they were. And perhaps he never was very wise, nor rose above the possibility of being taken in, which is a peculiarity of many generous spirits. But why should we say they were the happy ones? The really happy ones were Minnie and her Eustace, who never felt themselves to be in the wrong, or were anything less than the regulators of everybody's life and manners wherever they went. It was Mrs.

Eustace Thynne's conviction to the last that all the misfortunes which temporarily befell her sister were owing to the fact that she herself was not on the spot to regulate affairs; and that Theo, if he had taken her advice, would never have placed himself in the way of the trouble which had overwhelmed his life.

THE END.